He lifted one hand to tangle it in her hair.

"Stay away from me, you . . . you cur!" she cried. "I am a de Mont—"

The gypsy's lips came down on hers before she could finish. His kiss was deep, demanding, his chin rough and foreign against her cheek. For a moment she was too stunned to resist. Then her head cleared, and she began to struggle in his confining embrace. She tried to scream, but his mouth cut off the sound. This couldn't be happening, she thought distantly.

Not with a peasant.

Not her first kiss.

She pushed against the firm wall of his chest and tried to twist in his arms, but he held her fast. The kiss seemed to last forever. To her growing dismay, her breath quickened in her breast, and her heart began to beat erratically against her throat at the place where his thumb rested. Then, all at once, he pulled back. For one instant, as she looked up into his smoky eyes, he looked as dazed as she felt . . .

MY CHAMPION

GLYNNIS CAMPBELL

JOVE BOOKS, NEW YORK

MY CHAMPION

A Jove Book / published by arrangement with
the author

PRINTING HISTORY
Jove edition / December 2000

The Penguin Putnam Inc. World Wide Web site address is
http://www.penguinputnam.com

ISBN: 0-515-13048-6

A JOVE BOOK®
Jove Books are published by The Berkley Publishing Group,
a division of Penguin Putnam Inc.
375 Hudson Street, New York, New York 10014.
JOVE and the "J" design
are trademarks belonging to Penguin Putnam Inc.

PRINTED IN THE UNITED STATES OF AMERICA

10 9 8 7 6 5 4 3 2 1

For Blake, who opened the door,
Lynette, who pushed me through it,
and Richard, who held it wide

With special thanks
to two of the loveliest ladies in the world,
Helen and Cindy,
and my sisters at OCC/RWA

prologue

"BUT BEFORE YOUNG PERCEVAL LEFT HIS HOME TO SEEK KING Arthur and earn his spurs, his mother said to him, 'There are three things you must remember if you're to be a proper knight.'"

Lady Alyce had the boys' attention now. The three of them hung on her every word as they gathered at her feet in the solar, listening to the tale of Sir Perceval. At their age, there was naught they wanted more than to be knights. After all, it was the de Ware legacy. Theirs was a family rich with great warriors and rife with high adventure.

"I wonder," she mused, eyeing the lads in turn, "if you can guess what those three things are."

Garth, the youngest, the only one of them born of her own womb, screwed up his four-year-old brow and narrowed his gray-green eyes. "You got to wash your hose before the Sabbath."

Holden, the middle boy, snickered, earning an elbow in the ribs from his scowling older brother. Lady Alyce bit her lip, determined not to laugh.

"Well, aye, Garth, that is very important. Can you think of aught else?"

All three frowned then, their bright little minds busy. Deep in thought, they didn't hear their father come in. Lord James leaned against the doorway with his arms folded and his eyes twinkling, flashing that smile that always set Alyce's heart aflutter and made her grateful all over again that she'd been able to assuage the pain of his first wife's death, that the handsome Wolf of de Ware had married her.

She would have welcomed him to sit on the bench beside her, but he cautioned her to silence, content to listen to his sons' discourse in secret.

Holden was the first to look up.

"I know," he said.

She smiled wistfully at him. The path of life would not be easy for Holden. He'd never known his true mother, for she'd died birthing him. His past was stained, and his future was uncertain. Duncan, as the oldest, would inherit de Ware Castle. The youngest, Garth, would likely pursue the clergy. Middle sons had nothing handed to them. Everything they gained they earned. But if anyone could fight his way to the top, it was Holden, with his wild ways and those stormy green eyes that could glare down the most formidable foes.

"A knight must protect ladies . . ." he said.

"Exactly right!" Lady Alyce sang, delighted.

". . . because the silly wenches haven't got the least idea of how to wield a sword or ride a destrier or . . ."

"All right, all right," she interrupted, her initial pleasure somewhat diminished, more so when her husband grinned smugly in agreement. "Aye, a knight must always protect ladies. What else?"

Garth squirmed and glanced at his older siblings, clearly reluctant to make any more mistakes. He so admired his halfbrothers, and Alyce dreaded the time when he might be compared less than favorably to them. Duncan and Holden had inherited their father's stature and striking looks, and already they demonstrated prowess with wooden swords. But Garth was a beautiful child in his own right, possessing his unique strength by way of intelligence and a depth of character not usually found in one so young.

"A knight must . . ." he began tentatively.

"Go on."

"A knight must obey God."

"Excellent!" She clapped her hands together. "A knight must always keep the Holy Church in his heart. Ah, what brilliant lads you are."

They all turned to Duncan then. Clearly, a burden lay on their oldest sibling's shoulders. He was a handsome youth of eight years, with his father's raven-black hair and eyes as bright as sapphires. His charming wit and natural warmth earned him an easy camaraderie with everyone he encountered. But sometimes she fretted that he might never adapt his dreamy idealism to the harsh realities of the world.

"Hmm, a knight . . . must . . ." Duncan's lips slowly curved into a mirror image of his father's smile, and the spark in his eyes told her he was up to some mischief.

He cleared his throat and began very dramatically. "A knight must vanquish dragons and save damsels in distress . . ."

Holden smirked, and Garth giggled. They instantly recognized the meter of the jongleur's songs Duncan was always inventing.

"And kiss his lady's hand . . ." The boys cringed in revulsion. "And let his father win at chess . . ."

His brothers tumbled with laughter now, and even Alyce had to grin at the amusement in Lord James's face.

Then Duncan's eyes gentled into the serious gaze he would retain as a young man, and he continued thoughtfully. "A knight must save his fellow man from pain and poverty, for a noble knight, in thought and deed, a champion must be."

Alyce and the boys cheered and applauded his clever verse. But beyond them, Alyce caught a glimpse of her husband, still standing in the doorway, his arms now unfolded, his smile vanished. He stood tall and silent, and for a moment, she worried that James did not approve of his son's levity. But then she noticed the trembling of his chin, the mistiness of his eyes. Bless him, he was not angry. He was proud, proud as a father could be, of the little wolf cubs they'd reared together.

She gave him her own watery smile. Sooner than they imagined, the boys would be grown, with ladies and children and homes of their own. They'd live and love and hurt and mend and wind their way down life's path as young men with promise in their eyes, fire in their veins, and love in their hearts. And she couldn't help but wonder what fine adventures the future held for the Wolves of de Ware . . .

1

DUNCAN DE WARE TOOK A REFRESHING BREATH OF COOL, salty air and glanced toward the sea, over the heads of the people schooling like herring at the Dorwich dock. The crowd didn't bother him. In sooth, he liked the lively chaos.

Sailors swaggered, ill at ease on land, down the gangplanks of grand vessels. Little boys darted past him toward the crates of newly arrived goods, guessing excitedly at their contents. Cats roamed the walkways for discarded bits of fish. At the furthest edge of the pier, merchants flung orders like gauntlets toward shipmen, daring them to let harm come to their precious wares.

Foreign merchants comprised the largest part of the crowd, arriving by ship to sell their goods at the spring fair and to perhaps continue west to London. Amongst the throng were serfs of Duncan's father, earning a spare coin here and there by selling their home-brewed ale or freshly dug leeks to the hungry travelers. But a few of those strolling the wharf were knaves, and a few were trouble-makers, like the brash guildswoman for whom Duncan and his three companions kept watch.

The foolhardy wench had filed and won letters of marque from the King to collect compensation from a Spanish ship for goods stolen from her. Consequently, early this morn, the panicked harbor master had sent word to the lord of de Ware that there might be trouble at the dock, trouble that required a man skilled with a sword, and Duncan had obliged.

Letters of marque were a messy affair. No ship's captain liked to be held financially responsible for the underhanded business practices of his countrymen simply because they sailed under the same flag. And if this merchant had an ounce of sense, she'd hike up her skirts and run for the hills when she saw which captain she was about to face.

"You're certain the harbor master said 'letters of marque'?" muttered Robert, Duncan's oldest friend and constant companion, who stood, as always, close at hand. He nodded toward a spot where a particularly unsavory ship's crew mixed in among the wealthier merchants. "Not something else? Perhaps 'debtors disembark'?"

Duncan smirked, letting his gaze meander past the hordes of milling strangers toward the moored vessels creaking slowly on the gentle current like complaining old women. Then he saw it, just as the harbor master had said—the *Corona Negra*, the ship of the infamous El Gallo, its Spanish flag flapping in the breeze. And swaggering along the dock was the unmistakable villain himself.

Duncan's brother, Holden, stiffened. "Filthy bastard," he growled, his emerald eyes darkening. Holden had a history with a particularly vicious Spaniard, a woman-killer, and while Duncan couldn't condone his brother's blind hatred of all things Spanish, he could understand it.

"By the Saints," Robert said sardonically, "I believe the lad's grown since the last time we saw him."

El Gallo was roughly the size of a young elephant. And he had a temper to match. It was rumored that the notorious sea reiver had once torn a servant limb from limb for being late with his supper. No one with an ounce of common sense would pass within arm's reach of the hotheaded Spaniard.

Until now.

While Duncan watched in amazement, a little bit of a wench stepped of a sudden out of the crowd and planted herself brazenly before the beast, standing toe-to-toe with El Gallo like a tiny David facing Goliath.

Garth, Duncan's young half-brother, whispered a prayer of disbelief. "Dear God."

The woman turned toward them for only an instant, but that instant impressed itself indelibly upon Duncan's mind. Never before had he glimpsed such rare beauty—not in the blushing courtesans of France, nor in the wild Highland lasses, not even among the lovely golden concubines of the Orient.

She'd fallen from heaven. That was the only explanation for such translucent, ethereal skin. Her face, framed by a wimple of linen only one shade lighter than her flesh, was all cream and roses, surely too delicate to endure the harsh climes of this world. Her lips looked soft and vulnerable, as if she dined on nothing heavier than spun sugar, and her eyes were as wide and innocent as a fawn's. She was small, no greater than a child forsooth, and yet the jade-colored kirtle embracing her body left no doubt that she possessed the curves of a woman. Nay, not a woman, he decided—an angel.

Only this angel confronted the devil himself, El Gallo, the most notorious Spanish reiver of the high seas.

"If he touches a hair on her head . . ." Holden challenged.

"God save her," Garth petitioned.

"She needs my help," Duncan decided, starting forward.

Robert stopped him, gripping his forearm. "Lads, lads," he chided, "the girl seems capable of taking care of herself. Look you. She has the documents with her even now."

The angel clutched a sealed parchment in her small fist. But that didn't stop her from looking as helpless as a field mouse in a falcon's sight, trembling there beside the corpulent figure of El Gallo.

A breeze suddenly whipped mischief along the ocean's edge. It fluttered the angel's skirts and snatched the wimple from her head, startling her and nearly stealing her precious document. The girl made a wild grab for the wimple, but the winds had their way with it. It promptly sailed off the dock and into the water, where the greedy sea swallowed it whole.

Her shoulders slumped infinitesimally, and she ran a slender hand through her unbound hair, which had spilled free like long-bottled wine.

Duncan let the breath whistle out between his teeth. Her hair was utterly divine. There were long, golden masses of it, all silky and luminous, the color of ripe wheat shining in the afternoon sun and moonlight reflected in a still pool. It cascaded over her shoulders and down her back like a melting halo. He could almost imagine how the shimmering tresses would feel entwined around his fingers.

Then he frowned. The angel had lost her wimple. She could just as easily lose her head.

"She is mad."

"Utterly," Holden agreed.

"She's remarkable," Robert declared. "She's the first woman I've seen with the mettle to stand up to these despicable reivers. The King obviously supports her claim," he said smugly, "and it looks as if she's about to collect her due."

Duncan lowered his brows. "*More* than her due, I'd wager, if it's from El Gallo." He pursed his lips thoughtfully. "Mettle or not, I suggest, lads, that we make our presence known until this business is settled."

His men fanned out among the crowd, finding vantage points where they could see and be seen in their recognizable de Ware tabards. Their hands never strayed far from their hilts. Duncan drew his dagger, pretending to idly carve a chunk of driftwood, all the while letting the steel glint menacingly across El Gallo's field of vision. The reiver would know he was being watched.

Linet de Montfort swept the annoying curtain of hair away from her face. She wished she'd taken the time to pin the damned wimple properly. This encounter was difficult enough without the added distraction of her unruly tresses tangling about her.

"I have the letters here," she told El Gallo in what she hoped was a firm voice.

"What!" the overgrown, scowling Spaniard boomed at her through his scraggly red beard.

His exclamation did what normally only a thundertube could have—it effectively silenced the bustle of the docks. Merchants halted in the streets. Harlots turned lazy glances his way. Even fishmongers stopped hawking their wares to see who had dared vex El Gallo.

Linet prayed no one saw the quivering of her knees beneath her best wool surcoat as she stood on the dock within an ell of the Spaniard man called The Rooster. In the hush, she could hear now the lapping of the waves that had devoured her wimple and the snapping of Spanish sails. The sudden prankish screech of a swooping gull nearly made her jump out of her skin.

Her sweaty fingertips were smearing the ink of the royal writ. She ran her thumb once again over the wax of Edward's seal, trying to reassure herself that the letters were genuine. Before this behemoth of a man, the document seemed only a frail piece of meaningless parchment.

"You dare bring this to me!" El Gallo snarled, taking a threatening step forward.

Linet resisted the urge to retreat, despite the horrific stories she'd heard, despite the odor of garlic and cheese that suddenly assailed her nostrils and the beady black eyes that stabbed at her like a crow's beak. She squeezed the letters of marque even more tightly and forced her gaze to rise to his.

The man really did resemble a great rooster, she decided. He was enormous, a full foot taller than any man she'd ever seen, and nearly as big around as he was tall. More appalling than his size, however, was the fact that apparently no one had offered him any helpful advice regarding his attire. The Spaniard's clothing looked like an embarrassing accident at a dyemaker's shop. His sleeves were as yellow as brimstone, and his surcoat was of inferior russet velvet. Deep blue hose wrinkled down his surprisingly spindly legs, a green linen coif stretched across his huge head, and the striped sanguine cloak of nubby serge that attempted to cover it all looked remarkably like a pavilion tent. The orange fuzz of his hair escaped rampantly from the coif on his head and seemed to float about his ample chin in a scruffy beard, only partially concealing the red wattle beneath.

Certainly she had nothing to fear, she tried to convince herself, from someone who dressed so distastefully. She swallowed, lifted her chin, and cleared her throat.

"By order of the King . . ." she began.

El Gallo pecked the writ from her hand like his namesake fowl before she could snatch it back. He held it aloft, over her head, and for a moment his face beamed with gloating.

"You stupid *puta*," he bit out, "I recognize no . . ."

Then someone or something in the distance apparently caught his eye. His smugness faltered. His lip curled as if he'd tasted rancid meat, and he blew a disgusted breath out through his nose. He muttered a string of what sounded like Spanish curses. Then his sneer somehow evolved into an ingratiating smile.

"As I was saying," he whined out in the nasal tone common to his mother tongue, "I recognize no problem with these letters."

Linet blinked. Surely she'd heard wrong. The imperious El Gallo couldn't be surrendering so easily. Of course, he had to abide by the King's decree. The royal agent had assured her that any document bearing Edward's seal was considered law. But she hadn't expected her efforts to bear fruit so soon.

The outcome exhilarated her. In sooth, she thought, with the backing of King Edward, the infamous El Gallo was no more threatening than a cock crowing among a yard of cackling hens.

Ah, she decided, this revenge would be sweet.

"There," Robert said, clapping his hands together when the men had regrouped atop the hill. "You see, Duncan? She did it. Collected her debt without our help."

Duncan wasn't fooled. If it hadn't been for the presence of the de Ware knights and the silent threat of their blades, the Spanish reiver might have done the girl harm. Now, at least, he could rest easy. She seemed safe enough. Her old servant wheeled several casks of Spanish wine from the hold of the *Corona Negra* across the dock, payment from Spain for the merchant's previous losses. And El Gallo, apparently unwilling to witness the confiscation of his goods, had disappeared into his cabin.

"Now can we go home to supper?" Robert urged. "Watching that fat rooster strut across the docks has set my mouth awater."

Holden nodded surreptitiously toward a trio of moon-eyed young ladies making their way up the hill. "You're not the only one slavering over your next meal," he muttered.

Duncan glanced at the giggling maids and sighed. He'd wanted to stay, to get a closer look at the angel on the docks. But, Lord, the women were coming for him. They were *always* coming for him. Ever since his unknown nine-year-old

betrothed had fallen from a horse and died last year somewhere in France, every marriageable female in the country between the ages of five and ninety had sought him out.
Doggedly. Hanging on his every word as if it were a jewel.
Twittering over his most trifling comment. It was no wonder
he'd taken to disguising himself half the time.

"Garth," he murmured resignedly.

"Me?" Garth's young eyes grew round with panic.

"I believe it *is* your turn," Robert said, clapping Garth on
the shoulder.

"Make quick work of them, eh?" Holden added.

"But . . ." Garth looked horrified.

"There's a lad," Duncan said with a wink as the three of
them whirled away, leaving Garth to fend off the feminine
crush.

"What!" Lord James de Ware fired the word like a catapult's
missile, garnering the instant attention of the scores of diners
who sat at the trestle tables in his great hall. His eating dagger
hung in the air halfway to his beard, a thick slice of venison
balanced precariously on its edge.

Duncan pushed away his own empty platter. He leaned
back in his chair, stretched out his legs, and watched his father expectantly, vaguely amused. Apparently, Lord James
had paid little attention to the harbor master's news this morn.
To his right, his brother Holden, ever the warrior, had tightened his fingers reflexively on his knife. Beyond Holden,
Garth appeared to be holding his breath.

"Duncan, is it true?" Lady Alyce asked, her buttered knife
poised over a piece of pandemayne bread, unruffled by neither her husband's outburst nor the subsequent silence in the
great hall. "A woman obtained royal letters of marque?"

"A woman?" Lord James echoed in wonder. The slice of
meat had fallen from his knife, but he still held the blade aloft.

"Aye." Duncan crossed his arms over his chest. "We all saw
her."

Lady Alyce leaned forward, her gray eyes twinkling. "So
this Englishwoman claimed her wool was stolen at sea last
year by Spaniards, and King Edward gave her leave to collect
her due from any Spanish ship in port?"

"Aye."

"Well! And what did the Spanish captain have to say about that?"

Duncan shrugged. "Something . . . Spanish. Something about the merchant woman's parentage, I believe." A smile tugged at his lips. "Isn't that right, Garth?"

Young Garth, whose ecclesiastical studies had left him with a command of several languages and a reluctance to discuss such wickedness, colored and grew singularly obsessed with his trencher of pottage.

"A *woman* was given letters of marque?" asked Lord James, still confounded. "A woman?"

"A woman," Lady Alyce gushed, raising her pewter cup as if to toast the fact.

Lord James muttered something that sounded suspiciously like, "A woman merchant can only mean trouble."

"Agreed," Holden chimed in.

Lady Alyce fluttered her hands, waving away their inconsequential opinions. "Well, I believe it is quite marvelous. With the King's seal on the documents, there's really nothing the Spaniard can do, is there?" she said, popping a sweetmeat into her mouth.

Duncan scowled at that. He'd been there. He'd seen the hatred in El Gallo's eyes. There was always something an affronted Spanish reiver could do. They had notoriously long memories when it came to matters of revenge.

"How much did they owe her?" Lord James asked around a bite of venison.

"Five hundred pounds," Duncan replied.

Lord James let out a low whistle. "And all this on her word alone?" he said, louder than was polite. "The word of a merchant woman?"

Duncan's hackles rose, and he felt Garth's uneasy regard upon him. His father knew better than to prick him with that point. If there was one thing Duncan couldn't abide, it was prejudice against the lower classes. Many was the time he'd used his sword to protect a commoner's head. He admittedly had a weakness for the weak. In fact, Lord James liked to grumble that if King Edward himself were drowning beside a nameless orphan, Duncan just might save the child first. Duncan usually responded with a judicious shrug.

This time he couldn't let his father's attack go unanswered. "My lord, just because she is of the merchant class does not mean she is not entitled to the same justice as . . ."

"I'm certain your father means no slight to the merchants of the village," Lady Alyce intervened. "Do you, James?"

Lord James grumbled into his beard.

"But tell me," she continued, "what did the woman collect in payment?"

"Wine," Holden supplied. "Spanish wine."

"Wine?" Lord James asked. "What would a wool merchant want with wine?"

Duncan raised his brows. "She could sell it."

Robert nodded. "Good Spanish wine is a profitable commodity."

"She cannot sell it now," Garth murmured.

Everyone stared at Garth.

Duncan stopped mid-bite. "What do you mean?"

"She can't sell it. After you . . . left," Garth said pointedly, "she dumped the lot of it."

The back of Duncan's neck prickled. "Dumped?"

"She uncorked the casks and let the wine spill all over the docks," Garth told him.

A collection of gasps circled the table.

"What!" Lady Alyce crowed with glee. "Why, I'll wager the captain's face was as red as his wine by the time she'd finished!"

Sir James unconsciously licked his lips. "Good Spanish wine?"

Duncan felt all the breath go out of him. He didn't listen after that. The wench was mad—deliriously, raving mad. It was foolhardy enough that she'd publicly humiliated a Spanish reiver with her royal letters of marque, but to add further insult by dumping out good Spanish wine . . . that was pure lunacy. Didn't she know that her slight could bring the wrath of the Spaniards down upon not only her, but the entire village?

He suddenly longed to throttle the little fool.

"This could have serious repercussions," Duncan announced, glancing up at his father's grim face. Obviously Lord James had reached the same conclusion.

"England's relationship with Spain is strained as it is," Lord James chimed in. "An incident like this could . . ."

"It could devastate all trade," Duncan finished, "to say nothing of the threat to the townspeople. I hope the woman had sense enough to flee. Some of those Spaniards . . ."

"They're bloodthirsty savages," Holden interjected, his eyes narrowing in memory.

Lady Alyce gasped and brought a hand to her bosom.

"Although," Robert wistfully allowed after a moment of silence, "they do make a fine blade."

There were nods all around, and a short discussion ensued concerning the quality of the latest steel from Toledo.

Meanwhile, the cogs began to revolve in Duncan's head. He had to do something. The village was at risk, and the naive little perpetrator of the trouble was wandering about like a cocked crossbow.

"Robert! Garth!" he called out finally, throwing down his napkin like a challenge. "The spring fair begins on the morrow. The three of us will go. You can find yourselves new Toledo swords while I keep watch to see what hives that wench has poked a stick into."

"Spring fair!" Lord James harumphed. "Naught but rogues and swindlers to rob a man blind. Not to mention beggars and waifs by the score."

"Nonsense," Lady Alyce said sweetly. Then she added in a whisper, "I'll wager no more than six."

"Pah!" Lord James replied, then murmured, "My silver is on a dozen, madam."

"What's this?" Holden ventured. "Wagering?"

Robert leaned forward with a conspiratorial grin. "Aye. They've taken to wagering on how many strays Duncan will bring home with him each time he goes out."

Lord James grumbled into his beard, "'Tis the only way I can afford to feed them all."

Duncan chuckled. He couldn't be more content. With Holden temporarily home from the King's service, and Garth and Robert by his side once more, things were exactly as they should be. The great hall teemed with members of his extended family, velvet next to linen, unwashed faces beside powdered ones, everyone partaking of the rich harvest the land provided. The room reverberated with the panoply of sound, from the lewd heckling of randy knights to the murmured dreams of maidservants.

His father never truly understood Duncan's taste for the full palette of humanity, but that was no surprise. Lord James was a man of his station. He adhered to the belief that only nobles should sit above the salt, servants had little capacity for learning, and common wenches were to be bought for a penny. Yet, Duncan thought with admiration, Lord James had never turned away any of the unfortunates Duncan inevitably brought home with him. There was always an extra trencher at the table and a little room by the fire.

Duncan swirled the wine around in his cup. His chest swelled with pride as he looked over dozens of his loved ones, lost souls he'd rescued from the streets, orphans he'd brought in from the rain. Lord James might complain about the extra mouths to feed, but he was always there with relief for them. Duncan smiled at the graying wolf of a lord who was still muttering into his beard and hoped with all his heart that when the time came, he'd be as fine a leader of men as his father.

He wiped his mouth, then arose, rubbing his hands together. "Now," he called out, "who would like to hear the tale of the wayward miller's daughter and the enchanted frog?"

A high-pitched cheer arose in the hall, and a score of children came bounding up from the tables to gather around him. They clutched at his surcoat as he seated himself on the dais, begging him eagerly to begin the story. He grinned at them, placating them by holding as many on his lap as he could.

Some of the children had the same thick black hair as he. Some of them looked back at him with the sapphire eyes he saw in the looking glass each morn. Indeed, many of them were likely his own byblows. But he'd be damned if he could ever remember which ones they were. He felt as if they were *all* his.

Linet de Montfort elbowed her way along the crowded lane of the spring fair. All around her, patches of woaded linen, russet wool, scarlet velvet, and green silk fluttered on the breeze like a beggar's cloak. She took a deep breath. Cinnamon, pepper, and ginger wafted tantalizingly over the smell of fresh fodder and warm apple tarts. The smoke from roasting meat mingled with the musk of strong ale. Leather and tallow lent their familiar odors to an essence laced with the more exotic scents of Turkish chocolate and oranges from Seville. Sound filled the air around her: steel on steel as swords were tested, the bleating of ewes, the sweet tones of a jongleur's lute, and the everpresent haggling over coins and wares.

Despite the excitement of the morning, tears welled in Linet's eyes. She was alone. It was the first fair she'd come to without her father, Lord Aucassin. For the first time, she'd be selling her wares as a *sole femme* under the de Montfort insignia. Lord Aucassin, God rest his soul, would have been proud of her for that. She sniffled.

But he wouldn't have stood for her tears.

She quickly wiped the moisture away. She could almost hear her father now, chiding her for blubbering when there was profit to be made.

Shifting the precious bundle in her arms, she perused several rows of colored ribbon with the discerning eye that had assured her entry into the Guild two years ago. Still, not a single English dyer could match the wondrous new shade of blue she'd commissioned from Italy. She might have trouble selling the cloth, she thought, if proper trims were scarce.

She sighed and turned to go. She'd been away from the booth long enough. While she could rely upon old Harold to keep an eye on her goods, the servant certainly couldn't sell them. As the crowd tangled about her, she ducked in and out of the colorful tapestry of humanity, unaware that her own bright hair was like a thread of gold in the weave.

Halfway down the lane she felt it. Trouble. Following her.

She wasn't alarmed. It was all part of being a merchant in the lucrative wool trade. Usually the inconvenience was no more than she could turn aside with a word or two. Only a few times had she needed a more formidable weapon.

Yesterday, that weapon had been the royal letters of marque she'd presented to the sputtering Spanish captain. She was still astounded by how well it had gone. The letters had been fairly easy to obtain, thanks to the good name of de Montfort and the wide-eyed innocence Linet could summon up when dealing with royal officials. And she'd felt gratified, standing on the ship, directing Harold to bring up the casks of wine. After her knees had stopped shaking, of course.

In the end, good old English law had come through for her. There was justice after all. Once a debt was scribed on the King's parchment, it was a simple matter to collect one's due.

Dumping the wine had been honey on the cake of her revenge. She hadn't really needed the monetary compensation. Already this season she'd profited enough to more than make up for the lengths of wool stolen last year.

Nay, the revenge was a final tribute to her father and assurance that no thieving miscreant would make the mistake of troubling a de Montfort again.

Still, trouble rode close on her heels today. A stranger dogged her every maneuver as she wove her way through the marketplace.

He wasn't very subtle. Of course, anyone that tall and imposing would've been hard to miss. His mismatched, haphazard, tattered clothing marked him as a gypsy. He walked briskly after her, his oversized hat pulled low, his patched cloak billowing out like a sail behind him. She caught a glimpse of a black beard and dangerous eyes. Quickening her pace, she silently rehearsed the speech she'd given countless times before.

I, she'd tell him in no uncertain terms, *am not a villein to be toyed with. I am the daughter of a lord. The blood of de Montfort flows in my veins.* True, she thought, slipping as easily through the crowd as a Spanish needle through silk, the de Montfort blood was heavily diluted with that of a myriad other unnotables. But she'd make no mention of that. Her famous name was her one link to nobility, the frail thread establishing her exalted place in a world of coarse manners, the wall that protected her from the seaminess of the lower classes.

With that comfort, Linet raised her chin and pressed on, so intent upon the gypsy that she never noticed the two other commoners closing the distance.

Duncan cursed softly and loped after the unsavory pair. In his de Ware tabard, he'd have been swarmed by urchins calling out his name and clinging to his knees and by maidens fluttering coy lashes at their lord's eldest son. But no one paid heed to him today. Today he was a bearded gypsy, a peasant, and peasants, for better or worse, passed through the fair unremarked.

True to Duncan's fears, an inordinate number of rough-looking foreigners loitered in the marketplace this morning. And two of them were following his angel.

His angel? He shook his addled head. What was he thinking? No matter how innocent she looked, the girl was no angel, not with all the unrest she'd caused. And she certainly wasn't *his*.

As he watched, the rogues caught up with the girl. One of them called to her, and she turned. Duncan tugged his hat down over his forehead to watch unobserved. From beneath the wide brim and through a break in the crowd, he was favored with a closer view of her face.

His memory hadn't done her justice. She was absolutely stunning. Her eyes, which he'd been unable to see clearly before, were as green and sparkling as a dewy spring meadow. And that hair—a man could lose himself in that glimmering cloak. A corner of his mouth curved up in an approving smile. Ah, his work could be so rewarding at times.

Then he lowered his gaze. The girl clutched a small, swaddled bundle to her breast, cradling the tiny thing with utmost care. No doubt, he figured, bemused by his own misguided instincts, one of the men he'd thought a troublemaker was the angel's husband and the bundle's father.

He stifled a pang of disappointment and allowed himself the luxury of a small sigh. Why were men always most attracted to that which they couldn't have? He let his eyes rove over her once again, wondering what delights that fine dove-gray wool surcoat concealed.

True, he mused wickedly as the three subjects continued to converse, when he became lord, he could take whatever he wished, including the archaic *droit de seigneur*—the right to bed with whomever he chose of his vassals, married or not.

Then he grinned in self-mockery. He'd sooner sleep in the stables than lie with another man's wife, particularly since he'd never lacked for the company of *un*married women. He stole one last appreciative look at those beautiful golden curls, then turned to leave her to her husband's protection.

A clear, feminine shriek of protest jerked his head back around. Amidst the masking noise of the fair, most of the passersby remained oblivious to the cry. But Duncan knew the sound of a lady in distress when he heard it.

One of the villains had laid hands on his angel. The other grabbed at her infant, tearing the child from its mother's arms.

Outrage flooded Duncan's veins. He forced his way through the crowd, knocking a hapless merchant from his path in his haste. While he apologized to the merchant, the two villains took flight.

He nodded once to his angel, but dared not tarry. Justice had to be served. He strode after her attackers, the authority of his voice clearing a path. He swept his cloak aside, reaching for his sword.

And cursed.

Gypsies carried no swords. He was armed with but a dagger. With a sword, he could have easily dispatched the two knaves. With a dagger, the fight might prove a more even match.

Linet watched in wonder as the dark gypsy moved through the crowd. She'd suspected he was after her for some ill purpose. Now he was acting like her hero. But that was unlikely. Peasants didn't go out of their way to help others. He was probably counting on a healthy reward for his actions. She supposed she'd have to give it to him, as much as her father would have disapproved of her trafficking with his kind. After all, the gypsy appeared to be her only hope.

She glanced at her towering rescuer again as he strode off. He looked more muscular in his snug woolen leggings and sheer muslin tunic than she'd first noticed. The cloak swirled about him as he moved with the speed and grace of a knight's fine steed. His shoulders were broad, and something about those strong, capable hands clenched in determination made her heart flutter.

She stared silently after him, until she realized he was disappearing from sight. With a gasp, she picked up her hay-strewn skirts and scurried after her mysterious hero.

Duncan squeezed his fists in frustration. The Spanish reivers were as slippery as river eels. That was one of the few things he had to admit he despised about the peasantry. Many of them followed no code of honor, bore no respect for the rules of chivalry. They'd just as lief stab a man in the back as face him in fair combat.

He wove his way past the stalls, catching only a glimpse now and then of the two abductors as they cast anxious glances over their shoulders.

Then, abruptly, the stalls ended. Beyond lay a small meadow where spectators stood in a ring for a wrestling bout. The thieves had disappeared, as he'd feared, melted into the crowd. Carefully, he scanned the circle, narrowing his sharp eyes in concentration. His dagger inconspicuously palmed, he approached the ring with measured steps, studying each face he passed. The ground was soft and wet, he noted regretfully, too slippery for a good fight.

Suddenly, his gaze shot to a spot across the circle. There, huddled within the inner ring, was his quarry. One scoundrel still gripped the infant. It would be a miracle if the child was unharmed, considering the rough care it was receiving. But the babe uttered not a peep. Perhaps the poor thing was killed already.

He shuddered. He couldn't afford to believe that.

The Spaniards hadn't spotted him yet, but it was obvious from their nervousness that they expected to soon. When they did, the three of them would likely spend several minutes doing a silly bit of circle dance in pursuit and flight. Duncan didn't want that, not with the babe's welfare at stake. Nay, his move would have to be quick and sure.

Between the thieves and himself were two wrestlers, stripped to the waist and covered with the mire of the well-used meadow. Peasants and nobles alternately egged on and hurled insults at the fighters. A knife-wielding gypsy held little interest for them. Duncan focused on the Spaniards, waiting patiently for the best moment to strike. At last, one mud-covered giant of a wrestler flung the other into the muck. The crowd cheered. In the ensuing melee, Duncan tossed aside his cloak and headed straight for his prey.

Linet stopped to catch her breath, wincing at the slime that clung to her soft boots. Yet when the cheer rose from the circle of spectators, she shoved her way to the fore of the ring.

Once again, the village giant had overthrown a challenger from a neighboring town.

But before the downed wrestler could rise, the intriguing, ebony-haired gypsy entered the ring, a dagger in his grip. Linet gasped, following him with her gaze.

One of the scoundrels yelped like a kicked hound, backing out of the circle to flee. The other, the one holding her bundle, looked as if he wanted to stand his ground, but fear flickered across his face.

For one moment, her rescuer's eyes gleamed in triumph. Then his boot found a slippery patch of mud. His arms cartwheeled for an interminable span of time as he struggled to keep his balance. The villain, seizing the opportunity to escape, rapidly skirted the inner ring of peasants, clinging stubbornly to her bundle and skittering sideways like a crab. The gypsy's other foot finally came down to steady him, but it, too, slid on the wet ground. He landed with a thud on his hindquarters, his fawn-colored hat dropping down askew over his forehead.

Then, to her surprise, the gypsy rolled over twice on his side, completely covering himself with mud and coming rapidly to his hands and knees before the villainous Spaniard, knife at the ready. She'd never seen a man move so quickly. The knave squeaked as he beheld the savage dagger just inches from his throat. With nowhere to go, he tossed up the precious bundle in surrender.

Time slowed as Linet looked on in horror.

The cur used the distraction to escape.

Duncan's heart seized in his breast. He dropped the knife and dove forward, his arms outstretched to catch the babe before it fell. It seemed an eternity before his fingers contacted the soft blue of the babe's swaddling. He willed the infant into the safety of his hands, twisting his own body so he'd bear the brunt of the impact as they struck the earth.

The ground surged up to meet him. He landed hard on his shoulder. A knot and a bruise would be there on the morrow. But the babe was safe in his arms. He'd come to the angel's rescue.

When the angel rushed to his side, anxiety marring her delicate brow, the sun shone behind her head, painting her even more like a heavenly apparition. When she spoke, her voice was warmer, more earthy than he'd expected.

"Ah, thank God," she said, holding forth her lily-white hands for the bundle. "Let me see."

He gently offered the child to her.

Linet hesitated. The gypsy was unclean, probably infested with fleas. She wondered if it was possible to take the bundle from him without touching those grimy fingers.

Then she looked into his eyes. Their clear color, complemented by the blue wool he held aloft, startled her. They were the exact shade she'd been looking for all morning, the color of her cloth, the hue of sapphires and summer skies and cornflowers all blended into one. How rare, she thought.

Then she remembered herself. She remembered that the man was a gypsy. She remembered that she was here for business, and that her father would've had her hide for lowering herself to speak with a rag-picker.

Without further ado, she delicately pinched one corner of the bundled wool between a thumb and finger and shook it briskly from his grasp, unfurling it.

Duncan's breath caught in his throat. What was the woman doing? He reached out in shock to save the babe.

"Hardly a mark on it!" she exclaimed. "Well, that is surprising, considering the filthy fingers that have handled it."

He could only gape wordlessly. He didn't even care that his false beard was drooping oddly on one side. Or that his heart was banging against his chest like a blacksmith's mallet.

The woman was absolutely mad.

"This is the finest English wool you shall ever see," she confided, "woven in the Flemish style, colored with rare dye from Italy. Nowhere else could one find such a shade of blue . . . almost . . . nowhere else." She was looking at him strangely. Then she shook her head abruptly, as if remembering herself, and her tone cooled. "But of course, you'd have no interest in that." She fished in the leather pouch at her hip for a moment and drew forth a tiny coin. "For your trouble," she explained, tossing the coin to the ground beside him.

Apparently finished with him, she rolled her damned cloth again carefully and flashed him a curious smile. Nodding in farewell, she picked her dainty way back toward the stalls.

2

FOR A MOMENT, DUNCAN WAS PARALYZED WITH FURY. THEN he scooped up the coin, shoved his dagger back into his belt and scrambled to his knees.

Damn his eyes, he'd made a fool of himself! Nay, he corrected, *she* had made a fool of him. She'd let him risk life and limb for a mere piece of cloth. And furthermore, the townspeople, *his* townspeople, were making furtive sport of him, whispering and chortling behind their hands.

Crawling to firmer ground, he at last found his footing and broke through the circle of spectators. Peering easily over the tops of the merchants' heads, he glimpsed the wench bustling her way through the crowd as carefree as a lark.

Pressing the coin she'd given him into a dirty urchin boy's hand, he took off after her. His rage must have been clear in his eyes, for men made way, pulling their mistresses aside as he stormed past.

Oblivious to the chaos behind her, Linet strode happily toward Woolmaker's Row. She congratulated herself. She had emerged victorious. She had handled yet another messy situation with the grace of a lady.

At least she *felt* graceful. Until her sleeve was enclosed suddenly by what seemed an iron cuff and she was spun around with such force that she nearly lost her precious cloth again.

A fierce cobalt gaze instantly demanded her attention. She gasped. Never had she had such palpable rage directed at her, not even from El Gallo's beady black eyes.

"Damosel," the gypsy bit out, "I believe you owe me something."

Her fear soured to disgust. She supposed she should have suspected as much. Men of the gypsy's ilk were never content. Her father had warned her about that. If you gave a peasant one coin, he'd only want another. She looked with distaste at the smudge of mud the man was leaving on her sleeve, then sighed heavily.

"I suppose it's too much to expect to find chivalry in the lower classes," she smirked. "I gave you a farthing, and that is *all* I intend to give you."

"A farthing!" the gypsy roared, attracting the unwanted attention of several nearby merchants. Scowling furtively about, he lowered his voice. "Your coin does not interest me."

She looked up into his stormy blue eyes, undaunted. He really was quite handsome for a peasant, she thought, or at least he might be under all that mud and without that scraggly . . .

She frowned. Then she lifted a brow at him. "Perhaps you could purchase yourself a new beard."

The gypsy's fingers flew up reflexively to what remained of his false beard. When he discovered its bedraggled state, he ripped it fiercely from his face.

Linet winced. It must have hurt. The man said a very bad word, throwing the beard into the dirt and grinding it under his heel as if it were a loathsome, hairy caterpillar.

Then she could help herself no longer. An unladylike laugh escaped her as she looked up at his mud-spattered face, despite the two flinty daggers of his eyes. His hat was nowhere to be seen, and his once lustrous black hair was now caked with drying slime. The cloak had been left behind, and there was a huge tear in the shoulder of his matted linen tunic. To her discomfiture, she could see the considerable muscle beneath it flex as he breathed.

"Come with me," he grumbled at her, as their combative discourse was beginning to attract attention.

He paced off, clearly expecting her to follow. She stood her ground, regarding him with amused scorn. The man was apparently accustomed to being obeyed, because her stubborn refusal incensed him. Pressing his lips together in a nasty grimace, he turned and marched back to her. Then, with all the warning of a snake striking, he shot out his hand and snatched the precious wool from her. Mercilessly, he dangled his catch before her like an apple before a horse.

"Nay!" she gasped, reaching in vain for the fine material.

He kept it just out of her reach, gloating smugly at her futile attempts to grab the prize.

"Come with me," he repeated.

She swore she'd see him rot in hell for this. It was on the tip of her tongue to scream for the authorities. But the last thing she wanted was to attract the attention of the other Guild members by whining for help. Not now, not her first year as a *sole femme*. Muttering curses to herself, she accompanied him out of the marketplace and into the wood nearby.

The sounds of the fair were muted now by the trees, but Linet knew she could still be heard by her fellow merchants should she need to call for assistance, as a last resort.

"May I have my cloth now?" she asked as civilly as she could.

"Not until I receive my due," the gypsy replied, slinging the wool carelessly over one muddy shoulder.

She bit the inside of her cheek to check her temper. "I gave you a farthing," she said tautly. "I'll not give you more, you greedy rogue."

"I told you," he insisted, "I have no desire for your coin."

She forced her expression to remain calm. Dear God, if her father were alive to see her . . .

"What sort of payment do you expect?" she asked, although she was afraid she had a fair idea. He was a man, after all. But if he thought he could put those massive, grimy hands of his on . . .

He drew his broad frame up haughtily and dared to look down his nose at her. "An apology," he stated matter-of-factly, "and a little gratitude."

His answer surprised her. "What?"

He nodded. "You've made me look the fool. It's an unbecoming thing in a lady. I risked my neck for the sake of your . . . your . . ."

"My cloth," she supplied, entirely puzzled now. "Why *did* you risk your neck? Only a weaver or a dyer would know its value, and you are clearly neither. Even so, the way I had it bundled . . . the wool could have concealed a coffer of gold or but a dish of tarts . . ."

"Or an infant." His narrowed eyes accused her.

"An . . ." Mortified, she clasped one hand to her breast. Dear God, had he believed the bundle to be a babe? No wonder he'd gone to so much trouble, the poor fool. A babe!

The corner of her lip began to twitch. She was helpless to prevent the laugh that threatened to escape. And then, of course, once begun, her laughter couldn't be stopped. Each time she ventured a glance up at the gypsy, who stared at her as if she were addled, his comical appearance spurred a fresh round of giggles. How the Guild would roar, she thought, when she told them the tale of her wool's "rescue"!

The gypsy apparently didn't share her amusement. Calmly, deliberately, he lifted his muddy hands and proceeded to wipe them on her pristine dove-gray skirts.

She froze in mid-laugh, unable to assimilate what he'd done. There was a moment of stunned silence as their eyes met. Then the gypsy's eyes softened, crinkling at the corners, and he began to chuckle.

It was a deep, rich, pleasant sound, as warm as mulled wine and smooth as sheared velvet. But that didn't make it any more welcome. The knave had sullied her fine English worsted surcoat.

After the initial shock wore off, Linet forced herself to smile, nodding her agreement that his was indeed a good joke. She even began to laugh softly. Of course, it was a ruse. She hadn't survived in the merchant's world by losing gracefully.

Without warning, she reached out toward the gypsy's waist and drew the dagger from his belt. While he was still gloating, she raised the point of the blade up beneath his chin. She hoped he wouldn't notice that her fingers were quaking. With the other hand, she snatched away her cloth. There'd be time later to inspect it for damage. For now, she had to make good her escape.

"I . . . I've dealt with rogues before, gypsy," she warned him, though she was sure the tremor in her voice belied her words, "and I am . . . quite skilled with a dagger."

His eyes widened slightly.

It wasn't exactly true. The extent of her talent with a knife was that she'd been able to shave her father without spilling a drop of blood, which was fortunate, since the sight of blood often made her faint. Nay, she didn't honestly believe she could intentionally harm the flesh of any man. But that wasn't about to stop her from putting up a good bluff.

Duncan was struck speechless. It took every bit of his willpower not to burst into delighted laughter. How he could have ever described this little imp as an angel he'd never know.

He could easily knock the knife from her puny grasp. But if he did, he wouldn't find out what she intended next, and *that*, more than anything, he wanted to know. The little spitfire fascinated him. She piqued his curiosity. He chose to play along with her.

"Do not mistake me," she told him. "Your services were appreciated. But I will not apologize for making you look a fool. You did that yourself. Now, I have business to attend to, so you'll understand if I don't choose to linger. I'm sure someone will come along to free you soon enough."

Free you? Had she said *free you*? What the devil was she plotting?

She cleared her throat. He believed that was a blush stealing up her cheek.

"Now. Remove your tunic . . . slowly," she said.

"Remove my . . . ?" Just what did she intend?

"Silence! I can throw a dagger to . . . to kill a man at twenty paces."

She probably *could* throw a dagger, he thought, but he doubted it would knock a fly from a wall. He hid a grin and pulled the tunic slowly over his head.

Linet suddenly wished she could belay that last command. Without his tunic, the gypsy looked twice as intimidating. His shoulders were easily an ell wide. She doubted her fingers could meet around the muscular swell of his arm. Even his forearms were as big around as young trees. More muscle covered his broad chest and ridged the narrower plane of his stomach. Every inch of him bespoke danger and power. Every inch but the faint line of endearing ebony hair that made a straight path downward, disappearing coyly beneath the waist of his snug braes.

She could feel her face flame crimson. She had no business

thinking such thoughts. Studiously avoiding his eyes, she quickly tucked her cloth into the belt of her soiled skirt, then grabbed the linen tunic from him.

"Sit down here," she ordered, selecting a spot beside the biggest willow she could find. To her chagrin, its trunk still didn't equal the breadth of his shoulders.

Duncan was enjoying himself immensely. His blushing angel was obviously uncomfortable. This was probably the closest she'd ever been to a bare-chested man. And he'd wager silver she'd never so much as been kissed before.

"Wrap your arms behind." Her voice cracked with strain.

He did so, and she brusquely brought the sleeve of the linen tunic about his wrists, tying it in a knot and securing him to the tree. He wasn't sure if it was pity on her part or merely an oversight, but she didn't bother to gag him. Then she picked up his knife and stood cheekily before him.

He tried his best to look miserable and defeated. But when she slipped his dagger down the front of her surcoat between her breasts, the gesture shot an unexpected jolt of desire through him, tightening his loins and slackening his jaw.

With a quick adieu, the angel left with her precious wool. He watched her every step, admiring her nerve and her backside.

She was mad, of course. She'd never have bested him had he not allowed it. But her daring intrigued him. This angel had quite a bit of the devil in her.

When she was out of sight, he wiggled his fingers and shuffled closer to the willow. He wasn't concerned. The girl would be without his protection for a few moments, but he'd be out of his bonds and back onto her trail in no time. His brother, Holden, and he had tied each other up so many times as boys that there were almost no bonds he couldn't escape.

Yet a quarter hour later, struggling with the knot, he began entertaining the faint possibility of uprooting the tree. Sweat dripped down his temple and caused a tormenting itch at the back of his neck. He growled in frustration. What devil's handiwork was this?

He was stuck. And the merchant girl was running around defenseless. But he'd be damned if he would call for help. De Wares never needed anyone's help.

As it turned out, he didn't have to. In the next moment, he heard someone creeping through the bushes toward him. From behind the foliage emerged Robert and Garth, armed with their new broadswords.

"Well, Garth," Robert chirped with all the cheer of a morning sparrow, "what have we here? It seems your brother has gotten himself into the stewpot again." He clapped Garth on the back and sheathed his sword.

"Robert," Duncan called irritably, "cease your prattle and get me out of these bonds."

"Who was it this time, Duncan? A jealous husband? A vengeful nobleman?"

Duncan scowled at him. "It was a devil in the guise of an angel. Now loose me!"

Robert crouched to the knot.

"And hurry!" Duncan snapped. "There are two Spanish rogues afoot who may seek to do her harm."

"Her?" Robert asked, nudging Garth.

"The angel," Duncan replied.

"I knew there had to be a woman involved," Robert said. "Did I not say that, Garth? Did I not say . . ."

"Will you hurry?" Duncan bit out.

Robert shook his head. "She's a peasant, isn't she?"

"She's . . . a merchant," Duncan mumbled.

"Oh ho!" Robert exclaimed. "Not *the* merchant?"

Duncan's lack of an answer was damning.

Robert clucked his tongue. "Duncan, Duncan, Duncan . . ."

"She may be in peril, Robert."

Robert sobered immediately.

"From the Spaniards?" Garth asked. "So they *are* making trouble?"

He nodded. "Two of them were skulking about the fair. They tried to steal something of the angel's, and I don't believe they'll give up easily. I intend to keep an eye on them . . . and her."

Robert and Garth exchanged a meaningful look. He supposed he couldn't blame them. Whenever he said he was going to keep an eye on a woman, be she peasant or noblewoman, widow or virgin, he somehow ended up with much more than his eye on her.

He twisted his wrists in the bonds, which seemed to have tightened. "What the devil is taking you so long?"

"This knot is impossible." Robert threw his hands up in frustration. "What witch's work has she wrought here?"

Garth contemplated the handiwork. "Perhaps it is a weaver's knot," he mumbled.

"What?" Duncan and Robert asked in unison.

"A weaver's knot. They are nigh impossible to untie."

"Then cut the damned thing!" Duncan bellowed. "If you don't free me this instant, I'll dull your new blades on your brains!"

Slicing the tunic to ribbons was the work of a moment with Garth's virgin blade. Duncan borrowed Robert's cloak, and the trio set off at a run to search for the Spaniards.

His heart pounded. He felt as formidable as a wolf on the hunt. Nothing excited him more than saving damsels in distress. Unless it was, of course, receiving their undying gratitude.

Hours later, listless with disappointment, Duncan trudged up the steps leading from the great hall to the west tower. He supposed he should have been content to know that Linet de Montfort was safely ensconced in some noble household for the afternoon. That was if what he'd been able to pry from the stubborn old servant at the de Montfort booth was accurate. All the proud fellow would disclose was that his mistress had taken her wares to the home of a prominent lady who had requested Linet come herself. And, of course, no amount of cajolery would get the man to reveal the name of her mystery benefactor.

But Duncan wasn't content. He'd hoped to see her again, this devil-angel who'd dared to hold a dagger to his throat. She enchanted him. He wondered what she'd say if she knew just whose life she'd threatened.

Something about the intriguing wench set her apart from the other women he'd known. She was captivatingly beautiful, aye, but he'd seen more beauty in his years than most men saw in a lifetime. Nay, it was something else.

She was like a flower, like a rose. Not the insipid roses of the jongleurs, but a *real* rose. All soft, frail petals on top and a tough, prickly stem beneath.

As he approached his chamber along the hall, a round of feminine giggles came from the solar. That would be his mother and her ladies finishing up their stitching for the afternoon. Perhaps he'd poke his head in. Shocking Lady Alyce's bevy with his muddy countenance would surely take the edge off his disappointment.

However, as he drew near, he heard a voice that seemed oddly familiar. He stopped in the hallway, pressing back against the wall to listen.

Linet draped the fabric over her palm for Lady Alyce's inspection. "You see, my lady," she crooned, "how fine the weave is?"

Glancing about the room, Linet could scarcely contain her excitement as she thought of the profit she could make here. Velvet pillows were tossed onto two padded oak chairs. An ornately carved mahogany screen stood in one corner, and a massive chest bound with silver sat beside the hearth. The afternoon sun slanted down into the solar, giving an ethereal light to the pair of expensive hunting tapestries hung on the wall. That same light was perfect for showing Linet's fabric to its best advantage, and she used it expertly, keeping the cloth in the shadows, then at the right moment, revealing it dramatically in the golden luminescence.

Lady Alyce moved her delicate fingers across the soft cloth, and the gentle ladies clustering about her cooed in delight. Oh aye, Linet thought, she'd easily sell at least half of her goods to this household alone.

Peeping through the crack of the solar door, Duncan could witness every nuance of her clever techniques, the way she flattered and bargained and enticed the ladies into purchasing far more than they required. Linet de Montfort was very good, he decided, grinning in admiration.

She'd changed from her soiled gown into another equally rich but properly modest garment of moss-colored wool. Her glorious hair was now hidden beneath a proper linen coif, but her emerald eyes were bright with enterprise as she reveled in what was obviously her element.

"Have you ever seen such a rare and beautiful color?" she asked the ladies, carefully concealing the muddy handprint, *his* handprint, on one corner of the fabric.

"It looks as if you've captured a piece of the sky," Lady Alyce agreed, her eyes twinkling.

The angel clucked her tongue. "I regret I have only the one small sample today, my lady."

That was unlikely, he thought. She probably had yards of the stuff cached away in her wagon. It was all part of the politics of the sale.

"The dye is so new and popular that it has been difficult to keep up with the demands for it," she explained. "Why, even the King . . ."

The ladies gasped collectively. Duncan stifled a laugh. The wench had cleverly left the sentence unfinished, allowing the ladies to draw their own conclusions.

"I will take one length for myself," Lady Alyce decided, "as soon as you are able to procure it, and enough additional to make a surcoat for each of my ladies."

The women clapped their hands excitedly.

Linet smiled, indulging their enthusiasm. "I'll arrange for the weaving of three full lengths, my lady." Duncan could almost see visions of profits whirling in her eyes.

"Now, my dear," Lady Alyce said, "I'd like to see your more serviceable wools, your broadcloth, your worsted."

"Of course." She made a formal bow.

Linet de Montfort was amazing, he thought as he watched her spin her magic web around Lady Alyce and her ladies-in-waiting. She had them feeding from her hand and hungry for more. Pulling forth swatches from an enormous basket, she became a master of drama, regaling them with stories of the exotic beetles and rare flowers used for dyes, then drawing forth the colorful fabric with a flourish, letting it slip gracefully over her arm like a waterfall. The ladies sat spellbound as she told them which wealthy noble had ordered which fabric. They listened intently as she made flattering recommendations for each of them concerning their own coloring and style. Before she left, he was certain half of the de Ware coffers would line her pockets.

"That's settled then," Lady Alyce said, startling Duncan

from his thoughts. She rose above her ladies-in-waiting. "My steward shall pay you a sum for the fabric you'll be sending."

"Half payment will suffice for now, my lady. I can have the cloth for you in a fortnight, by your leave."

"Splendid."

Gathering up her ladies like a goose collecting goslings, Lady Alyce left the solar. No one observed Duncan lurking behind the door.

After they'd gone, he watched as Linet began the tedious work of folding the swatches and tucking them carefully back into her basket. For a long while, he merely waited, enjoying the view. Then he slunk around the door and inclined his shoulder against the entry. Linet, intent on her work, didn't notice him.

"A piece of the sky?" he asked casually.

Linet gasped, nearly upsetting her basket.

"It's fortunate," he purred, "that she didn't see that muddy cloud across it."

"You!" Linet hissed when she'd collected herself. She wondered how long he'd been there. The gall of the man was unbelievable. He leaned insolently against the door, every part of his body projecting amused arrogance. "How did you . . . what are you doing here?"

He didn't respond at once, and Linet regarded him incredulously. She'd seen cutpurses and highwaymen, but never had she met a scoundrel so bold or self-assured. Smudges of dirt still decorated his face. His long hair was matted with a crust of mud. His clothes were tattered. But his eyes regarded her with the easy authority of a king.

Before she could protest, he eased into the room and closed the door behind him.

"Oh, I managed to escape," he said with a rueful smile, folding his arms across his chest, "although it did cost me my tunic."

Linet narrowed her eyes. He wore an obviously stolen wool cloak that only partially covered that formidable bare chest. She looked away, clenching her fist in a swatch of worsted. "Then I suppose our accounts are settled, since you ruined my surcoat." She forced herself to continue her work as she furtively searched the room for exits.

"Your surcoat will wash," he said. "My tunic, alas . . ."

"Why have you followed me here?" she blurted out.

"Perhaps I've come for the dagger you stole from me," he suggested. His eyes traced a path down to the space between her breasts where they both knew his blade was cached.

She would have liked to poke those insolent eyes of his, no matter that they sparkled like a summer stream. It had better be only his dagger that he'd come for. She supposed she ought to return it to him. After all, it might be that the blade was the peasant's only weapon. She'd not be so stupid, however, as to hand it over to him now, while they were alone. Her father had raised no fool. She nodded once, then carefully drew the dagger forth from its hiding place.

Duncan's breath caught in his throat. Desire washed over him as he imagined his own hand doing the deed. Sainted Mary, her skin was likely as soft as a dove's breast. A few tresses had escaped her wimple, turning from honey to amber as she stepped into the sunlight, light that made her eyes shine as clearly as gems. Her lips curved upward into a coy sort of smile, and he realized instinctively, catching her gaze, that she would be unimaginably enticing in bed. His loins swelled at the thought.

As he watched, she shyly lowered her lids. He wasn't surprised. Women often grew diffident beneath his frank regard. Then she took a timid step to the open window. Holding the haft of his dagger daintily between her thumb and two fingers, she peered down over the edge and dropped the blade onto the grass below.

His illusions shattered like a cathedral window under a naughty boy's sling. He stared at her in disbelief. This was no coy maiden. She had deliberately discarded his knife.

"If you hurry down," she told him sweetly, "you may retrieve it before someone else does."

He continued to stare at her, appalled yet fascinated. Hurry down? He thought not. He had no intention of leaving her to retrieve the dagger. He could have a hundred more daggers just like it made at his command. Nay, he thought with dawning amusement, he'd much rather stay here with this extraordinary woman, parrying wits.

Recovering his aplomb, he said smoothly, "There is also the matter of the tunic I was forced to destroy."

She glared at him in impatience, but the merest hint of guilt glimmered in her eyes, and he intended to exploit it.

"I did, after all, retrieve that . . . what was it? 'Finest Italian wool' for you."

"English," she corrected.

"Ah," he nodded, rubbing his chin thoughtfully. "Perhaps you might give me some of *that* for a new tunic."

She froze. That cloth, of course, was worth a fortune. It was clear from her expression that she considered him naive or mad or both.

"Well, what say you?" he asked, all innocence.

Linet could feel an ache starting at her temples. She rubbed a crease into her wool skirts with agitated fingers. The gypsy must be addled in the head to think she'd give him her best . . .

She took a deep breath. Losing her temper would gain nothing. Instead, she forced a regretful smile to her lips. "Alas, that piece has already been sold. Lady Alyce just purchased it."

The gypsy shrugged. "Ah, with such a large order, she won't miss a few inches off the end."

That did it. That broke her control. She could feel her eyes blaze in fury. "How dare you suggest such a thing—taking advantage of a fine lady in that way!"

"I?" he exclaimed with a bark of laughter. "Who has taken the advantage here? What of your prattle about the King? I warrant you've never sold Edward so much as a thread of wool!"

Her face went hot. She slammed the lid of her basket down.

"What about," he said, chuckling, " 'the blue makes your eyes shine like sapphires,' or 'that fabric will not do for you— you deserve a much finer weave'? I'd be amazed indeed if Lady Alyce has so much as a farthing left!"

Linet trembled in embarrassed rage. Curse the peasant! A nobleman would never deign to speak to her so rudely, to laugh at her. She fought to maintain her calm. "Shall I summon the guard, or will you leave of your own accord?"

The gypsy grinned in spite of her threat. "I will take my

leave," he promised, his azure eyes warm with amusement, "when *you* do."

"Who *are* you?" she whispered fiercely.

His smile remained an enigma. His gaze dropped sensuously to her mouth. "At this moment? An admirer of beauty."

Linet resisted the urge to roll her eyes. She'd heard this type of gushing sentiment from noblemen before who were misled by her delicate appearance. She certainly wasn't going to put up with it from a peasant. She was no wide-eyed maid to let herself be distracted by flattery, no matter how silky his voice was. "I see. And does this pursuit keep food on your table?"

"It appeases my hunger," he replied cryptically, looking at her from beneath lowered lids.

Linet cursed the fair complexion of hers that showed every subtle flush of emotion. Damn the rogue! She'd dealt with such gibberish before. Why was she blushing?

"What is it you *really* want?" she blurted in frustration, folding her arms before her.

"Aside from a new tunic?"

She managed to keep her gaze steady, but she felt a tiny muscle in her jaw tense.

"You may make little of it," he said, sniffing. "You are a wealthy merchant. But I, I am only a poor wretch with no tunic on his back."

Linet felt her poise ebbing away as surely as the tide. This scoundrel had gone too far. He was cocky and arrogant and underdressed, and all she could think about was getting rid of him as quickly as possible. With a flustered sigh, she rummaged through her basket and tugged out a short length of cheap woaded wool. The Guild would have given her a tongue-lashing for this, but she was desperate.

"Here," she bit out, shoving the cloth at him.

The knave had the audacity to inspect the fabric, as if he would've known fine worsted from Kendal cloth.

"Anything else?" she asked, her voice dripping with sarcasm.

He tucked the fabric beneath his cloak, brushing it with annoying intimacy against the bare skin of his chest.

"As a matter of fact, aye," he replied, drawing himself up to his full imposing height before her.

She felt suddenly overwhelmed. His presence dominated the room, and she regretted her hastiness in dropping the dagger out the window.

"I'd like to offer you my services for the duration of the fair," he told her.

"Your . . . services?" Her voice sounded high and brittle in her ears. She didn't want to think about the pictures his words had just conjured up. His speech was innocuous enough, but somehow his body was imparting another message altogether.

"You need me," he murmured.

Her breath froze in her throat. She must have heard him wrong. To her chagrin, another flush stole up her cheeks.

"You shouldn't be out alone," he told her, folding his arms decisively. "I fear those two knaves in the marketplace haven't finished with you. I'm offering you my protection."

"Protection?"

"Yes," he confirmed, wrinkling his brow in concern. "A prosperous merchant like yourself is at great risk from thieves." He shrugged. "A poor gypsy like me could use a spare farthing or two for a good day's labor, keeping them at bay."

Linet could only stare at him. His smoky, sapphire eyes and that deep triangle of his chest were making it difficult to concentrate. "I can manage well enough on my own," she choked out at last, irritated with herself and eager to distract him.

"Keep me in food and clothing, and you can defer paying my wage until you've sold the season's goods," he offered.

"Nay, I . . ."

"I insist," he said in a voice that, while soft, brooked no argument.

She wasn't about to enlist the services of this too proud, too smooth, too smug peasant who wore a fake beard. He was as suspect as a smelly herring. In sooth, he was likely to *cause* more trouble than he could prevent. She didn't need a guardian. Harold was protection enough. She'd simply tell him so.

She glanced up at the dark gypsy again and noted the firm, stubborn line of his jaw. Somehow he didn't look like the sort of man who would comply with a woman's wishes. She supposed she'd have to use her merchant's wits.

"You think you can protect me from thieves?" she asked, pretending to consider his offer.

He spoke solemnly. "You may rest assured."

"And you have experience in this?"

"My dagger has tasted the blood of many a varlet."

"So you can singlehandedly defend me from two, three, four attackers?"

"Aye," he said with easy confidence.

"Then let us put it to the test," she told him, linking her arm through her basket of wool. "Guards!" she screeched abruptly. "Help! Guards!"

The gypsy flinched, and his right hand flew reflexively toward his belt. It came up empty. He had one brief moment to glare at her in baffled accusation. Then the solar door burst open beneath the shoulders of two de Ware knights.

3

Robert and Garth leaped into the room. Their bright new swords, already drawn, flashed in the sunlight as the oak door banged against the wall, sending a puff of dust into the pregnant air. They glanced in confusion back and forth from Duncan to the wool merchant, awaiting an explanation.

"Well?" Linet asked, eyeing Duncan expectantly.

So this was her game, he thought, narrowing his eyes. She wanted him to prove his skill. Very well, he decided, dropping the length of woaded wool and tossing off the cloak—he would oblige her. Weaponless, he slowly turned to his brother and his best friend. He crouched like a wolf about to spring. Then he winked at them.

Garth was accustomed to maintaining a sober expression in the face of his brother's wiles. Robert was not. He smothered a laugh, clearing his throat importantly.

"Do you require assistance?" he asked Linet.

"Yes," she replied. "This man has gained entry here without the consent of Lady Alyce."

"I see," Robert nodded, tapping his thumb on the hilt of his sword.

"Come on!" Duncan goaded them with a snarl, a feral gleam in his eyes. "Come on and fight!"

"'Twould hardly be a fair fight, sir," Garth remarked. "You are unarmed."

"I care not!" Duncan recklessly declared. "I can best you both!"

Robert and Garth exchanged quick looks that indicated otherwise. It was clear that even the best swordsman alive, without a weapon of any sort, against two armed guards who were also his bosom companions, didn't have a prayer.

"Do not . . . hurt him," Linet requested, studiously avoiding his eyes. She collected up her basket and made her way to the door. "He is fairly harmless. Just make certain he doesn't follow me, please."

Robert, the traitor, decided in a moment of mischief to side with his antagonist. "As you desire, my lady," he bobbed, flicking the point of his sword up to touch the tip of Duncan's chin.

Duncan shot Robert a clandestine look that would've singed his friend's brows had Robert not been so highly amused by the whole affair.

Damn their betraying hides, there was nothing he could do. He was trapped in his own masquerade, and it was apparent that his companions weren't about to rescue him. Robert was deriving far too much enjoyment from having his blade poised at Duncan's throat. Curse the wench! She'd bested him again, coolly and completely humiliated him without a hint of remorse. Where was her gratitude? Where was the appropriate awe he always inspired in the gentler sex? He had nobly offered her his sword arm, and she had hurled his own gauntlet back in his face. *Fairly harmless* she'd called him. She hadn't wanted to test his mettle at all. She'd simply wanted to be rid of him.

And the little princess hadn't given him a second thought as she smugly made her way out of the room.

The instant the door closed behind her, Duncan hissed out an expletive that startled Garth. "Put up your swords, both of you!" he snarled.

They sheathed their blades, but Robert remained uncowed, his eyes dancing merrily. "Well, we have fodder for the jongleurs now, do we not, Garth?" he teased. "A woman has fled Duncan's side! Perhaps she is daft, touched by the moon, eh?"

"Cease!" Duncan thundered.

He paced across the floor, clenching and unclenching his fists, drawn to the window every few moments as he checked for the girl's departure. A glint of metal from the sward below caught his eye. Before he could blink, young Wat, the scrawny peasant lad, scooped up Duncan's discarded dagger, furtively tucking it into his jerkin. Duncan opened his mouth to protest, then merely kicked the wall in frustration instead and resumed his pacing.

"The fool wench wants to be rid of me," he muttered. "By all rights, I should oblige her. She's laid out her own damned pallet. She should sleep in it. If she wants to risk life and limb for a pile of wool, what concern is it of mine? If she wishes to tempt fate by . . . by flaunting her power in front of the most notorious sea reiver in all of Spain . . ." He stopped in his tracks. God's wounds—what was he saying?

He couldn't let her go back to the fair alone. It was a de Ware's duty to protect ladies. He'd never turned his back on a woman in need. And she was in need. Even if she didn't know it.

He swept Robert's cloak from the floor and whirled it across his back. "Your sword, Robert!" he demanded.

Robert looked crestfallen. "My . . . but . . ."

Unwilling to waste time, Duncan unbuckled Robert's swordbelt himself and fastened it about his own hips. Shouldering his way past Garth, he bolted for the door. "Don't wait supper for me!"

Linet couldn't have been more pleased with herself as she made her victorious way across the de Ware courtyard. She'd bested that meddling gypsy again. Her first year as a *sole femme*, and already she was proving the de Montfort cleverness her father had always praised. If only, she wished, Lord Aucassin had lived to see her accomplishments.

The castle yard was nearly deserted. She supposed most of the craftsmen had gone to the fair. There were but a few armorers hammering hot steel over the forge and a thatcher repairing a rotted roof. In the midst of the courtyard, draped across three trestle tables, an enormous pennant was being stitched by several young ladies. Drawing near, she could see the figure of a great black wolf depicted on the green serge, the Wolf of de Ware. The eyes were fierce and chilling, the mane bristling. Suddenly she was very glad she'd be done with her business here in a fortnight.

She'd heard the stories. Everyone had. The three sons of

de Ware were warriors not to be trifled with—powerful, cunning, ferocious. In sooth, the eldest was considered by many to be the most dangerous swordsman in all England. All three had earned their spurs at an early age, and it was said they indeed possessed the hunting instincts of the wolf so boldly emblazoned on their crest.

She shivered involuntarily. She hoped Lady Alyce would be content with the cloth she'd purchased. Spanish captains she could handle, and an overzealous gypsy. But Linet wasn't sure she could face a trio of disgruntled, sword-wielding, lupine knights. She wondered how sweet Lady Alyce managed to keep her pups on their leashes.

She cleared the portcullis and nodded to the guard for her cart. Beyond the wall, the balmy spring breeze soughed through the elms and maples and wafted the fragrance of bay up the hill. It was the best time of year, with the grass new and sweet, sprinkled with periwinkles and daisies, and the willows tipped with vivid green. The sky was riddled with tufts of clouds, reminding her of shearing time, which reminded her in turn that she had little time to waste on savoring the spring day. There was business to attend to before night dropped its dark cloak over the land.

As she slipped her basket into the cart's bed, she couldn't help but think about the gypsy with the azure eyes. Who was the cocksure knave, she wondered, and what did he want? Of course, his story about protecting her was nonsense. After all, he was only a peasant. He was probably just eager to get his hands on her cloth or her coin. He wouldn't be the first to entertain such a notion. Like the others, however, he'd find himself in peril of his good health should he attempt to cheat Linet de Montfort out of her hard-earned living.

She shook her head as the breeze tugged at the edges of her cloak. She should've slapped the cur, she thought, for his insolence. Her father had warned her about dealing with peasants, how they were not to be trusted, how they possessed few manners and fewer morals. The de Montfort family was not to stoop to their level—so he'd drilled into her time and time again. Despite their own fall from grace, he never let Linet forget that she was a real lady.

She smirked. A real lady would never have endured the way

that peasant had stared at her, his eyes perusing her figure as if he planned to devour her, his sly smile mocking her dignity. He was a rogue, a scoundrel with cocky airs and more in his sapphire eyes than avarice, something far more dangerous than greed.

She definitely should have slapped him.

Her basket settled, she gathered her heavy skirts to climb up on the cart.

"Wait!"

Her foot hesitated on the step. Dear God, she thought, it couldn't be. No one was that audacious.

"Wait!" repeated the all-too-familiar voice, still several yards behind her. "I cannot let you go!"

Damn his persistence. She took a deep breath and turned, prepared to give the gypsy the scolding of his life. Then she froze.

Somehow the peasant had managed to wrest a sword from one of the guards. The heavy-laden sheath slapped against his thigh as he loped toward her. Dear God, she thought, did he mean to kill her?

She wasn't going to wait to find out. She heaved herself onto the cart. Then she took up the reins and snapped them smartly, startling the old nag into bolting down the castle road, nearly upsetting the wagon.

Recklessly she fled, determined to leave the gypsy in her dust, urging the horse on with curses. The wagon rollicked over a stone, and her wimple flew off her head, making her hair tumble out in wild tangles behind her. But she paid it no heed. Her heart racing, she half-stood to drive the nag onward.

The wagon careened around an egg merchant, scattering his flock of chickens in its wake. Then it bounded perilously over the rutted road, narrowly missing a fishmonger on his way to the castle with a basket full of herring. Only when the road cleared did she hazard a glance back over her shoulder.

"Jesu!"

He was tearing after her like a plundering berserker.

She cracked the reins down again. A squeal of panic rose in her throat. The cart rumbled over the road like an undulating pack of hunting hounds, growing more frenetic with each passing moment. The right wheels pitched into and out of a deep rut, rocking the cart perilously askew. The basket of neatly folded fabric toppled like a drunkard.

Then, suddenly, the entire back of the wagon dipped down. The gypsy was aboard.

She turned to him, her eyes wide.

Grim determination hardened his square jaw. The muscles of his forearms bulged as he hauled himself forward over the piles of wool. He was coming after her as relentlessly as a wolf after a fawn. And like the doomed prey, Linet couldn't drag her gaze away from her pursuer.

Alas, she had picked a poor time to shift her attention from the cart's path. The gypsy's eyes widened as well as he glanced beyond her at the abrupt turn in the road. Before she could mouth a protest, he dove to the front of the cart and grabbed the reins from her, hauling back on them so hard that the nag yelped and the wagon skidded to a halt in a cloud of rocks and dust.

She would have fallen forward, out of the cart and over the horse, but the gypsy barred the way with his arm. She let out a great "oof" as his elbow caught her in the stomach. Coughing and sputtering hysterically, she rounded on him.

"G-get away from me!"

Duncan's lungs hurt to bursting, and Linet's piercing shriek only added insult to the pain. Why in God's name he'd chased afoot after a wool merchant's cart driven by a reckless hoyden, he couldn't begin to fathom. Chivalry certainly had its queer moments.

By now, several interested travelers had stopped to look on, slack-jawed, but none seemed to want to get involved in what appeared to be a household squabble.

"Get away!" she squeaked, her eyes wide with fright.

He cocked an affronted brow at her. What was wrong with the woman? She had no cause for fear or hostility. After all, he'd likely just saved the little wretch's neck.

"Don't touch me," she gasped, scrambling to her feet. But this time, like a panicked hound biting its master's hand, she hauled back her arm and slapped him. Hard.

The crack of flesh on flesh stung his cheek and split the air like summer lightning.

He was stunned. He'd never been struck by a woman before. No one intentionally riled the temper of a de Ware. It was like poking a sleeping wolf. Worse still, there wasn't a shred of apology in her eyes, only mortification at what she'd dared.

He ground his teeth, wavering between shock and anger. For one ignoble moment, his fingers itched to return the slap. Instead, he grabbed her by the forearm, forcing her to sit down next to him on the wooden seat. Then he snapped the reins to set the old horse in motion. Ignoring the curious stares of those who pointed at the odd pair of them wrestling atop the cart, he drove onward toward the fair.

He'd never felt such anger—never! It wasn't like him to handle women roughly, but the urge to throttle this one overwhelmed him. She should be grateful to him, he thought. It was likely due to him that her neck was still attached to her shoulders, considering the company she'd kept lately. But nay, the silly wench probably thought she could walk through *hell* unscathed.

They rode along in frosty, bone-jarring silence until the castle diminished and slipped from sight behind a hillock. Then they reached the cover of the trees, and he drew back on the reins to stop the nag in the middle of the road.

Linet held her breath, her trepidation rising. Sweet Jesu, the gypsy had stopped in this isolated spot apurpose. What in the name of God did he intend?

His hand felt like a shackle around her arm. Mayhaps, she dared to hope, he only intended to rob her. Mayhaps he'd take her coin and be gone.

But her worst fears seemed confirmed as the rogue reached into the pouch at his waist with his free hand and pulled forth a small vial, uncorking it with his teeth.

Poison!

She tried to jerk her arm from his grasp.

"Cease, woman!" he commanded, his eyes blue steel beneath the dark brows.

Casting her pride to the wind, she sucked in a great breath and began yelling at the top of her lungs. "Murder! Help me! Murder!"

"Quiet!" he snarled, shaking her.

Some of the contents of the vial dripped out onto her cloak. She gasped in horror. What if the fabric melted away?

The gypsy glanced about to insure that no one had heard her cries. Then he glared at her, not in anger, but rather a kind of bemused disappointment. "Murder?" he asked.

Her heart still beat wildly, and she stared at the spot on her cloak, waiting for the material to dissolve. He followed her gaze. One corner of his mouth crooked up in a sardonic smile.

"Pine sap," he replied to her unasked question.

Then he released her arm to pull something else from his satchel, something black and hairy and dead. She recoiled instinctively. But it was only his fake beard, worse for wear from the stomping it had endured. He must have retrieved it from the fair.

"Perhaps this will cushion the blow next time," he grumbled. With that, he dabbed some of the sticky sap onto his cheeks and chin and affixed the scraggly beard to his face.

A bit of the tension drained out of her shoulders, and she felt suddenly foolish. It was clear the gypsy meant her no harm. Still, she wasn't about to let down all her defenses. She sat on the verge of the seat, ready to bolt.

"If you wish to retain custody of your horse and cart, wench," he said calmly, as if he could read her mind, "I suggest you remain where you are."

In sooth, she had little choice. She could ill afford to lose her wagon or the nag. She sat helplessly by while he patted his beard into place.

Suddenly the craziness of the whole episode struck her. Here she was, the hostage of a man who claimed to want only to protect her, who had no use for coin, and who possessed a penchant for wearing false facial hair. Slowly her fear began to diminish in the face of burning curiosity.

"Why do you wear that . . . that ridiculous thing anyway?" She waved toward his beard. "Can you not grow your own?"

"A beard?" He glared at her. "I used to be able to grow one," he said pointedly. "Although a few more harrowing days like this one may leave me both beardless and bald."

She peered at his thick ebony mane. He obviously spoke in jest. Jesu, he could lose half his hair and still have enough left for two men. It curled sinuously about his ear and teased the broad column of his neck. It looked soft.

He curved a brow at her, and she realized suddenly she'd been staring. She jerked her head around and trained her eye on the nag. "I suggest we dispense with this . . . whatever nonsense you have in mind as quickly as possible. I have work to do," she said, more to herself than to him. "So if you will leave off your morning ablutions and tell me just what it is you want from me . . ."

His cursory perusal of her from head to toe made her regret her choice of words. But thankfully, he didn't rise to the bait. He took a deep breath as if to collect his faculties. "I made a promise when I earned my spurs to protect all women," he announced. "I intend to honor that promise."

She could only stare at him. For all his strange antics, it had never occurred to her that he might be genuinely mad. Until now. "Your . . . spurs?"

"I do not take my vows lightly." His eyes took on a faraway cast. "Wherever there is one in need, there will I go."

Linet was silent for a moment. Then she burst out laughing. "You expect me to believe you are a knight?"

He thrust his jaw forward haughtily, which only made her laugh all the more.

"Well, Sir Whatever-You-Call-Yourself, you are the first knight I've met with no horse, no armor, and absolutely no sense of honor."

The flicker in his eyes warned her she had just tread on perilous ground.

"I have more honor in my little finger," he ground out, "than you have in your entire de Montfort body."

"Oh ho!" she cried. "My father was Lord Aucassin de Montfort of Flanders." Her hand went reflexively over the family medallion she wore beneath her surcoat.

His laugh was a snort of disbelief. "Forsooth? Yet he allows you to toil in the wool market?"

She blanched. He had no right to question her, none at all. A nobleman would've taken her at her word. She owed him no explanation, and she certainly had no intention of divulging her family's blemished history to him.

"Ah, I see," he said, his eyes softening. His voice grew curiously gentle, the amusement gone. "You are a byblow then?"

"No!" she exploded. "I am not a byblow! Don't ever call me that! My mother and father were properly wed! It wasn't my father's fault if . . ."

"If . . ." he prompted.

The care in his eyes seemed genuine. But she wasn't about to let a stranger know the humiliating circumstances of her birth. She straightened on the seat.

"We will drive to Woolmaker's Row," she informed him coolly, "and you will leave me there . . . alone."

He shook his head. "I'm not *leaving* you anywhere. You may be in grave danger. I've taken a vow to see you safe, and . . ."

"Safe? And who is to keep me safe from the likes of you?" She shook her head. "Nay, I have no need of your protection. I have my servant, Harold . . ."

"The old man?"

"He's . . . stronger than he looks."

The gypsy coughed.

She clenched her fists in the folds of her surcoat.

He clucked to the horse, and the cart lurched forward.

"I'll allow you to escort me only as far as the fair," she told him, pretending she had a choice in the matter.

He made no reply. She knew better than to mistake his silence for assent, but it was useless to argue now. Once they turned down Woolmaker's Row, she'd have Harold and the entire Woolmaker's Guild to back her up. Then she'd be rid of him.

Aye, she'd likely never see him again.

Never know the reason he wore that infernal beard, or why he claimed to be a knight, or why he was singularly obsessed with protecting her. But it was no concern of hers. She had her own life to live—a life of warp and weft, numbers and accounts, profit and tax—a comfortable, secure, predictable life. She had no time for eccentric gypsies and their crackbrained, chivalrous fantasies.

She sighed and clasped her hands in her lap as they bounced along the road, wondering uncomfortably if her father was scowling down from heaven. This was the closest

she'd ever been to a commoner. Likely the closest she'd ever
get. And as long as she was never going to see the gypsy
again, she supposed it would do no harm to take a quick peek
at the man, just out of the corner of her eye, solely for educa-
tive purposes.

Who was he? she wondered. The fists holding the reins
were massive, the veins prominent. They were hands accustomed to hard work. His thighs, too close to hers for comfort,
were long and heavily muscled beneath the crumpled hose,
like those belonging to a laborer. And yet there was a laziness
about him, a sensual languor that made him seem as if he
worked at nothing.

Then there was his behavior. He was certainly as vulgar and
boorish as the crudest peasant, and yet he possessed the natural authority and speech of a nobleman.

His clothing, of course, revealed the truth. While the wool
of his trews was coarse and riddled with tiny moth holes and
his leather boots worn nigh through, his cloak was fashioned
of finest English worsted. No coin had been spared in the
making of that garment.

There was but one conclusion to be drawn. The man was
obviously a thief. "You must have paid handsomely for that
cloak," she muttered, raking him with a knowing glare.

He smirked. "In sooth it was given me."

She rolled her eyes. "Given you! No doubt given at the
point of a dagger. 'Tis too fine a garment to give away. In
sooth, sirrah, you do the thing an injustice by wearing it."

"Indeed?" The corner of his lip curved up. "You think I
should cast it aside?" Then he clucked his tongue. "Ah nay,
you little wanton. I perceive your trickery now. You'll not get
me out of my clothing that easily."

She was sure she turned the color of Norwich scarlet, especially when he began to chuckle deep in his chest.

"And as to doing the garment an injustice, I must object. I
was grateful of the gift, and I respect its value." His lip
twitched with repressed humor. "Unlike some I could name. I
heard tell of a ship's captain who generously gave away four
casks of his best Spanish wine to a merchant who didn't respect its value. The foolish wench spilled the whole of it
across the docks right before his eyes."

Surprise slammed like a rock into her chest. She whipped her head around. "What do you know of that?" she asked sharply.

"Enough."

She fidgeted with her skirt, shifting her gaze between the two azure orbs of his eyes. "I was correcting an injustice. El Gallo stole goods from my father." She meant to stop there. She owed the gypsy no explanation. But something about the silent encouragement in his face bade her continue. She stared at her hands in her lap. "I didn't want the wine at all. That wasn't the point. But somebody had to stop the thieving. That's why I dumped it out."

She ventured a glance at the gypsy. Damn her ready tongue, she'd said too much. His gaze had melted into some utterly indescribable emotion—something between amusement and pity and admiration. She didn't like him looking at her like that. It was far too . . . intimate. If it killed her, she swore she'd not breathe another word to the man.

She was close enough to him now to see that silvery streaks shot through the cobalt of his eyes, as incongruous as silver thread worked into the blue woad of peasant's cloth, as enigmatic as the man himself. A lock of hair crooked across his forehead and between his brows like black lightning, giving him a dangerous air. His wide mouth had parted the merest bit, enough so she could see the tips of his strong, white teeth.

He was beautiful, she realized with a start. And just as quickly, she remembered he was a peasant. She trained her eyes on the path ahead.

Duncan endured Linet's curious perusal in silence most of the way. By the time he hauled the old nag up behind the de Montfort pavilion, she'd so thoroughly studied him that he wondered if the poor wench had ever laid eyes on a man at all before.

"Harold!" Duncan called, bringing the servant scurrying out of the booth in surprise. He tossed the reins to the old man. "Thank you," he said with a nod.

Linet alit daintily from the cart, clearly peeved by his familiarity with her servant. She smoothed her skirts and cleared her throat.

"Listen," she said quietly. "If it's coin you're after . . ."

He grinned. She was ever offering him coin. "As I told you before, I have no need of money. My family is quite rich."

She looked at him with such frustration that it was nigh comical. He supposed the amused glint in his eyes didn't help to soothe her irritation. "You won't go?"

He shook his head in mock sorrow.

She muttered something behind her teeth and began hauling forth bolts of cloth from the wagon with a vengeance. As much as she clearly longed to be rid of him, they both knew she could hardly afford to start a heated exchange in the marketplace. Besides, he had every right to be there. The fair was public thoroughfare.

Still, it didn't stop her from voicing her opinions under her breath. She muttered as she worked, and he heard bits and pieces of her complaints—"spiteful peasant," "meddling gypsy," "just take the coin and be on your way."

Chuckling, he climbed down from the wagon and positioned himself at the front of the stall to watch.

She selected the materials as if she were an artist choosing pigment—gray patterned worsteds and russet woolens, creamy broadcloth with deep green stripes, and some in several shades of blue, even a dark Spanish scarlet. All the while, her hair shimmered about her like a Saracen dancer's veil. When her nimble fingers caressed the varied textures of her wares, he found himself imagining those fingers upon his own varied textures.

He heaved a languorous sigh.

She'd scarcely completed displaying all the cloth when a golden-haired nobleman approached, eyeing a piece of yellow cloth.

"Ah, the saffron worsted," she told him, summoning up a convincingly charming smile in spite of her ill temper. "The color comes from a rare and exotic flower, sir. If I may say so, it is a perfect choice for your fair coloring."

The man was obviously flattered by her nonsense. His eyes gleamed, and he stroked the material speculatively.

Duncan didn't like him. And he didn't like the way Linet was speaking to him, almost as if she were enticing the man to purchase somewhat more than her cloth. He straightened and scowled at the patron from across the row. The man sheepishly backed away and moved on.

Linet whipped around after he had gone, her fists clenched at her sides. "What do you think you're doing?" she hissed.

"I've never trusted a man who would wear yellow," he invented simply, crossing the distance between them.

She looked at him as if he'd fallen from the moon. "You have just cost me a fortune! Do you know how much that worsted is worth?"

He narrowed his eyes. "I'll not tell you how to sell your goods, and you'll not tell me how to protect you."

"I've told you I need no protection," she bit out.

Then two young ladies approached, and she was forced to grit her teeth and smile again. Duncan nodded politely to the pretty maids. They giggled. Linet elbowed her way in front of him to show them a length of something in pale blue, but they gave it only a cursory glance. They weren't interested in Linet's cloth. They were interested in him. He gave one of them a wink. The maid blushed, murmuring something to her friend behind her hand.

"Does anything catch your eye, ladies?" he quipped, gesturing to the cloth draped about the booth.

The girls gasped and giggled again. Then, either too shy or muddled of wit to pursue further conversation, they scurried off, fluttering their eyelashes in farewell.

Linet gave him a withering glare. "You are interfering with my work."

He bowed and retreated to a less obvious post beside the counter. "My apologies." But he didn't feel apologetic in the least. He was enjoying himself.

"*You* may have no need of coin, gypsy, but I depend upon it."

He snorted. "After what you took from the de Ware coffers, I should think you could live comfortably the rest of your years. Though that may be a short time for one who bargains with sea reivers."

Her mouth dropped open. "Lady Alyce was charged fairly for her cloth," she huffed defensively. "As far as sea reivers. . . ."

"Sea reivers?" a fat woman with red cheeks aped as she

picked up a piece of green broadcloth. "Are these stolen goods?"

"Nay," Linet hastened to assure the lady, giving Duncan a warning glare. He obediently returned to the far side of the lane, but not before flashing her his most charming grin. He heard her continue, "They are all come by honestly, my lady, and what a clever woman you are to have spotted that green."

It was going to be a long day, he thought, leaning back against an elm and folding his arms across his chest. And it was going to be a Herculean task to keep troublemakers away from her—his angel with the dancing eyes, the dazzling smile, the heavenly curves.

A smile touched one corner of his mouth. It was going to be hell all right. But he supposed somebody had to guard angels here on earth.

4

L INET HAD BEEN SO CERTAIN THE GYPSY WOULD LEAVE BY
day's end. Surely by then he'd have tired of his game, seeing how intently she focused on her work, how seldom she
paid him any heed. But still he remained, standing across
from the stall with his arms crossed, watching the merchants,
watching the passing crowds, but mostly watching her. It
seemed as if every time she glanced up, he was watching her.

It had affected her business. She'd sold less than ten ells of
cloth today, and there was little hope of selling more. Already
the sun sank in the half-wooded copse, dancing in dappled
patterns across her fabric. The acrid smells of the dying fair
hung on the air—rusting apple cores, horse dung, stale beer.

Soon a great fire would blaze in the nearby clearing. All
were welcome to roast their own meat and apples over it or
perhaps purchase a joint or a pork pie from a vendor. Some of
the merchants packed up their wares and carted them home.
But the village of Avedon, where Linet kept her mesnage and
warehouse, was too far away for the daily trip, so she'd bed
down in her pavilion.

"What will you have for supper tonight, my lady?"

Linet pressed a startled hand to her heart. She hadn't even
seen the gypsy cross the lane.

"A pasty? Mutton mortrews?" he asked.

"Nay. I have a little dried herring and . . ."

The gypsy made a face. "Dried herring?" He shook his
head. "That is not food. That is a punishment. You must have
a proper meal."

She opened her mouth to stop him, but he snagged a passing squire, mumbled some instructions to him and pressed several silver coins into the boy's hand before she could speak. God alone knew where he'd come by the money, but she doubted he'd see it or the boy again.

Thus it was a complete surprise when, even before she and Harold had finished folding the cloth away, the lad returned juggling a veritable feast. The gypsy must have purchased a half dozen pasties and fruit coffyns. There was a great joint of beef, a wedge of hard cheese and even a jack of ale. Her mouth was still agape when the gypsy shoved a pasty into it.

"I hope you like lamb," he said.

Before she could reply, he called out, "Harold! Give those old bones a rest. I've got supper."

Harold dropped the cloth he'd been folding and toddled eagerly forward, not about to question a free meal.

"Weary of that nasty herring, are you?" the gypsy asked.

"Oh, aye." Harold licked his lips.

Linet would have protested the gypsy's meddling, but she was still chewing on the lamb pasty. It was admittedly delicious, the meat succulent, the crust flaky. It was far better than another meal of dried herring and hard bread. But she'd be damned if she'd tell him so.

"Herring's not much good for anything beyond Lent, I say," the gypsy confided. "Here, my good man, have a pork pie and a swig of ale to chase it down."

"Thank ye, m'lord."

M'lord? Linet choked on the pasty. Had Harold actually called the peasant *m'lord*? Her eyes watered, and she began to cough.

"Or perhaps *you* had better have the first drink," the gypsy offered with a wink, clapping her on the back.

She seized the ale from him and downed a big gulp. When she'd swallowed properly and could finally catch her breath, she returned the jack. "Harold, he is *not* your lord," she scolded. Then she turned to the gypsy. "My servant and I were quite content with our herring."

"Ah." He was laughing at her. She could tell.

"I won't pay you for what my servant eats," she informed him.

"I won't ask you to."

Fine, she thought, as long as they understood one another.

She dusted the crumbs from her skirt and surreptitiously eyed the fruit coffyns. They looked delicious, all golden and shiny and flaky. She wondered whether they were apple or cherry. The thought of the sweet fruit within made her jaw tingle. Her tongue flicked once lightly over her lip. Apple or cherry?

She bit the inside of her cheek. Perhaps, she considered, if she played along, if she *did* partake of his food, the gypsy would leave willingly.

"The only payment I'll ask," he said with a shrug, interrupting her thoughts, "is a small measure of gratitude."

"Thank ye, m'lord . . . again," Harold repeated, his mouth full of pork, his eyes confused.

"He is not a lord, Harold!" Linet hissed, bristling. Then she turned on the gypsy. "And just what do you mean by 'gratitude'?"

"I've purchased you a fine meal," the gypsy explained, "and I've kept the robbers from your stall. Surely that warrants . . ."

"Robbers? Aye, you've kept the robbers away, and the lords and their mistresses and everyone else with coin in their purse! I've not sold enough today to keep a beggar alive since you took up residence across the lane, watching me like . . . like some hawk on the hunt."

"Really?" he drawled with that irritatingly smug smile. "Well, if *you* had kept your eyes on your *patrons* instead of letting them rove in *my* direction every few moments . . ."

The blood rushed to her face. "*My* eyes!" she gasped. "I never . . . *You* were the one . . . Oh!"

Linet could see by his knowing smirk that the gypsy didn't believe anything she said. And she knew she'd only dig herself further into that pit of shame if she continued. She shoved the half-eaten pasty at him, dusted off her hands, and, with as much dignity as she could muster, resumed her task of folding the cloth.

The man was an arrogant imbecile, she thought, snapping a square of broadcloth, if he thought she'd have any interest in looking at him. He was a peasant, for God's sake—a filthy, unscrupled peasant, and she—she was a lady. Or nearly a lady. Nay, no matter what he said, *he* had been staring at *her*. She was sure of it.

She slammed the folded broadcloth down on the counter and began with another.

Harold continued to eat with untamed enthusiasm, licking his fingers and rolling his eyes in ecstasy. She should have made him stop as well. He was her servant, after all. She could order him to cease eating that ill-gotten food. But he looked so happy. And the pasty had been delicious. The gypsy was eating the rest of hers now, but there were plenty remaining. Her stomach growled in complaint.

She smacked the broadcloth into quarters atop the counter.

She glanced at the fruit coffyns. They were balanced precariously on the gypsy's thigh as he leaned against the booth. If he wasn't careful, he might drop them and waste all that delicious fruit. Apples wouldn't be so bad, but cherries . . .

Her mouth watered.

She smoothed the material with wide, brusque strokes.

She glanced up. A drop of rich brown juice hovered on the gypsy's lower lip.

She bit the inside of her cheek and creased the fabric.

"Mmm, there's naught like tender English lamb, is there, Harold?" the gypsy crooned, lapping up the juice.

"Nothin', m'lord," Harold agreed. Then he glanced up quickly at her in apology. "Er . . . nothin'."

Linet gripped the edge of the counter to keep from screaming. Her supper of dried herring seemed less and less appetizing by the moment. "You may leave as soon as you finish your meal," she told the gypsy tautly.

"I cannot eat all this myself," he said reasonably. "Come have a bite. I promise I'll not make you blush again."

Of course, those were the very words to set her flesh pinkening once more. She tried to ignore it and those teasing blue eyes of his.

"I'm not hungry," she lied. "Especially not for . . . for apple coffyns."

His smile was like honey poured slowly over pokerounce. "They're cherry."

She swallowed hard. She loved cherry coffyns. But they'd

been purchased with the gypsy's coin, coin no doubt pilfered from innocent purses.

"And they're still warm." His languid eyes were as tempting as the sweet he offered, no doubt as tempting as the devil's when he enticed Eve to taste the forbidden fruit.

She wavered in indecision.

"I won't even make you eat all your nasty herring first," he teased, wiggling his dark brows.

She had to crack a smile at that. "Just this once," she decided, "and then you'll go. I don't make a habit of living off the charity of others."

Duncan tried to contain his amusement. The toplofty merchant acted as if she did him a favor, taking the coffyn off his hands. But with what eagerness she came to retrieve it! She bit gently into the pastry, her eyes closed with delight. A smudge of cherry lingered on her lips, and Duncan longed to taste it there. But her tongue flicked out to catch the stray juice, savoring it with almost improper ardor. He'd seen that expression a hundred times on the faces of the children he'd saved from the streets—that ecstasy at their first taste of an orange or a piece of sugar loaf. But Linet was no starving waif. Surely she'd eaten her share of sweets.

Then again, he was certain she'd never experienced the touch of a man. And with her sparkling eyes, her flawless skin, her supple lips and glorious mane of hair, that seemed harder to believe.

She was an enigma, this wool merchant who could be so world wise and yet so enchantingly innocent at the same time. The combination was intriguing, but dangerous. It was indeed fortunate he'd undertaken to see to her safety.

She licked the last drop of sticky juice from the tip of her finger.

"Would you like another?"

An endearing blush rose to her cheeks. She'd finished the pastry off as quickly as a starving hound did a bone, and she knew it. "Nay." She lowered her gaze. "Thank you."

He smiled. She'd said it. She'd said thank you. "It was my pleasure." And had been, indeed.

Linet looked up and felt the warmth of the gypsy's smile all the way to her toes. Then she endured an awkward moment of silence when her hands seemed to turn to useless extensions, fidgeting with her skirts. "Hadn't you better go while there is yet light?" she finally blurted out.

"Go?"

She stiffened.

"I told you I was here to protect you. The night can be even more dangerous than the day."

"But surely you can't mean to . . ."

"I couldn't possibly leave you now. To abandon you when you need me the most? Nay, it would be unchivalrous."

"But I don't need . . ."

"Nonsense." He scooped up the leftover food and placed it on an empty space on the counter. "I'll stretch out right here before the pavilion. You needn't worry about me. This cloak will keep me as warm as a nesting cuckoo. And I'll keep at least one eye open for trouble."

She supposed it would have been rude to suggest that she hadn't been worried about his comfort at all, that she really was more concerned about her reputation. Still, how would it look to have a vagabond sleeping on the de Montfort doorstep? Unfortunately, there was naught she could do. A peasant could sleep where he willed as long as it wasn't within another's private domain. The lane belonged to everyone.

The gypsy yawned and stretched his arms. At least, she thought, he was right about one thing. A troublemaker would think twice before crossing the path of a man with arms like that.

The sky was darkening faster than indigo dye dropped in hot water. There were still accounts to go over, cloth to fold, and coin to count. She had no time for this nonsense. She supposed she'd just have to grit her teeth and endure the night. It was too late and she was much too tired to discuss the gypsy's meddling. Ousting him would have to wait till the morrow. On the morrow she'd have a fresh outlook and more resolve. Aye, she'd know just what to say to the man to send him packing come morning.

Hours later Linet finished her work inside the pavilion, and Harold began snoring from behind the linen modesty screen. But she was wide awake. She nibbled on a morsel of pasty left from dinner, listening to the crickets drilling the night air with their wings, thinking about the man slumbering but a single serge panel away.

She wondered if he was cold. The pavilion's walls kept her as cozy as fleece kept a sheep. But outside the pavilion, the cruel English mist, even in spring, could cut through a man like shears. She looked guiltily about her at stack upon stack of thick, warm wool. Even one ell of it could mean the difference between freezing to death and getting a good night's sleep. And she seemed to remember that somewhere there was a piece of woaded wool, stretched a bit askew, dyed a little unevenly, that probably wouldn't profit her more than a pound or two at most. She supposed she could afford to part with it. Besides, it was likely the only way she'd get a good night's sleep herself.

Before she could reconsider, she dug the piece out from under a pile of cheap cloth. Silently she stepped through the pavilion flap and into the dim night. The cool grass chilled her bare toes, and she curled them protectively. Holding her breath, she tiptoed toward the front of the stall and leaned over the counter. Just below her, the bulky shape that was the gypsy huddled on the ground. Unfolding the cloth, she took a few practice swings, then tossed the fabric over his slumbering form.

The material landed askew, half atop him, half on the ground. She cursed under her breath. Balancing precariously on her stomach upon the ledge of the counter, her toes inches above the ground, she stretched out an arm and painstakingly tugged the cloth up over what she presumed were his shoulders.

Her task completed, she began to scoot backwards.

But something snatched her wrist before she could withdraw it. She let out a loud gasp.

"Shh."

How dared he hush her? He'd frightened the wits out of her! "What do you think you're . . ." she hissed.

He squeezed her wrist to silence her, then turned her hand purposefully over in his. He let his thumb nest in the palm of her hand, his fingers splaying across the back. Then a moist warmth enclosed the tips of her fingers.

Dear God . . . he was kissing her.

She should have done a million things—slapped him, snatched her hand back, cried out for Harold—but the contact seemed so innocent . . . and so fleeting that on the morrow she'd think it had been a dream.

"Thank you," the gypsy murmured against her fingers.

Then he released her.

It was over as quickly as it had begun. And then the chill of the night descended, making her shiver, calling her back to the safety of the pavilion. But for a long while, until she finally drifted off in slumber atop her straw pallet, her fingers tingled with a current she could neither name nor understand.

It was summer. Duncan was swimming in the south pond, letting the cool water slide over his naked body, coursing like a breaching whale upward into the sun's warmth, then falling again into the refreshing depths. The current caressed his flesh, swirling about him in waves that turned from blue to green to gold.

And then it was her hair—silken waves of amber brushing against his skin, cloying like honey between his legs, wrapping like spun gold around his chest, until the delight of liquid sunlight brought him to the brink of ecstasy . . .

The crickets stopped.

His eyes popped open.

Night crashed down around him as black as a hood over a condemned man. His heart thrummed in the calm but quick beat of a seasoned warrior. He placed his right hand over the pommel of his sword.

Someone was near. He could feel their presence. Slowly, stealthily, he peered out from beneath the cocoon of his cloak and the wool coverlet.

It was not yet dawn, but enough morning light filled the sky for him to recognize the silhouette of a rascal up to some mischief. The man stopped less than a yard from where Duncan lay hidden. Though he didn't dare take a closer look, he'd have wagered his blade it was one of El Gallo's men. He'd known the reiver would not surrender so easily. Just as he'd been fairly sure the slimy bastard would strike in the anonymity of night.

And he was ready for him.

At least he'd thought he was ready. Until the man let out a low whistle, summoning two companions from the wood.

Duncan narrowed his eyes. One man he could take by surprise. Two he could play against each other. But three . . . three were going to be messy.

The familiar harsh whisper of steel against leather told him the men had unsheathed. They were splitting up, sidling around opposite ends of the counter to get at the pavilion. He would have to subdue the first man, then leap over the counter before the other two could gain entrance.

He grinned. It was a good thing he liked challenges.

He let three heartbeats pass. Then, like a wild beast, he pitched forward, bowling the first ruffian over. The man started yammering in Spanish, kicking at him. Duncan threw off the cloak, entangling the man's legs in the fabric, and shot to his feet.

Wheeling about, he drew his blade. Too late. The other two had disappeared. Mother of God, were they already inside? His heart in his throat, he leaped atop the counter.

It wasn't as sturdy as it looked. The wood creaked and whined as he tottered on its edge. Then he catapulted free, and the whole thing crashed in splinters to the ground.

He dove for the flap of the pavilion and flung it aside. The interior was as black as pitch. The odds were against him. It was no longer a question of frightening the Spaniards away now. When he found them, he'd have to slay them.

He could hear Linet's sleep-befuddled murmuring from the midst of the pavilion.

He shouted, "Harold! Linet! Stay back, both of you!"

He swung his left arm blindly about and touched heavy wool—a man's garment. Snatching viciously at the sleeve, he stabbed forward. But his target seemed to vanish.

He whipped his sword to the right. Damn it! Where were they? His foot nudged what felt like a boot, and he sliced outward, slashing through another tabard. But there was no scream, no falling body, not even a whisper of protest.

"Come forth, you cowards," he growled, squinting against the impossible black.

Something toppled to his left, something heavy. He drove the point of his sword downward, impaling the foe.

"What's going on?" Linet demanded.

"Stay back!"

He waved the sword in a wide swath before him. One was down. Where was the other one hiding? He strained his ears for some telltale sound, but all of Woolmaker's Row had come awake at the disturbance and were making a clamor outside. He swung around and backed up one pace, and another.

Then he stepped straight into the folds of the Spaniard's cloak.

He dropped like a stone, raising his blade behind him. With one violent backward thrust, he skewered both the man and the pavilion wall.

The breath he expelled was shaky. It had been a long time since he'd killed a man. Tonight he'd slain two. But his angel was safe. That was all that mattered.

Linet swore that lunatic gypsy was making enough din to rouse the dead. "What is going on?" she persisted.

"Nay!" he exploded. "Stay there. You don't want to see this."

Linet pursed her lips. No one would tell her what she could or could not see, not in her own pavilion. She gathered the selvages of her dressing gown together tightly and made her way forward.

"Nay! Remain where you are!"

"What have you done?" she said, ignoring his command. "All of Woolmaker's Row is awake."

She breezed past him and tossed open the pavilion flap, shedding what little glow lightened the sky on the scene within. A pile of worsted slumped in the middle of the pavilion like a destitute beggar. She frowned. What was it doing there?

"Ahem," intruded a voice from outside. "May I be of some assistance?"

Linet turned. Standing just beyond the ruins of what had been her counter was a tall, dark gentleman—a foreigner, by the sound of his voice. He held aloft a candle, and by its fulvous glow, she saw a gaunt face framed by an impeccably trimmed sable beard. His eyes were so dark as to be colorless, shining like ebony beads in the candlelight. She could make out enough of his attire to see that his velvet surcoat was lined with fur and that he wore a large silver medallion on a long chain.

"Do you need help, my lady?" he asked again.

My lady. The words took her aback for a moment.

"Nay . . . sir . . . or aye." She smiled sheepishly. "I'm afraid I'm a bit confused. If I could borrow your candle?"

A drop of wax slithered down the candle and onto the man's hand, but he didn't so much as flinch. "Of course. Allow me." His eyes glittered as he passed her and ducked into the pavilion.

Nothing could have prepared Linet for the utter devastation the light revealed. Ruined cloth lay everywhere. Rent wool was strewn across the pavilion rug. Stacks of broadcloth had been knocked over and bore multiple imprints of muddy boots. A pile of worsted was run through like a boar for supper. And her best Italian blue—the cloth she'd promised Lady Alyce—hung skewered by a sword against the pavilion wall, like a dying butterfly pinned by a naughty boy.

Only this naughty boy was one meddling gypsy, crouching in bafflement at the foot of his handiwork, looking for all the world as if he'd no idea how this had happened.

Linet's eyes began to tear. So much work. So much time. Ruined. And all because of that peasant. It would take months to replace the cloth. Years to repair her reputation.

"Get out!" Her voice wavered. But she clamped her jaw. A de Montfort didn't cry.

The gypsy rose to his feet. "But I . . ."

"Get out!"

"Will you listen . . ."

"I think the lady has made herself clear," the man with the candle said.

"Linet, you don't understand," the gypsy implored.

"Nay," the man said, the threat thick in his voice, "it is you who do not understand. The lady asked you to leave."

The gypsy turned to her. His look of hurt confusion was almost convincing. But then she should have known better. She should never have trusted him. He was a peasant. Just like her mother.

"Linet, listen to me. Three of El Gallo's men came here to do you harm. I had to protect you. I followed them into the pavilion. You must believe me."

The foreign gentleman stepped between her and the gypsy in challenge. "Three men? I see no men."

"They came in here. They had to have." Duncan scanned the pavilion in desperation. This was mad, he thought. He knew what he'd seen. But had he seen them? Not really. He'd never really watched them enter the pavilion. "Wait. There was one outside. Surely you saw him as you came in. I left him trussed up in my cloak . . ."

"I saw no one, peasant."

Duncan wasn't about to take the simpering gentleman's word for anything. He pushed past the man and through the pavilion flap. A flock of merchants had gathered before the booth, their curiosity overpowering their grogginess. He milled through the mumbling crowd, scanning the ground for any sign of the missing Spaniard—his cloak, a coif, the woolen blanket. Nothing.

How could three full-grown men vanish like mist? Something smelled as rotten as a twenty-year-old barrel of salted herring. And Duncan wasn't about to leave Linet unguarded until he got to the bottom of that barrel. He turned from the questioning onlookers and prepared to face her with the news.

But the scene he glimpsed through the crack of the pavilion flap left a bitter taste in his mouth that silenced him. Strong, willful, independent Linet de Montfort was in tears. Drops streamed down her cheeks despite the battle she fought to suppress her weeping, and her shoulders jerked in mutiny.

The foreigner reached for her, drawing her in like a fisherman hauling in his net, bringing her slowly up against his spare frame until her sobs were muffled in the folds of his cloak. "Hush now, my lady," he murmured. "He is gone." Then the bastard lifted one black-gloved paw and ran his spidery fingers over her golden locks. *Duncan's* golden locks.

Duncan's jaw tensed.

"Shh," the man continued softly, stroking her hair. "He will trouble you no more, my lady. You have my word on it as a gentleman."

Duncan longed to burst in upon them, just to give the lie to the man's rash promise. If that lout was a gentleman, Duncan would eat his scabbard. But at that moment, Linet lifted her eyes, all dewy and full of suffering. She looked up at the stranger before her with all the trust and hope Duncan deserved but had never received.

And he grew infuriated. Those should have been *his* arms around her. *His* words of reassurance. *He* had been the one sleeping on the cold, hard ground before her pavilion all night. It had been *his* body at risk against three armed attackers. And if they hadn't somehow managed to disappear, it would've been *his* eyes she'd be looking into now with such gratitude.

Damn the wench! She had no heart. He'd purchased her supper with his own coin. He'd kept El Gallo from devouring her on the docks. He'd saved her cloth and her cart and her horse from certain destruction. God's wounds! He'd risked his very life for her! And yet, one flip of a velvet sleeve, one flash of a silver medallion, and she clung to an utter stranger as if the sun revolved around him.

So she didn't believe she needed his protection. Very well. He'd withdraw it. Far more important matters awaited. Whole villages of his father's vassals endured much more pressing problems than she. And *they* would accept his help gratefully.

Clamping his jaw, he turned and strode off with all the dignity his noble upbringing afforded him, past the rows of curious faces, down Woolmaker's Row, along the road leading back to the castle.

The concealing shadows of night fled before the approaching dawn, laying bare the familiar hills and dense forests rolling out across de Ware land. As he trudged home, Duncan tried to banish Linet from his mind. Instead, he thought about his people—the crofters who worked these fields, his noble kin who guarded them, the peasants who slept in the wood, the servants and merchants and beggars who would one day depend on him.

But everything he passed reminded him of her. The distant sun-kissed wheat was the exact color of her hair. The shiny young leaves of the hedges dividing the field matched her eyes. A wild rose climbing over a crumbling stone wall wore the soft pink of her lips. Even the somber hue of her gray surcoat was mimicked in the surface of the still, silvery pond south of the castle.

Somewhere in the distance, a spirited wench with a mane of amber and wide emerald eyes sought comfort in a nobleman's arms. She'd likely forgotten all about her worthless gypsy.

If only he could dismiss her as easily. After all, he tried to convince himself as the sun scaled steadily up the distant castle walls, it really was no concern of his what happened to her. She wasn't even his vassal. She wasn't his responsibility.

He ran a callused hand through his hair. It was no matter that the blushing clouds of morning were the exact color of her skin. No matter at all.

He shuddered and climbed the hill toward the castle. It promised to be another long day.

Linet was mortified. Not since her father's death had she wept so freely, and then only in the privacy of her chamber. Here she was, staining some poor gentleman's velvet sleeve with her tears, her season's cloth in ruins about her, and all she could think about was how that cursed gypsy had betrayed her.

She'd trusted him. Though her intellect had warned her otherwise, she'd believed him. In sooth, she'd not had so restful a night since she'd left her own mesnage in Avedon, simply knowing he was slumbering just outside.

But he'd played her false.

She should have heeded her father's advice. She should never have even exchanged words with a peasant.

"There," the nobleman cooed. "You feel better now, no?"

Suddenly she realized the impropriety of the situation. Sniffing delicately, she extricated herself from his embrace.

"Much better, my lord. Thank you." She gave him a quick smile.

His dark gaze fell sharply to the wet spot on his sleeve, startling her. Even the reassuring shrug that followed couldn't erase the instant of displeasure she glimpsed on his face.

"Oh, forgive me," she said. "A little water . . ." The basin of wash water still stood atop the small trestle table amidst her things. She rushed to it, wet a linen rag, and returned to scrub vigorously at the stain. "This should rinse out most of the salt. The water shouldn't harm the fabric. Of course, you'll want to brush it when it's dried, and . . ."

He grabbed her wrist as suddenly as a spider catching a fly. She gasped. Then he turned her hand over and bent to kiss it.

"My lady," he breathed, his lips barely sweeping the back of her hand, "I would consider it an honor to wear your tears upon my sleeve."

She gave him a tremulous smile. What a relief it was to exchange pleasantries with one of her class, one who understood courtesy and chivalry, one who wouldn't twist her words. Or gaze lustfully at her. Or claim to be something he was not. She wiped away one final tear and took a deep breath.

"Besides," the gentleman added, "I have several garments just as fine."

Linet blinked. Most men could ill afford *one* such garment.

The man passed off the smoking candle to Harold, then rubbed his hands together, the gloved one against the ungloved, his long fingers interlacing like contrasting threads on a loom. "And now, my lady, if I may introduce myself?" He made a courtly bow. "I am Don Ferdinand Alfonso de Compostela."

"You're Span . . . Spanish?"

"Yes." His brow wrinkled in concern. "Does this trouble you?"

"Oh nay," she was quick to assure him. Certainly she had naught to fear from the kind gentleman. Still, she gave him her name on a murmur. "I am Linet de Montfort."

"It is an honor, my lady." He sketched another half-bow, then turned briskly about to survey the room, his black cloak whirling like a great bat. He pulled the sword protruding from the pavilion free. The precious blue cloth dropped as heavily as a dead beast. "I fear your goods have been damaged beyond repair, my lady."

She knew that, but somehow hearing it spoken aloud made it all the more horrible. The taste of hopelessness was bitter. Her reputation would be destroyed now. Her weavers couldn't possibly fulfill all the orders she'd taken, even if there was the faintest hope she could lay hands on that much raw wool. And that didn't even allow for spinning, carding, and dyeing. Her first year as a *sole femme* was ruined.

Of course, the Guild wouldn't let her go hungry. Woolmakers always took care of their own. But the compensation she'd get from them would be nearly as difficult to accept as the smug, pitying looks that would surely accompany the coin.

"I'll have to go back to Avedon," she murmured.

The gentleman stepped forward at once. "Then I insist on sending my guard with you. A beautiful lady as yourself should not travel without protection." With a snap of his fingers, he summoned a servant to assist her.

She gave him a bleak smile, too stunned by loss to be more gracious. Then, with the help of Harold and the Spanish gentleman's servant, she morosely collected her possessions for the journey home.

It was mid-morning when Linet clucked to the horse to start the heavy-laden cart forward. Even in the noble company of Don Ferdinand's mounted escort, it was all she could do to hold her head high, ignoring the prying stares of her fellow woolmakers as she departed the fair a full fortnight early.

Don Ferdinand, bless his gallant heart, had provided well for her. Not only had he sent four well-armed knights to accompany her, he'd also included a basket of bread and Spanish wine for her breakfast.

Not that she had the stomach for it.

But Harold took to the food eagerly enough. In sooth, when his wine was half gone, Linet noticed her servant lolling drowsily beside her on the cart seat like a too-well-fed pig. He slumped against her, and in disgust, she tried to elbow him back. But instead of awakening him, she shoved him clear from the cart and into the waiting arms of one of the riders.

Still Harold didn't rouse. Dear God! What was wrong with him?

The guard hissed something in Spanish to his cohorts. Then they all looked at her. Linet blanched. Had their eyes been so black, so flat, so scheming before? A lump of sickening fear rose in her stomach as she began to ask questions she should have asked all along, questions she *would* have asked had she been thinking aright. Who was Don Ferdinand? How had he appeared at just the right time to come to her rescue? Why was he being so generous with his aid?

Before she could answer, someone's hairy hand closed over her mouth, and she was dragged backward by an arm around her waist.

Suddenly, every sense came alive. She fought against the human bonds as the guard lifted her from the cart like a basket of laundry. She kicked and struggled with every ounce of her strength. She chomped down hard on her captor's hand.

The man screamed. She tasted sickening blood. Then something landed heavily at the back of her head. There was a brief flash before she slipped into dreamless oblivion.

5

DUNCAN STOOD UP IN THE STIRRUPS ATOP HIS GALLOPING
destrier and swung the studded mace over his head. The
great helm was suffocating. Sweat dripped down his forehead,
and his shoulder ached, but he hadn't yet exorcised the
demons that cursed wool merchant had set upon him. A twist
of his arm, a splintering crash, and the wooden target was de-
molished. He turned the steed and hauled off his helm, tossing the mace to the ground.

From the corner of the list came a smattering of applause.

"Well done, Duncan!" Robert called. He shook his head
and elbowed Holden beside him. "Your brother's generosity
is indeed amazing," he quipped sardonically. "See how he
bashes apart the target just to give some poor idle soul employment tomorrow building a new one?"

Duncan dismounted and gave Freya a dismissing swat on
the flank. He wasn't in the mood for Robert's sarcasm. Neither, apparently, was Holden. His brother's eyes darkened as
he strode across the field toward Duncan.

"Where is the wool merchant?" Holden demanded, scowling.

Duncan spat in the dust. God forbid Holden should waste
time on such a triviality as a polite greeting.

"Where is she, Duncan?" he repeated.

"And what concern is it of—"

"Duncan!" Holden caught hold of his shoulder, his eyes
steely. "Sombra . . . travels on the *Corona Negra*."

Duncan's heart skipped a beat. He looked back and forth

between the two. He hoped Holden was jesting. But neither cracked a smile. "Sombra . . . is alive?"

Holden punched his fist against his palm. His nostrils flared. "I don't know how he did it. I saw the bastard myself. No one should have survived that beating."

A sickening knot formed in Duncan's belly. Sombra, the notorious Spanish whoremonger, the woman-killer, had deserved to die, if half of the stories about him were true. That his brutal beating had been at the hands of a man who'd lost his only daughter to the monster was fitting. In sooth, had the poor man's crime been discovered, no jury of his peers would have convicted him for it.

But if Sombra was alive . . .

The thought chilled him. Sombra was a merchant of flesh, earning his name, Shadow, by working on the heels of El Gallo. While El Gallo intercepted ships to steal their goods, Sombra boarded the vessels to see what human treasure they offered. There were Spanish nobles who would pay a considerable sum for Sombra's discriminating taste in women and his effective methods of taming them.

Holden's eyes were haunted, remembering. "I helped the man hide the body. We left Sombra in the bracken near the shore where no one would find him." He ploughed a hand through his dark hair. "Jesu, I should have buried the Spanish bastard beneath twenty feet of rock."

"We can correct that oversight now," Robert said grimly. "The *Corona Negra* is still in port. Sombra's bound to be close."

Holden nodded. "Duncan, your merchant wench is safe, aye?"

"Safe?" He snorted. "Aye." Linet was safe forsooth. Safe in another man's arms. A Spanish nobleman who had swept her off her feet with honeyed flattery and dripping wealth . . .

Duncan's gut twisted as a horrible possibility wormed its way into his head. It was too awful to contemplate, but . . .

"Holden," he barely breathed, "describe Sombra."

Holden frowned. "When I saw him, he was a bloody mess. Thin as a lance, black beard, dressed like a damned lord, all in black."

Duncan's breath froze in his chest. Linet's nobleman. . . . "Sweet Christ!"

• • •

Everyone gathered at The Pike's Head. Within the crowded alehouse, gossip was exchanged, bargains were struck, and impoverished villeins rubbed elbows with wealthy merchants. One had only to wait to learn any piece of news. Including the whereabouts of a missing wool merchant.

Duncan had found nothing all day. No trace of Linet's pavilion remained. All the other wool merchants could say was that she'd left earlier in the company of four guards.

Robert, Garth, Holden and he had ransacked the surrounding woods, probed every bole of every tree, overturned rocks a person couldn't possibly fit beneath, and waded for miles along the banks of the treacherous river nearby. They'd searched till the last of the sun's rays dwindled, turning the woods a hopeless tangle of murky gray. To no avail. She'd simply vanished. He'd failed. He'd promised Linet protection, and he'd failed.

Robert had bade him let it go. Garth had tried to absolve him of blame. Only Holden had understood. Duncan would die before he'd give up the search.

He discreetly summoned the alewife for another cup, then sank back into the shadows of the darkest corner of the pub. He pulled the threadbare wool cloak tighter about his shoulders, watching, waiting, listening.

The room was alive with chatter. Two velvet-clad youths conversed in gently indignant voices about the price of silk. A wheezing old woman huddled in the corner against the chill of her own bones in a bundle of filthy rags that seemed her only possession. A sailor regaled the serving wench with bawdy roundelays. A reeking leather merchant calculated his day's earnings by candlelight, rapidly scrawling figures across a ledger. But Duncan was only interested in the Spaniards.

The black-bearded fellow in the middle of the room had drunk far too much. His red-haired friend told him so as Black-beard tipped his ale back yet again, sloshing it over the rim of his cup and onto his crudely bandaged hand. Before he could begin to wail in pain, another Spanish mongrel stumbled into the alehouse, distracting him. The red-haired man made a grand gesture of welcoming the new arrival to their table.

Most of their talk was idle chatter—boasting, ribbing,

shared obscenities. Duncan supposed if he wanted informative conversation, he was going to have to prod it along.

Taking one last swig of ale from his cup, he wiped the foam from his mouth with the back of his sleeve, then sprinkled the brew generously over his garments. Tousling his hair into wisps over his forehead, he pulled the hood of the cloak forward to conceal his face and staggered to his feet. Hiding his hands in the folds of worn wool, he hunched and tottered toward the trio of Spaniards.

"*Perdon*," Duncan croaked in the cracked, feeble voice of an old woman.

Black-beard frowned at the intrusion. Red-hair made a show of waving away the odor of ale wafting from Duncan's garments.

"What do you want, you stinking crone?" Red-hair snapped.

Duncan pretended great secrecy, bending close to Red-hair's ear and whispering in Spanish. "El Gallo has sent me."

"Sent you for what? To polish my boots with your wrinkled backside?"

The Spaniards laughed uproariously.

When they had settled again, Duncan resumed. "He wishes me to find the one called Sombra."

The three reivers gaped at this piece of news.

"Sombra?" Black-beard murmured.

"Shh!" Red-hair looked nervously about, then bunched the front of Duncan's cloak. "El Gallo told you to go to Sombra?" he whispered.

"*Sí*," Duncan said. Then he emitted a nasty wheezing cough that made Red-hair snatch his hand back in revulsion. "He said I might find employment."

"Employment!" the third fellow barked.

The three Spaniards looked quizzically at Duncan's huddled form, then at each other. At last, Red-hair nodded, smothering a snort of laughter behind his hairy knuckles.

"Ah, now that I think about it, *sí*, Sombra might have room in his employ for a pretty young thing like you."

The other two snickered into their ale.

Duncan had guessed aright. It probably wasn't the first time El Gallo had played such a jest—sending a withered old crone to Sombra.

"Go down to the docks, *abuela*," Red-hair continued. "Ask for the *Corona Negra*. Sombra will be aboard."

Duncan mumbled his thanks and shuffled toward the door of the alehouse while the Spaniards speculated on the outcome of the joke.

"He'll dump her into the sea directly," Black-beard guessed, "the toothless old crone."

"Wait," Red-hair said. "Toothless? She is toothless?" He hacked out a dry laugh. "Eh, maybe Sombra does have employment for her after all."

Duncan could easily imagine the crude gesture accompanying that remark. Ignoring them, he surreptitiously pressed a silver coin into the palm of the destitute old woman in the corner as he passed, then made his way out of The Pike's Head.

"You think she's aboard?" Robert whispered.

Holden and Garth followed Robert's gaze toward the huge ship listing menacingly at the moonlit dock.

"Aye," Duncan replied stonily. But he didn't want to think about what had become of her there. If Sombra had touched one hair on her head . . . He ground his teeth as rage and fear threatened to break the thread of his calm. Whatever had happened to Linet, it was his fault. He shouldn't have let her out of his sight for a moment. Not for a moment.

His only hope was that Sombra recognized her value, that the whoremonger wouldn't pass up the chance to turn a profit on such a prize by . . . damaging her.

From his vantage point high on the hill, Duncan could see the *Corona Negra* etched in shadows against the dark sea. Its furled sails exposed three masts like the skeletal remains of giant fingers. He shivered as the cold mist penetrated his worn garments. Then, taking a deep breath, he stepped forward.

Holden caught him by the shoulder. "You're not going aboard." It was a statement, not a question.

Duncan tensed his jaw. "You know what kind of things that bastard is capable of."

Holden compressed his lips into a grim line and nodded. "But Sombra is *my* unfinished business, Duncan, not yours."

"Listen, you two," Robert hissed. "Your father will have

my head if I let either of you board El Gallo's ship." He straightened his shoulders and cleared his throat. "I'll go."

Garth whipped his head around. "Nay! Absolutely not, Robert. *I* can understand their language best. *I* should be the one to . . ."

Holden grabbed Garth by the front of his jerkin. "Don't even think of it, little brother."

Robert shook his head. "Impossible, Garth. Your *mother* would have my head if I let *you* . . ."

Duncan seized Robert by the front of his cloak and spoke under his breath. "You'll not breathe a word of this to our mother, Robert, or I'll break every bone in your body! In fact," he added, releasing Robert, "I'll have your oaths, all of you. None of this will pass your lips. Do you understand?"

Holden cursed softly, but gave his assent.

Garth nodded solemnly.

Robert reluctantly agreed. "All right, but I'm not letting any of you board that reiver's vessel."

Garth sighed. "Robert, be reasonable. You couldn't . . ."

"Wait." Duncan looked at his trio of determined cohorts. There was only one way to end their dispute. No one could ask for more loyal companions. But this was his fight. He alone was to blame. He alone would enter the dragon's lair.

"Perhaps Garth *should* go," Duncan said, rubbing his chin thoughtfully. "After all, he *is* the best swordsman."

"Don't be absurd!" Holden cried.

"What! The best . . ." Robert choked. "Garth couldn't slice the end off a roast joint!"

"Are you insulting me?" Garth asked incredulously. "I believe you're insulting me! And who managed to unhorse you at the last tournament melee?"

"Sheer luck! By the time you'd come round with a blade . . ."

"*I* had come to your rescue," Holden informed Robert. "You were fighting like a woman . . ."

Duncan stole off, leaving them to argue. He knew full well he was the only man for the task. By the light of the moon, he made his way swiftly down the lane toward the *Corona Negra*, toward his maiden in distress.

• • •

Slipping aboard the *Corona Negra* was easy for Duncan by the shadow of night. His cloak enwrapped him like a dark cloud. As a precautionary guise, he'd obscured one eye with a makeshift patch cut from his boot, but he doubted any of the reivers would cross his path. Most of the ship's crew were still deep in their cups at the several alehouses lining the harbor.

The watchman at the main mast took him completely by surprise. Duncan had almost stepped on the man's shadow before he noticed him. His heart leaped into his throat and he stopped in his tracks. Fortunately, the man hadn't let his duties as the watch prevent him from imbibing as freely as his more lucky companions. As Duncan stood frozen in silence, the reiver knocked back a jack of ale in several long gulps and let out a hearty belch.

Duncan stepped carefully backward over the warped wood planking as the watchman grumbled about his sudden shortage of liquor. Then Duncan's cloak caught on a grappling hook, rending the quiet of the night with a loud rip.

"Eh!" the watchman grunted, whipping around.

It was too late to run. Duncan let loose with a string of the foulest Spanish words he knew and began grappling drunkenly with the snagged garment as if it were the devil himself. The watchman visibly relaxed, chuckling at the obvious misfortune of one of his fellow reivers, and Duncan tore the cloth free.

"*Tonto!*" the watchman guffawed.

Duncan couldn't have agreed more. He *was* a fool. But now wasn't the time to discuss it. "*Bastardo,*" he muttered back, spitting at the watchman's feet. Then he stumbled off in the direction of the hold.

She had to be there. Sombra wouldn't risk carrying his precious cargo in view of the crew. But he had one chance in two of choosing the right compartment of the hold. Eyeing the twin hatches, he measured the suspense with two breaths, whispered a hasty prayer, then hauled open the one on the left.

One grateful wool merchant was nowhere to be seen.

Instead, Duncan stumbled onto a lively game of dice. Three drunken Spaniards crowded around an oak barrel, fingering piles of silver coins. He cursed under his breath. Mumbling an apology, he tried to extricate himself, but it was too late. They'd spotted a mark.

"Eh, we need a fourth, right, Cristoforo?" one of them said.

"*Sí*. Come in, come in. Your first voyage with El Gallo, no?" He winked at the first.

Duncan grunted.

"Then you are a virgin, no? We break you in right. Slow. Gentle." He smiled. Two of his teeth were missing. "Come sit here," he beckoned. "Antonio, pour our friend a drink."

He had no choice. He had to join them. He only prayed they'd tire of the game before the ship sailed.

That prayer went unanswered. A full hour passed before any of the players so much as yawned. And then, without warning, the ship's undulations grew more pronounced. Above, he could hear the creaking of the winches as the sails were unfurled. With dawning horror, he realized the *Corona Negra* had already cast out to sea.

Linet jerked awake. Dear God—it was night! Somehow she'd fallen asleep at her work. The Guild would give her such a tongue-lashing . . .

She tried to stretch. But her arms and legs were bound tightly against her. Fear plunged her beneath drowning waters for a moment. She fought for air. Musty cloth plugged her mouth. Then by sheer will, she forced herself to take several calming breaths through her nose. She was all right. She could breathe.

And she remembered—her ruined goods, the Spanish gentleman, the guards' attack, the taste of blood . . . She swallowed down an urge to retch. The last thing she recalled was a dull thump and an explosion of bright stars. Then this . . . prison. Her head swam dizzily as her surroundings seemed to list gently from side to side. Then she realized where she was. A ship's hold.

A scraping sound came from the darkest corner of the shadowy confines. Rats come to torment her, no doubt. Squinting hard, she peered in the direction of the noise and was startled to see the gleam of two human eyes staring at her. They blinked agitatedly as if to convey some urgent message. Harold, she realized. It was her servant, bound and gagged, but thankfully alive.

Gradually her eyes grew accustomed to the feeble light, and

through obscuring shadows she could discern some of the hold. The rest she could well imagine. She'd been in ships' holds innumerable times.

She wiggled half-numb fingers and tried to adjust to a more comfortable position against the stack of wool-wrapped parcels. Against one wall were crammed several wooden chests. An oak barrel sat near her head.

By the vessel's subtle movements, it was yet moored. But for how long? she wondered with rising anxiety. Sweet Mary, she'd done it this time. Trussed up like a fly for a spider. Captured by God-knew-who for God-knew-what purpose. Her servant just as helpless as she. For the first time, she had to admit she might have gotten herself into more trouble than she could handle alone.

And she was indeed alone. Her father was dead. The servants at home wouldn't expect her for another fortnight. The guildsmen saw her leave. No one would even miss her. No one, she suddenly realized, except the gypsy.

Some guardian he'd turned out to be, she thought waspishly. He hadn't kept her safe for a single day. Unless . . . unless that had been his intent.

But of course! She felt like a fool. The gypsy was part of it. *He* had sent the Spaniards after her. He probably worked for the Spanish gentleman. They'd planned it from the beginning.

The scrape of a boot sounded overhead. Men's voices wafted down, muffled at first by the wooden planks of the deck. Then the hatch door abruptly lifted. Moonlight streamed in like bolts of the sheerest silk. Linet pressed her eyes shut, pretending sleep. It took all her willpower not to open them when she heard the woody squeak of a man descending the ladder to the hold.

He shouted to the men above in Spanish, nearly startling her into confession. Then he said something she could translate easily, for she'd heard it so many times.

Holy Mother! They were casting off.

The door fell closed with a grim finality. She opened her eyes and grappled wholeheartedly with her bonds, a scream building in her throat. Harold cast pitying glances her way. He'd no doubt already spent hours in that fruitless pursuit.

Moments later, covered with beads of sweat and rope burns

from her struggles, she felt the ship jerk free from the dock. She looked over at Harold in dread. As the vessel rocked slowly out to sea like a grand old lady, Linet alternately prayed for and cursed the peasant gypsy who might, or might not, be their salvation.

At the foot of the docks, Garth closed his eyes and made the sign of the cross. Holden cursed. Robert stared in open-mouthed wonder, for once at a loss for words.

They watched in silence, helpless, as the *Corona Negra* carried off Duncan de Ware as inexorably as a shark with a seal in its belly.

"I knew I should have gone," Holden snarled, clenching his fists in frustration.

"What will we do now?" Garth asked.

"There's only one thing to do," Robert said. "Lie like the devil."

"What?"

"Oh, I know the word is foreign to you, Garth, but there's no other way. Your mother and father would worry themselves ill if they discovered the truth."

"He's right, Garth," Holden said. "This is our fault. It's up to us to follow him, to get Duncan out of this mess."

Garth looked decidedly uncomfortable. "So we'll lie? What will we tell them? That we're all going off on pilgrimage?"

"We're not all going off anywhere," Robert replied. "You and Holden will tell them that Duncan and I escorted the wool merchant home."

"You're not following him alone," Holden decreed. "It's too dangerous."

Robert clapped him on the shoulder. "I'd far rather die at the hands of sea reivers than face your father's wrath for losing all three heirs to his title."

Holden's lips thinned, but he had to agree.

"There's a ship bound for Spain in the morning," Robert said. "I plan to be aboard her."

"How do you know El Gallo is going to Spain?" Garth asked.

"I don't," he said with a shrug. "It's a risk I'll have to take."

"I don't like this," Holden sulked.

Robert nodded. "I know."

Holden clasped him by the elbow.

There was a moment of silence. Then Robert flashed his biggest grin. "You just can't abide someone else getting all the glory, can you, Holden?"

6

LINET BLINKED AGAINST THE BRILLIANT FLOOD OF LIGHT AS the hatch creaked open. It was day. They must have sailed all night.

"So you are among the living, eh?" someone said. The accent was thick and nasal.

She glared toward the intruder as fiercely as she could.

The man laughed. "Ah, you *are* full of fire, *doncella*, thinking to burn me through with those pretty eyes!"

She tried to show neither trepidation nor revulsion as the man descended to the bottom rung. He was oily and rumpled, his velvet surcoat too fine not to be stolen. His hair was flattened to a nondescript shade from lack of washing, his eyes sunken from too many years of heavy drink.

He suddenly dropped down beside her. She gagged at the stench of onions on his breath. He ran one grimy finger beneath the rope across her shoulder.

"It would appear one of our men may have a future as a weaver, eh, wool merchant?" he said, chuckling at the maze of ropes around her. "But we are far from harbor now. There is no reason to keep you trussed up. You would not be so foolish as to fight while I hold a knife, eh?"

He drew forth a nasty-looking jeweled dagger, no doubt pilfered from a nobleman. Her breath caught in her throat, but she managed not to flinch as the man sawed at the ropes, a hair's breadth from her skin. When her arms and legs were free, she stretched them out slowly, wincing in new pain as the blood coursed through them.

"Sombra wishes to see you now," the Spaniard informed her, helping her to her feet with one bony paw.

Sombra! She knew that name. But then who did not? Sombra, the scourge of the seas, the flesh peddler from Spain. Dear God, was she in the clutches of that demon? She reeled dizzily for a moment, then forced herself to straighten, summoning up the strength to confront her captor.

Perhaps, she thought desperately, she could reason with the man. Sombra had been a noble once. Perhaps she could use her merchant's wits to bargain for her life. She had faced far worse, after all. She had faced El Gallo and triumphed.

Removing the man's hand distastefully from her arm, she reached behind her head to untie her gag.

"I am not so certain," the shipman sneered, "that he wishes to *hear* you."

As soon as the gag was off, she nodded to Harold. "What about my servant?"

"Ah, shark bait?" he snickered. "Perhaps you should be more concerned with your own destiny, *doncella*."

Linet stiffened. The Spaniard waved his dagger before her. The jewels winked ominously, but she refused to recoil from the friendly but obvious threat.

"I would advise," he confided in a loud whisper, "that you do not ask Sombra such a question, or you may learn the answer sooner than you wish."

The Spaniard hauled her up the steps to the deck. She was momentarily blinded by the sun as she poked her head out of the hold. But the cool, salty breeze was refreshing in her lungs, and she drank it in eagerly.

Suddenly, black leather boots stepped into her field of vision, boots that had to have come from Cordoba. Her gaze traveled upward. Black hose, surcoat, sleeves, girdle—the fine raiment hung upon a painfully thin frame she instantly recognized.

"Don Ferdinand."

"Sombra," he said with a curt nod, "if you please."

Linet felt sick to her stomach. Sombra. The nobleman in whom she'd blindly placed her trust was in sooth one of the most savage villains to scour the seas. Of course she could see it now, now that she had the benefit of hindsight. He looked

so much more gaunt in the harsh light of day. His face bore
the unmistakable signs of a life of debauchery. Dark circles
haunted his narrowly spaced, beady eyes, eyes that seemed to
fix on her far too intently. Tiny scars crisscrossed his face like
badly tangled threads on a loom. There was a cruel twist to his
thin lips today, an unnerving precision in the cut of his beard
and the lank, inky hair that clung to the sides of his head. He
looked, Linet decided, shuddering, as sleek and unruffled as a
raven.

"How lovely to see you again," he said, his nasal accent
butchering the words.

She parted her parched lips to deliver a caustic retort, but
the words stuck fast in her throat. Behind Sombra, like a
whale sneaking up on an eel, loomed another familiar figure.
Sweet Mary—it was El Gallo. This must be *his* ship.

"What have you to say now, my thieving little merchant?"

Linet's heart hammered away at her ribs. But it would do
no good to let them see her fear. Haughty noblemen never respected you unless you spoke to them as equals. Despite her
fluttering pulse, she stepped brazenly out onto the deck before
them and burst out with the first thing that popped into her
head.

"Did you enjoy drinking our English wine in port?"

"What!" El Gallo exploded.

Sombra's nostrils flared once. He held up his hand to calm
El Gallo. "She is mine," he hissed.

Linet had hit her mark. El Gallo boiled with anger.

"Leave her to me," Sombra said.

El Gallo muttered something foul under his breath but followed Sombra's advice, disappearing into his quarters.

Sombra forced his features into a semblance of nonchalance. "Spanish grapes will always grow back, *doncella*," he
assured Linet silkily, gaining control, his lips curving into a
disingenuous smile. "Flesh, however . . ." He let the sentence
dangle before her like an executioner's axe. He seemed almost disappointed when she displayed no fear of him.

She hid it well. She was terrified. It was only by an act of
pure will that she kept her knees from giving out and her face
unperturbed. She'd been so confident at the docks before El
Gallo, her royal letters of marque rippling proudly in the En-

glish wind. Where were they now? Out here, adrift, far from the arm of English law, the papers might as well have been chaff on the breeze. Here she was completely at the reivers' mercy. Even now she could feel the crew members' gazes slithering like snakes up and down the length of her, and for once, she was glad she'd only a minimal knowledge of the Spanish tongue. She'd no desire to know what crude remarks they whispered to one another. Mother of God—here she was, not a year yet from under her father's protection and already in the clutches of criminals. If only she'd listened to that over-bearing gypsy, she despaired in silence.

If only she'd listened to me, Duncan thought in disgust as he peered down through the rigging with his one uncovered eye. And if only she'd curb her tongue now. The little merchant had mettle, that was certain. He only wished she would keep it to herself. There she stood, as cocky as ever, her eyes challenging, her hair blowing as freely as a pennon of gold, like a holy saint dropped onto a shipful of demons.

He knew better. Only the handmaiden of the devil could cause so much trouble.

He rubbed his weary eye beneath the patch, gripping the ropes with his legs as the ship swayed gently, wondering for the hundredth time how he was going to get them out of this. God's wounds—he was but one man against a horde.

Below him, Linet had said something that amused Sombra. The whoremonger threw his head back and cackled heartily. Linet, however, didn't share his levity. She glared at him with eyes of stone.

"What do I want?" Sombra echoed with a garish grin. "How about a little of this?" He reached out a gloved hand and gave one of her breasts a squeeze.

Duncan ground his teeth together. He could have split the ship in twain with the powerful bolt of rage that seared through him. But Linet was already moving to defend herself, quickly slapping the bastard's hand away.

Fortunately Sombra didn't take offense. It was rumored that the Spaniard had little appetite for women himself. He apparently only wanted to humiliate Linet. And he'd succeeded. Linet's face was as red as a ripe apple. Sombra's grin widened.

He wouldn't have been so smug had he stood face-to-face with Duncan.

"No," Sombra leered, "I do not like skinny little girls. I have friends in Spain, however, who do. Wealthy friends."

Linet's bravado faltered briefly, and Sombra fed on her fear.

"Ah, yes," he purred. "My friends have rather . . . exotic tastes. Don Alfredo, for example, has a fondness for the whip. De Blanco likes to perform for an audience. And then there is Lady Marietta, sweet, virgin-loving Lady . . ."

Linet clapped her hands to her ears.

Sombra laughed. "Tomorrow we begin your instruction. You see, my friends prefer their mares . . . tamed to the hand. Meanwhile, enjoy your last day of freedom." He gestured grandly to the ship. "Ah, and be advised that I am no stranger to, shall we say . . . inventive punishments should you prove uncooperative."

Linet felt as if she were drifting in an endless nightmare. This couldn't be happening, she thought. But at a nod from Sombra, the shipman beside her climbed into the hold and hauled Harold up. The poor old servant's legs could barely support him, his tunic was in tatters, and he flinched against the bright light. For a moment, her gorge rose, for Harold's back was crossed with the nasty slashes of a recent flogging.

"Of course," Sombra said, "I would not wish to mar the precious flesh of a beautiful woman."

Without warning, he lifted his gloved hand and cracked the back of it hard across Harold's mouth.

"Nay!" she gasped.

Harold moaned, and his head fell forward. Tears gathered in her eyes. She felt as if she'd been struck herself. Never had she witnessed such cruelty. But after the shock of the Spaniard's brutality wore off, she turned upon Sombra with eyes grown as hard as emeralds. She hated him, more than she'd ever hated a man before.

High above the sordid scene, Duncan faunched like a warhorse at the bit. He yearned to rip the patch from his eye, cut loose a rope from the rigging, and swing down to kick that villainous swine in black overboard once and for all.

But the moment wasn't right. Aye, he had the blade at his

hip, and he had the skill. His brother Holden might have tried to take on the whole shipful of reivers—Holden was as reckless as he was brave—but then Holden didn't possess half the wiles Duncan did.

Even now a bold proposition worked its way into his head. Perhaps his accidental journey could prove worthwhile after all. If only Linet and Harold could hold out, there might be a chance he could snare El Gallo and Sombra in their own greed. He smiled grimly. At this moment, there was naught he longed to see more than both bastards swinging from an English gallows.

Below, on the deck, Sombra apparently tired of taunting Linet. He turned his attention instead to a spot on one of his precious boots, dismissing her as easily as a swatted fly. But only after Sombra retired to his quarters below did the little wool merchant relax her defenses. Then her shoulders slumped, and her legs began shaking violently. Her bravado had been a ruse, and it appeared to have cost her much. Strangely moved by his discovery, he battled the overwhelming urge to take her in his arms, to coax away her fears with tender words of comfort.

His reverie was cut short as immediately below him on the deck, a man began muttering to his shipmate.

"Just for sport," he was saying. "We would not hurt her. No one would have to know."

"The woman is a beautiful she-cat," his friend agreed, "but this she-cat, she took a bite out of old Oso, did you not see?"

"I fear old Oso is not long for this world," Duncan chimed in, his Spanish flawless. His voice, coming from the rigging above, startled the two Spaniards.

"Who are you?" the first one asked, his eyes squinting in suspicion. "I did not see you aboard before."

"Venganza I am called," he answered, climbing down to the deck and carefully turning away from Linet in a show of conspiracy. "I have seen this wench before. She is like a spider, deadly poison," he confided. "She bites a man, and he dies. Three men I have seen her kill this way."

The two Spaniards shuddered.

"Bah, I think it is the pox," Duncan said, spitting. "Still, it is not a pretty way to die."

The Spaniards nodded agreement.

Duncan let out a long sigh. He certainly had his work cut out for him. Unfortunately, there was little for the crew to do but drink, and with their stomachs full of ale, they were as dangerous as loaded catapults. His most effective weapon was a well-placed rumor like the one he'd just planted. But rumors had a way of fading over time.

As if she could sense his worry, Linet wheeled and made her way back down the ladder to the hold, out of view. Duncan wished he could lock her in there for the length of their journey.

But only moments later, she emerged again, rising like a wraith from the bowels of the ship. Her lips were white where they were pressed tightly together.

The poor thing was going to be sick.

Linet made the trek to the railing with as much dignity as she could muster. The shipmates gave her a wide berth as she staggered weakly by. She was almost as disgusted as she was nauseous. She was a seasoned traveler. She'd sailed between Flanders and England dozens of times. There was no cause for her to be sick.

Other than the fact she hadn't eaten since yesterday. And her faithful servant Harold lay below deck, bleeding half to death. And she was going to be sold as a slave to the highest bidder by the end of the week.

Heat flashed across her face as she hung her head over the side. She focused intently on taking deep and steady breaths, then trained her eyes on the horizon until her stomach ceased its mutiny.

Wispy white clouds stretched across the sky like carded wool. The winds blowing up from the Spanish coast were warm and not unpleasant. The ocean, its garment like Arabian samite, shifting and catching the light in shimmering hues of jade and cobalt and turquoise, was kind for the moment to the frail beasts sailing so tenuously across its bosom. But she knew it could change its garb in an instant. Just as kind Don Ferdinand had changed into the villain Sombra.

She peered down in the ship's shadow at the deepest water rising and falling in undulating waves of ebony. The gypsy's hair fell in similar black curls, she recalled. And farther off, where the sun sparkled on the surface, the sea became the exact color of his eyes—a clear, vibrant sapphire. She sighed shakily. Rogue or not, she would have given anything to have that guardian now, even if it meant listening to his cocksure voice chiding her for getting herself into trouble.

As she wallowed in regret, a queer prickling began at the base of her neck, not seasickness this time, but a sensation that told her she was being watched. She shouldn't have been surprised. It seemed the entire crew watched her every move. After all, she was as obvious and out of place among them as a black thread on white linen.

Something made her turn anyway.

There, by some amazing miracle, at the opposite end of the ship, he stood. The gypsy. Her guardian. Hope.

She blinked. Perhaps it was a trick of the light or just her eager imagination.

Nay. That eye patch and stubbled chin were no foil for his broad shoulders and arrogant stance. Wonder coursed through her veins. He had found her. He had come for her.

The gypsy held her gaze for an instant. But he gave no sign of recognition. Instead, he turned to speak to the two Spaniards beside him, nodding in her direction. One of the outlaws made the sign of the cross. The other shuddered.

Her stomach lurched painfully. She was going to be sick again. But it wasn't from the roll of the sea.

He wasn't her rescuer after all. He *had* helped plot her abduction. The damned knave was one of them.

Duncan cursed silently, agonized over deluding Linet this way. Glimpsing the raw hope in her gaze, it took all his will to tear his eyes away, to resist the urge to go to the pitiful waif and sweep her up in his arms. Now she'd believe him a traitor. She'd believe he intended her harm. But there was nothing else he could do. It would avail nothing to have both of them tossed into the hold.

His jaw tightened as Linet swung back around, her fists clenching the railing as if to strangle it. He knew there would be tears of hurt in her eyes, tears she'd be too proud to shed. God—how it tormented him to ignore her silent plea.

But ignore her he did, nearly the whole day. He spent every

spare moment slipping extra bread into the hold when it was empty, making certain there were plenty of blankets for the prisoners, and continuing to spread rumors about the pox, driving Oso to check his skin hourly for telltale marks of the disease. But he spared her not a glance.

Until twilight, when the stars emerged overhead like tiny jewels and the moon hung low, sending shimmering ripples of silver along the waves. When she stood, haloed by the opaque light of the heavens, staring off across the endless water, a tear glistening on her cheek. Then he watched her from the shadows of the mainmast, miserable with regret. He watched her until the moon rose, until her tears dried and the only remaining evidence of her pain was the haunting sorrow in her eyes.

Heavy chains encircled Linet's waist and arms, binding her to the mast like a meal for the scavenging crows who called themselves the crew of this vessel. She'd been stripped to her underdress. The sheer linen, plastered against her body in the damp breeze, afforded her little modesty. The sun had begun to burn her fair skin, and the wind slapped tendrils of her hair across her face.

Duncan scowled from the midst of the rigging, clenching the ropes of the mainsail so tightly he was sure they'd fray within his fists.

How long did a sleeping philter take anyway? He was sure he'd dissolved enough of El Gallo's medicinal powder into her morning wine. Linet should be drifting off to the land of dreams by now, safe from her own sharp tongue, to a place where Sombra couldn't touch her. But, damn the stubborn wench, she was still standing.

Linet shivered once. Her head was swimming with wild and foggy colors. She knew she should be afraid, but it seemed too much of an effort. Besides, it wasn't as if anything was going to happen to *her*. Sombra was only interested in the woman chained to the mast, the poor woman shuddering with cold in her shift.

She blinked her eyes several times to clear them and spat a strand of hair from her mouth. In one terrible moment of clarity, she realized the truth. *She* was the woman chained to the mast. And then the gentle mists closed again, mercifully obscuring her thoughts.

Sombra circled her like a spider considering its next meal. He clucked his tongue. "I understand you insulted my captain in England." He tossed the words over his shoulder. "Is that not so, *señor*?"

El Gallo, standing behind him, hooked his fat thumbs into the armholes of his surcoat and rocked up on his toes. The weathered boards of the deck groaned. He nodded.

"It is a very bad thing to insult a man," Sombra continued. "It is death to insult a Spaniard. However . . ."

Linet wanted to explain about the letters of marque, wanted to tell him that El Gallo had stolen her wool, but her eyelids flagged, and then she couldn't remember what she was going to say.

"We have other plans for you, far more profitable plans." He rubbed his black-gloved hands together. The leather squeaked. Then he swung around to El Gallo. "Do we not, my captain?"

El Gallo scoured her with greedy eyes and made a crude gesture which amused his companions on board.

"Who will pay the most, eh?" Sombra purred, taking her chin in his gloved hand. "The Saracens? Some French lecher with gentlemen friends to entertain? Or perhaps a bishop with secret vices?"

The crew volunteered their opinions. Linet tugged her chin from his grasp.

"Of course," he added, peeling the glove languidly from his right hand, "the price will double if I find you a virgin."

Linet's eyes went wide for a moment. Surely he didn't mean to . . . She stared as he flexed his pale fingers. Then a wave of gray light washed over her. She faltered forward.

"Eh, Sombra, see how she swoons with anticipation!" El Gallo crowed.

The last thing she saw was the gypsy leaping impossibly out of the sky onto the deck.

"Leave her be!" he cried.

And then the world went black.

7

LINET'S EYES ROLLED IN HER HEAD, AND SHE SLUMPED BACK-
wards against the chains.

Mother of God! Duncan thought. If he'd killed her with the
sleeping draught . . .

In the next instant, Sombra whipped around like a snake,
his face blanched with fury. "Who dares command me?" he
snarled.

Duncan scanned the expectant faces around him. Some
were outraged. Some were annoyed. Some were thirsty for
blood. Everything depended on his answer to Sombra's question.

"A friend perhaps," he answered with a casualness he didn't
feel, intentionally fracturing the Spanish words with a French
accent. "An opportunity without a doubt."

"You interrupt me for . . ." Sombra began, clenching his
naked hand into a claw.

"The woman carries the pox," Duncan said calmly. "I
would keep my distance if I were you, Monsieur Sombra. It is
not a pleasant death."

Sombra pressed his thin lips together and took a judicious
step away from Linet, who, to Duncan's relief, seemed to be
breathing.

El Gallo swaggered forward, crossing corpulent arms
across his barrel chest. "What is your name . . . friend?" He
sneered the word.

"I am . . . Gaston de Valois, cousin to King Philip," Duncan
announced, presenting his own de Ware crest ring with a hasty

flourish. "And this," he said, gesturing to Linet, "is my prisoner."

"Is that so? And what would the King's cousin be doing aboard my ship?" the captain grumbled, his eyes oozing suspicion.

"Philip has a very lucrative proposition for you, Monsieur El Gallo," he suggested, subtly fingering the money pouch at his waist, "one that might sound better perhaps over a cup of wi- . . . er, pardon, ale?"

The taunt was not wasted on El Gallo. He hesitated, clearly torn between the pleasure of watching Sombra further torment his female captive and the prospect of increasing the weight of his purse. Finally, he growled for two cups.

"Sombra, take our prisoner below," El Gallo ordered. "The Frenchman and I have things to discuss."

"But . . ."

"Do it!"

Pure venom shot from Sombra's eyes at the dismissal, but El Gallo took no notice. Duncan struggled to feign disinterest as the slimy Spaniard unchained Linet and had her hauled into the hold.

When the ale had been poured, El Gallo raised his cup in salute. Duncan swept up his own drink, draining every drop at once. There was impressed muttering among the shipmates. Not to be outdone, El Gallo answered the unspoken challenge and tossed back his cup of ale. The crew chuckled in admiration.

"Away!" the captain shouted, slamming the cup down. The curious crew scattered across the ship like dice on a table. "Now." El Gallo wiped his sleeve across the foam clinging to his beard. "What is this proposition King Philip has in mind, eh?"

Duncan looked furtively about him and spoke for El Gallo's ears only. "Word of your exploits has reached Philip. He is interested in hiring your services."

"Hiring my . . ." El Gallo grunted, belching loudly.

"France has enemies," Duncan confided, the deception coming easily to his lips, "enemies Philip would like to see meet with . . . misfortune."

"Misfortune?" the captain wheezed, narrowing his eyes.

"Only of a minor nature," he hastened to assure El Gallo. He chose his words carefully. "France would not be averse to granting you a pardon should you, for example, mistakenly . . . lighten the burdens of some of her enemies' ships in French waters. I believe a small fine, as little as half of what you may collect, would appease His Majesty for such actions."

El Gallo didn't bother to conceal the greedy glint in his eyes as he stroked his beard speculatively. Duncan was sure that the crafty sea reiver was already scheming to kill him and somehow collect all the profits himself. But it didn't matter. Things would never get that far.

"How did you find me?" El Gallo asked, mistrustful.

"The wench," he just as quickly replied. "Philip was made aware of the unfortunate royal letters she secured in London last month. He knew you would not let her go unpunished. I was to follow her, to wait for you to make your move."

El Gallo poured them each another cup of ale.

Sweet Mary, Duncan thought, he'd burn in Hell for the lies he'd told over the past day alone. The fiction seemed to roll off his tongue as if it were God's truth. He'd have to spend hours in confession when this was all over. Still, all of it would be worthwhile if he could at last put the notorious El Gallo and Sombra away and save Linet de Montfort. Why, he thought wryly, perhaps his daring would earn him the position of Patron Saint of Wool Merchants.

"The *doncella* is of no further use to you then. Why did you prevent Sombra? She belongs to him now," El Gallo abruptly challenged, shattering Duncan's train of thought.

"Indeed?" Duncan tossed back his ale to give himself time to think, then shook his head. "Philip will pay you handsomely himself for her return. You see, he has his own quarrel with her, and for that, she will suffer, believe me. I fear this Sombra, he may . . . damage her. Philip will not pay so highly for damaged goods."

El Gallo grunted in agreement.

"I think it best that the girl remain under my watch until we reach . . . Flanders." It was a stab in the dark. There were de Montforts in Flanders. They had to be Linet's kin.

"Flanders!" El Gallo exclaimed. "We sail for Spain!"

Duncan picked at imaginary lint on his sleeve. "Of course Philip would prefer *your* services," he intimated, "but if you have more pressing business elsewhere . . ."

"Oh no," the captain was quick to deny, as if he could imagine all those coins slipping through his fingers, "nothing that cannot wait."

"*Eh bien!*" he announced, saluting El Gallo with his half-empty cup. "To our alliance!"

It was twilight. The rim of the sun eased itself into the cool crimson sea, burning it to a deep blue. The stars began to wink down at the landing boat, and the calm of the evening was ruffled only by the occasional scree of a gull and the rhythmic lapping of oars pulling against the water.

Sombra stood recklessly, defiantly, as his captive, Harold, rowed the small vessel over the waves toward the Normandy coastline. He glared across the distance at the retreating silhouette of the *Corona Negra*, which had turned tail and now headed east. Hatred etched cuts into his gaunt face, and the veins on his neck stood out like the roots of a starving tree.

El Gallo had foiled his plans.

She was the one who could have supported him the rest of his days, this sweet-faced innocent with hair of spun gold. For years his wealthiest patron had been searching for just such a prize. And to find one who was yet a virgin . . .

He knew she was intact, even without examining her. Only a maiden blushed like that. The Spanish nobles would've drooled over their Cordoba boots, emptying their purses in their frenzy to bid on her. And in the end de Seville would've outbid them all, bringing Sombra untold riches.

But that wretched one-eyed Frenchman had interfered.

Blood coursed in Sombra's temples. In one day, Gaston de Valois had destroyed a partnership he'd spent six years cultivating.

El Gallo would profit handsomely from his new alliance. There was no mistake about that. As long as the political climate was stable, one always profited by serving as a king's agent. But a king would never openly condone the merchandising of flesh, the taking of another king's subjects for profit.

To do so was to flirt with the possibility of real war. Sombra's days of shadowing El Gallo were over.

He suppressed an angry sob as he thought of his special quarters on the *Corona Negra*, the room he'd so meticulously furbished for the methodical taming of his female captives. It was a work of art. He'd labored long to perfect it. Now it would serve no purpose other than to stow the pilfered goods of France's enemies.

If, indeed, that was Gaston de Valois' true intent. Sombra didn't trust him. There was something unsettling about the man's face, some nagging memory that kept picking at the back of his brain like a pesky flea. Something told him that more than just a royal contract awaited El Gallo at the Flanders dock. Of course, the captain would listen to none of Sombra's skepticism. El Gallo couldn't think straight when there was silver involved. Somehow, Sombra knew, El Gallo was about to trap himself in the Frenchman's clever web of deception. Sombra didn't intend to be caught in that web. He'd cheated death once already and intended to survive, even if it meant leaving El Gallo like a rat abandoning a sinking ship.

He could make his way back from whatever foreign shore he found. He had a hostage, and enough silver could pave one's way anywhere. And he'd seek retribution. Not today, not tomorrow, but someday. He'd destroy that one-eyed bastard and steal his angel-faced whore.

His lips twisted with malice as he sank down upon the hard bench and fingered the bronze medallion he'd lifted from the merchant girl's unconscious body. This was the key, he thought, rubbing a gloved knuckle across the worn crest. There was a mystery attached to Linet de Montfort. Someone would pay dearly for the owner of this medallion. He was sure of it.

He closed his fist around the medal and let his grimace evolve into a voracious grin. Without warning, out of pure spite, he hauled back and clubbed the girl's servant in the jaw with all the strength of his rage, oblivious to the crunching of his own knuckles as bone met bone.

Robert rubbed his gritty eyes. He hadn't shut them for more than a moment all night long. He was worried. Not for himself, as anyone who knew him might suspect, but for Duncan. Though he'd been the de Ware brothers' companion all his life, exchanging blows and words and even women with them, he'd never misunderstood his role. Lord James de Ware counted on him to keep his pups out of too much trouble.

He'd failed this time. And if it cost him his life, he'd rectify that mistake. It was his unspoken duty.

With a firm resolve and a soberness that was a better disguise for him than the merchant's clothing he'd donned, Robert climbed the gangplank of the *Rey del Mar*.

It seemed an eternity before the vessel finally weighed anchor, an eon before it lost sight of land. All day long, every wave that sluggishly lashed the side of the ship tortured him more than a flogging. But, as Garth would have told him, there was no more he could do. He was on his way to the place where, God willing, the *Corona Negra* had sailed. The rest was up to the winds.

Robert took a deep, tingling breath of salt air and exhaled slowly, leaning back against the aft railing, squinting into the setting sun. He'd been so preoccupied with his mission that he'd hardly spared a glance for his fellow passengers. He did so now.

A weathered old sailor with a shock of white hair captained the vessel. A young lad with eager black eyes hovered about him like an excited puppy, jumping up to fetch the captain's eyeglass or to bring him a drink of ale. The rest of the crew, a crusty, threadbare lot, roamed the decks like loose rats. A pair of spice merchants engaged themselves in some animated argument about the best source of cinnamon. A dozen or so bawdy Spanish boys stood at the forecastle, regaling each other with outrageous tales. Three Spanish nobles stood apart from the others. One of them looked desperately ill, his face a deathly shade of green as he watched the ship roll over the lurching waves. Beyond them, a youth in a hooded cloak and tattered hose stood gazing out to sea, his face a haunting study of . . .

Robert blinked. The angle of the chin, the delicate nose and small mouth, those huge, dark, soulful eyes . . . God's teeth—it was a woman.

He sauntered across the deck to get a better look, whistling softly.

She was beautiful. Her face, framed by the coarse woaded wool of the shabby cloak, seemed like a priceless jewel set in cheap metal. Her skin, illuminated by the last gold rays of the sinking sun, was the color of honey, smooth and even. Her features were delicate, her bones fine. Her lips had a sensual pout to them, and there was the most intriguing dimple at the point of her chin. Her head was hidden by the hood, but he could see by the gentle arch of her brow and her long, curling eyelashes that her hair was as black as onyx.

She was a fool if she thought she could pass for a boy.

He stopped at the railing a few yards away and watched as two gulls fought over a fish in the distance. The woman pulled the hood tighter about her and turned aside to conceal her face.

"So you're running away?" he asked offhandedly, still gazing out to sea.

Her head whipped around like a startled doe's. Then he saw the dagger in her white-knuckled grip. Something in her tragic, liquid eyes told him she meant to use it on herself.

But not if he could help it.

He casually returned his gaze to the ocean. "A young lad like you sailing for Spain—no belongings, no companions—you must be running from something . . . or someone."

The woman shifted her eyes forward. "Spain is my home." Her voice was low and husky, the accent subtle.

"Ah, so you ran away to England, and now you've seen the error of your ways," Robert said with an understanding nod.

"No." Her brows drew together in a tiny frown. "I am just going home. That is all."

"Ah," he said with a knowing grin, chucking her on the shoulder. "It's a woman then, isn't it, lad? Some English wench stole your heart and left it in pieces on the cobblestones, so now you're going home to see if you can make anything of what's left of your miserable life." He clucked his tongue.

The woman was staring at him as if he were mad, but not too far from the truth. He would have wagered his armor that she was running away from a man—a betraying lover, perhaps, or a cruel husband.

"No," she said. "That is not . . ."

"Say no more, lad. I know the tale all too well. Here you'd come after your lady love—one of those pale as cream, plump as a peach English dainties, no doubt, the kind with skin like velvet and a love nest as sweet as . . . But why am I telling *you*?" he chuckled. "*You* know well enough, eh, my lad? I'll wager that young stick of yours has stirred the honeycomb oft enough."

A sidelong glance revealed that the woman had blanched to the color of parchment. Her eyes were wide, her lips parted in shock. Now he had her attention. Her fingers had loosened on the dagger.

"So you're bound for Spain now, is it?" he continued. "Well, I can tell you how that will go, my boy. You'll drown your woes in Spanish wine for a while. And then you'll get yourself in a fight or two—black your eye, bloody your lip. And finally you'll decide your English poppet wasn't so irreplaceable after all, and you'll scour the streets looking for some cheap harlot with honey hair and skin like milk. But you won't find her, lad. You won't find her."

He glanced down at the dagger as if noticing it for the first time. "Is that Toledo steel? Mind if I have a look at it?"

By now the woman was so caught up in his chatter that she readily handed him the knife. He turned it over in his hand, pretending to study the blade.

"But you know, if it were me," he confided, twirling the point of the dagger atop the wood railing, "I'd head for France. If you think the English ladies are delectable . . . lie on French linens sometime with a perfumed whore on each arm." He rolled his eyes in mock ecstasy.

"I beg your . . ." she choked.

"But Spain . . ." He shuddered dramatically and handed the dagger back to her. "It's a fine blade, lad. You'd be wise to keep it sheathed."

She took the knife and his advice. Then curiosity got the best of her. Her chin came up. "What about Spain?"

"What? Oh. Well, you know what they say about Spanish women."

He could almost see her hackles begin to rise. "No. What do they say?"

Robert shrugged. "It's nothing. Probably rumor."

She was facing him now. A fire had begun to smolder in her enormous dark eyes. "Rumor?"

"Some say they're, well . . ."

"Yes?"

"And of course, having no real experience myself with . . ."

"What?" she asked impatiently. "What?"

Robert tried not to smile. So the woman had a quick temper. He loved quick-tempered women. They were so spirited, so full of life, so passionate. "They say they are as cold as frost, as passionless as eels."

The woman blinked.

"They say their hearts are like stone."

Her eyes narrowed.

"They say kissing them is like kissing a dead herring."

She nodded. Anger emanated from her like heat from a gray coal. "Is that what they say?"

Robert expected a long tirade in Spanish after that, or a healthy slap across the face, or some other expression of her rage. He expected to comfort her afterward, to confess that he had known all along she was a woman, and then offer her what succor he could.

He never expected her to kiss him.

Robert had never tasted such heady drink.

The woman's lips were as soft and sweet as ripe berries. Her cheek was like velvet against his. A cloud of fragrance surrounded her and enveloped him, like the first whiff of unkegged apple wine. She had taken his head in her hands, bending it down to hers with a strength she'd not looked to possess, like a Siren pulling him to his doom. And yet he had no desire to escape that fate. He'd willingly let her drown him beneath waves of seduction.

She'd caught him so by surprise that his arms still hung limp at his sides. In one instant, his world had been reduced to just the delicious pair of lips pressed to his and the warm breath stirring his stubbled jaw.

Only gradually did he become aware of the silence around him. She must have, too, for she pulled back, releasing him.

But her eyes didn't let him go for one moment. They held onto him, smoky with desire, as dark and liquid as two great pools, reflecting his own sense of wonder, of amazement.

It was then he lost his mind.

He tossed her hood back and coiled his hand in the rich, weighty cascade of her hair. Then he swooped down on her like a hunting hawk, claiming her mouth as if he deserved it, as if it had always belonged to him. He crushed her to him, arching her back impossibly and pressing the evidence of his lust against her like a rutting animal.

And she clung to him. It was like tasting fire—dangerous and compelling. She never fought him. Even when he knew he was scraping her frail skin with his bristled, devouring jaws. Even when he squeezed her so fiercely that he left her gasping for air. The only time she cried out in protest was when he paused, wrenching her tunic aside to sample the supple curve of her shoulder. But that moan was followed by a purr of such longing that he felt as if he'd been pushed over the precipice of madness.

How they managed to make it to the hold, he didn't know. How he came to be unclothed, he couldn't remember. But by the time the moon dropped its silvery threads down through the cracks of the hatch, lighting the cabin with an ethereal glow and illuminating her eyes—her beautiful, shining, happy eyes—Robert knew he'd found a treasure.

He knew he'd found his bride.

8

LINET DRAGGED HERSELF UP THE LADDER OF THE SHIP'S HOLD.
Good Lord, she thought, what had happened to her? And
where was Harold? She felt as if someone had sent her
through a fulling mill. Every muscle in her body ached, and
she was as muzzy-headed as an old sot. She fought to get her
bearings in the fading sunlight, but her eyes kept refusing to
focus. When they at last stopped swimming in her head, she
wished she'd kept them closed.

More than a score of dangerously drunk reivers gathered
near the mainsail, stuffing chunks of hard bread and cheese
into their maws, washing them down with ale. The low-slung
moon turned their leering faces to lurid gold masks.

Linet self-consciously clutched at the neck of her shift as
their eyes raked her, but still the lawless knaves of the sea
bore their lust like a banner. They gestured crudely, calling
out what she was sure were vile propositions.

A gull screeched overhead, garnering her attention, and she
followed its path of flight with her eyes.

Then she saw them. Not ten paces from her, silhouetted by
the purple sky, El Gallo and the gypsy stood together like life-
long friends, toasting one another, laughing. Pain closed her
throat. What treachery was this? she wondered. Did the
gypsy's loyalties shift with the wind? She could have sworn
he'd swooped down earlier like some guardian angel to save
her from the reivers. Then again, perhaps she'd simply imagined the whole episode.

She closed her eyes and pressed her fingers to her throbbing temple. Patterns of color descended upon her head like a shower of fabric. Dear God—she must be going mad. Or maybe she was only dreaming. Aye, that was it—she was having a bad dream. She'd simply return to the hold until she awoke.

But before she could turn, the gypsy pinned her with his cobalt gaze. "Thank God . . ." he breathed. For an unguarded instant, naked relief shone in his eyes, dazzling and disarming her. Then he added loudly, "Thank God you are awake at last, you wretched wench. I have waited long for our reacquaintance."

The ragged crew hushed. Linet frowned. What was he talking about? And why was he speaking with the ridiculous accent?

"How know you this man, eh?" El Gallo demanded, his pig eyes slipping drunkenly from one to the other.

Her mouth felt as dry as dust, but at least the colors in her head were fading. "He . . ." She stared at the gypsy, still bewildered by the genuine concern she'd glimpsed briefly in his eyes.

"I fear I am not a very welcome sight," the gypsy said, smirking. "We were lovers once, you see, until she decided to make off with my coffers."

She gasped at the ridiculous lie. "What?"

The reivers watched with growing interest, though few of them could understand the exchange.

The gypsy continued. "She is part of the reward Philip promised me for my part in this."

"Reward?" she exclaimed, outrage replacing caution. "What are you talking about? I am no man's reward!"

"Silence!" El Gallo barked, rolling his eyes in disgust. "I am beginning to think no truer words could be spoken. Women's prattle is tiresome," he said to the gypsy. "You would like me to cut out her tongue for you?" he offered, sneering.

"Oh no," Duncan whispered silkily in Spanish, gazing steadily into her eyes. He strolled up to her until his chin was mere inches away from the top of her head. "I have other uses for that tongue of hers."

The band of reivers cooed at his words, some raising their

cups in salute. Linet hadn't the slightest idea what the gypsy was talking about, since he'd said the last in Spanish. But the message in his penetrating gaze and the lascivious invitation of his lips were unmistakable.

He lifted one hand to tangle it in her hair.

"Stay away from me, you . . . you cur!" she cried. "I am a de Mont—"

The gypsy's lips came down on hers before she could finish. His kiss was deep, demanding, his chin rough and foreign against her cheek. For a moment she was too stunned to resist. Then her head cleared, and she began to struggle in his confining embrace. She tried to scream, but his mouth cut off the sound. This couldn't be happening, she thought distantly.

Not with a peasant.

Not her first kiss.

She pushed against the firm wall of his chest and tried to twist in his arms, but he held her fast. The kiss seemed to last forever. To her growing dismay, her breath quickened in her breast, and her heart began to beat erratically against her throat at the place where his thumb rested. Then, all at once, he pulled back. For one instant, as she looked up into his smoky eyes, he looked as dazed as she felt.

Duncan *was* dazed. Never had a kiss felt so right to him, so perfect.

"Ho!" El Gallo bellowed, his eyes narrowed suspiciously. "You said she had the pox!"

Duncan's voice was ragged. "I am a . . . a jealous man. Would you not have said as much?"

The crew hushed in apprehension, awaiting their captain's response. The silence grew uncomfortably long. Then El Gallo's eyes crinkled, and he burst out laughing. He slapped his thigh. "Indeed!"

The laughter seemed to bring Linet around. Duncan had let his arm creep casually across her shoulders. But a silent battle ensued now between the two of them as he left his fingers dangling suggestively above her breast.

"Eh, Frenchman!" a black-bearded, sly-eyed fellow beside El Gallo said. "In my country, it is a sign of courtesy to share one's good fortune." He fingered the buckle of his belt. "I would not mind a piece of this treasure." He took a bold step forward.

Duncan felt Linet tense beneath his arm.

But El Gallo stopped the reiver short, whacking the man's belly with the flat of his eating dagger. "In your country, Diego, it is a sign of courtesy to respect the property of others." He motioned the man away.

Duncan resisted the urge to scoff. Since when did a reiver respect the property of others? Still, he thanked El Gallo with a subtle nod of his head. The captain wasn't stupid. He might be greedy. He might be twisted. But he wasn't stupid. Until he held Philip's gold in his hands, he'd have to appease Duncan's wishes.

"Wench," Duncan barked out, "bring me a trencher." He swatted her enthusiastically on the backside.

He should have been prepared for her reaction, but nothing could have readied him for the speed at which she swung around with her fist, slamming it into his stomach. All the air went out of him. He coughed once and turned ashen. But he refused to acknowledge further how much she'd hurt him.

"*Ay, Madre de Dios!*" a man yelled. "There's fire in her!"

"Fire that begs to be quenched!" Duncan laughed to cover his pain. His eyes watered. He gripped the top of Linet's shoulder tightly.

"Come and have a bite, my friend," El Gallo called from beyond the mainsail, his mouth full of cheese. "You'll need your strength with that kitten, eh?"

Duncan nodded vaguely. The last thing his bruised stomach wanted was dinner. Nonetheless, he pressed Linet with a firm hand toward the food.

Linet wasn't about to cooperate. She was a de Montfort. De Montforts followed no one's orders save the King's. She pushed against her captor, intent on standing her ground, no matter what manner of threat the rogue concocted.

But a whiff of something sweet, something irresistibly familiar, changed her mind. An orange. The black-bearded reiver was biting into an orange. And there was a whole basket of them.

Her mouth began to water. She realized she hadn't eaten since morning. Suddenly she was ravenous. She let the gypsy lead her forward, then reached out to snatch one of the fruits for herself. But before she could, the gypsy reined her in abruptly beside him.

The words he bit out were for her ears alone. "You will pay one day for that blow, wench. But for now, you will do precisely as I command."

She squirmed in his close hold.

"Unless, of course," he added, "you wish to be their last course for supper."

His words hit her like a dash of cold water. She scanned the faces around her, faces of predators—toothless grins, gluttonous eyes, foreheads slick with sweat, chins slimy with grease. She shuddered and relaxed marginally against her captor. At least, she thought, glancing down at the hand that yet clamped her arm, there was no observable grime beneath the gypsy's nails.

The gypsy maintained a smile for the reivers' benefit, but his voice was clipped as he murmured into her ear. "You will serve me—bring me bread, cheese, an orange, a cup of ale. You will fetch me these before you sit down for your own supper, and any time my cup grows empty, you will fill it. Do you understand?"

Who did he think he was? she wondered, incensed that he'd command her as a lord would a servant. Her body fairly vibrated with ire. But she knew she had no choice in the matter. Unless she wanted to become the crew's plaything, she had to obey him.

"Aye, my lord," she muttered sarcastically through her teeth. Scowling fiercely, she gathered his supper, juggling the orange atop the bread in one hand, cheese and ale in the other. When she presented the food to him, he didn't so much as give her a nod of acknowledgment. He behaved as if he were accustomed to being served. She longed to pour the ale down over his head.

Instead she tore off a hunk of her own hard bread with her teeth. She wolfed it down with a piece of cheese as if it were her last meal. She hadn't realized how hungry she was. She hardly tasted the orange. The strong ale made her head buzz pleasantly, mercifully numbing her to the humiliation of serving a peasant.

When she rose to fill her cup for the fourth time, the gypsy halted her.

"Come, wench!" he announced loudly. "I don't wish you too drunk for what I have in mind. The food has only whetted my appetite."

Before she could argue, he stood and with one hand wheeled her around and into the wall of his chest. He pulled back on her hair with that hand and pressed her hips to him with the other. Then, with no further warning, his head descended to her upturned face, and his mouth captured hers in a sensual devouring.

His kiss was all-encompassing, blotting out sight and sound and reason. It left her breathless. And naturally, the ale made her slow to resist him. It must have been the ale, she reasoned, for it left her weakened to the point that she swayed into his embrace.

Duncan felt as if a lance had struck him dead center. He'd expected resistance. He'd braced his body for the wench's struggles, tightened his stomach against her inevitable pummeling. But the soft petals of her mouth opened beneath his. She leaned against his chest like a hungry kitten seeking nourishment. Need surged inside him, and he found welcome in her embrace, welcome and danger. Sweet Jesu—he felt as if he'd leaped upon a runaway destrier. He just hoped to God he'd be able to rein it in once they were alone.

He did intend to get her alone. He had to tell her the truth—how he meant to rescue her and turn El Gallo over to the authorities in Flanders. How he would turn Normandy upside down to find Sombra, the eel who'd slithered from his grasp, bring him to justice and rescue Harold. How he'd help her find her way to the de Montfort castle and deliver her straight into the arms of her grateful kin.

She'd thank him then. Once she understood. Once he got her alone.

If he could only get her to stop kissing him.

The reivers had begun a rhythmic chant, drunkenly encouraging him to dare more. Steeling himself, he finally broke free of the little wanton's grasp, holding her away from him by the shoulders. At arm's length, her senses seemed to return. She shook her head as if shaking off the remnants of a dream.

"You will make her pay, eh, Frenchman?" one of the crew-men asked.

"*Doncella*, with that purring of yours," another chimed in for her benefit, "he will end up owing you change!"

Linet blanched. Had she heard the man aright? Purring? Surely she hadn't been . . . She drew a deep breath to tell them just what she thought of their taunts, but the gypsy squeezed her shoulder in warning. She bit her tongue and waited for him to rise to her defense.

He answered smoothly in English. "It will take many nights of purring and screaming and begging for mercy before she can begin to pay me back for the fortune she stole." His fin-gers idly caressed her chin.

Her jaw dropped. What in God's name was the knave doing? She felt as if she were in the midst of a storm at sea, that the piece of wood she'd clung to had turned out to be rot-ted away and sinking fast.

"I wish she had taken *my* family fortune!" one sailor cried.

"For *your* family fortune, you would be lucky to get a peck and a tickle!" his friend chortled.

Then El Gallo roared with laughter. Duncan held onto Linet as tightly as he dared, but it was all he could manage to keep her from bolting overboard. The reiver captain leaned toward him, sloshing ale down his own surcoat, and gestured Duncan closer.

"I like you, Gaston," El Gallo decided in a loud whisper. "Eh," he confided in Spanish, his voice slurred by drink, "how would you like to use Sombra's cabin? You wreak your revenge on the wench now, eh?"

"Now?" Duncan choked out. His mind raced. Why would El Gallo make such an offer? And how was he going to get out of it? He glanced at Linet. She was desperately trying to de-cipher El Gallo's sloppy Spanish.

The captain shrugged, but there was a queer hunger in his eyes. "Sombra has some . . . toys . . . that can be quite amus-ing. Go on." He nudged Duncan.

Duncan lifted his cup to buy time. Something wasn't right. It looked as if he and Linet were going to get that solitude he desired, but the circumstances couldn't have been more suspect. With great misgiving, he nodded to the captain. "Your hospitality is overwhelming."

Linet didn't like the sound of their voices. She looked nervously from one man to the other. The gypsy rose suddenly to his full height, a head taller than she, his ominous eye patch making him look particularly villainous. She realized she was in real peril.

"Come," he commanded.

She locked her knees.

"Come with me," he warned her, glancing with obvious unease at the witnesses around him.

She wasn't going to budge.

Then, before she could voice a protest, he bent and tossed her over his broad shoulder, and her world turned upside down. She shrieked.

A great cheer went up.

After that, it was all she could do to keep her balance as her wretched captor strode purposefully across the deck.

"Unhand me!" she cried.

Her face burned as the gypsy raised a hand to her bottom, steadying her for the climb down into the cabin. She batted frantically at him, but he seemed undeterred, continuing to clutch her where he willed. At last he stepped through the hatch and into the candlelit cabin, securing the door after them with one hand.

When he pivoted, Linet got her first glimpse of the den of the infamous Sombra. Blood-red brocade was draped everywhere, its luxurious folds making an odd canopy in her inverted perspective. A huge black leather chair seemed suspended from the ceiling, and next to it a great silver-banded chest. A fat candle on a stand flickered near one sloped wall of the cabin, lighting up an assortment of leather and iron devices that looked to Linet like instruments of torture.

She would have screamed in horror had the gypsy not tossed her abruptly onto Sombra's enormous bed. The breath was knocked out of her, and for one awful moment, she couldn't speak, much less scream.

Suddenly he was there, over her, too near. As he bent close, she could smell the musky ale on his breath mingled with the other—a mysterious, masculine scent she'd tasted before in his kiss. She could feel the heat emanating from his body, sense the sheer strength of his limbs as he placed one arm at each side of her head. She felt like a trapped animal.

"Thank God you're safe," he said softly.

"What?" she gasped. What game was he playing now?

Duncan had little time to explain. "Sombra jumped ship. He took Harold with him. If I'm ever to find . . ."

He put a finger to Linet's lips to silence her and listened for sounds outside. A low creaking behind the wall told him what he feared. One of the several knotholes in the wood-paneled room was fake. El Gallo had an observation room off Sombra's cabin. The reiver captain intended to watch. Duncan sneered in disgust. Quickly, before Linet could speak, he clapped a hand over her mouth and placed his lips close to her ear.

"Listen," he whispered. "You must trust me."

Her struggles against him proved she trusted him not at all.

"I am trying to protect you."

She squirmed even more.

"We are in *my* lists now," he said under his breath. "You are going to *have* to trust me. You must do exactly as I tell you. This is going to require a bit of playacting." He murmured, "I want you to scream."

He slowly removed his hand from her mouth. He never dreamed she'd refuse. She glared at him with mutinous eyes, but made no sound.

"Scream," he hissed. "Loud."

"Nay," she bit out.

He gaped at her. She was positively mad. Surely she knew they would have to be convincing for his plan to work.

"El Gallo is watching," he muttered.

"I don't care if the whole world . . ." she began.

But he never let her finish. Before she could utter another lethal word, he swooped down upon her like a falcon on a mouse, claiming her lips with his own. He captured her pounding fists against his chest with one arm and nudged her jaw open with his so he could deepen the kiss. Then he let his tongue lash out, let it lap full across hers, and he felt her gasp into his mouth. Her arms went limp beneath him, and she answered him with a tentative stroke of her own. Desire ripped through him like an arrow from an unseen bow. He cupped her face in his hand so he could explore the sweet recesses of her mouth more fully.

Then the creak beyond the wall reminded him of his purpose. He pulled away abruptly and gazed incredulously down into Linet's passion-softened eyes. Dear God—El Gallo was watching. And whatever this looked like, it certainly bore no resemblance to revenge. How was he going to convince El Gallo that the wench despised him when her desire was so painfully obvious? He had to do something fast to allay any suspicions El Gallo might be entertaining.

He squeezed his eyes shut, bent close to Linet and whispered, "Forgive me." Then he became vengeance-seeking Gaston de Valois. "You will pay for what you stole from me, harlot!" he shouted. "Pay with your own flesh!"

Before she could assimilate what he was doing, he grabbed hold of the neck of her shift with both fists and ripped the laces loose. Then he plunged his hand beneath the open garment, seeking and finding the soft, full treasure within. Surely, he thought, Linet's shocked expression and her scream of outrage would satisfy El Gallo, convince him that Gaston was indeed taking full payment for the insult the wench had dealt him.

What he hadn't counted on was his own reaction.

He glanced down at the lovely, pale skin of her throat, her delicate shoulders, the innocent curve of her breast. A pang of guilt joined the desire flooding his body. Suddenly he knew he couldn't share that sight with anyone, least of all a lecherous sea reiver. Let the captain simmer—he'd do the rest in the dark.

With one arm, he hauled up his kicking, pummeling captive and started for the wall of shackles and lashes that Sombra evidently used for his own perverse pleasure. Linet shrieked as he plucked what looked like a horse's bridle and a whip from the wall.

Then he snuffed out the candle.

9

Linet's mind screamed. Sweet Christ, she had leaped from the claws of danger straight into the jaws of hell. The last thing she saw before the room plunged into darkness was the one-eyed gypsy towering over her, brandishing his leather devices like a devil set on taming a wild beast.

He was mad. That was it. How else could he have been kissing her one moment and threatening her the next? The gypsy was stark, raving mad.

She had to get away.

Blindly she floundered on the bed, seeking escape. But the voluminous coverlets prevented her. She scrambled to her knees, only to find herself engulfed in the arms of her antagonist. She flailed and kicked at him, using every trick she'd learned watching street urchins as a girl. But the superiority of his strength was inevitable.

Duncan swore as his captive's fist connected with his ribs. Damn the girl, she was like a wild kitten in his arms, clawing and scratching everywhere she could. He'd surely bear the wounds of battle on the morrow.

He tumbled her to the bed again, dropped the leather harness onto the floor, and murmured against her hair. "I won't hurt you. I just want you to scream when I tell you."

"Nay," she gasped. The cursed wench was still determined to defy him at every turn, to stretch his patience to the limit.

"I'm supposed to be ravishing you, you little fool!" he said through gritted teeth.

She swore and wriggled anew.

He sighed, exasperated. The reiver captain was listening at the wall like a naughty squire at a brothel. If she didn't cooperate soon . . .

"Stubborn wench!" he hissed. "Do you not realize this is a matter of life and death?"

But her petty oaths and irate struggles would never convince El Gallo that she feared for her life. He was going to have to take drastic measures. At last capturing her arms, he pressed her down upon the bed with his own weight. With an evil laugh, he unfurled the whip.

"This is for the coin you stole!" he cried.

He raised the lash high. He could hear Linet's shuddering intake of breath. Then he dashed his arm down, cracking the whip smartly on the floor. The loud snap startled a cry from Linet. He chuckled as if savoring his victim's pain.

"And this is for the jewels!"

Again he brought the lash down. Linet shrieked.

"And this, this is for making a cuckold of me!"

Twice more the switch split the empty air, wringing terrified gasps from Linet. But by the fifth time, when she realized he wasn't going to strike her with it, she remained silent. He was forced to discard the thing.

He cursed under his breath. He couldn't very well ravish the wench, no matter what his body was telling him. He had more honor than that. Still, there was El Gallo to consider. The man wasn't stupid. A snap of his corpulent fingers and the two of them could become sharks' supper.

His own lust he could fake. But hers—hers would have to be real. There was no help for it, no choice at all. The wench's propriety had to be sacrificed for her welfare. He smiled grimly. For the first time in his life, he truly regretted having to play the seducer.

Linet shivered in the dark, her other senses heightened by her blindness. She heard the gypsy growl deep in his throat, smelled the salty tang of his skin, tasted fear on her own tongue. Then she felt his teeth along the neck edge of her shift, nipping at the cloth, tugging persistently downward over her throat and bosom until, to her horror, one breast tumbled free. Her face went hot. Dear God—what did he intend?

He'd dropped the whip to the floor. She'd heard it fall. But there was much pain a man could inflict with his bare hands. She braced herself for the worst.

And then it came.

Her breast was suddenly engulfed in warmth. Something soft and wet closed over her nipple . . . sweet Mary—his mouth . . . and he began to suckle gently there. The blood rushed to her ears. Her humiliation was so great that she almost wished he would attack her with the lash instead. She groaned in protest. But to her shame and against her will, her body began to enjoy the lavish attention. Her nipple hardened with desire.

She cursed her tormentor in three different languages, trying to put an angry edge on her arousal. But he only responded with cruel laughter, nuzzling the cloth from her other breast, bathing her with his slick tongue. She moaned in helpless rage.

Duncan's heart pounded in his temples. God, but she tasted sweet, he thought guiltily. Her skin was warm and soft and fragrant. But damn the Fates, he couldn't afford to think about it. He had to keep his mind clear.

He captured both of her wrists in one hand. With the other, he inched up the hem of her shift. She shrieked and kicked out wildly, but he subdued her with a thigh thrown over her bare legs. His hand traced the soft contours of her calf, rounded her knee, and slid stealthily upward.

"Nay!" she yelled in panic. "Nay!"

"Oh, yes," he promised.

When at last he found her soft curls and his palm squeezed gently between her legs, her hips moved instinctively against him. His mouth went dry as he felt her searing heat and tenderly searched the mysterious flower of her womanhood. He opened the petals with nimble fingers. When he touched the tiny bud in their midst, she bucked and gasped with surprise. Yet even as he felt her shudder away from his touch, that part of her strove upward to meet his hand.

He stroked her expertly, wetting his fingers with her juices and murmuring encouragements to her as she moaned helplessly. He lay half astride her and rocked slowly, deliberately, against her body, making the bed creak for El Gallo's benefit.

Linet groaned. She'd never known such an agony of pain

and pleasure. She should fight him, yet her limbs refused to cooperate. Her entire body was aflame, and she forgot whether it was shame or passion that had made it so. The world shifted in her as she lost complete control over her body—the thrashing of her head, the rocking of her hips, the primitive sounds growling from her throat.

And yet it didn't matter. She found a strange contentment, a freedom in riding on the crest of that unknown wave. A warmth emerged inside her like the birth of a new sun, filling her with heat and light stronger than she'd ever known.

Duncan endured an agony of his own. He thanked God he was clothed, for it took all his moral strength not to plunge into that softness with more than just his fingers. Aroused to the point of pain, he knew there was no relief to be had for him tonight. It was all for the woman writhing beneath him.

Sooner than he expected, he sensed her reward was imminent, and that knowledge made him rock hard. Linet clutched at him with fingers he'd long ago freed and begged him wordlessly to finish it. Groaning, he pressed his head to hers, and when she sobbed out wildly in fulfillment, he echoed her with a deep growl of his own.

It was over. And he still ached with need.

He pulled the shift back over Linet for modesty and staggered back. From behind the wall, Duncan could hear the heavy creaking of El Gallo vacating his observation quarters. He ran a shaky hand through his hair. He hoped the reiver was more satisfied than *he* was.

"He's gone," he murmured.

Fumbling his way, he sat back on the large trunk and hung his head. He was miserable, physically unrequited and mentally shaken. Never had he felt such a strong response to a woman. Never had he had to deny that response with abstinence. He certainly hoped Linet appreciated the torment he was enduring for her.

For a long while the only sound in the room was Linet's ragged breathing. He hadn't expected much else. The poor thing was probably too astounded to speak.

Gradually, his heartbeat evened, and his loins eventually gave up hope. He stood on unsteady legs. Groping in the dark, he found his way to the candle and the flint that hung below it. He struck the flint and lit the wick. Then, as the cabin was suffused with gentle light, he stole a guilty glance at the bed.

Linet lay curled into a protective ball. Her hair concealed most of her face like a coif of golden mail. To look at her lying there, small and defenseless, one would think he had truly beaten her.

He'd beg her forgiveness now, of course, though it would be the first time he'd ever offered up an apology for bringing a woman's desires to fruition. Still, it was the chivalrous thing to do.

He rose and neared the bed, unsure how exactly to convey his remorse. He crouched by the bedside and awkwardly cleared his throat. "I am sorry if my actions have caused you distress," he murmured.

There was no response.

"I am certain El Gallo was convinced," he continued, hoping to assuage her with praise. "Your responses were most . . ."

A cry of rage erupted from Linet, a culmination of all the shame and self-loathing that had bubbled up inside her as her body reverberated with the echo of her climax. Damn his soul, she didn't want to hear about her responses. She wanted to pretend it hadn't happened.

"You bastard!" she hissed beneath her hair. "Leave me alone."

Duncan stiffened. What was wrong with her? Hadn't he apologized? She didn't sound properly grateful for his help at all.

Perhaps she didn't understand. "I had to convince El Gallo you were mine," he patiently explained. "I had to lay claim to you before one of *them* did."

Her silence irritated him.

"I'd think you'd be grateful," he muttered.

"Grateful? *Grateful?* What makes *you* any better than one of them?" Linet spat, lifting her head to glare at him, an action she instantly regretted. She couldn't very well pretend it hadn't happened now, that he didn't exist. He seemed to fill the room. His gaze was sultry, his hair tousled, and she could remember all too well the feel of those skilled fingers upon her so intimately only moments ago.

Her cheeks turned to flame. She scrambled up to her knees

on the bed, clutching her shift to her chin. "Get out," she mumbled, trembling.

What sympathy Duncan possessed escaped him quicker than a bird from an opened cage. He controlled his temper only by sheer dint of will. With forced patience, he bent to retrieve the diabolical-looking harness and hung it back on the wall. He coiled the whip and hung it up as well.

"You know, it is partly your own fault," he grumbled. "If you'd only gone along with . . ."

"*My* fault! You have the audacity to drag me into this devil's lair and threaten me with a whip and . . . and have your way with . . ."

"Have my way!" Duncan's irritation blossomed into full-blown anger now. "I did not, my lady, have my way with you! I had *your* way with you!"

"How dare you insinuate . . . you Satan's spawn! This was all *your* idea! You used me, lied to me, forced me to enjoy your pawing, and now you . . ."

"Ah ha!"

"What!" she snapped.

He cocked a brow at her. "Enjoy?"

"What?"

"You said I forced you to enjoy my pawing."

Linet reddened. "I did not. I said 'endure.' You forced me to endure your pawing." Surely she hadn't said "enjoy." Sweet Mary, she wished she hadn't drunk that last cup of ale. She couldn't stand much more humiliation at the hands of this commoner tonight.

"In sooth," he explained, "you left me no choice. I did what I had to do for your safety."

She ran a shaky hand through her tangled hair. "Get out."

Duncan swore. "I'm not leaving without you."

Her gaze flashed at him. "I wouldn't leave with you if you were the last man alive."

Duncan gnashed his teeth. The combination of Linet's unthankfulness and his own unrequited lust vexed him sorely. He had half a mind to take the whip back down. "You prefer to wait here for El Gallo?" he asked, quirking a brow. He looked pointedly at the wall of devices. "Very well. He no doubt knows the proper use for those things." With that, he wheeled and headed for the door.

"Wait!" she cried, her voice raised in panic.

She scrambled to her feet with as much haste and dignity as she could muster. God—she hated being dependent upon anyone, most especially a toplofty peasant. "You will escort me to the hold then," she informed him.

Duncan blinked, incredulous. Now she thought to order him about. Was there no end to the woman's nerve?

He waited for her to clamber off the bed, his lips clamped together. Her ruined shift fell away from the top of one creamy breast as she neared, causing a twinge of desire to torment his loins. He averted his gaze and rubbed a weary hand across his forehead. "This way," he muttered. Maybe the brisk evening breeze would cool his ardor.

"My garments," she gasped, fumbling with the laces.

He shook his head. "As you are."

She flushed in horror. "Sweet Jesu—you're serious." If she had any qualms about sacrificing her dignity to save her life, they proved futile. He caught her wrist and tugged her forward.

"El Gallo believes we have just trysted in Sombra's cabin. You must look the part. As far as the reivers are concerned, you belong to me, Linet de Montfort. After tonight, no one will dare question that fact."

Her heart raced, as if she half believed his words. She drew back her arm, and he let her go. But she knew resistance was pointless. Reluctantly she followed him, creeping onto the deck close at his back. The evening wind lifted the edges of her gown away from her damp bosom. She sucked in her breath, praying for invisibility.

Duncan sucked in his breath as well. The most difficult part, he grumbled to himself, would be convincing the crew he was sated from his tryst below.

The gypsy didn't exactly throw her into the hold, but he might as well have, for all the dignity he left her. On their trek across the deck, he pinched her backside, remarked lewdly and loudly on her performance in Sombra's bed, and cupped her breast in full view of the crew. The last earned him a sharp elbow in the stomach that she hoped he'd feel for days.

But instead of reacting with anger, he paid her back with more humiliation. Standing before the hatch of the hold, he spun her toward him, took her face in his hands and planted a long, slow, wet kiss on her lips.

If she had trouble thinking after that, it was small wonder. The churlish peasant was making a spectacle of her, mocking her good breeding by treating her like a wanton, as if she were his for the asking. He was making her feel things . . . God, no, she wouldn't think of that!

"How dare you lay hands on me!" she cried breathlessly. "I am a de Montfort! And you . . . you are . . ."

But he swept her off her feet and below deck before she could finish. "I am your rescuer," he whispered fiercely, plopping her down upon a wooden chest. "Me! By whatever name I choose, whether I am nobleman or slave, nothing changes that fact. I've risked much in coming here, and I'd die to protect you. The least you can do is treat me as an equal."

Then he left her to ponder his words. An equal? He would never be her equal. She was a de Montfort, damn it, and he . . .

Moonlight pierced through the planking overhead, striping her shift with stark white. She lifted tremulous fingers to her mouth. Her lips were still soft from his kiss. And warm. She flicked her tongue lightly over them. God—she could still taste . . . him. What other havoc had he wrought upon her body? A tear welled in her eye, and she brusquely wiped it away. There was naught to cry about, she scolded herself. It wasn't as if she'd invited his attack or encouraged him in any way. She'd simply forgotten herself for a moment in the excitement of it all. She was, after all, in dire circumstances. Any noblewoman would've reacted so in the clutches of ruthless sea reivers. She was in danger and drunk and naturally thankful for an ally, even if it was a pretentious gypsy. She wouldn't allow herself to think about the warmth that suffused her when his lips closed over hers, the thrumming in her breast when his thumb brushed her skin, the breathlessness she suffered when his sapphire gaze held her in his regard.

Instead she clung to more consoling memories—memories of her well-appointed cottage in Avedon, of the thriving wool trade she and her father had built from nothing, of the stirring lectures Lord Aucassin had given her, assuring her of her birthright, high on the ladder of society. She raised her chin, certain she could survive anything, comforted by the fact that she was a grown woman, far removed from the cruel-tongued playmates who'd taunted her as a child. She knew her place now. Lord Aucassin had made sure she would never forget.

With one hand, she reached up to fondle the de Montfort medallion, tangible proof of her breeding. To her horror, it was gone.

It wasn't as if the piece was particularly valuable. It had been a Christmas gift from Linet's father when she was five winters old. Since that time, the cheap bronze had been worn almost smooth, the finish dulled with handling. Still, it was a symbol—a symbol of her inheritance, her status. Removed from her father, far from her bolts of wool, adrift among a pack of savages, it proved to her that she was a de Montfort, that she could rise above whatever misfortune fate handed her.

Without it, she was only Linet. Without it, men like the gypsy could look at her the way they would any tavern wench, the way he had when he'd kissed her.

She buried her face in her hands. In one cruel stroke, some lowborn reiver had reduced her to the insignificant child she'd once been. Without her medallion, she was a little girl again, suffering the ridicule of ruthless teasing: Linet the bastard child, Linet the whore's daughter, Linet the black sheep of the de Montfort flock.

Ah God—if she got out of this alive, she vowed, she'd never again even speak to a commoner outside her own servants. Once Harold was found, she'd return to her warehouse and live inside the safe, protected, isolated walls of her mesnage, never to set eyes on that damned gypsy or his thieving kind again.

With that small comfort, she curled up against a bale of linen rags, punched them into a more desirable shape and drifted off to slumber.

Duncan wondered, gazing up at the dawning cloud-scattered sky, if someone would saint him when he died. Two days of hell had passed on the back of a snail. Two days of suffering the torment of a martyr. Oh aye, he'd fondled and kissed Linet to his heart's content on deck. The reivers expected it of him. But below deck, the woman had forced the celibacy of a monk on him. The stubborn wench still adamantly resisted the natural longings of her own body. Thus, his desire remained unrequited.

Chivalry certainly came with its challenges.

Never had he been so frustrated. How his brother Garth had made it to the age of ten and eight as yet untried in the ways of love, he'd never understand. Duncan felt the gnawing ache of unmet lust like a rat chewing at a brimming keg of ale.

But Linet de Montfort was not the sole source of his frustration. The *Corona Negra* was nearing the coast of Flanders now. The difficult task of helping Linet escape and assuring El Gallo's capture lay ahead. Much was at stake. Much could go wrong.

He rubbed his cheek beneath the eye patch and let his gaze drop from the distant horizon to the dark water below, where a school of fish glittered by. If only, he thought, there was some way to get Linet safely off ship before they got to the harbor at Boulogne.

"Nay!" Linet whispered fiercely, shuddering in the loose jerkin and hose.

The afternoon sun sparkled on the gray-green water, making the waves wink up at Linet as if they were teasing her. But she was not amused. She was terrified.

True, this close to shore, the ocean was calm and shallow. And she knew how to swim. But this was the sea. The men's clothing was cumbersome, and it was a long dive from the side of the ship to the water below. Who knew what savage creatures lurked below the guileless surface? Certainly the savage creatures of the slave market could be no worse. At least those she was accustomed to. After all, she was a merchant. She was used to bargaining her way through life, not making reckless, foolish, daring escapes like this one.

"You must!" the gypsy hissed.

Linet bit her lip and stalled for time, holding up the selvage of the jerkin. "Do you have any idea what seawater will do to this dye?"

The gypsy clenched his teeth. She could tell what he was thinking. After all his trouble of digging up a disguise for her, she'd better not disappoint him.

The rest of the crew bustled about the fore of the ship as they neared the harbor, some watching for hull-ripping reefs, others trying to make out the insignias of the anchored vessels. They were preoccupied now, but there was no telling how long they'd remain so. She knew it was imperative that she jump now . . . if she was going to do it.

The gypsy placed a rude hand on her backside and shoved her a foot closer to the rail. She gasped. But why the intimate contact startled her, she didn't know. After all, it wasn't as if the man hadn't touched every part of her anatomy at one time or another in the past two days. It seemed he was ever finding an excuse to swat, squeeze, pet, or maul any piece of her he could get his hands on, all in the name of lending believability to their ploy.

"Hurry!"

"Nay!"

Some of the reivers were beginning to wander back to midship.

"Can you not swim?" the gypsy demanded pointedly.

"Of course I can swim," she haughtily replied.

Before she could draw breath to expound upon her talents, the gypsy lifted her bodily from the aft deck and dropped her without ceremony over the edge and into the sea.

It was fortunate that Linet gasped in a great draught of air as she tumbled overboard. The water was freezing and much deeper than it had appeared from above. Still, she feared her lungs would burst before she finally emerged from the briny drink. She shot through the surface, coughing and sputtering and swallowing more than a little seawater in the process.

Salt stung her eyes. Icicles stabbed into her veins. The heavy clothes weighed her down. But anger moved her to stay afloat. She fought the current, swimming in the shadow of the great ship, and swore she'd see the wretched gypsy hang for his devilry.

How dare he treat her like so much baggage! After all she'd

endured—all his pawing, all the painful pretense—she deserved so much better, she thought as a wave rose and plastered her woolen coif in an unflattering fashion to her head. She was glad to be rid of him, she told herself. After she escaped, she'd collect the tangled threads of her old life and weave a new one—one free of men like that devil whose presence she'd been forced to enjoy . . . *endure*, she corrected peevishly.

She shivered. The chill of the sea sobered her and made her focus on her own survival. She clamped her chattering teeth shut and with a firm shake of her head, swam a steady course for an empty stretch of shore. And by the time she hauled herself, dripping, exhausted, onto the beach, she'd almost forgotten about the one-eyed gypsy. Almost.

Duncan dusted off his hands. Linet would make it to land. He was sure of it. She was a fighter. She'd survive, if only to spite him. For now, he had to trust in her talents and concentrate on his own end of the plan.

By the time the *Corona Negra* furled her sails and dropped anchor in the harbor, Duncan could no longer see the tiny speck that was Linet. She had either found her way ashore or . . .

He didn't dare think about it. It was time for action.

He clapped El Gallo familiarly on the shoulder. "Philip's man is staying not far from here. I will fetch him, and he will draw up the papers for your clear passage."

El Gallo squinted dubiously. "If you leave the ship, my friend, how will I be certain you will return?"

"I thought we trusted one another."

"Only fools indulge in trust."

Duncan nodded. "Then it is good I have locked the girl in the hold. If I do not return, she is yours to sell."

El Gallo scratched at his bushy beard. He glanced at the hatch of the hold, no doubt calculating the worth of one flaxen-haired wench. "Done."

Duncan strolled casually toward the dock, silently congratulating himself on another successful deception. Of course, he wasn't so naive as to believe El Gallo wouldn't have him followed. But he intended to give the captain no reason to suspect him of foul play.

The Spaniards were all eager to disembark and find the nearest alehouse. It would be at least a quarter of an hour before anyone began to seriously wonder about him, and even then, they wouldn't think to check the hold for a long while. By then he would have informed the Flemish officials of El Gallo's presence and his crimes, and Linet and he could be at least a mile away on their journey to the de Montfort castle. Then, with Linet safe, he'd seek out Sombra and rescue Harold.

That was his plan.

Unfortunately, at that moment some wayward crewman chanced to want access to the hold. When El Gallo saw the hatch flung wide, he knew he'd been gulled. The reiver captain's roar of rage stopped Duncan in his tracks.

Duncan fingered the haft of the sword he'd pilfered from an inattentive shipmate. He wondered if he'd be needing it. He whirled and faced El Gallo's look of murderous wrath with quiet determination. Swiftly, he assessed the situation. El Gallo had all the wits and fury about him of a bear wakened early from its winter nap. There was no point trying to talk his way out of this one. He'd have to use a cruder weapon.

It wouldn't be easy. True, most of the crew had left ship, but those who remained posed no mean threat. He'd have to strike like lightning.

He flipped up his eye patch and tore his sword from its sheath. With the pommel of the weapon he knocked aside a reiver standing too close before El Gallo could even draw steel. Then he took a step backward and nearly stumbled over a coil of rope.

El Gallo, unsheathed now, came hurtling forward with murder in his eyes. Duncan dove away and rolled across the deck. He tripped another oncoming crewman, who slammed head-first into the railing. He barely had time to bolt to his feet before El Gallo came for him, confident and menacing.

The giant lumbered forward. Duncan skirted away. A man of El Gallo's size could crush a man's ribs without a thought. The tension thickened as they circled. Finally, El Gallo stabbed blindly forward. Duncan dodged and turned the heavy blade aside with some effort. Then the captain hefted his sword high and brought it down hard toward Duncan's head. Duncan ducked out of the way. The weapon made a breeze through his hair as it sailed past. But its point lodged harmlessly in the wood of the deck, making the planks shudder.

While El Gallo seesawed the blade to work it free, Duncan tossed his sword to his left hand, elbowing back a crewman who'd crept up behind him. When he pivoted back to El Gallo, he had to resist the unchivalrous urge to immediately lop off the unarmed captain's head with a single blow. Instead, he glanced up into the rigging and found what he needed. Swinging his blade in a wide arc, he slashed the key rope, which brought an enormous crate of hoisted plunder crashing down. Wood and treasure exploded outward, coins and bright jewels skittering like colorful beetles across the deck between Duncan and El Gallo.

Finally, El Gallo's blade came free. But by then Duncan was already leaping over boxes and ropes and on his way down the plank. He discarded his sword, replaced the eye patch, and immersed himself in the densest part of the crowd before El Gallo could even pick his way across the scattered spoils.

If he'd been on his own, Duncan would have simply set off for the nearest authority, then made an easy escape through the wood. But he had Linet to think about. He couldn't leave without her.

Where was the lass?

Shouldering his way through the crush, he found a narrow passageway between two shops. He melted back into it, secreting himself in the shadows.

She could be anywhere. Hundreds of faces swam in this thronging human sea. Fishermen flung their largest catches over their shoulders as if they were babes to burp. An old rheumy-eyed man shuffled by, muttering to himself and swilling ale. A boy chased a chicken down a cobbled street past a flock of preening strumpets. But nowhere did Duncan see a pretty peasant wench in men's garb, soaked to the skin.

He listened to the noisy throng surrounding him. Fishmongers hawked their wares in raucous rhyme. Muffled, drunken singing could be heard through the open door of a nearby ale-house, even though it was scarcely midday. Lambs bleated, babies squalled, sailors argued. And then he thought he recognized the shriek floating over the crowd from down the lane.

He was about to follow the sound when he spied El Gallo coming from the opposite direction. Peering cautiously over the heads of the passersby, Duncan watched as the Spaniard was halted by a small retinue of Flemish knights. It was obvious from the captain's bluster that he'd attracted trouble, what with charging through the crowd with a drawn blade.

Good, Duncan thought. That would slow El Gallo down while he sought out Linet. He emerged from the niche to find the source of that scream.

As predicted, Linet was in trouble, cornered in an alley. Apparently, three drunken sailors had taken a fancy to the voluptuous woman trying to pass herself off as a lad. One had stolen her sodden coif and was entertaining himself by keeping it just out of her reach. Another couldn't keep his hands off of her. The third insisted on singing bawdy songs that made Linet blush to the roots of her hair. They didn't notice Duncan until he was upon them.

"Och, thank God ye've got her!" he sang out in his best Scots brogue. "The laird would have my head if the witch escaped again!"

The three sailors stood frozen in their last comical positions.

"You!" There was undeniable relief in Linet's tremulous voice, though her eyes plainly blamed him for her predicament.

"What?" was all one sailor could manage, dropping Linet's coif.

"She didna harm ye lads, did she?" Duncan rolled his exposed eye dramatically.

Linet frowned. It was clear she wasn't enjoying his theatrics. She slapped away the man's hand that seemed to be affixed to her hip, making him jump.

"Harm us?" one sailor repeated.

"Nay," another answered.

"Ye've got her dagger then, eh?" Duncan asked.

"Dagger?" the third echoed.

Linet was fast losing patience.

"Don't tell me she's still got her . . ." he began, his voice shrill. "Stand back, lads! Watch her! She's a wily one!"

The sailors didn't need a second warning. They backed up instantly. Then Duncan deftly palmed his own dagger and appeared to draw it from within Linet's jerkin. Linet gasped in amazement. The sailors stepped back, awestruck.

"She had a . . ." one of them began.

"I told ye she's a wily one," Duncan nodded, tucking the knife into his belt.

"Wily," one sailor aped sagely.

Then Duncan took hold of Linet's elbow, anticipating a struggle. She didn't disappoint him. She'd obviously decided she was having no part of this nonsense. Also, her face had taken on a greenish cast. If she'd swallowed seawater . . .

"Where are you bound with her?" one of the curious sailors interrupted.

"Destined for the hangman, she is."

The sailors gasped collectively.

"What's she done?" one of them asked.

"What *hasn't* she done?" he replied enigmatically, winking.

The sailors backed away another step, regarding her with new respect. Duncan pressed forward.

"Shall I tell ye what happened to my eye?" he confided softly, bending close.

The lads nodded. He glanced at Linet. She was swaying. She didn't look well at all.

"The witch waited till I was fast asleep."

The sailors leaned forward, hanging on his every word.

"She used this very dagger . . ."

Linet moaned.

"Plucked out my eye and swallowed it, she did," he crowed.

The sailors paled. Linet's stomach rebelled then. She heaved salt water forth all over the ground at their feet. The sailors shrieked like scullery maids and scrambled off as if they half expected to see the gypsy's eye looking up at them from the stones.

"I couldn't have timed that better myself," Duncan chuckled when they had gone. He laid a sympathetic hand on the poor girl's back.

Linet obviously didn't share his amusement. She cringed from his touch, shivering as with the ague. "Leave me alone," she murmured miserably, leaning back against the rock wall to let her stomach settle.

Duncan could no more suppress the guilt and empathy that surged inside him than he could stop the tide. The pathetic wench looked exhausted and hurt. His heart went out to her as it always did to helpless urchins. She must feel wretched, the pitiful thing.

Still, despite the pale cast to her skin, she looked rather charming in her oversized, waterlogged clothes. Her hair, drenched to a deep gold, was drying in tantalizing tendrils about her face. She looked to him like a water nymph just emerged from the sea. He told her as much in his softest, gentlest voice.

Linet curled her lip. His compliment didn't seem to please her at all. Seething, she swung her arm round to strike him as hard as she could.

The blow fell upon his sleeve like a wet fish. Then she collapsed in his arms.

From deep beneath the blankets of slumber, Linet heard the familiar crackle of fire on a hearth, felt its comforting burn upon her face. She was back home in Avedon, she thought, safe within her demesne. Her cocoon, though warm, was lumpy. She snuggled further down into the rough wool, trying to get comfortable.

A low chuckle coaxed her awake. Eyes like two blue sapphires sparkled down at her. She groaned. Her memory came back in a rush. Immediately, she tried to extricate herself from the gypsy's lap.

"Easy," he encouraged as she struggled from him.

She fell with a painful thunk to the wooden floor and tried to fight her way out of the blanket. "I'm all right now! I can take care of myself," she informed him, thirst making her voice surprisingly husky.

He handed her a cup of watered wine without comment. To her own mortification, she swilled it down faster than an alewife. At least it rinsed the sour taste from her mouth and the fog from her brain.

"More?" he asked when she'd finished it off.

"Nay." She shoved aside the cup, then resumed her battle with the blanket, searching for the crux of the problem. She could feel his prying eyes on her.

He reached out for a corner of the material and easily pulled it loose. With muttered thanks, she gathered up her sagging garments and her dignity and stood tall before him. The fact that the top of her head scarcely reached his shoulder did not discourage her. She'd tell him in no uncertain terms . . .

"Where are we?" she blurted out, aware for the first time of her surroundings.

There was a merry hearth and a worn wood floor, a chamberpot half hidden by a screen of pauper's lace, bread, cheese, and more wine on a tray, a lit candle, and a bunch of daisies placed on a mean table at one end of the room, which was small but tidy. The shutter to the window was open, and she could see they were on the upper story of the building. The gypsy sat on the edge of a straw bed of mammoth proportions that was covered with several cheap wool blankets.

"A . . ." He cleared his throat. "An inn." Duncan stroked his chin. He'd paid handsomely for this "inn." He'd chosen this place, knowing a bath and anonymity would be easy to obtain at just such an establishment. And he'd made certain the place was too rich for a sea reiver's purse. The ladies who served here were accustomed to the bizarre antics of their customers. So when he showed them his coin, they jumped to do his bidding, not even questioning the fact that he carried a wet, unconscious woman in his arms.

A soft scratching came at the door. Linet whirled to glance at him in askance.

"Your bath, sir," a young servant announced through the door.

"Bring it in."

Four boys hauled in a large wooden tub, their schooled eyes ignoring the young lady. Within minutes, they had filled it with steaming water and taken their leave. When they'd gone, the wistful longing in Linet's eyes assured Duncan that his silver had never been so well spent.

"You may have the first bath," he said with a chuckle.

Linet sighed. The last thing she'd do was argue with him. The bath was too inviting. Even the sound of the peasant's laughter was like warm waves already upon her back. Later, after she was dressed in dry clothing and her hair was combed, she'd upbraid the knave for dumping her off the ship. Then, of course, she'd forgive him. After all, he *had* saved her life. And he'd ordered her a bath.

"I'll let you know when I've finished," she said.

She paused, expectantly, for the gypsy to leave, but he only leaned against the door, his arms folded across his chest. She swallowed. She wished he wouldn't look at her like that, all handsome and imposing and amused.

His black hair dropped over his shoulders in unruly locks, and one particularly stubborn curl fell across his forehead. He needed to scrape his chin, but the whiskers there added an intriguing, dangerous cast to his face. Now that the leather patch was discarded, his crystal eyes seemed to burn into her soul, reminding her all too vividly of the night of passion they'd shared in Sombra's cabin.

She quickly averted her eyes. "You may go now," she said by way of explanation, though she was almost certain he understood and just as certain he had no intentions of leaving.

"Go?" He lifted a brow.

"To your room," she whispered.

"This is my room," he whispered back.

She took a breath to steady her nerves. "Then where is *my* room?" She was afraid she knew the answer to that, too.

"I am not a greedy man," he told her with a magnanimous bow of his head. "What is mine is yours."

God help her, she tried to be patient. "We are no longer aboard El Gallo's ship. There is no reason to continue the farce. I need my *own* room."

"Oh. Have you more coin?" he asked innocently enough. But then he grinned, and she could see he'd manipulated this whole situation to his own advantage.

Of course she had no coin of her own. The reivers had seen to that. Even her medallion had been taken. She wanted to scream in frustration. Damn it all! She was not helpless! How could she prove to the gypsy she could take care of herself when she kept needing him for things?

She flounced down upon the bed and began peeling off one of the thick leather boots clinging to her ankles. She muttered to herself as she worked, calling him every name she could think of from "filthy cur" and "shandy knave" to "heartless bastard."

The last one he took issue with.

"I am not heartless," he told her, coming away from the door. For just a moment, he looked rather like a hurt little boy.

"All right," she grumbled. "Perhaps not heartless." She struggled with the other boot. "But you are a churl and a knave. And a bastard."

He smiled at that, infuriating her more. Her boot finally slid off with a sucking noise. She dropped it to the floor, wiggling her toes to make sure she could still feel them. Then she crossed the room and began wrestling with the screen.

"After all we've shared, you're still shy?" he remarked.

She blushed. It was ignoble of him to remind her of all they'd *shared*. She muscled the screen of pauper's lace up in front of the tub and deftly moved behind it. There, she thought—that would hamper his curious eyes. She proceeded to spend several long moments fumbling with the laces of her jerkin. The damned things were still soaking wet. The more she worked, the more snarled they became. Even brute force didn't work. She cursed quietly.

"Trouble?" The gypsy poked his head around the screen.

She nearly jumped from her skin.

One corner of his mouth lifted in a coy smile. "I am fairly handy with garments."

She glared at him. "No doubt."

He raised both hands in surrender. "I'll only untie the laces," he promised.

She had little choice. That luscious bath was growing colder by the moment. She would just steel herself against the sensation of his callused fingertips against her skin . . .

"That's quite a snarl you have here," he said, carefully disentangling the knot beneath her chin, "almost as nasty as a certain weaver's knot I recall."

A reluctant smile slipped across her lips.

"I could cut the laces, but I fear this is your only garment," he said.

She resisted the urge to remind him that that was his fault. If the fool hadn't . . . but she couldn't reprimand him now, not when he was helping her.

She stole several furtive glances at him as he labored. His brow furrowed as he picked at the knot, his dark lashes fell thickly upon his swarthy cheek. His fingers were warm against her skin, tickling her throat while he worried the laces. She wished he would hurry. She didn't know how much longer she could endure his proximity. She was having difficulty concentrating, as if his nearness somehow affected her senses. Perhaps, she dared to hope, it was only the wine.

"I do apologize for the lack of privacy here, my lady," he murmured in all sincerity, "but I dare not leave you alone."

"Why not?" Her voice had grown curiously rough.

"Why not?" he repeated, finally freeing the laces and tugging gently at the front of the jerkin to loosen it.

He met her eyes then, and she could see in their smoky depths that he was hiding something. She grew instantly alert.

"El Gallo *is* in the hands of the authorities?" she demanded evenly.

He averted his glance for only an instant, but that gesture told her everything.

"What has happened?" she asked, not entirely sure she wanted to know.

Duncan frowned, not entirely sure he wanted to tell her. He poked at the pauper's lace in the screen with his thumb. "All did not go well."

"You failed?"

That was the wrong word to use. He straightened to his full height and scowled down at her. "Nay, I did not fail," he bit out. "I got us both off the ship. You have a roof over your head, food in your belly, and a warm bath waiting."

"But El Gallo is free and probably sniffing about for us with his pack of reivers."

He compressed his lips. "As long as you stay by my side, we shall be safe enough here."

"In an inn? God spare me from half-witted peasants," Linet

mumbled to the ceiling. "Do you not suppose that an inn is the first place he'll look?"

Duncan clenched his jaw. Now she was calling him names again. "You faithless little witch," he muttered, "I am not entirely a fool. I would not bring you to a place of danger."

"But it's so obvious! An inn?" She raised an incredulous brow.

"This is not just an inn," he declared triumphantly. "It is a brothel."

The silence that met that revelation was so complete that he could hear the water dripping from Linet's jerkin onto the floor.

10

"HE WILL NEVER THINK TO LOOK HERE," THE GYPSY EX-PLAINED, "and the ladies that ply their trade at such places are quite discreet."

Her voice came out in a strangled whisper. "You brought me to a . . ." She couldn't even say it.

She shouldered past him, plucked up her boots and stalked to the door. There, she turned to give him one final piece of her mind. But she could find no words to express her outrage. She flung the door wide and stepped out.

Nothing could have prepared her for what lay beyond the door. Down one end of a sloping hall stood a pair of plump, painted whores wearing nothing but what seemed to be a few bits of lace placed strategically about their anatomy. From the other end, a drunken, leering nobleman stumbled, a strumpet on each arm. Yet when the man saw Linet loitering in the doorway, he appeared to take a sudden amorous interest in her as well, indicating with a coarse gesture what he'd like to do with her.

Linet immediately ducked back inside the room, slamming the door with such force that she made herself jump.

"I cannot . . . leave just now," she whispered in horror, dropping her boots to the floor.

Duncan suppressed a grin. He wondered what she'd seen.

"Of course, neither can I stay," she said, pacing. "Do you know what goes on here?"

He lifted his brows.

"Of course you know," she answered herself. "You probably frequent places like this every time you get a spare penny."

Duncan mused briefly that he'd have little time for anything else if that were true, considering all the "spare pennies" he had.

"I assure you," he told her, "we'll leave on the morrow."

"On the morrow?"

"Until then, we must make the best of what we have—a tray of food, a warm bed . . ."

"On the morrow?" Her eyes grew wide. "I'll not sleep in a . . . in a place like this."

"And I suppose you've also changed your mind about that bath?" he asked dryly.

She hesitated, clearly tempted by the thought of warm, soothing water. Then she reluctantly nodded. "Absolutely. I am a de Montfort," she said, as if that explained everything. "You must take me from here as soon as it is . . ."

While she rattled on, he sat down upon the bed and removed his boots.

"What are you doing?" she asked.

"You said you didn't wish to bathe."

"Aye. I wish you to take me away from . . . What are you *doing*?" she asked again, worry making her voice strident, as he began to unlace his jerkin.

"The water grows cold," he explained.

"Surely you're not . . ."

"I see no reason to waste a good bath."

"But . . ." Linet was clearly in a quandary. She dared not go out into the hallway again. But she couldn't very well remain, not while the gypsy . . . dear God—he was pulling the jerkin and shirt off over his head. Her breath caught in her throat. Sweet Mary—the brazen knave wasn't even bothering to conceal himself behind the screen. Not that that magnificent chest should be hidden. His body was perfect—his shoulders were wide, his arms well-muscled, his belly flat and lightly furred with dark hair. In sooth, she found it difficult to tear her eyes away.

"You could always turn around," he teased, as if he could read her mind.

She could have kicked herself for overlooking the obvious.

She spun away immediately. Glancing, to her credit, only once or twice as he removed his hose, she was rewarded with a view of incredibly strong legs and a thick nest of black curls from which she recoiled just in time.

When she heard the splash of water from behind the screen, she deemed it safe to turn around. She began bustling about the chamber, creating imaginary duties to keep her mind off of the gypsy.

"After you've finished your ablutions," she said with shaky sarcasm, rearranging the daisies on the table, "I expect you to take me from here at once."

"Do you?" he yawned, pulling the screen aside and out of his way so he could see her.

Linet froze. She would not look at him. She would not. No matter that his imposing dark form against the white plaster wall beckoned to her like a candle in a cellar, she would keep her eyes averted. She'd look anywhere but at the man in the tub.

Slowly, she sucked in her breath. She walked straight to the bed and began smoothing the coverlet. She could hear his small groans of pleasure as the water soothed his sore muscles, smell the sage as he lathered the scented soap over his head.

She would have given her golden tresses to have that bath. But she wasn't about to admit it to him.

This was amusing, Duncan decided, thoroughly enjoying himself. This little bit of a wool merchant was more delightfully complicated than anyone he'd ever met. God's wounds—he'd nearly bedded the woman, and yet she was afraid to look upon him. He could tell she ached for a bath. She no doubt itched from salt water, and long days on a grimy ship had taken their toll on her hair, which hung in dull strings. Still, he knew pride kept her from accepting his hospitality. He'd have to force it on her.

Linet fluffed the bolster on the bed and bit her lip. If she heard just one more contented sigh out of that wretched peasant . . .

"Ah!" he suddenly cried out.

She immediately looked his way. He was seated modestly enough in the tub, bent forward, scrubbing at his eye. Before she could think, her instincts came to the fore. She crossed to him. "Did you soap your eye?" she demanded, bending down to him. Her father had done the same thing countless times.

He nodded, grimacing.

"Let me see," she insisted. She brushed his hands away, muttering, "The French put so much ash in their soap."

He looked up at her and blinked a few times, but she didn't notice the spark in his eyes until it was too late. Before she could do anything, he had hold of her arm in a steely grip.

"There is no soap in your eye," she stated, realizing her error.

His smile was grim and full of promise. "You need a bath."

"What?" she gasped.

"You stink. I refuse to share my room with anyone smelling of seaweed and wet wool."

She gave him a satisfied glare. "Good. Then I shall *never* bathe."

The glint in his eye told her otherwise. Without warning, he rose like Neptune from the sea, the water sluicing down his body. Before she had time to be shocked by his boldness, he caught her by the waist and bent her over his thigh into the tub. Water splashed up over the edge and onto the floor.

"Y-you!" she sputtered, struggling and splashing more.

He laughed, pulling her wet jerkin and tunic off in a matter of moments. While she shrieked, desperately trying to cover her top half, he tugged off her hose as well, leaving her completely naked.

Duncan tossed the dripping garments onto the floor. Then he wrapped a linen towel around his hips, crossed his arms, and stepped back to admire his handiwork.

His breath stilled in his chest, and his mouth went dry. His grin melted away, and his arms relaxed out of their fold. Before, he'd seen her only partially unclothed in the dim shadows of the hold. He'd only imagined by the feel of her what she must look like. But now the gold light of day left nothing to his imagination.

She was Venus bathing in the sea. The fair crescents of her breasts skimmed the top of the water like twin moons, the nipples shielded from his eyes by one modest arm. Her hair floated like a storm cloud in the swirling water around her body. Her long legs glistened with water drops, and beneath the water, peeping out from between her concealing fingers, he could see the darkened curls of her womanhood waving gently in the subsiding current. Only the crackle of her eyes destroyed the illusion.

He thanked God he'd wound the towel around him, for he was about to show the effects of her beauty upon him in a most blatant fashion.

Linet felt a giddy flush stain her cheeks, the kind that came when she'd drunk too much wine. Her body seemed to tingle beneath his gaze. No one had ever looked at her like the gypsy did. She knew she should be indignant. She tried desperately to act so. But the truth was, it was oddly pleasing to be looked at this way. It gave her a peculiar feeling of power to note the heaviness of his eyelids, the deepening of his breath.

Without meaning to, she watched him as well, mesmerized, as a drop of water fell from a lock of his dark hair onto the broad swell of his shoulder. It trickled slowly over his wide, smooth breast and down his lean stomach. She had the strangest longing to reach out and retrace its path with her fingers. Then she realized she was staring. Briskly, she tore her gaze away.

"You've got me in the tub then," she mumbled breathlessly. "At least have the decency to let me bathe in peace."

"As you wish," he replied with a mockery of a bow.

Only when he'd gone to the far side of the room did she settle back against the damp wood of the tub. The warm water began to work its magic instantly, easing her muscles, soothing her temper, even melting her inhibitions. Never mind that the gypsy had used it before her—the tepid swirls and eddies were divine.

Before long, she began to feel positively remorseful about the way she'd treated the man across the room. Aye, he'd offended her propriety. And he'd taken unspeakable liberties with her person. He'd flung her off a ship and brought her to a brothel. Yet he'd saved her from the hands of ruthless sea reivers, and, thanks to him, however he'd accomplished it, she had shelter tonight and a hot bath. After she finished, she decided, she'd give him that simple gratitude he seemed to so desperately want. Satisfied, she smiled and glanced over at the man by the window.

The smile fell from her face. In profile, clean from his bath, the gypsy was magnificent. The afternoon sunlight shone full on his face, muted in the hollows beneath his cheekbones. Strands of his hair, blacker than ink, seemed to tease at the powerful cords of his neck. His eyes, staring off into the distant sea, were almost transparent in the bright sun, and his lips parted slightly as he pondered some profound matter.

She swallowed hard. On the ship, by the meager light of Sombra's cabin, he had seemed a phantom come to pleasure her and leave, as insubstantial as a dream. The man before her now was real. He was flesh and blood. He breathed, he moved, and she already knew what he was capable of doing to her senses. The memory made her shiver.

Duncan felt Linet's eyes upon him. He turned to her. She was trembling.

"Are you chilled?" He offered her the second linen towel from the bed.

"Nay." Her voice was curt, at odds with her smoldering eyes.

Duncan knew that look. Lord—did he know that look. "God's blood, lady," he groaned, "you test me sorely. Do not gaze upon me like that."

Her mouth fell open, then snapped shut. She dropped her regard at once, too mortified to speak.

He rubbed his hand across his stubbled cheek and forced his own gaze away. Perhaps, he thought, some mundane activity would keep his mind off of the goddess bathing not three steps distant. He walked stiffly across the room to the table and rummaged in his pouch, fishing out a pumice stone. Turning his back, he briskly scraped it across his chin to eliminate the whiskers there. The rough sensation helped to distract him.

Still, his ear was keenly aware of each swash of water she ladled over her body, the erratic currents she created as she shifted in the tub. He swore he'd rub his cheek raw before he could begin to ignore her completely.

After what seemed an eternity, blessedly, the splashing ceased. He tucked the pumice back into his pouch and stole a glance at the wooden tub. What he found there suffused him with a tender warmth. He felt a smile tug at his lips.

She was asleep. The water was quiet around her, but for the small ripple her chest made as it lightly rose and fell. Her head lay back against the wood, and her mouth lay open like a babe's in slumber.

What was he to do now? he wondered, wryly shaking his head. The bath would grow cold soon.

He approached with stealth, sweeping up the linen square from the bed. He slowly knelt in silence beside the tub and gazed at his sleeping angel. How innocent and sweet she seemed. One would hardly suspect there was a haughty spit-fire beneath that silken skin.

Without meaning to, he let his eyes slip to her breasts, to the nipples that waited coyly just beneath the surface of the water. His stomach tensed, and he fought the desire to cradle one of the perfect curves in his hand.

Then he sensed he was being watched. He peered up and found himself looking into two slumber-glazed jewels of willow green.

Linet blinked sleepily. She had no desire to move. The bath was so comfortable and warm, the man staring down at her so pleasant to look upon. She saw no reason to disturb the languor she was enjoying by thinking too deeply. She didn't even budge when the gypsy's head lowered and drew near. His mouth seemed to whisper down to hers, alighting there as lightly as a breeze, demanding nothing. She could smell the dampness of his hair and the sweet musk of ale on his breath.

Duncan believed he was tasting heaven. His loins quickened as rapidly as a boy's, and he intensified the kiss, grasping the back of her silky head and covering her delicate lips with his own. She *was* an angel, he thought in a rush as he sampled her soft, yielding flesh and began to engage her without restraint.

But all at once his angel pulled back, then resisted, then struggled, pushing against his shoulders.

Linet felt panic thrum in her veins like the pounding of a fuller's mill. Everything was happening too fast. God—his mouth was delicious, but she was losing control. Her father's warnings sounded an alarm in her head.

At last, she broke free of the gypsy's embrace and exhaled sharply. She should slap him for his impertinence. She should. It was what her father would have told her.

As if he could read her thoughts, he grabbed her by both wrists.

"Do not strike me again," he bit out.

"Do not . . . kiss me again," she answered tremulously.

Duncan had never had his ardor cooled so quickly nor so completely. For one moment he had sampled Paradise. Now he was Adam cast from the garden.

"I have no desire to," he assured her, his voice flat. "But you're a fool to deny *your* desire to kiss *me*."

"How dare you . . ." she gasped.

"Don't attempt to gainsay it. Your body speaks well enough for itself." His eyes raked her in accusation.

"Unhand me!" she cried, her face turning crimson.

"I will unhand you when you admit to desiring me."

"Let me go," she warned, "or I shall scream."

"In a brothel?" he barked. "No one would take notice."

"If you don't release me this instant, I will have you . . . put in stocks!"

This amused him. "Stocks? On what charge—kissing you?"

"You are a . . . a peasant." She spat the word. "You have no right to lay a finger on me. I carry the noble blood of de Montfort."

He instantly released his grip on her. "Is that it?" he asked incredulously. He couldn't believe the turn of events. Had he really kissed this woman a moment ago? "You think my kiss will taint your bloodlines?" he seethed. "Forgive me, my lady," he snarled sarcastically, "if my breeding offends you!" He couldn't resist adding, "It certainly didn't seem to offend you when you had your arms locked about my neck."

The sound of her slap was as stark as a whip in a chapel.

He recaptured her wrists, ground his teeth, and silently counted to ten, slowly. Then he shoved her arms back at her in disgust and stood up.

He supposed he shouldn't be angry with her. After all, she had no cause to believe he was a noble. In her mind, he'd insulted what were considered perfectly normal prejudices.

She'd simply voiced what practically everyone held to be truth—that common folk were somehow inferior to those of noble blood. Yet somehow he'd expected more from her, especially considering her own dubious bloodlines.

Linet's hand stung from the slap, but not as much as her pride. "You will stay away from me! I do *not* want you to touch me a—" She began to lie, then was horrified at the sudden catch in her voice.

The gypsy's eyes lingered on her mouth, and he gave her an infuriating smirk. "No," he murmured, "you *do* want me to touch you. And therein lies your trouble."

Her heart plunged at the ring of truth in his words. She could summon up no reply.

He snatched up his clothing and donned it briskly. Combing his hair with his fingers, he slung the pouch around his hips, grabbed up two bottles of wine, then stalked to the door.

"The bed is yours, Highness," he mocked with a bow.

"Wh-where are you going?" she asked offhandedly, trying to mask the anxiety in her voice.

"Out."

"But there are men here who . . ."

"I was mistaken. You seem perfectly capable of fending men off," he replied, and with that, he slammed the door, leaving her alone with her slowly chilling bath.

Fool, Duncan chided himself as he leaned back against the closed door. He couldn't believe he'd actually let his damned principles interfere with an opportunity to bed the divine creature on the other side of the door.

Of course, that was mostly his unrequited body speaking. He knew in his heart it would have been wrong. He could have seduced her easily, but he'd never been one to use women for brief pleasure, as many nobles did. And it wasn't that he hadn't had his share of them. But he'd never bedded a woman until her heart, not just her body, belonged to him.

For that reason, although he was ironically in a brothel filled with willing wenches, he'd seek no satisfaction tonight. Nay, he decided, slumping against the chipped plaster wall, tonight he'd drown his torment in drink.

Linet couldn't stop trembling as she rose from the bath. She snapped the linen cloth about her and rubbed vigorously, as if she could wipe away the remnants of his touch. A wayward tear coursed down her cheek, mingling with the drops of water there, as she wrapped the linen with punitive tightness around her betraying body.

It couldn't be true, she thought with rising desperation, echoing the fear that had been pummeling at her soul's door from that first kiss. She was a de Montfort. She was a lady, not some wanton villein, diving into the arms of the first man to whisper come hither.

Aye, it had been desire flooding her body as he bent to bestow that kiss. But surely she was better than her harlot mother, even if that woman's peasant blood did pollute her veins. She'd conquered that desire, hadn't she? Hadn't honor prevailed?

In the end, she got the privacy she wanted. She struck the gypsy for his insolence, sent him storming from the room. She had won then, hadn't she? Somehow, the tears brimming in her eyes as she perched on the edge of the pallet felt less than victorious.

She absently reached for the comfort of her medallion, remembered its loss, then clasped her hands together before her in a brief plea for strength. She had betrayed her father. She would not do so again. Even if it meant she might remain a maiden the rest of her life. She could not disappoint Lord Aucassin. She was a de Montfort. She was a *de Montfort*.

Over and over she repeated the words, until they became a litany, lulling her to sleep at the foot of the bed, still wrapped in the damp linen.

The sun set, and the moon rose in a sky salted with stars while she slept. Sometime in the night, with the unerring accuracy of a rooting newborn, she worked her way out of the toweling and up and under the coverlet to snuggle down into the cozy bed, where self-doubt couldn't disturb her dreams.

Long past midnight, Duncan staggered into the chamber. He banged his shin on one of the tables, but felt no pain. He wrinkled his nose. His clothes reeked of wine. Pulling his jerkin and shirt carelessly from his body, he let them drop to the floor.

He seemed to recall he'd made some arrangement about

sleeping, but he couldn't quite remember it. Only half-undressed, he fell headlong onto the bed and fast asleep.

El Gallo prowled anxiously across the flagstone floor of the Boulogne magistrate's manor. He hated being confined. And though the manor was generous in size, it wasn't the bow of his ship where a man had room to walk, where he could breathe, for God's sake. Even now, his prey was escaping. And there was nothing he could do about it. He was trapped here like a moth in the fist of the magistrate's guard.

What did they want with him?

There was no solid evidence of his reiving onboard the *Corona Negra*. He'd always made sure of that. All jewels were pried loose from their settings. Coin was ultimately melted down. And until that unfortunate incident with the wool merchant, it had been almost impossible to trace raw goods to their maker. Even Sombra, who might have attracted some suspicion with his reputation, was not aboard this time.

As for his brandishing his weapon at the docks, he was certain his story had been plausible. He'd told the magistrate that a one-eyed scoundrel had made off with his passenger, Linet de Montfort. He'd drawn his sword to go after her abductor.

The magistrate had grown very interested then. But he'd not let El Gallo go. He'd sent a handful of his own guards to search for the girl. And he'd left El Gallo to stew in this well-appointed gaol for hours.

"This way, please," came the magistrate's voice at last through the front entrance.

A tall, grim-faced man in an expensive woolen surcoat accompanied the magistrate.

"This is Bertrand Gaillard, steward to . . ."

"What did she look like?" Gaillard eagerly interrupted.

El Gallo frowned.

"Linet de Montfort," the magistrate explained. "Tell Monsieur Gaillard what you told me."

El Gallo pursed his lips. The girl was important to this Gaillard. He could see it in the man's eyes. Coin would be made where such emotions flourished. "She was under my care," he lied. He hung his head guiltily. "And now she has been stolen. What will I . . ."

"What did she look like?" Gaillard repeated. "How old?"

He didn't have to lie about that. "She was a young woman, like an angel—pale and blonde. And her figure . . ."

"Did she have a . . . a crest?" Gaillard asked, his gaze piercing. "A medallion of some sort?"

El Gallo frowned in concentration. He couldn't remember the color of the witch's eyes, much less what jewelry she'd been wearing. But it seemed important to Gaillard. "Yes, I seem to recall . . ."

"And the crest. Was it a crowned mountain peak?"

El Gallo nodded. "Yes. I think that was it."

"It's her," Gaillard said. "It has to be."

"Who?"

"The daughter of Lord Aucassin de Montfort. For months now, since Lord Aucassin wrote to us from his deathbed, her uncle has been searching for her, trying to make reparations for the damage done to her family. He has even announced a reward for the one who finds her. But Lord Aucassin gave us no clue as to where she lives, only that she carries the de Montfort medallion. If you've seen her . . ."

El Gallo's mind reeled with visions of reward money. "Let my men and me search for her. It is the least I can do, considering it was I who . . ."

"Very well," Gaillard said. Then he handed a pouch of coins to the magistrate. "The magistrate will provide you with four men to aid in your search."

El Gallo bowed to the magistrate, a gesture that was foreign to him in his life of unquestioned power. But a pint of humility now might be worth a barrel of gold later. He could suffer through it.

Fingers of sunlight poked at Linet's eyes to wake her irritably from her slumber. Whatever was tickling her ear wasn't helping her mood. Squinting, she turned to brush the offending object away and found herself face to face with the softly snoring gypsy.

Her eyes flew wide. She scrambled away from him. "Get out!" she hissed with morning harshness.

He winced and eased over onto his back.

"Get out!" she shouted in high panic.

He groaned and covered his ears.

She kicked frantically at him. But the pathetic misery in his red eyes as he bore her punishment moved her to mercy. She ceased, pulling the coverlet high under her chin.

"What are you doing?" she demanded more reasonably, though she still trembled.

He opened his mouth to speak, but his parched throat could make no sound. "Drink," he finally croaked.

She supposed she'd get no cooperation from him until she complied. She slipped the wrinkled, still damp jerkin over her head. "Close your eyes, then."

Duncan didn't need the admonition. He had no desire to open them again until the sun set. After a moment, a cup of watered wine was pressed to his lips.

"Here," Linet breathed.

He half sat up. The wench nearly spilled the cup in her haste to be rid of it and away from him. When he'd drained the tankard, he fell back again, all his energy expended on that one motion.

"Well?" she squeaked.

"Please . . ." he began, then flinched at the volume of his own voice and continued in a whisper, "please ask me later."

"Later?" she cried, making him squirm in discomfort. "But you . . . you had no right . . ."

"Wait," he pleaded.

" . . . to sneak into my bed . . ."

"Not now," he begged.

" . . . like I was some strumpet . . ."

"Please . . ."

" . . . you had purchased!"

He'd had enough. He sat up and rounded on her. "Look you! I paid for this room and the bed in it with my own coin! Sleep elsewhere if you do not like the arrangements." He groaned, holding his throbbing head in his hands.

Linet balled her fists, thoroughly frustrated. Was there no end to this peasant's audacity? She hated being in his debt. It was too much like being . . . owned. And she *really* hated that a tiny part of her was attracted to the idea of being possessed by the handsome gypsy.

She picked up his cup and slammed it onto the table, vow-ing she'd take no more of his charity and no more of his kisses. She kicked his boots from her path and stomped across the cold oak floor to collect her things.

Duncan would never have believed that such a tiny woman could make so much noise. There was no point in trying to get any more sleep this morning. Between Linet's crashing about the room and the blacksmith hammering at his head, he knew he wouldn't get a moment's peace. He flung off the covers and stood up, reeling as a wave of dizziness hit. Whatever had possessed him to drink so much? he wondered.

"I won't encumber you any further," Linet haughtily announced when she'd finished her noisy ablutions. She had dressed, he saw, in the rumpled clothes, and she stood straight now before him, her eyes carefully averted. "You are hereby released from your vow to watch over me. I need neither your protection nor your charity." She paused. The next words she muttered in a rush. "I thank you for your assistance thus far, and I promise that payment for your services will be forthcoming."

He couldn't help but laugh at her little merchant's speech, even if it did make his ears ring. How unconvincingly contrite she sounded. Unfortunately for her, she didn't know how single-mindedly persistent he could be.

Once when he was a boy, he'd boasted he could fight as well with his left arm as his right. That boast cost him no few nicks and bruises. But in the end, his skill with either arm became equal. His stubbornness triumphed.

A few years later, he similarly undertook the obligation of knighthood. Nothing could distract him from the responsibility that entailed. Chivalry was everything.

"You would not last a minute here without my protection," he grumbled, pulling up his sleep-wrinkled hose. "Besides, you have no coin . . . unless, of course, you'd planned to seek employment here." He indicated their room. He could see her temper struggling at the bit like a peevish mare. "The proprietor usually does, however, require you do something more than *slap* the patrons," he couldn't resist adding.

Her eyes flared like emerald flames, and she could scarcely speak to him in a civil tone. "If you could spare a small amount of coin to see me home," she choked out, "I promise

I will repay you in full for your trouble. I shall be getting a goodly sum from Lady Alyce de Ware. I can send your money to you within a fortnight."

Duncan studied her thoughtfully. She was furious, that much was clear. But beneath that fury something else flustered her, some war she waged upon herself.

"Nay," he said. The idea of letting her go on alone was, of course, absurd.

"Nay?"

"Nay." He calmly pulled his tunic on over his head.

"You do not trust me?" she gasped. "I am of noble blood."

"Trust does not reside in the blood," he said, reaching for his belt. "Nay, it is not a matter of trust. It's a matter of obligation. You will stay by my side until I have fulfilled that obligation. And then you can pay me, if you like . . . for my inconvenience."

"Inconvenience!" she stormed. "These accommodations have been quite convenient for you! How many harlots did you purchase last night, by the way?"

The ensuing silence was excruciating for Linet. She clamped her teeth together so tightly that her jaw ached. She didn't know why she'd said that.

Duncan knew why she'd said it. She was jealous. She may have scorned him, the high and mighty queen, but she didn't want anyone else to have him. That discovery warmed his heart. And nothing Linet could do or say afterwards, no amount of denial or protest on her part, could alter the profound effects this newfound knowledge had on him. "I purchased no harlots. In sooth, they offered to purchase *me*," he lied matter-of-factly.

11

THE POCKMARKED CUTPURSE SQUIRMING AT THE POINT OF
Sombra's dagger nodded rapidly. "Aye, I've seen it!" he
said, nervously licking his lips and staring at the bronze
medallion.

Finally, Sombra thought, someone recognized the crest.
He'd been in Normandy for two days now, and this miscreant
was the first one he'd questioned to give him anything close
to the answer he wanted.

"Where?" he demanded.

"It's de Montfort. From Flanders. I don't know where."

"Fool!" Sombra bit out, nicking the man's throat.

"Wait! A . . . a man from . . . from de Montfort came
through," the wretch stuttered, "m-months ago. He had a
drawing like that—a m-mountain, with a crown." The man
squeezed his eyes shut. "Now please let me go, sir. You can
have your purse back. You can have *all* the purses I cut this
morn."

Sombra growled. He wasn't done with the man yet. "What
did the man say?"

"Oh." The man screwed up his face, trying to remember.
"Something about a m-missing heir, a girl, something like
that."

Sombra let the breath seep out between his taut lips. This
was good news indeed, more than he'd anticipated. "And was
there a reward offered?"

"Oh, aye, a reward, yes," the man gulped as Sombra caressed his throat with the dagger.

Sombra snorted. The fool probably couldn't really remember if there was a reward or not. He'd likely been too busy cutting purses to hear. But where there was a missing heir, there had to be a reward.

Sombra had what he needed now. Someone, somewhere, was looking for Linet de Montfort, someone willing to pay for her return. He could hardly contain his pleasure. Not only would he collect the reward for restoring a missing heiress to her rightful place. He would also wreak sweet revenge on Linet de Montfort by replacing her with an imposter.

"C-can I go now, sir?"

Sombra glanced at the thief. In his excitement, he'd forgotten about him. He reached down with a gloved hand and retrieved his stolen purse dangling from the thief's belt. Then, with an easy twist of his wrist, he slit the man's throat, leaving him to gurgle out the last bewildered moments of his life at the end of the alley.

Sombra carefully wiped his fine Toledo blade on the victim's cloak and sheathed it. He dusted off his Cordoban gloves. All he had to do now was find a pretty, green-eyed, blond-haired young wench willing to sacrifice her sagging crofter's cottage for a spot at the high table of de Montfort castle. All the way back to the inn, where Harold lay in chains, Sombra couldn't stop grinning with delight.

Linet heard a soft scratching at the door.

"Sir," some woman whispered. "Sir."

"Ah," the gypsy said with a broad smile, "that must be one of the women desiring my services now."

Linet wished she had something to throw at him.

He opened the door a crack. "What is it?"

"The magistrate's men are coming. They are searching all the establishments."

"Damn!" He pounded his fist on the edge of the door.

"I have an idea," the woman offered.

Linet didn't hear the rest of the conversation. It didn't concern her. She'd done nothing wrong. If the magistrate's men were coming, she'd turn herself over to them. What could be safer than . . .

"Linet!" the gypsy said urgently. "Take off those clothes! We have to leave at once!"

The man was clearly mad. "*You* have to leave at once," she told him. "*I'm* waiting for the authorities. And I'm staying *dressed*."

"Linet, El Gallo is traveling with the magistrate's men. I don't know why. But I know it doesn't bode well for us."

"It doesn't bode well for *you*. *I* shall be safe enough. I am Linet de Montfort, daughter of Lord . . ."

"It doesn't matter if you're the daughter of King Neptune!" His eyes snapped. "We have to leave. Now!"

"But where will we . . ."

"Now!" He caught the neck of her jerkin and yanked it down hard, ripping the fabric down the middle and nearly knocking her off her feet. While she stood open-mouthed, the woman at the door rushed in with two other young wenches, carrying a bundle of cheap, flamboyantly dyed garments.

"The green one will fit her," the woman said, quickly sizing her up. "But you, cherie . . ."

The gypsy rummaged wildly through the clothing himself, finally seizing an embroidered, berry-colored piece.

"But that is a cloth for the table," the woman protested.

"Now it is a cloak," the gypsy declared, whirling it about his shoulders.

The two young girls had thrown the ugly green gown over Linet's head now and were helping her inch into it. But it was far too small.

"We need a veil for you," the woman told the gypsy. "Celeste, fetch my plum veil." She eyed Linet. "And one for the girl. The deep green one." She clucked her tongue. "Ah, if only we had time to darken her hair."

Linet squirmed in the tight surcoat. Dear God—were those her breasts pushed up above the low neckline of the garment like two over-leavened loaves of bread?

The gypsy wrapped himself in the huge square cloth, and the woman secured it at his throat with a bronze brooch. Celeste returned and began fussing over Linet's hair, coiling and pinning it into a knot, then covering it completely with the green veil and a wire circlet. The other young girl took hold of the laces at the back of Linet's surcoat and tightened them, ignoring Linet's protests, until the garment fit like a second skin.

But no matter how indecent she felt when they finished with her, she was certain she couldn't look as absurd as the gypsy. The makeshift cloak hung unevenly around his feet, its embroidered floral border contrasting painfully with his large, heavy boots. The plum veil, held in place with a yellow cord hastily knotted for the purpose, was draped and tucked so strategically around his hair and face that his head resembled a huge grape wrinkling on the vine. But when he turned to her in all sobriety to inquire as to her readiness, when she beheld his swarthy, masculine face—his dark brows, his shadowed jaw—peering out from beneath the delicate fringe of plum-colored sendal, she began giggling uncontrollably.

The streets were chill and as yet uncrowded when the bevy of unengaged harlots escorted them from the brothel. Somewhere, sailors still snored beneath the rumpled sheets of whores' beds. Merchants were only beginning to stretch before their crackling hearths, filling their stout bellies with bread.

Then, marching importantly down the street toward them came El Gallo and the group of local lawkeepers, and suddenly Linet was grateful for the harlots' effective camouflage. The officials passed within arm's reach of the women, who seemed, to Linet's horror, to be inviting their attention, cooing and waving and flashing their bare legs. But in sooth, their actions had the opposite effect. The magistrate growled at them, ordering them to move aside. She and the gypsy traveled virtually unnoticed in the midst of the ladies.

By the time they reached the edge of town, Linet was beginning to reconsider her opinion. This pack of harlots, women her father had always condemned as the worst scourge of nobility, the highest offense to God, had helped her. Without reward, without ulterior motive. Simply out of the goodness of their hearts. They had given her a garment, and now they handed the gypsy a wedge of cheese and a loaf of bread for the journey. Nor would they take compensation for any of it, though the gypsy dug in his pouch for coin she knew wasn't there.

"Perhaps you will remember us one day, eh?" the proprietor of the brothel said, her old, wise eyes sparkling suggestively.

For answer, the gypsy whisked off the veil and cloak, handing them to the proprietor. He lifted the woman's hand to place a kiss upon the back of it—a noble kiss, the kind a knight might bestow upon a lady. Then they turned expectantly to Linet.

She hardly knew what to say. She'd never spoken to a harlot. God's eyes—before she met the gypsy, she'd spoken fewer than a hundred words to any peasant, save her own servants. But though she was much discomfited by their presence, she realized they'd done her an enormous service. She straightened, looking the woman directly in the eyes. "My thanks to you."

The woman smiled gently, almost as if she understood Linet's difficulty, then bade them farewell.

Duncan couldn't have been more pleased. The harlots had broken down a barrier in Linet that he could not.

As they traveled along the winding, rutted road that meandered down to less than a path at times, stepping through mounds of sweet clover and stands of majestic elms, Linet seemed deeply lost in her own thoughts.

"She was . . . kind."

"Who?"

"The . . . that harlot woman."

Duncan grinned. "Aye, she was."

"I don't believe they are the *worst* scourge."

She frowned then and asked softly, "Do you suppose Harold is still alive?"

Duncan spoke with more surety than he felt. "Sombra no doubt has a purpose in holding him. But fear not—I'll find him if I have to search the four corners of the world."

She returned to silence then, and the only sounds were the steady brush of their boots along the path, the random whistles and flitting of birds. And the distant footfalls of the two men following them.

Duncan didn't want to frighten Linet with the news, but someone had been trailing them for some time now. His first inclination had been to wait for them. He had his sword, after all, and he could easily best any pair of men, save his two brothers.

But he had Linet to think about. If the pursuers were part of El Gallo's crew, killing them would eventually bring others even more bent on vengeance, and that would jeopardize Linet's safety.

There was only one solution. He had to get Linet to de Montfort at once. Once she was secure behind the walls of her family castle, then he'd deal with the reivers. For now, he'd lead them on a merry chase at a healthy distance. As long as the two men believed the fugitives were nearly within their grasp, they'd not bother to summon assistance. Meanwhile, he'd keep his eyes focused, his ears alert, and his lips sealed.

The moon rose in the heavens like a fierce, white saber. The shadows of twilight washed the landscape into a purple blur of foliage and sky. Through the leafy copse, Duncan could discern the faint glow of firelight through an oiled skin shutter. It was a crofter's cottage, and beyond it stood both a bakehouse and a barn.

Thank God, he thought, they'd found lodging at last. For the past hour, he'd gently urged Linet on despite her fatigue, knowing it was foolhardy to sleep in the open with men following them. Now the poor wench looked exhausted. Her eyelids drooped, and she could barely lift her feet to shuffle along.

His heart went out to her. Although hers was not a life of leisure, Linet de Montfort was probably accustomed to far more sedate labor—bidding on wool, sitting at looms, tallying accounts. She was simply not made for traipsing off across the countryside to flee attackers. In sooth, so weary was she, she voiced not a single protest when he guided her by the elbow toward the crofter's barn, pushing open the creaky door.

A shaft of moonlight slanted down through a hole in the thatched roof, illuminating the interior. The straw was clean, and a milk cow was tethered in the far corner. Chickens roosted in the rafters, and geese wandered underfoot, but they seemed to take no notice of their guests. Their clucking made a pleasant counterpoint to the gentle lowing of the cow.

The cozy, sweet-smelling stable reminded Duncan of his

childhood. To the dismay of his father, he'd spent many a boyhood summer night dozing among the stable lads on a pile of fragrant straw. He gave Linet a smile of reassurance and carefully closed the stable door.

"We should be safe enough here for the night, as long as we're away before the crofter rises tomorrow."

Linet wrinkled her nose and peered up at the moonlit dust filtering through the hole overhead. "I've never slept in a stable before. Are these your . . . usual accommodations?"

"I'd take you to my castle . . ." One corner of his mouth quirked up. "But it's too distant."

Fatigue made Linet chuckle easily.

"Hungry?" he asked.

"We ate the last of the bread at midday," she said ruefully.

"There's a bakehouse behind the cottage. There's bound to be a morsel there."

"You cannot steal bread from a crofter."

"Who said anything about stealing?"

Her eyes narrowed. "You said you had no more coin."

It was true. He had no more coin. But what he could purchase with the jewels from his dagger could feed all of London for a month. And if a man used his wits, much could be procured for little more than a good deed. "As I told you before, I have no need . . ."

"I know. You have no need of coin," she finished.

He grinned.

She crossed her arms. "And just how do you . . ."

"Wait here."

He could feel her eyes on him all the way to the bakehouse. It was a good feeling. He gave her a brief wave of assurance. Then he ducked in through the low door, as swift and quiet as a shadow, closing it behind him.

He counted on being in and out of the bakehouse in the wink of an eye. He counted on finding some poorly risen loaf or over-baked roll left behind. He didn't count on intruding upon the crofter's wife.

The woman looked as shocked as he. But then he supposed it wasn't every day an oversized Englishman, salivating with hunger, came bursting in through her bakehouse door after dark. Her eyes grew round, and she opened her pudgy mouth to scream.

He acted without thought, following instincts that never seemed to fail him. Rushing forward, he placed a hand on each side of the woman's generous jowls and planted a resounding kiss square on her still open mouth.

She squeaked once like a mouse caught by a cat. But after an obligatory protest, she melted predictably into his embrace. The poor woman must have been starved for affection. She leaned against him, savoring the moment as if it were her last.

When Duncan felt assured she'd not cry out, he withdrew, smiling down at her with tenderness. By the candlelight, he could see her flushed fat cheeks and the dreamy quality to her eyes as she smiled weakly back. Not for all the silver in the world would she cry out now.

"I mean you no harm, my lady," he assured her. "It is just that I have traveled far and eaten little. When I smelled your fine bread baking, I admit I . . . lost control."

The woman's blush deepened. "Please, sir," she gulped, "help yourself to what you will."

He grinned. The woman swayed on her feet.

"I believe I already have," he said.

Her eyes danced with pleasure for a moment. Then panic creased her brow. "Paul, my husband . . ."

"I will be brief."

She grabbed up three still-warm loaves of brown bread and eagerly pressed them into his hands.

He closed his fingers over hers. "Be not surprised if by sunrise the milking is done for you, my lady." He tucked the loaves beneath his arm and winked at her. Before she could utter a word, he gave her a courtly bow and made his exit.

Linet could almost smell the loaves the gypsy cradled as he stole across the yard. Sweet Mary, she was so hungry she could eat alms bread. Her stomach growled like a pack of hounds.

He was still a dozen yards away when the door of the cottage began to swing slowly open. He was forced to make a mad scramble for the safety of the barn. Just as he dove past her and out of sight, the crofter emerged from the cottage, rolling his sleeves down over his forearms and heading off for the bakehouse.

"Mathilde!" the farmer called out.

Linet peered back through the crack of the door. Mathilde? Was there a woman in the bakehouse? She frowned. "How did you . . . ?" she whispered.

"Come," the gypsy said, ignoring her question and easing the door shut. "I've brought a feast." He broke off a piece from one of the loaves.

She eyed the bread, involuntarily licking her lips. She hated taking it from him. Her father would have burst a vein to know a de Montfort was relying on the charity of a peasant. But the demanding trek had left her famished. She accepted the tidbit, murmuring her thanks, and perched on the edge of a milking stool to eat.

The bread was still warm. Between savory bites, she gave the gypsy a sidelong scrutiny. He appeared untouched by the fatigue that plagued her own bones. While his hair hung in unruly curls and his clothing was hopelessly rumpled, there was a sparkle in his eyes that the long day hadn't dimmed. His sigh was contented as he fell to the coarse bread like it was the finest pandemayne.

And for the hundredth time, she furrowed her brow and wondered what he wanted from her. Why would a gypsy peasant risk his life for her?

It could only be for profit. Though why he thought she had any reward to give him she didn't know. Still, there could be no other reason, no matter how he protested that he had no need of coin. No need of coin. Pah! Even a king could not make that claim.

But the gypsy had managed to procure much in the last few days—camaraderie from El Gallo, assistance from the harlots, bread from the crofter's wife—all without silver, save that which fell from his tongue. Mayhaps he was right. Mayhaps he did have little need of coin. But never in all her years of lucrative business had she seen such a thing.

Popping the last morsel of bread in her mouth, she wondered how the gypsy had convinced the crofter's wife to part with her loaves. She peered speculatively up at him for a moment as he licked his lips between bites. And with the sudden clarity of a seer, she knew. After all, how did he get his way with *her*?

"You kissed her."

He almost choked on his bread. "What?"

"The crofter's wife. You kissed her. That's how you got the bread."

A lazy grin stole over his face. "Now why would you think that?" he asked, raising a brow.

"How else could you keep her from caterwauling for her husband?" She crossed her arms importantly, sure she was right. Yet she couldn't stop the sense of irritation that bristled at her like a teasel comb at wool.

He shrugged, and a lock of hair fell enticingly over his forehead. "Perhaps I threatened her."

She knew better. "You kissed her," she accused.

He slowly licked a crumb from his thumb. "You sound jealous."

"Jealous?" she squeaked. "Don't be absurd." Her fingers knotted in her lap, and she felt color flood her cheeks. "It's only my . . . my disgust you see."

"Disgust?" he smirked, his eyes twinkling. "I doubt the crofter's wife found me disgusting."

Outrage simmered in her veins. How cocky the gypsy looked, grinning down superiorly at her with that wry mouth, a mouth no doubt still warm from that Mathilde's kissing . . . Curse his hide, she didn't want to think about it. And she wasn't going to let him unnerve her with mere words.

"The crofter's wife," she stated, folding her hands in her lap, "is no doubt accustomed to the crude embraces of a peasant."

A laugh exploded from him. " 'Crude' is it now? I believe you are insulting me, my lady!" Then he turned on her with a sudden interest that made her want to squirm. "Hmm, so you think I was crude with her?" he murmured.

He took a step closer.

She shot up from the milking stool. Had the stable walls always been so narrow, so confining? "I care not how you were with her!"

He took another step. "Oh, I think you do, my lady. I think you care a great deal."

She made a valiant attempt to stare him down with a haughty scowl. But she was no match for those sultry azure eyes of his that melted her like butter on a hot cross bun. She quickly averted her gaze to the straw at his feet.

"In sooth," he added, coming so close to her that she could feel his warm breath on her face, "I think you enjoy those . . . crude embraces yourself."

He must have guessed she'd try to slap him for that remark, for his left hand snaked out and caught her wrist before she could raise it. An instant later, his right hand secured her other wrist. She was trapped.

Time stood still as he turned his smoky, teasing gaze upon her. For an eternity he studied her, his eyes flickering over her face, memorizing each detail, burning into hers as if he could divine her very soul. Then, with an abrupt chuckle, he released her.

She sucked in a cool breath. She didn't realize she'd stopped breathing. Or that his eyes crinkled so charmingly at the corners when he was amused.

"You, Linet de Montfort," he said, "are afraid of me."

Her mouth fell open, and for a moment she could think of naught to say in her defense.

He shook his head. "You, who so boldly insulted El Gallo on the docks, who dared to confront Sombra himself, you are afraid of . . . of a lowly gypsy."

"I'm not afraid," she whispered in denial. Yet deep in her heart, she knew it was true.

"Yet you withdraw from me. You pretend it is disgust, but I hardly think . . ." he announced with self-mocking arrogance.

"I *do* find you disgusting," she stated. But she couldn't look him in the eyes with this falsehood, not while that wild black curl fell across his forehead, not while his eyes shone with blue mischief.

The last thing she expected was his roar of laughter.

"Oh, aye—disgusting! And just what is it you find disgusting?" he inquired, closing in on her again.

She eased backward. Nothing about the gypsy was disgusting. Everything about him was fascinating—fascinating and dangerous.

"My nose? My eyes?" His voice softened, luring her in even as she retreated across the barn. "My mouth?"

She started to take another step away, but a spade abandoned on the stable floor tripped her up, making her stumble backwards. The gypsy reached out for her elbow just in time to keep her aright. But by then her back was against the planking of the stable.

"Perhaps it is my . . . touch that disgusts you," he said.

She was trapped now, pinned between a wall and a man whose sheer, raw masculinity rivaled the wood's strength.

"Shall I show you," he whispered, "how I kissed the crofter's wife?"

"Nay." She stiffened like a stick. Not a kiss—anything but a kiss, she thought, even as her lips tingled in anticipation. No matter what he did to her, no matter how her heart raced, she swore she'd not bend beneath his onslaught.

"I placed my crude thighs just so." He stepped between her legs, nudging them apart with his knee until his body was pressed intimately against hers, leaving her breathless, leaving no doubt as to his desire. "Then I placed my disgusting arms thus." He transferred one of her wrists to catch both within his left hand, trapping them against the solid wall of his chest. Then he slipped his right hand gently around her throat. His fingers were like Lucca silk against her skin as they slid up the side of her neck and tangled in the curls at the back of her head.

Her breath grew shallow. She dared not look at him.

"Then," he breathed against the corner of her mouth, "I pressed my crude . . . lips . . . so."

His mouth closed over hers as if she were a chalice of sweet wine, his tongue flicking lightly along the rim of her lips, tasting her, tempting her. She closed her eyes tightly, fighting her own desires, willing the embers glowing inside her to subside. But it was useless. His kiss stole the very thoughts from her brain.

At last he withdrew, granting her respite from the chaotic emotions clouding her mind. For a moment she could almost think.

Then he kissed her again. This time he embraced her completely, plundering her senses, devouring her with all the ardor of a starving man. Her blood rushed through her ears, as if he'd summoned it all the way from her toes. Every inch of her skin responded to his touch like iron filings awakening to a lodestone. And even when he finally pulled away, when his thumb brushed her bottom lip, she felt the lingering molten heat of his kiss. She could no more silence the ragged sigh that slipped out between her teeth, the sigh that pleaded for more, than she could stop the tides.

She never meant to surrender. But once she felt the demand of his searching mouth, once the muscles of his body contoured themselves to her, all care ceased. She knew only that she wanted . . . something more.

Duncan knew what she wanted. And he fully intended to appease her. He released her hands, hands grown limp in his, to wrap one possessive arm around her back. Then, to his amazement, before he could muster his forces for another onslaught, the hungry little vixen threw herself with abandon against him, into a kiss of her own making. She crushed her breasts against his ribs and opened her mouth to him, exploring his shoulders, his face, his hair with frenzied hands.

And he lost control.

Never, *never* had it happened before. He'd made love to dozens of women, kissed scores more. Christ's bones, the de Ware brothers were the envy of the barony when it came to seduction. But always he was in control. It was he who set the pace, planned each move, each word, knew the moment of surrender. He always knew how far he could go and how to gracefully back away. Now, for the first time, he was utterly and completely powerless to stop himself.

She'd astonished him by responding to his kiss with an eager passion as heady as fine wine. Her body clung to him like a well-made garment, and her lips were musky-sweet as they murmured and kissed and sighed against his. Her hair felt like silk between his fingertips, and the warmth of her belly pressing against his loins made him throb with longing.

God—he craved her.

Holy Mother, Linet realized, coming up for air, she wanted him—his kisses, his caresses, his bold, powerful arms about her. The blood sang in her veins. She wanted him with every fiber of her being. And she might have surrendered, might have let him take her at once . . .

Were it not for the chickens.

The soft clucking of roosting hens suddenly seemed to fill the close air of the barn, reminding her of the world this man belonged to. It was a world her father had striven relentlessly to claw his way out of. A world where the name of de Mont-fort was utterly insignificant. A world she'd sworn to Lord Aucassin on his deathbed that she'd never enter.

She pulled back, gently at first, then with increasing urgency, ultimately bringing her hand around to his cheek and pushing his lips from hers. "Stop," she gasped.

His passion-glazed eyes were laced with pain. "You want me," he whispered. "Why do you resist?"

"I don't want you," she choked. "I . . . I despise you."

"Liar."

"Let me go!" she insisted, pounding on his chest.

He caught her fists within his palms and said hoarsely, "You don't despise me, Linet. You only fear me. Nay, you fear your own desire . . ."

She struggled against him, against the urge to succumb again to his embrace. It was the most difficult thing she'd ever done. He felt like heaven. But it was a heaven not meant for her.

"I do not desire you," she insisted. The lie came hard to her lips, and she couldn't meet his accusing stare. "And I do not fear you. 'Tis only that you . . . you refuse to keep to your place."

Much of the ardor left his eyes. He quirked an annoyed brow at her. "My *place*?"

"You are a . . . a peasant," she explained shakily. "I am of noble blood. You have nothing to offer me."

"Nothing to . . ." The gypsy released her hands. He looked truly incensed now. "What about love? What about loyalty?"

"Love is for fools." Her father had told her so a thousand times. Still, her voice cracked as she repeated the words and her eyes filled with tears. "I deserve far better than to live . . . like this." She sniffed, indicating the stable. "You should seek out one of your own—a milkmaid or . . . or a serving girl—to marry."

Her eyes only flitted over his face, but in that brief moment she glimpsed his enormous pain. She had hurt him, far worse than she'd hurt anyone before. Guilt crushed her. And yet there was naught else she could do. If she let the gypsy believe they had a destiny together, she'd only prolong his agony, and hers. It was better this way, even though her heart cried out bitterly in protest, better to end it now.

"I want no part of you," she lied.

The gypsy's eyes narrowed to slits, smoldering anger quickly replacing the pain. "Oh, there's a part of me you do want, my lady," he said nastily, "and that part makes no distinction between noblewoman and peasant." He snorted. "And what made you think I intended marriage? You must have let your imaginings get the best of you."

A damning flush burned her cheeks. They were cruel words, but she should have foreseen them. She should have known by the gypsy's glib tongue that he was the type of man to use a woman for his own pleasure and then abandon her. He was a self-serving peasant, just like all of his ilk were, just like her own mother.

She blinked back hot tears and let familiar memories bring her solace.

She'd heard the story a thousand times—how young Aucassin de Montfort had broken his own betrothal by marrying, for love, a peasant girl, how his family never forgave him, how they disowned him in the end. All of it her father bore with the grace of a penitent priest. But what transpired afterward he could never speak of without bitterness in his voice and a flat hatred in his eyes awful to behold.

The peasant wench, his beloved Anne, the joy of his existence, had married him for his wealth and title. Once those were stripped from him, she had no further use for the man she'd purported to love. She abandoned him and left the fruit of their brief union, the newborn Linet, on his doorstep.

Gradually Lord Aucassin recovered. He took up a trade to support himself and his child. Later he learned from Anne's sister that his wife found a richer, less scrupulous nobleman to live with, one who eventually killed her with the pox.

And each time her father told the story, he made Linet promise the same thing, a promise that once seemed ridiculous to her. No more. He made Linet vow that she'd never fall in love with a commoner.

She steeled her trembling jaw and stared at a spot over the gypsy's shoulder, letting dignity fuel her words. "On the morrow we will part ways."

"Eager to leave my care?"

She drew herself up proudly. "Eager to be with my own people."

Duncan spat. He didn't know whether to be disgusted or amused. "Your own people?"

"Aye. Noble people, honorable people, people who . . . who buy bread with coin, not kisses."

Duncan nodded, biting back his anger. He studied her—the determined thrust of her chin, the sheen of her eyes, the rosy lips that pressed together with stubborn pride—and he couldn't dispel the pall of despondency that came over him. It seemed that was all women cared about—wealth and lineage. He'd dared to hope Linet de Montfort would be different.

When he spoke at last, it was with the calm of defeat. "Does it mean so much to you then?"

"It is everything," she whispered fiercely.

Duncan studied her a long while. Finally he nodded and lowered his gaze in surrender. A single white feather floated down from the loft between them as if to signal a truce. Then Linet gathered her skirts about her and retreated quietly to bed down in the straw.

Duncan felt the day's long journey now. He was sad and tired, like a soundly vanquished warrior. The dim silence of night stole over the stable. The first tentative chirps of crickets intruded upon the dark. The beasts calmed and nestled down to sleep. Duncan lay awake for a long time, staring at the moonlit black rafters in deep contemplation.

He'd meant to tell her tonight, to reveal his name and his title. He'd planned to assure her that his intentions were honorable, that she'd be safe with him until he could convey her to the de Montfort castle.

He'd never meant to fall so completely in love with her. And he still didn't know how it had happened. After all, she'd been but an obligation he'd taken upon himself. If he felt a certain compassion for her, it was surely no more than what he always felt for those he took under his wing. That explained the softening he experienced when he looked into her sweet face. It was mere compassion.

And yet . . . she had responded to him, and he to her, as if they were forged upon the same anvil. When he held her in his arms, she was fire to his tinder and wine for his thirst. She embodied much of what he found noble in a lady and all that he found ingenuous in a wench. No woman had ever had such a profound effect on him—amazing him, arousing him, challenging him at every turn, captivating him with her curious blend of intellect and innocence.

Damn his eyes, he'd fallen in love with her.

But that was before, he chided himself, before she'd revealed her true colors. She'd exposed a fatal flaw, one that made him grind his teeth in frustration. Linet de Montfort bore an appalling prejudice against commoners.

He turned onto his side, bunching the straw beneath his head for a pillow, and closed his eyes. How could he possibly feel affection for a woman who based every interaction of her life upon the very thing he fought most fervently against? No one could be more wrong for him. He couldn't love her.

He sighed. All he had to do was convince his heart of it.

Until then, he'd keep her at arm's length. He still intended to protect her until she was safely behind de Montfort walls. But then he'd disappear. She'd never know the gypsy who had saved her life was in sooth a nobleman of the highest order.

It had been years since Duncan had milked a cow, but it was something that, once properly learned, one never forgot. He perched on the three-legged stool, resting his forehead against the beast's warm, sweet-smelling flank, and massaged her udders to start the flow of milk. Once begun, the rhythmic movement was soothing. The sounds of the milk spraying into the pail, the munching of fodder, and the occasional soft stamp of the cow's hind hoof comforted him after a restless night. His eyelids began to grow so heavy that he could scarcely keep them open.

Until he heard noise from outside. Then his senses came alert. He hopped up from the stool to press his eye to the crack

of the stable door. By then it was too late. Two horsemen had
dismounted and were already coming his way. The crofter had
arisen as well, chattering away angrily at them to be off.

By the first footstep, Duncan recognized the pair—Tomas
and Clave, reivers from the *Corona Negra*. By their second
footfall, his mind had raced through a series of possibilities for
escape. By the third, he bolted back from the door, dove for the
still slumbering Linet, rolled with her into the shadows of the
stable, and laid hands upon a pitchfork leaning against the wall.

The plan would have worked flawlessly had Linet been
some straw-stuffed quintain's dummy. But as soon as she felt
the weight of Duncan's body pressing her into the hay and
then tumbling her roughly across the stable, she let loose a
spate of indignant protest that likely alerted the next village.

"Unhand me, you . . . you cad!" she cried. "How dare you!
What do you think . . ."

Too late, Duncan clapped a free hand over her mouth.

12

LINET BIT DOWN HARD AS THE STABLE DOOR FLEW OPEN WITH a vengeance that rattled the rafters. Her victim howled with pain, shaking his injured hand free.

In the doorway, dust scattered in a maelstrom around two of El Gallo's reivers. They stood in a pool of morning light, their swords at the ready. Linet spit the straw from her mouth, rapidly blinking her eyes against the bright rays in the fervent hope that this was just another dream. But the reivers didn't disappear. They were as substantial as the hard ground beneath her.

How two of El Gallo's men had managed to track them across the countryside to this stable she didn't know. She only knew that the reiver captain must want revenge very badly to send his men so far afield.

"So what do we have here, eh?" the smaller, ferret-like man chortled. "A fine pair of chickens, no, Tomas?"

Tomas, lumbering forward like a big bear, only grunted, apparently misliking the fact that the gypsy had armed himself with a pitchfork.

"One of them looks to be a *laying* hen, no?" the ferret said with a gap-toothed smirk, winking at her.

The crofter plunged in through the door just then, loudly protesting the reivers' intrusion. But before he could speak his full piece, the bearish reiver cuffed him soundly alongside the head, knocking the poor man senseless to the ground.

"Come on out now, chickens," the ferret crooned. "El Gallo is calling you."

Linet's head still reeled from the shock of her rude awakening. A glance toward the gypsy confirmed that he, at least, possessed all his senses. His face seemed carved of granite, his eyes stone cold. She could feel the tension in him, as keen as lightning about to strike.

He murmured so softly that she could barely hear him. "Go above when I rush forward, into the loft."

She frowned. She had no intention of cornering herself in the loft when the gypsy fell to the two reivers. "Nay," she murmured back.

"Do as I say," he pressed.

"Nay," she repeated through gritted teeth.

A muscle in his cheek twitched. He looked as if he'd like to throttle her into compliance. "Then at least stay back," he growled.

The ferret sneered, "Make your move, coward."

The gypsy obliged him, skulking forth from the shadows like a stalking wolf, brandishing the pitchfork with cool menace. The two Spaniards came at him together, swinging their blades in wide, slashing arcs that the gypsy deflected with the tines of the pitchfork. They scuffled across the stable floor, sending dust and bits of straw flying.

The cow lowed once and kicked over a half-full pail of milk in her bid to saunter out of harm's way. Chickens squawked at the sound of metal hitting metal.

The gypsy half crouched, holding the pitchfork like a quarterstaff, ready for an attack from either side as the reivers circled. When their jeweled swords came flashing around simultaneously, he dropped to the ground. The two villains engaged each other in a tangle of steel as he rolled free of their arena.

Linet cursed softly. She supposed she couldn't very well stand idly by while this fool gypsy got himself killed. Snatching up a spade from against the wall, she tossed her hair over her shoulder and advanced on the combatants. The men moved about so quickly that she wasn't sure where to begin. She jabbed experimentally forward, poking at empty air. Then, just as she reared back to swing the spade at the one called Tomas, the gypsy stepped into its path, and it took all her strength to stop the blow's completion. She skidded on the straw, waving the spade wildly for a moment.

By the time she'd gained her balance, she was in the midst of the fighting. Swords whistled about her head. She sucked in a terrified breath.

Nothing won Duncan's attention faster than the gasp of a woman in distress. He wheeled about to see what was wrong. What for the love of God was Linet doing? She stood holding a spade before her as if it were some magic shield that would render her invincible to wounds. Had he not commanded her to stay back? He scowled at her, and that split second of inattention to the fight cost him a shallow gash across his ribs. He winced, then grabbed the spade from her, roughly shoving her away with it as he did.

Linet's backside was bruised by that shove, though not as badly as her pride. She had little time to lick her wounds. She scrambled backwards in the dirt just as a blade flew past her head. She'd have to find another weapon. Quickly, she scanned the stable.

Duncan could feel the linen of his shirt growing wet with blood, but he doubted the wound was severe. Hopefully, with two weapons in hand, he'd be able to end the skirmish soon.

The planting stick Linet found was too brittle to make a good weapon. She was just creeping forward, considering the merits of the half-empty milk pail, when a reiver's sword sang through the air toward her.

She experienced no fear. There wasn't time for it.

"Nay!" the gypsy cried. Then he dove with impossible speed in front of her, turning the blade deftly aside with his pitchfork.

His heroics took her breath away, and she staggered back to watch. To her amazement, even without her help, the gypsy singlehandedly held the Spaniards at bay, armed with little more than farmer's tools and his wits. She stared in awe as he lunged and leaped, feigned and struck with spade and pitchfork as brilliantly as any knight with sword. Where, she wondered, had a peasant learned such combat?

The ferret swung his blade high, and the gypsy dropped beneath its path, then came up abruptly, slamming the broad pan of the spade against the back of the reiver's head. The resulting dull ring made Linet groan in empathy. The gypsy didn't wait to see the damage, but turned immediately toward Tomas, who gaped at his fallen companion. Hefting the spade upward, the gypsy sent Tomas's sword sailing across the stable, where it landed mere inches from the cow chewing her cud with bovine nonchalance.

Now he had them, Duncan thought. He narrowed his eyes as he closed in for the final coup. He casually dropped the spade. His prey retreated step by shaky step. Then a movement glimpsed from the corner of his eye reminded Duncan that Linet was watching him.

By all rights, he should slaughter this scoundrel. Common sense told him so. The man was a sea reiver, one of El Gallo's brood. By the devil's beard, he probably deserved far worse even than a quick, clean death. Yet Duncan couldn't bring himself to kill so cold-bloodedly, not in front of the angel.

A revelation took sudden hold of him. Here was the perfect opportunity to teach Linet de Montfort something about the lower class and honor. After all, he had discovered chivalry amongst the poorest of peasants and pride in the humblest of hovels. Here was a chance to prove to her that wealth and title did not a gentleman make.

He raised the tines of the pitchfork against the reiver's bobbing Adam's apple.

"I should slay you, knave," he proclaimed, "but I will not. I do not wish to cause my lady further distress at seeing your blood spilled."

Tomas's eyes remained nervously focused on the long tines before him.

"You two," he continued, waking Clave with a kick to his skinny butt, "will return to El Gallo. You will tell him that you have looked into the face of death, and that I let you live. And you will warn him that should anyone so much as touch a hair on the head of Lady Linet de Montfort, they will have to deal with . . ." He straightened, suddenly inspired. "With the only man to ever have defeated Sir Holden de Ware."

"De Ware . . ." Clave gaped. "But no one has ever . . ."

"And the next time, I will not be so merciful." With that, he lowered the pitchfork.

Tomas cowered back and turned to go, not even bothering

to collect his sword. Clave scrambled after him. Duncan prodded the reivers' backsides with the tines just hard enough to
make the Spaniards yelp as they hurtled toward the safety beyond the stable door.

Linet stood with her mouth open as the dust settled. She
could do no more than stare at her unlikely hero's back—his
rumpled linen clothing and straw-bedecked, disheveled hair.
Had she heard him aright? She'd have sworn he'd called her
Lady Linet. He'd shown the reivers a nobleman's mercy, releasing them with a warning, little worse for wear. Could it be
the gypsy had some scruples after all?

Nay, she decided with a shake of her head, not after that
outrageous lie he'd concocted about defeating Holden de
Ware.

She dusted the straw from her jerkin. "If you are going to
make a practice of lying, you would do well to be more subtle about it. Holden de Ware indeed—"

He turned toward her, and horror froze the words on her
tongue. As she watched, a tiny wet thread of scarlet worked
its way down the front of the gypsy's shirt, staining the white
linen.

"You're wounded," she breathed.

Duncan frowned and glanced down. That? It was only a
scratch. A bit of cloth for binding and the cut would heal in a
sennight. "It's noth—" Dear God! Linet was as white as a snow-
drift. She looked as if she might collapse. His heart leaped to his
throat. Was she hurt? Forgetting his own scrape, he strode forward to clasp her shoulders, his eyes wide in concern. "Are you
all right?" His voice was ragged.

She recoiled from him, her eyes rolling like a frightened
palfrey's as she stared at his chest. "You're hurt," she murmured.

He narrowed his eyes, quickly inspecting her for injuries.
She seemed unharmed, thank God. A warm rush of relief
washed over him.

Still she looked pale. "So much blood," she said weakly.

Her concern moved him. "I have enough to spare, my lady,
never fear," he assured her, wadding the bottom of his shirt
against the cut to stanch the flow. "It's but a scratch."

Linet swallowed hard and forced herself to bridle her panic.

If the gypsy could endure such a wound, so could she. She turned away, reaching beneath her surcoat, and tore a large piece of linen from her undergarment. Biting down on her lip to stop its quivering, she marched over to him. But she wouldn't look at the ghastly injury. Averting her eyes, she donated her cloth to the cause and the pressure of her hands to the task.

He caught her hand in his where it rested on his chest. Curiosity played in his eyes. "You have never thrown a dagger to kill a man," he said, recalling her boast.

"Nay," she replied, too queasy to lie.

"You're really made of the sheerest sendal, aren't you, beneath all those layers of thick wool?"

Her silence condemned her.

"Then I'm glad I spared those two," he said softly. He removed her bloodied hands from their reluctant task with gentle fingers and nudged her away. "Go, wipe your hands on the straw. I can bind this myself," he murmured.

She glanced at her hands. She tried to imagine the tips of her trembling fingers were stained with carmine dye, not his blood. "I've never been able to abide the sight of blood," she muttered in self-disgust.

"For a woman with no taste for blood," he said, wincing as he wrapped the linen tightly around his ribs, "you certainly seem to engage in more than your share of violence." He glanced meaningfully at his palm, which still bore the faint marks of her teeth.

Linet flushed, but was spared having to think of a defense, for barreling in through the stable door came the crofter's wife.

"Paul!" the woman shrieked when she beheld her fallen husband. Her voice startled the poor man from his unnatural slumber. Wild-eyed, she turned on the gypsy in accusation. "You! You ungrateful wretch! I give you bread, and this is how you repay me—by beating my husband? Get out of here! Get out! You devil's spawn! You thieving bastard . . ."

"How dare you!" Linet cried, whirling her skirt regally before her. "Listen, you addlepated woman! If it weren't for this man, your husband might be dead! And you! You might be tossed over a sea reiver's shoulder, bound for the slave market!"

Duncan felt a grin tugging at the corner of his mouth. His arrogant angel sounded absolutely indignant. This was a peculiar turn—Linet de Montfort leaping to his defense.

Mathilde was clearly taken aback. She curved a brow toward him. "Who is *she*?"

It was all Duncan could do to keep a solemn face. "This," he announced, "is Lady Linet de Mont—"

"Mathilde?" the crofter called weakly.

Mathilde rushed to his side at once. All else was forgotten as she murmured endearments to her groggy husband and tried to explain to him the presence of boarders in his barn.

Duncan whispered to Linet, "I have yet to pay for the bread and lodging." Then he thoughtfully furrowed his brow. "Though I fear my wound may make the work difficult."

"Work?" she whispered back. "What work?"

"On the other hand . . ."

"Should we not be making our esca—"

"Have you ever milked a cow?"

She blinked twice.

"Have you?" he repeated.

"Milked a cow?"

"Aye."

"You jest."

"Come," he told her. "I'll teach you. It's not difficult."

Surely he wasn't serious. She wasn't about to soil her de Montfort hands on the teats of a beast. She whispered as much to him.

He murmured back, "So you'd rather have it bandied about that a de Montfort stole three loaves of good bread and a night's lodging?"

She pursed her lips. He had a point. And by the glimmer in his eye, he seemed to be enjoying making it.

In the end, she supposed it wasn't so terrible. In sooth, once she became accustomed to the rhythm, milking a cow proved almost pleasant. It wasn't unlike weaving—a simple motion repeated over and over, slowly but surely achieving results. The pail was already three-quarters full. But she didn't want to stop. And it wasn't only because the gypsy had convinced her that doing the service was the noble thing to do, that paying her debt honestly would demonstrate her de Montfort honor. Nay—as against her nature as it was, as foreign to her upbringing, she had to admit the experience was enjoyable. She leaned her cheek tentatively against the cow's flank. The beast had a sweet odor, like summer, and her hide was warm and as soft as brushed wool.

The gypsy crouched behind her and murmured against her hair, "Are you sure you haven't done this before?"

"Certainly not. My father would've rather seen me dance with the devil than set foot in a barn."

The gypsy's chuckle sent shivers up her back. "Then perhaps I should've asked you to dance instead."

She stiffened and stopped the milking.

Duncan mentally chided himself. Arm's length indeed, he thought. He could scarcely keep his hands off her. Only last night he'd sworn to keep his distance, and yet here he was in close contact with her again. Patiently, he eased her back into the rhythm of milking, squeezing her supple fingers in a downward motion.

God, she smelled wonderful—earthy and sweet with the scent of fodder and sleep and fresh milk. Her hair tickled provocatively beneath his chin, the curls tucked behind the delicate shell of her ear hanging inches from his lips, taunting him. Her fingers continued to work their magic on the cow, pulling, squeezing, drawing the bounty forth. Waves of desire assaulted him like a raging tide as he imagined what magic those hands might work on him.

By the time the cow ran dry, it was all Duncan could do to keep from tumbling Linet off the stool and into the hay. He'd never ached with such an agony of longing. He felt nigh to bursting. Now he understood why cows late to milking lowed so miserably. He, too, felt like moaning in protest.

As it was, he settled for far less. And still it was too much. When he loosed Linet's hands from the cow's teats, a drop of milk trickled across the inside of her wrist. Acting solely on instinct, he lifted her arm and lapped the sweet liquid up with his tongue.

It was the wrong thing to do.

She snatched back her hand as if he'd scalded it and shot to her feet, knocking over the milking stool. Fortunately, Duncan thought to give the cow a reassuring pat before Linet could entirely spook the animal. But the peaceful moment they'd shared had passed. Tension once again rippled through the air.

Duncan righted the stool and rescued the brimming milk pail from beneath the cow.

"We should leave before El Gallo's men find us again," Linet murmured, still awkwardly holding her wrist.

Duncan only nodded, too frustrated to speak.

The sun had begun to slide toward the afternoon. Linet could remain silent no longer. They'd walked for hours. For hours she'd listened to the creak of the gypsy's leather belt and the soft slap of his sheathed dagger against his thigh, endured the occasional brush of his cloak against her leg, caught the wondrous scent of him as a breeze wafted past. And each moment spent near him made it more difficult to imagine life without him.

It wasn't his fault. She knew that. But the torment inside her made her peevish and cruel. "Do you have any idea where we're going?" she asked breathlessly, slowing as the stitch in her side begged for relief. "I would vow we'd marched to Jerusalem by now."

The gypsy looked at her almost apologetically and called a halt to their breakneck progress. He stopped at a place where the stream they'd been following widened into a deep pool. She supposed it was a beautiful place—green and shady, overhung with lush elms—but she was too exhausted and irritable to notice. She flopped down onto the mossy bank against an old tree overhanging the water. Then she removed her boots, wiggling her toes, half in pain, half in relief, as they tugged free of their leather prison. Never had she been so miserable.

The gypsy rummaged through the provisions Mathilde had packed for them once their innocence was confirmed, offering her a hunk of bread and cheese. So hungry was she, she fell upon the fare with a haste and lack of manners that brought tears of shame to her eyes.

"Why did you not tell me sooner that you hungered?" the gypsy asked as she choked on a bite of bread.

Weak and humiliated, she fought the sob that longed to

burst forth from her throat. "I shouldn't have to be hungry," she muttered, pathetically sorry for herself. "I shouldn't be traipsing about in rags, miles from civilization, blistering my feet on this cursed rocky Flemish ground." She knew she should keep her feelings to herself. A lady didn't complain about such things. But once begun, she could no more stop the words than one could cease the flow of ale from a cracked keg. "I should be working peacefully at the spring fair right now, selling my wool, raking in a tidy profit." To her dismay, the sob escaped her. "I want to go home, back to my life."

The gypsy was silent for once, leaving her childish, selfish sniffles to echo foolishly, endlessly, across the water. He didn't speak to her until the well of her tears ran dry. Then he took a long pull at the jug of wine and spoke in a taut voice. "We'll be safe in a day or two. I'm sorry you've endured such . . . hardship."

She could tell by his tone that he'd seen far worse in his lifetime, and suddenly she felt quite ignoble.

He lifted the jug toward her. She compressed her lips, stifling a new bout of weeping. Even now, the gypsy refused to show her the slightest favor. He should have let her drink first. Damn him—everything he did was against convention, against nature. Why did he find it so difficult . . .

"Well, are you thirsty or not?" the gypsy asked impatiently.

She *was* thirsty. She sniffed and took the jug from him, wiping the mouth of it with her sleeve before she perched her lips atop it.

"I had no idea you were so fastidious," the gypsy said wryly, sitting down beside her. "I must be certain to scrub my lips before I kiss you the next time."

She choked on the wine. There wasn't going to be a next time. He was a peasant. She was a noble. There was *not* going to be a next time. She started to tell him so.

"So tell me, Linet de Montfort," he smoothly intervened, "what makes you so despise the common man?"

She looked warily at him, sure he was baiting her. But his expression showed mere interest. She folded her hands in her lap. She'd be only too happy to oblige him.

"Peasants are untrustworthy and disloyal," she began, enumerating the faults her father had named of her mother, "conniving and filthy and coarse-mannered . . ."

"Ah," he interjected, slicing a morsel of cheese for her, "and you have found me to be thus?"

She declined the cheese, taken aback by his question. Was the gypsy untrustworthy, disloyal, conniving? Thus far, he had kept his promise to protect her almost like a religious vow. Filthy? He was clean enough now. His skin was golden, his chin smooth. His black locks glistened in the dappled sunlight. Coarse-mannered?

"You *are* coarse-mannered," she decided.

He smiled. "It seems to me that *you* are the one I must keep reminding of your manners." He nibbled at the piece of cheese. "You know, you have yet to thank me for saving your life back there."

Linet shifted her focus back to the deep stream, her cheeks warm. She *had* been remiss.

"Well, no matter," he said with a shrug. "Do not let it trouble you overmuch. I know scores of nobles even less honorable than you, Linet de Montfort."

Linet gasped and shot up to her feet. He couldn't insult de Montfort that way. "Honorable? And what about *you*?"

He cocked a brow up at her.

"What about carting me about that ship as if I were your doxy?" she asked. "What about tossing me overboard like . . . like so much laundry? What about forcing me to enjoy your pawing at a brothel?"

The gypsy came lazily to his feet. A smile flirted with the corner of his mouth.

"Well?" she demanded, her hands on her hips. God—the man was infuriating. "What do you find so amusing now?"

"Naught, naught at all." He grinned. "God's bones—you are in a foul humor today."

"I am no such thing! It is *you* who—"

"I think you need to cool your head, my sweet," he said in mock concern.

"I am *not* your . . ."

Before she could rake his face with the claws her hands had formed, he placed one great palm in the middle of her chest and pushed.

Duncan swore she sizzled as she plunged backwards into the stream. The icy water took her power of speech away. She came up sputtering, her hair plastered to her face in long wet streamers. Her face registered shock, then outrage.

"How dare . . ." she managed before the water bubbled up above her chin, cutting off the last word with a gurgle.

He crossed his arms and watched her. "Has your temper cooled yet?"

Despite her attempt at righteous indignation, she couldn't maintain her anger for long. The water *was* refreshing. And the situation was ludicrous. She fought back a grin. "You devil-spawned son of a . . ."

He clucked his tongue. "Such language from a noble-woman." He stroked his chin thoughtfully. "I think I shall leave you in the stream. Aye, you shall stay there until you thank me for saving your life."

"You would not dare!"

"Come, come, my lady, I have served as your champion."

She found her footing on the slick, pebbled streambed and took a step toward the bank. But he wasn't about to let her out, not without just payment.

He tugged his jerkin open and drew it over his head.

She cursed as she stubbed her toe on a rock.

He carefully peeled the bandage from his chest, then pulled off his boots.

She scrabbled her fingers over the slippery grass of the bank, looking for purchase.

He slipped out of his hose.

She was halfway out of the water, balanced on her stomach across the muddy bank, when he stepped in front of her. She glanced up fleetingly, and her mouth uttered an astonished "oh." Then she fell back into the water like too small catch.

Naked and unashamed, he rose above her like a Norse god. In one brief moment, every detail of his strong, sleek body imprinted itself upon her brain as indelibly as dye on raw wool. It was an image she'd never forget, even if she lived to be an old crone. Then he dove over her head and into the pool, and she welcomed the dousing splash shocking her back to her senses. He surfaced immediately, shaking his dark head like a wolf, spattering her with yet more icy drops.

"Are you ready to thank me?" he said breathlessly as the water dripped off his nose.

Linet struggled to find her voice. Her own emotions were confusing her. She should be furious with him. She *had* been a moment ago. But now she felt as giddy as a new lamb. She should be outraged by his unabashed display. Her cheeks *did* burn, but not out of anger. And suddenly she didn't want to know the truth.

He was too close—too close to her body, too close to her soul. He made her forget who she was. She couldn't let him do that. She had to do something. Without thought, she turned aside to embrace an armload of water. Then she hurled it, catching him square in the face.

Almost instantaneously, he returned the favor with a sweep of his arm and a great howl, soaking her yet again. She spat the tresses from her mouth and tried to kick away from him. He caught her by the knees of her waterlogged hose, but she cleverly wriggled out of them to freedom.

At least, she *thought* it was clever.

Until he tossed the hose up on the grass out of her reach and continued his pursuit.

"You will have to thank me, one way or another," he promised, stalking her.

When he captured the hem of her surcoat, she knew she was doomed. He'd snatch her to him in no time now, and the last thing she wanted was to be any closer to him. She had to make a desperate move.

He had both hands on the floating garment now, ready to haul her in like a pike in a net. Before he could get a better grip, she ducked down under the water, loosened the laces, and slipped backwards out of the garment. By the time he brought the empty surcoat out of the water, she was safely distant, peeping triumphantly at him across the waves.

The gypsy laughed and, like a laundress, slapped the garment onto the bank. "How cunning you are, my lady," he said with a mocking bow, advancing again.

Linet could have kicked herself. She'd succeeded in delaying him a moment, no more. She'd surrendered her clothing. And she'd allowed him to position himself between that clothing and her. Nothing could be worse.

Nay, she amended, giving up would be worse. And she'd be damned if any peasant would get the best of a de Montfort. She tossed her head and prepared to fight.

The gypsy came within arm's length of her, and the battle began in earnest. Linet swam away from him, kicking up a steady wall of water. He grabbed one of her ankles and turned her onto her back. Splashing him mercilessly in the face, she was able to squirm free, but he pursued her instantly. He dove beneath her and pushed her up out of the water like a spawning salmon. She shrieked in outrage and went under, her cries making bubbles in the water.

Half wild with desperation, she decided she was going to have to take stronger measures. While the gypsy stood searching for the spot from which she would emerge, she swam down and, with all her strength, yanked his feet out from under him. He succumbed perfectly, falling backwards like a boulder, and she surfaced with a victorious cheer.

Suddenly, something wriggled along her leg. She had a feeling it wasn't a fish. Squealing, she skipped away. It came for her other leg, toying with her knee, but she escaped again. Then the gypsy's head emerged slowly from the water before her, and the look in his eyes and that wicked smile told her that vengeance was his. Her heart thrummed like a hundred looms in concert. She didn't know whether to laugh or scream.

He dove under. She panicked.

She kicked frantically against his attack, as if her very life depended upon it. More than one blow of her feet landed heavily against his body. Then he halted abruptly.

She cast about, expecting him to break through the surface beside her any moment. But not a ripple betrayed his presence. She held her breath. Nothing. She shivered. He was taking a long time to come up. Too long. And it was impossible to see through the murky water. They'd kicked up so much silt with their battle that the stream was hopelessly clouded.

Then she saw a pale island of flesh slowly breach the dark waves. It was the gypsy—his motionless back to her, his face still in the water.

Something was wrong.

She took a fearful step toward him, a worried whimper rising in her throat. She'd kicked him, she was sure, kicked him unconscious. And he was drowning.

Her heart bolted. Triggered by fear, with a burst of strength and speed, she reached across the gypsy's back and flipped him over. She gasped. His eyes were closed, his jaw slack. Sweet Jesu, she prayed, let him not be dead! No matter what vile names she'd called him, no matter what ill she'd wished him before, let him not be dead!

13

UNMINDFUL OF HER STATE OF UNDRESS, LINET SEIZED THE gypsy under the arms to haul him toward shore. She'd gone but two feet when he suddenly flipped back over to grab her by the waist. In the blink of an eye, he snatched her to him, smacking her smugly on the lips. Then he laughed. He might as well have kicked her in the stomach and been done with it.

"Get away from me!" she screamed. She batted furiously at him, shaking with rage. At least that's what she told herself it was.

He recoiled. "What is it?" he demanded. His guilelessness was almost convincing.

"Just go away!" To her surprise, tears sprang to her eyes.

Duncan heard the waver in Linet's voice. It wrenched the laughter from him and plucked at his heartstrings like fingers upon a lute. Remorse settled heavily upon him. "Oh, my lady, I didn't mean to frighten you," he said tenderly.

"I wasn't frightened." Her chin quivered.

"Then I didn't mean to cause you concern," he amended.

"Concern? I wasn't . . ." But she couldn't finish the lie.

God's wounds, Duncan realized, the wench had been genuinely frightened for him. Though she was trying valiantly to deny that she cared not a whit whether he lived or died, the truth was in her unguarded expression, in her instinctive response. He moved forward to take her in his arms, to comfort her.

She flailed at him in aggravation.

"Shh," he soothed, gently catching her fists.

Her emerald eyes were moist, her lips clamped to still their trembling. Only gradually did her arms relax in his patient grip. He tucked her wet hair behind her delicate ears, stroked her soft, rosy cheek. He nudged a drop of water from her eyelashes with his thumb, watching as it trickled down. It dripped from the point of her chin onto the swell of one pearly breast peeking through tendrils of her darkened hair, calling him, beckoning him like an irresistible Siren song.

She never flinched when he lowered his head to hers. He could tell by the faint smoldering in her gaze that she desired the contact as much as he. Their lips touched. Her mouth felt as pure and cool as the stream. Delicately he tread, tasting her like a bumblebee after honeysuckle—sampling tentatively at first, returning again and again for the fascinating nectar.

Then she answered his soft kisses with the tip of her tongue. He groaned deep in his throat. He shouldn't be doing this, he thought as he drew her wrists about his own waist and hugged her to him. It would only complicate things. In another few days they would part ways and possibly never cross paths again. He was mad to . . .

God—her breasts were heaven against him.

He was mad to begin something he couldn't consummate, that she'd never allow him to consummate. But his body paid no heed. It fed on the sweet, readily delivered harvest like a banquet. The velvety pillow of Linet's bosom cushioned his ribs. Her long tresses swirled about in the rollicking waves, tickling the sides of his stomach. His wet hair dripped down onto her face, and he licked the water drops from her cheeks and forehead. With the pads of his fingers, he stroked her spine, from the base of her neck down to the sensual curve of her buttocks.

Linet moaned. The voice warning her to cease grew faint. She could scarcely hear it over the low roaring in her ears. All she cared about was the man embracing her—the man who was warm, gentle and, thank God, alive. Her flesh seemed to kindle and burn. The cold water eddying between the two of them only accentuated the places that his steaming, naked body pressed against hers. And though the firm staff nuzzling her belly left no doubt as to his desire, the dappled golden light, the whirling current, the heaven of skin on skin made everything seem ethereal, unreal somehow. She turned her head and clung to his waist, sighing against the strong contours of his chest.

"My little water nymph," he murmured. "What a tempting sight you are."

The hair along his arms brushed her skin as he reached beneath the water to cup her breast, letting the current tease at its peak. He kissed her forehead, her eyes, her ear, settling again upon her lips.

She gasped, but the sound was lost within his mouth, altered into a soft moan as his fingers tugged purposefully at her eager nipples. He nibbled and sucked at her lips, showing her what he could do with those nipples, until her entire body swelled with a nameless aching. She shuddered as his mouth breathed flame into her body. She grew weak, as if a whirlpool had come to dance with her and drown her in its watery embrace.

Unable to get enough of him, she let her hands roam over his wet body. She stroked his broad shoulders, felt the pulse that pounded in his throat, tangled her fingers in the thick curls at the back of his neck. No longer was she a noble's daughter. No longer was he a peasant. They were kindred spirits of the woodland stream. The world around her receded as she surrendered to the enchantment of the moment.

Then, without warning, he froze. With cruel abruptness, he tore his hand from her bosom and clapped it over her mouth. He stilled her twisting movements with his body, and his nostrils flared as he fought to silence his own erratic breathing.

Linet saw instantly in the smoky wariness of his eyes, in the tilt of his head, that he'd heard something. She listened as well, willing the tingling distraction in her body to subside. Then she heard the faint whicker of horses. Someone was approaching.

The gypsy mouthed a curse of profound regret, releasing her and motioning her to silence with a finger against his lips. As the riders neared, her heart mimicked the dull thump of hooves on the hard-packed ground. She tried to scramble away, but the gypsy grimaced, holding her fast. Soundlessly, he swept her off her feet, carrying her up the bank of the stream, his eyes vigilant.

It took all of Linet's resolve not to dive for her clothing, but the gypsy motioned for her to step quietly into the bushes as he scooped up their garments. Dragging his jerkin to cover their footprints in the dust, he joined her in the thicket, and they waited.

Within a moment, two sable mares ambled to the water's edge for a drink, followed by their wary masters.

"See? Nothing." It was the reiver, Tomas, and he looked relieved to find the place empty.

"I tell you I heard something," the ferret insisted.

"Probably your ears ringing. That gypsy crowned you well with that—"

"Still your cursed flapping tongue, Tomas!" He yanked on his horse's bridle and spat into the stream. "They can't have gone far."

"But they could be anywhere," Tomas grumbled. "We could be searching for days."

"You heard El Gallo. She is a de Montfort. She could be worth a fortune. Once we have her and that medallion . . ."

The breath froze in Linet's throat. A fortune? The medallion? She suppressed a hysterical giggle. She could barely claim the title, let alone the wealth of the de Montfort estates. Not only that, but the medallion was no longer in her possession.

"So what do we do with that guardian of hers?" Tomas asked.

The ferret ground his teeth. "The bastard is mine." He pressed a hand to his head. "I owe him for that blow. It is a wonder I can still think properly."

He wrenched his horse from the stream and led it off along the path, with Tomas in close pursuit.

After they'd gone, Duncan let out the breath he'd been holding. He rubbed his hands through his wet hair. Somehow, some way, he had to get Linet to safety.

"Tell me, what is this medallion they speak of?" he said, snatching up Linet's garments and shoving them toward her. She looked so delectable, huddled there in the curtain of her damp hair, that he almost regretted handing her the clothes.

"The de Montfort crest," she said, hugging the wet things to her chest. "I've worn it since I was a little girl." Then her eyes dimmed. "But it was taken from me on El Gallo's ship."

"Taken? By whom?" He pulled his jerkin on over his shoulders.

She shook her head.

He nodded at her bundle of clothing. "We must leave at once."

"But where will we go? We cannot traipse around Flanders aimlessly like we have been."

"Aimlessly?" Was that what she thought? "I know exactly where we're bound."

She lifted an inquisitive brow.

"The de Montfort castle, of course," he said.

Linet could only stare at him. The de Montfort castle? The place of her father's birth . . . and exile? She'd be about as welcome there as a rat in the buttery. "We . . . cannot," she said lamely.

"What do you mean, we cannot?" he asked, pulling up his hose. "You are a de Montfort. They are your family. They will offer you protection against El Gallo."

She looked at him. There was such kind comfort in his face, such optimism, such faith, such simplicity. She hadn't the heart to tell him that even if they succeeded in making it to the castle, they'd be turned away at the gates of de Montfort like lepers.

Duncan could see Linet was worried. "Do not fret about your medallion. They will know you. That is the way of families." He smiled reassuringly. "But it might be to your benefit to be wearing something when we arrive."

She glanced at the wet clothes and wrinkled her nose.

He chided her with a look. "Someday, my lady, you may hire servants to fan your garments with griffin feathers until they are dry," he said sardonically. "Until then, I suggest you slip these on."

She grimaced as she tried to smooth the clammy garments clinging to her curves into some semblance of modesty. She didn't succeed, and the effect was most engaging. But there were miles to cover and no time to spare. He donned the rest of his garments, detailing in his mind their next move.

They needed a refuge. The forest wasn't safe. Hopefully, there'd be a castle or manor house nearby where they could find shelter without arousing too much suspicion, without divulging their identity.

Getting in would be easy enough. He'd never found a keep whose portcullis didn't fly open once he announced to the lady of the castle that he was a jongleur.

He shouldered their bag of meager belongings. "Tonight, my lady, I promise you shall sleep on a real pallet in a real manor house."

Linet folded her arms skeptically. "And how do you propose to pay for it, this real pallet?"

"Ah, my lady," he said with a dramatic flourish of his hand, "this day we become jongleurs. Tonight, we shall sing for our supper."

Linet's heart dropped with a resounding thud. "Sing?" she asked bleakly. Dear God, she thought, if they were going to sing for their supper, she'd surely starve. She couldn't hold a note if it were handed to her on a silver platter. "Nay!" she said, trying to keep the dismay out of her voice.

"Nay?"

"Nay."

The gypsy clamped his jaw tight, and she could almost read the murderous thoughts in his eyes.

"Surely there is another way," she said, fidgeting with the hem of her surcoat. "You've come thus far, having no apparent source of income or marketable skills . . ."

He raised a brow. "No skills?"

She supposed she'd insulted him, but at least she'd managed to change the subject. "Other than a talent for deception."

"Really?" he drawled, pulling her after him along the path.

"Mmm," she answered, then began to muse aloud nervously to herself as they ambled onward. "Where *do* you come by your sustenance? I daresay I can think of only two possibilities. From what I can tell, either you have a tremendous amount of money cached away from whatever wealthy family thrust you from its bosom . . . or you are a thief."

When she looked over at him for his opinion, he only smiled enigmatically at her.

"Well, which is it?" she asked.

He frowned as if in deep thought. "The only thing I have ever stolen was a heart. And I don't believe I was ever thrust from anyone's bosom," he added suggestively, "save yours, of course."

The corner of her lip curved up in spite of her efforts at gravity. "If you'd spent as much time sharpening an axe when you were growing up as you did honing your wit," she quipped, "perhaps you'd have a useful occupation."

"Ah, but tonight, my lady, you'll see what sustenance that keen wit can provide."

She glanced away. How quickly the conversation had turned against her again. "I do not intend to participate in your silly games. I am a wool merchant," she muttered, "not a minstrel. I am *not* going to sing for my supper."

The gypsy's voice took on a subtle hard edge, and his eyes grew serious. "You have no choice in the matter. It's not safe here in the forest. El Gallo's men may surround us for all we know. We need to find lodging where . . ."

"I said I will not sing," she said, halting in her tracks. "It is . . . beneath me. You, as always, may do as you wish, but . . ."

"As I *wish*?" A humorless laugh exploded from the gypsy. "Do you think I wished to be put out to sea? To face the notorious El Gallo? To battle a pair of outlaws with a pitchfork?" He grabbed her by the wrist and hauled her forward after him. "I do not do this because I wish it. I do it because we are in grave danger, lady. Unless we can find a way to take refuge for the night behind castle walls, it is possible we'll not wake on the morrow! Do you understand?"

His words and his tone startled her, but she wouldn't let him see that. "I will not sing," she insisted, raising her chin.

He wheeled to shake his finger at her. "You will!"

"I will not!"

"Give me one good reason!"

"I cannot sing!" she hissed.

There was a shocked moment of silence.

"I cannot sing!" she snapped. "Do you understand now? I cannot sing matins! I cannot sing madrigals! I cannot sing roundelays! I cannot sing anything that requires more than one blessed note! So *you* may sing for your supper, but I, I shall remain silent, thank you!"

She turned on her heel, mortified that she'd made that admission to him. It had always been an embarrassing secret she'd kept hidden away. Now it was out. She braced herself for the mocking laughter she was sure would follow.

Duncan felt no urge to laugh. He looked at Linet de Montfort's stiff back in disbelief. "Is that all?"

He shook his head. Everyone could sing. She was only being modest—modest or shy. He smiled with warm confidence. There was no doubt in his mind that, with a little encouragement, he'd have her singing like a lark.

He couldn't have been further from the truth.

Linet was sure her knees would buckle beneath her. Her limbs were as useless as wet wool, and her tongue sat like lead in her mouth. Her head felt odd, like it no longer belonged to her body. Her eyes kept going out of focus as she tried in vain to count the row upon row of nobles clad in silk, velvet, and samite, and beyond them, the common folk in Kendal cloth and rags seated at trestle tables.

"Damn," she muttered sluggishly, losing count again. She fanned her face with her hand. Good Lord—it was hot in this castle, even with the laces of her kirtle undone. Perhaps she'd just remove the stifling wool garment altogether.

Sweet Mary—what was she thinking? A giggle bubbled up from her well-lubricated throat, nearly throwing her off balance, and she clutched at the gypsy's sleeve for support.

It was all his fault—that gypsy devil. She punched him once, ineffectually, on the arm. Damn the handsome scoundrel. He'd given her far too much to drink. And now she couldn't count past twenty.

Ah well, she decided, perhaps the counting could wait. She fluttered forgiving eyes up at him and sighed. There was something wicked about the way she felt, like the nap of her skin was being combed up by a teasel. By the Saints, the gypsy was handsome. And what a delectable-looking mouth he had, she mused, licking her lips.

Duncan felt every supple curve of Lady Linet de Montfort's body as she inclined against him on the dais in that sheath-snug bit of wool the harlots had seen fit to call a kirtle. It hung perilously low across her shoulders now. God forbid she should take a deep breath . . .

There—she was doing it again—slipping her tongue out between her lips, looking at him from beneath heavy lids with those dazzling green eyes. Sweet Jesu—if she didn't stop it, he swore he'd take her atop the high table right here and now.

Entertainment? He'd show the lord of the castle entertainment.

He strummed a brisk chord on the borrowed lute, then proceeded with a melody he could play almost without thinking.

He should never have gotten her drunk. At the time, it had seemed a rational solution. After a sip of wine, a lot of cajoling and a bit of painful experimentation, he discovered that Linet's reticence toward singing was well-founded. Never had he heard such atrocious attempts at melody. Still, undaunted, he reasoned that singing wasn't everything. All he had to do was to get Linet relaxed enough to at least join him on the dais before the castle folk. Once the men laid eyes on her, her voice's shortcomings would be quickly forgotten and forgiven.

He was right. No one seemed to care that Linet was humming along with the tune a full fourth above pitch, nor that she sounded like a rusty portcullis. Their attention was doubtless drawn to her emerald eyes, her honey hair . . . her alabaster skin . . . that tiny dot of a birthmark low on her breast . . .

He blinked his eyes. God's bones—what was wrong with him? He couldn't remember the next chord, and he must be on the ninth verse by now. Not only was his playing suffering, but his cursed body was responding to Linet's nearness with all the finesse of an untried squire. Lord—it was going to be a long evening.

From a dark crevice of the hall, far from Duncan's eyes, Tomas and Clave huddled together in stolen monks' cassocks. They gnawed on the hard crusts begged from the kitchen and pulled their cowls closer about their faces.

"I told you we'd find them," Clave whispered. He tore off a hunk of bread in his teeth.

"I hope she does not mean to sing again," Tomas complained around a doughy bite. "Her caterwauling in the forest was awful enough to frighten the animals away."

"Her caterwauling led us to her," Clave reminded him.

"I see no medallion."

"She's probably hidden it somewhere."

Tomas licked his fingers. "You mean we'll have to search her?"

"*I'll* have to search her. *You* will be busy holding her guardian at swordpoint."

Tomas started to protest, but Clave shoved a piece of bread into his mouth before he could speak.

Linet was absolutely enthralled by the moment. Not in all her years of merchanting could she remember having so much fun. The free-flowing wine had gone swiftly to her head, warming her all over, making her feel as light as down. Before long, her foot was tapping in rhythm with the gypsy's roundelays. She forgot her reticence, forgot their differences. She even forgot, for a short span of time, that she couldn't sing.

And the gypsy—he was magnificent. His fingers fairly flew over the lute. When someone pressed a harp into his hands, he proved to be a master of it as well, running his fingers across the strings as smoothly as water over pebbles. His wit was charming and lightning quick. He regaled them all with daring tales of adventure and sweet love songs, with ribald poems and turns of phrases that made her dizzy. She laughed at the droll repartee he exchanged with the lord of the castle. Then, just as easily, she was moved to tears by a particularly tragic ballad.

She stared at him—the dark-haired gypsy jongleur who held such sway over her emotions—and realized in a flash how narrow her own world was. She lived a life of numbers and tallies, a life motivated by profit and expense, a life devoid of dance and song and other gratuitous pleasures.

But the gypsy . . . he had been places, he had seen things, even through his pauper's eyes. He had drunk deep the draught of life. And yet he sang about the beauty of a rose with the same relish as he told the tale of a Crusader's last battle. Listening to him, she could almost taste the wine of the Holy Grail. Watching him, she could almost imagine what it would be like to awaken in his arms.

In the midst of a humorous madrigal comparing the moon to a faithless woman, Linet began to notice the expressions on the faces of the other women in the hall. Peasant girls and noblewomen alike regarded the gypsy dreamily. Some fluttered their lashes, smiling coyly. Some looked as if they'd devour him. Some even impudently wet their lips.

She had to protect him, keep him from these women who

planned to make him their next meal. After all, he was *her* gypsy. Overcome by a surge of possessiveness, she sidled closer as he played. She ducked under his arm, insinuating herself between him and the harp, and rested her head against his chest. There, it seemed he was singing only for her. She reveled in the strong, soothing vibration of his voice as the song reverberated against her ear. It was *her* song, and he was *her* gypsy. She sighed happily.

Duncan felt his fingers falter on the harp, and his voice caught in his throat. What the devil had possessed the wench? All evening she'd been staring at him. The desire couldn't have been more evident in her smoldering eyes. And now she was practically sitting atop his lap. God's bones—if she remained there much longer, *his* desire would become evident, painfully so. As best he could, he brought the song to a rapid conclusion and extricated himself from Linet's possessive embrace. Then he stood and bowed toward the high table.

"Is my lord's appetite well-sated?" he asked politely when he finally found his voice.

Fortunately, the plump lord yawned and nodded in contentment. "Certes you have earned well that chamber with the soft pallet you so desired." His timid wife whispered something in his ear. "Ah, my lady wife wishes to obtain the verses to that last madrigal. Might you recite them for our scribe before you take your rest?"

"It would be my pleasure," Duncan lied, approaching the high table as a servant fetched parchment and quill for the scribe.

The lord and lady took their leave. Behind him, the diners at the lower tables guzzled down the last of their ale and shuffled up from the benches to go. From the corner of his eye, Duncan saw several ardent admirers beginning to stalk Linet like hunters sneaking up on a defenseless hart. He cursed under his breath. In her condition, she didn't have half a chance.

The scribe dipped his quill in the ink and waited expectantly.

"How like the pale and shining moon . . ." Duncan recited.

Linet giggled behind him. Duncan clenched his teeth.

"How like . . ." the scribe repeated, scrawling slowly across the page, " . . . the pale . . ."

"And shining moon," Duncan prompted impatiently.

Linet's shocked laugh grated on his ears like a blade on a grinding wheel.

"And . . . shining . . . moon," the scribe said.

"Listen. Give me the parchment. I'll write them out myself," he told the scribe, unmindful of how odd it might seem that a peasant could read and write. With careless haste and a hand that would've shocked the chaplain who'd taught him to write, Duncan scribbled out the words to the song and shoved the finished parchment toward the scribe.

By that time, Linet was completely surrounded by them. She hiccoughed loudly, then was off and giggling again, leaning with drunken grace against a nobleman whose fingers rested rather boldly upon the low neckline of her dress. Anger flared in Duncan quicker than fire on a thatched roof. A muscle jumped in his cheek. His fingers itched to clout the nobleman who'd dare lay hands on his angel. But he wisely counted to ten before he tapped the man on the shoulder.

"Good pardon, sir," he sang out with deceptive cheer, though he could scarcely keep the malice from his eyes. "I cannot fault you for your fine taste in wine and wenches. But methinks this vintage is yet young."

The men laughed all round. But the nobleman peered slyly down his nose at Duncan. "I see your game, my fellow," he retorted, digging deep in his waist pouch. "How much coin to add a few years to her vintage then?"

Duncan silently thanked God Linet was too drunk to follow the conversation. "Why, none, good sir, for you see it is a family recipe, this wine, and not for the selling at all."

The nobleman scowled.

"She is my own dear sister, my lord," Duncan whispered loudly, his hand over his heart, "and I assure you, our father would beat far more out of me than you could possibly pay were this wine to lose its cork."

After the nobleman digested his words, he guffawed heartily, releasing his hold on Linet. His friends clapped him on the back, swigging the dregs of their ale, and the lot of them left to seek more docile game. Duncan heaved a sigh of relief.

He swept her then from the golden warmth of the hall's roaring fire, following the servant through the starlit courtyard bathed in shades of azure and slate. She listed tipsily on his arm as he led her across the grassy expanse glowing eerily in the moon's light.

"You were wonderful," Linet gushed.

He grinned. Lord, was she drunk. "And you thought I had no marketable skills," he said.

She stumbled. He caught her.

"And I thought I couldn't sing," she beamed, tripping again.

"That remains to be seen," he told her. In one swift movement, he swept her off her feet into his arms. "However, I seem to remember you could walk at one time."

She tittered. It was a delightful sound. "You shouldn't be carrying me, you know," she chided, wagging her finger at him. "You are a peasant, and I am . . ." She frowned, puzzled.

"You are?" he prompted, carrying her up a set of curving stone steps and dismissing the servant with a nod.

"I am . . . drunk." She buried her giggles against his chest.

When he pushed open the oak door of the bedchamber, she made a soft sigh of approval. She scrambled out of his arms, padded across the floor, and flounced down upon the pallet, kicking off her shoes and wiggling her toes.

As Duncan bolted the door shut, he couldn't help but smile at the pretty bundle of contradictions perched on the edge of the bed. With her hair springing every which way in a riot of curls and her gown slipping provocatively off one shoulder, she was the picture of a fallen angel. Her bare feet dangled and kicked innocently over the side of the pallet even as she studied him with a curious mixture of inebriation and desire. Such heady passion resided in her heavy-lidded eyes that he felt the heat of her regard even as he bent to stir the banked fire on the hearth.

The flames of the fire lapped upward like petals of an orange flower under his prodding. When he turned toward his angel again, the soft planes of her skin were bathed in golden light—the apple of her cheek, the hollow of her shoulder, the cleft between her breasts. God—she was lovely.

Linet sighed happily. The gypsy was most pleasant to look upon, she decided. The muscles of his shoulders strained the seams of his tunic as he poked at the cinders, and his long legs were as sturdy as trees. His inky hair glistened in the glow of the wakening coals, and his hands as he picked up a log to toss on the fire were strong and sensual. A delicious dizziness washed over her, and she leaned back onto her elbows to take in her surroundings.

"What is this place?" Her words came out in a breathy slur.

" 'Tis the real bed I promised you."

"Mmm," she reveled, laying back to enjoy the softness of the straw pallet. "It's wonderful."

She threw her arms with abandon over her head. Not since she was a child had she felt so carefree, so content. There was something else, though, something languorous and hungry and sensual that hadn't been part of her youth. The curious sensation made her laugh, a throaty laugh that felt like it came from another woman hidden deep inside her.

That unexpected sound shot a bolt of desire through Duncan's body that took his breath away. He stood stunned for a moment, his eyes locked onto the tempting bit of woman sprawled on the bed. She rolled her head to the side and peered at him through lowered lashes, and he felt his tongue rise to the roof of his mouth. God help him, he wanted her.

Linet let out a rich sigh. He was so handsome and gallant. The firelight burnished his skin to copper and lent a warmth to the rougher planes of his face. His eyes glowed, their sapphire depths mysterious. She ran her tongue lightly over her lips as she stared, transfixed by his sensuous mouth.

"You," she mumbled with a hiccough, "gave me too . . . much to drink."

His eyes softened. "Aye."

Duncan smiled. Linet was right. She was well and truly sotted, too drunk to be responsible for her behavior. He knew that. He knew that bedding her now would be a mistake, even if he'd at long last found appropriate accommodations. Nay, he told himself, no matter how she stared at him with those lust-filled eyes, no matter how much willing flesh she exposed, he must take control of the situation. He must curb his own passions. He'd pull the coverlet over her and douse those fires at once.

He took a step closer to the bed.

Her face was flushed with desire, her lips curved in a ripe and inviting smile. Her hair fanned out about her and dripped like amber honey over the edge of the bed. As her bosom rose and fell, the fabric of the damned kirtle stretched taut across her breasts, and he saw the tantalizing outline of her nipples against the cloth.

He swallowed hard and, closing his eyes, groped blindly for the coverlet. With a rapid swoop of his arm, he flung the blanket over her like a child trapping a pet coney.

She promptly kicked it off. " 'Tis far too hot," she explained.

Dear God, he lamented, now the gown had ridden up, exposing her knees and a length of lovely thigh. He reached across her to grasp the coverlet again.

Linet wondered distractedly what all the fuss was about. She was perfectly comfortable as she was. Her belly was full, the bed was soft—she couldn't wish for anything more. Well, she amended, perhaps a taste of that delicious mouth would be nice. It would taste as sweet as mead, she knew. She waited until he drew near. Then she captured his head with her arms and brought him down, pressing her lips full against his.

Duncan was paralyzed for an instant. All his chivalrous instincts told him to pull away, but when her lips rose to him like eager, grateful blossoms toward the rain, he was lost. He plunged into her mouth with reckless abandon then, tossing aside his better judgment as readily as the coverlet, twining tremulous fingers in the fragrant ocean of her hair.

Linet cleaved to the gypsy like a nursing babe, and his musky, wine-sweet breath mingled with hers as she drank in delights that were even more intoxicating than the wine. His lips seemed to sear her, his tongue to trace fire across her mouth. His hands rustling through her hair made her shiver, and the strong, masculine, leather-and-smoke smell of him engulfed her senses.

Beyond thought, she reached up and tangled her hands in his thick ebony curls. She answered his kisses hungrily, slanting her own lips against his in a primitive dance of passion. Her head reeled with feelings unknown to her. She trembled with desire as her body pressed upward, seeking she knew not what. For the first time in her life, she let her emotions have their head and take her galloping off across undiscovered country.

Duncan closed his eyes against the flood of sensations that threatened to usurp his control. Never had a woman driven him so mad. She moaned for more, and he gave it willingly, kissing her eyes, her cheeks, her throat, her shoulders. He clasped her tenderly about the neck, his large hand easily encompassing the slim column, his thumb stroking the line of her jaw. He slipped his fingers beneath the neckline of her gown and fondled the peach-soft flesh of her bosom.

He knew he should cease. It was not his practice to take advantage of innocents too drunk to think clearly. He knew it. And yet, when she began answering his caresses, writhing intuitively against him, clinging to him as if for dear life, all his good intentions counted for naught.

"God forgive me," he murmured against her hair.

He slid his hand up the length of her silky thigh and kissed his way down her body to nip at the peaks of her breasts through the cloth of her gown. He groaned as they hardened for him.

Linet whimpered in answer. Suddenly, she wanted out of the kirtle. No matter that it might have taken someone weeks to weave—she would tear it from her body if she had to. She wanted to feel all that warm male skin against hers again. She fumbled frantically with the laces of the gown, straining against the stubborn cloth.

Duncan wasted no time. He tugged the dress up to her waist, revealing curving hips and a golden nest of curls. He helped her to sit up, then pulled the gown off over her head. The sudden tightening in his groin moved him to free himself of the constraints of clothing as well. Fiercely, he tore the tunic from his back. His breathing felt ragged and desperate in his chest, and he tried to slow it, afraid he would frighten Linet.

Linet wasn't in the least afraid. She floated in euphoria, studying the play of each muscle he flexed, sighing as he relinquished the last of his garments, yearning, reaching, flirting with emotions she'd never experienced till now.

At last, he came to her on the pallet. Flesh met flesh in a tender forging. His limbs entangled with hers. Both of their mouths sought bare skin to press against. The flicker of the fire seemed to urge them on, licking their bodies with frenzied gold light.

Duncan gasped in astonishment. His body moved with a will of its own, nuzzling and kneading and enveloping the perfect creature beneath him. It was as if he sought not only a joining of bodies, but a consummation of souls.

Linet had long since turned a deaf ear to her conscience. Desire ran as rampant in her veins as the wine. She wanted this man with the crystal eyes, needed him to fill her empty arms, to complete her empty spirit. She moaned with her hunger, pressed eagerly against his hips, incredibly aware of his arousal. Her moans became wordless sobs, demanding relief. She wanted him. Now.

Duncan cursed weakly, forcing himself to slow his pace. With enormous constraint, he pulled away, ignoring his angel's protests, and bunched the fur coverlets beneath her, elevating her hips. He moved one hand down over her stomach, past the tawny thatch below her navel, seeking and finding the soft lips that guarded her womanhood. Tenderly, he stroked her, teasing the petals apart. Then he touched the core of her passion with a single fingertip.

Linet sucked in a shocked breath and tried to squirm away, but he showed her no mercy. He left his hand where it was. Slowly, patiently, he began his onslaught, circling gently at first, until she grew accustomed to the intimate touch of his hand. Then he pressed his fingers more purposefully, sometimes with aching leisure, sometimes like an elusive butterfly, over the nubbin that focused her desire.

He used his hands to prepare the way, stretching her yielding flesh, moistening her with her own juices. She tossed her head from side to side, mumbling incoherently as he stroked between her legs.

Then her breath came sharply, her body grew rigid, and her fists clenched atop his shoulders. He rubbed his throbbing member against her swollen flesh and watched her eyes closely for the signs that she was crossing the threshold of desire.

At last, a recognizable expression of bittersweet wonder came over her face. Duncan lifted her knees high and wide, delving into her at the precise moment of her climax. His own came upon him with astonishing haste, hurtling him beyond reason and thought into a realm of sheer sensation as pure and powerful as the sun.

Linet gasped. The sharp, brief pain that accompanied her release was no worse than the prick of a needle, mercifully softened by the waves of ecstasy that washed over her. She squeezed her eyes tight. Yards and yards of the most beautiful fabrics exploded across her vision—bold, bright colors and patterns the like she'd never seen, angels' garments whirling and flashing by her on their way to heaven. She reached out for them, but they spun out of her grasp.

Gradually, as her breathing calmed, the colors grew muted, softer, more distant, swirling slowly in her mind's eye. Their hue became a memory and their movement a soothing balm, sending her gently to sleep.

Duncan felt his gaze soften with tenderness. He stroked the halo of hair about his angel's face while she slept. Never had he felt such a joining—of body, of mind, of spirit. Never had he felt so powerless and powerful at the same time, surrendering his very soul to her and yet tenderly receiving hers in that most intimate of bonds. Even now, he trembled with awe.

This was the one he'd been waiting for all his life. This was his truth, his strength, his destiny, this wool merchant's daughter lying beneath him. This was the woman he must marry.

It was absurd. It went against all rational thought. Yet he knew with the certainty of a prophet that their joining this night had sealed them together forever. This woman had accepted him into her body, into her heart, without knowing of his riches or his power. She'd given him the greatest gift of all, a gift he'd never before received—the gift of unconditional love.

Now he owed her the truth.

He'd tell her who he was. And he'd tell her he was hers.

Unfortunately, he discovered, he'd have to tell her another time. His little angel had fallen asleep, exhausted no doubt from travel and wine and lovemaking. He supposed the good news would have to wait.

Instead, he slipped the de Ware crest ring from his finger and slid it carefully onto Linet's, her middle one, the one leading to her heart. He smiled as he nestled beside her under the coverlet, curving his thighs beneath her bottom. He buried his face in her hair, relishing the fragrance that would scent his dreams from now on.

Satisfied, he closed his eyes and let contentment lull him to sleep. His life was in order, the wind was at his back, and nothing could disrupt the smooth sailing of fate.

14

WHEN LINET OPENED HER EYES, SHE FEARED SHE WAS ON board ship again. The room listed dangerously. She clutched the edge of the pallet and experimentally slipped one foot out from under the coverlet. Once she was able to anchor that to the floor, the motion ceased. Her head throbbed as she squinted into the shadows, trying to ascertain her where-abouts.

By the glowing embers of the fading fire, she saw she lay on a pallet in a simply appointed room. Then memory rushed down over her senses like a crushing waterfall. Sweet Jesu—she'd lain with the gypsy! She'd given herself to him. Completely. Willingly.

It almost seemed like a dream. And yet the smoky, leather essence of him lingered on her skin. She licked her lips. The musky flavor of his kiss remained, the memory of a joining nothing short of ecstasy. And she felt . . . different. He'd changed her somehow, like an alchemist turning lead to gold. Her body, her soul, had come to life in his arms. He'd guided her past care, transported her to celestial realms she'd never even imagined. She ran trembling hands over her breasts, past her stomach, there, between her legs, where it was slick, wet with his seed and her blood.

A log shifted on the fire, sending forth a shower of gold sparks, startling her and briefly illuminating the gypsy's sil-houette on the pallet beside her. He slept peacefully, his face turned toward the ceiling, his brilliant eyes cloaked now with dark-fringed lids, his generous mouth relaxed in slumber, as innocent as a cherub. But he was far from innocent. And now, so was she.

The truth wormed its cruel way into her thoughts. No matter what heaven he'd brought her, no matter how right she'd felt in his arms, she'd committed a horrible sin. She, Linet de Montfort, a lady by blood, a prominent merchant, a respected member of the Guild, had let herself be seduced by a gypsy. A gypsy—that was all—a nameless, homeless vagabond living by his wits and the will of the wind. A gypsy with no family, no title, no trade.

Her eyes brimmed with scalding tears. Dear God—what had she done? All of her life she'd listened to her father, obeyed him without question, heeded his advice. All of her life she'd been a good daughter. How then had she come to this? Sweet Mary—she'd broken his strictest commandment. She'd given herself to a peasant.

Her mother's blood ran rich in her veins after all, she despaired, that peasant blood that boiled at the sight of any man. She was no lady, she wept silently. She never had been. She'd only been deluding herself. One could no more make oneself a lady than calling linen silk could make it so. She'd fallen prey to the very devil her father had warned her against. She'd betrayed Lord Aucassin—betrayed his title and betrayed his love. With one careless act, she'd wiped away years of his selfless devotion to her.

She raised a shaky hand to brush a tear from her cheek. Then she noticed the ring upon her finger. Sniffling, she held her hand up into the dim firelight to examine it.

It was made of silver, rich and heavy. The design, a wolf's head worked cleverly into the band, looked worn, as if it were ancient. But it was hauntingly familiar.

Her heart skipped as she realized what the ring signified. The gypsy must have placed it there. For a peasant, that simple gesture was akin to the rite of marriage. He was pledging himself to her.

As if it were flame, she jerked the ring from her finger and cast it to the floor. It glimmered up at her with its taunting leer. Muffling her sobs with the back of her hand, she rose and stumbled blindly about for her clothing.

She was doing the right thing, she kept telling herself. She was doing what she had to do. She had to think rationally. It was the only way to get past the pain.

The de Montfort castle could not be far now. And though there was no reason to believe her father's family would recognize her, much less take her in, it was her only hope. If she left tonight, when El Gallo's men least expected it, there was a good chance she'd make it safely to de Montfort by the following afternoon. She'd need suitable clothing, she thought, wiping a tear from her cheek. She couldn't arrive at the de Montfort's door dressed like . . . a common woman. Her lip quavered, and she bit it to still its mutiny.

She was strong. She could do this.

She'd need coin. Somewhere the gypsy had to have money. She began to dig through his bag. Surely it was no crime to steal from a thief, she reasoned. But there was no coin there. Twice she checked the pockets of his jerkin. She combed every inch of the pallet for some trace of silver.

But none was to be found. Either he had secreted it away so cleverly that even a tax collector couldn't uncover it, or he'd told the truth—he had none.

Just as she was about to give up hope, her eye caught again the dull gleam of metal staring up at her from the floor. The ring. It was made of silver, solid and finely wrought. She could purchase a surcoat fit for a lady selling that piece, she was sure.

She wavered on the edge of morality for an instant that seemed an eternity. The gypsy had given her the ring as proof of his devotion. To sell it indiscriminately . . .

Quickly, before her conscience could make a coward of her, she scooped up the ring and slipped it into her pouch. Then she looked her last upon the gypsy. Her flurry about the room had coaxed a final flame from the dying hearth, flame that lit one side of his upturned face with a warm glow. The other side lay bathed in the moonlight pouring in through the narrow window. It was a beautiful face. The fine structure of his bones, his lean jawline, the clean symmetry of his brow all seemed to belie his peasant stock. And the sweetness of sleep that lay upon his head made her reluctant to betray him.

But she was a de Montfort. She had her family honor to consider, her father's name to protect.

As for the gypsy—he would recover. He belonged to a different world, a world of sour ale and hard cheese, a world of patched wool and haystack trysts and handfast brides. No doubt he'd be wedded to some milkmaid within the year, she told herself, with a son well on the way. It was foolish to feel pity—either for him or herself. She wiped at a wayward tear, then turned to depart.

Creeping to the door, she realized that the gypsy would misconstrue her leaving. He'd awaken, find her gone and worry. He might think the reivers had taken her. Knowing the gypsy, he'd stop at nothing, but track her with dogged persistence until he found her.

She couldn't let him do that. She couldn't face him, not after betraying him. If he found her, she'd have to tell him she felt nothing for him. And he'd see the lie at once in her eyes. Nay, she'd have to make sure he wouldn't follow.

If she only had the time, and he the ability to read, she'd leave him a missive explaining that she was safe, that he need not worry about her, that he should continue along with his life and . . . and what? Forget her? He hadn't crossed the sea and half of Flanders to be sent on his way with no explanation.

She'd have to take drastic measures. She'd have to make certain he couldn't follow her.

Rummaging through the supply bag, she found what she needed. She pulled forth the thick leather binding cord from the crofter's bundle. Drawing it tediously across the edge of the gypsy's dagger, she cut it into four pieces. Quaking with fear and stealth, she wrapped cord gently around each of his wrists and both ankles. While he dozed on, she secured the remaining ends to the bedposts, finishing each with a weaver's knot.

Now she had to make certain he couldn't call for help. Eventually, she knew, a servant would discover him and free him from his bonds. But by then she'd be long gone. She gazed at him, lying there as guilelessly as a child. Sweet Christ—she hated what she was about to do, but there was no other way. Using his dagger again, she sliced two strips out of her linen undergarment and wadded one of them into a ball. Before he could rouse and fully comprehend what was happening, she pulled down his jaw and swiftly shoved the thick ball of cloth into his mouth.

The gypsy gagged on the dry material. He involuntarily raised his head, giving her room to tie the gag in place. His eyes widened in alarm. He yanked on the cords once, twice, bidding for freedom. Her heart missed a beat. Had she made the bonds strong enough? He fixed her with a glare of incredulous hostility. It seemed he might tear the very bedposts from the bed to get to her. That look charged the air. It would be imprinted on her memory for a long time. It was a look of sheer rage and utter bewilderment.

She sobbed once, partly in fear, partly with raw guilt, partly from heartbreak. Then she turned away, unwilling to witness the shame she'd brought upon him, unwilling to face the accusation in his eyes. She threw open the bolt and scurried out of the chamber before remorse could try to drag her, kicking and screaming, back to his side.

Duncan thrashed in panic. The leather cord cut into his wrists as he struggled to be free of it. What the devil had the wench done to him, and why? The last thing he could remember was utter joy as Linet lay slumbering against him and the certainty that he'd at last found the woman with whom he belonged for all eternity. Evidently he'd been wrong. Very wrong. And he had the punitive bonds of a vengeful woman to prove it.

He'd looked into her eyes. What had he seen there? Fear? Guilt? Sorrow? Regret? He'd taken enough willing virgins to know that their emotions were as unpredictable as the weather. Some wailed and carried on. Some lashed out in anger. Some were convinced they'd burn in hell. But with Duncan's forbearance and understanding, all of them eventually came to have no regrets.

Until now.

Damn Linet, he'd been gentle with her. He'd been patient, delaying his own needs to fulfill hers, causing as little pain as possible. And she'd wanted him. He had felt it in her. Why then had she done this? He curled his fists upward against his bonds, staring at them as if the answer lay there.

A draft blew in through the open door and across the hearth, rattling the cinders to life. And all at once he knew.

Linet de Montfort had used him. The thought left an acrid lump in his throat. The wench had used him, made him believe she desired him so he'd play into her hands. She intended to leave him behind. The little fool was going on alone. She figured she no longer needed him—a peasant who had become so much excess weight. He'd seen her safely this far, and now that they were near to the de Montfort castle, he'd apparently outgrown his usefulness. She'd discarded him as callously as an old coverlet. She'd intended to get rid of him, he thought bitterly, all along.

Her passion had been fake, her cries of ecstasy a sham. The way she'd clung to him, called to him, joined him on that soul's flight to heaven, all a pretense. His heart twisted with pain. He wrenched in vain the bonds that seemed to knot tighter with each movement. Sweat popped out from his forehead, and the veins in his neck bulged with the effort. Again and again he strained, becoming angrier and more desperate by the minute.

As he paused momentarily, panting, gathering his strength for the next onslaught, he remembered something that turned his blood to ice. He'd given her his ring, the de Ware crest ring. And the wench had taken it with her.

His cry of frustration was muffled by the wad of linen, and his thrashing scarcely made a whisper upon the straw-filled bed. Still, he froze as someone, alerted by the noise, slowly pushed the door to his chamber open, widening the crack with a faint creak.

A twinge of hope streaked up his spine. Mayhaps Linet had come back, repentant. Then he grimaced in self-disgust. How readily he would have forgiven her.

But it wasn't Linet. And he suspected, despite the shadowy profiles that appeared to belong to men of the cloth, that he was about to find himself in a great deal of peril. He watched through slitted eyes, barely breathing, as a pair of men stumbled across the room. One of them lifted a timber from the hearth, blowing upon it till it blossomed into a firebrand that lit up the whole chamber.

He'd never felt so helpless. As he lay there, bound and gagged, Tomas and Clave threw back the cowls and swaggered up, leers on their lips and revenge in their eyes.

• • •

The moon gilt the crests of the waves lapping the Spanish shore, making golden gems on the water. Ships rocked against their moorings—stately ships, old rusted skiffs, vessels that sunk, barnacle heavy, low in the waves. But nowhere did Robert see the imposing sails of the *Corona Negra*.

"The ship—she is not here?" Anabella clung to his side, placing one delicate hand on his chest.

Robert sighed. How natural she felt in his arms. It hardly seemed possible that they'd known each other but a few short days. "I don't see her," he said.

"What will you do?" She looked up at him with huge, dark eyes—eyes that trusted him, eyes that made him believe he could do anything.

"I'll find him. Somehow I'll find Duncan. If he is not in Spain, I'll return to England and . . ."

"No, not there," she pleaded. "I don't want to set foot in that country again, not after . . ."

"Shh, Anabella," he soothed, stroking her silky black hair. "I am not the one who broke your heart. I could never leave you. You know that."

She smiled faintly.

"Besides," he added, running the tip of his finger down her nose, "I know several priests in England who will marry a couple without the usual fortnight of banns."

Anabella's eyes shone. She stood on tiptoe and kissed his cheek. Her lips were like velvet, her breath as sweet as honey.

"How I adore you, Roberto," she whispered, "and how lucky your friend is to have a companion so loyal. I only hope you find him."

"I *have* to find him," he said with a wry grin. "Otherwise, how can I gloat over my good fortune and show him my beautiful prize of a bride?"

He enfolded her in his arms once more and let his gaze ripple over the inky, endless sea. The smile faded slowly from his face. Somewhere out there, his friend, his lord, the heir to de Ware, floated in the hands of fate. Duncan might as well have been a needle dropped amid rushes.

• • •

Linet shivered. The moon peeped through the leafy canopy, leaving stepping stones of light along the winding path of the forest. Crickets ceased their songs as she trespassed into their shadowy world, and mice scurried off to safer corners of the wood. Every twig snapping beneath her step quickened her heart.

This was by far the most reckless thing she'd ever done. If she didn't freeze to death or lose her way in the dark, she might fall prey to wolves or their human counterparts—the thieves who frequented the high road. She was as vulnerable as a coney loosed among hounds in an open field.

But remorse numbed her to fear. The chill embrace of night was a welcome penitence as she slogged through wet leaves, struggling with her conscience. She dared not even think about what had passed between them—the intimacy, the murmured words of passion. The memory was as painful as a fresh wound.

She'd betrayed her father. And she'd never be able to rectify that mistake. It was like a poor stitch taken in weaving. No matter how many more stitches one took to cover it up, the flaw still remained, and more often than not, each subsequent row of weaving only served to magnify the error. She'd just taken such a stitch. And she feared that flaw was going to haunt her for the rest of her life.

The first blow was always the worst.

This one was no exception. The fist slammed into Duncan's stomach, folding him near in half with nausea. After that, the body's level of tolerance was set, and nothing would get much worse. They split his lip, opened his cheek, and blacked both eyes, but he grew oblivious to the pain. He focused instead on the image of Linet burned into his mind, those culpable eyes looking down at him in anguish and betrayal before she left him.

He had to understand. He had to make sense of her cruelty. If it was the last thing he did, he'd strip her very soul bare to discover the truth. It was this obsession that kept him alive as the reivers beat him without mercy.

Finally their enthusiasm and strength began to wane in the face of their sense-dulled victim. The rogues ceased their bludgeoning and chortled to themselves over their victory as they waited for him to revive. He jousted with the fog of unconsciousness for a while, whether for seconds or hours, he knew not. When he awoke, the two Spaniards were engaged in a stifled verbal battle.

"We must find out where she has gone," said Clave.

"Let me beat it out of him."

"You've already beaten him half to death, imbecile! Besides, I do not think it will work. The fool will go to the grave with his lips sealed." There was a long pause. "No, we must use our heads."

"Why not kill him now, eh?" said Tomas. "If he is not going to talk, what good is he?"

"You have the brains of an ass!" Clave hissed. "He may not tell us where she is. But if we let him go—if we make him think he has escaped—he will lead us to her."

"Let him go? We cannot let him go," Tomas whined like a petulant child.

"How else will we find the wench?"

Tomas spat in response.

"We will do it my way," Clave announced. "Later we will kill him."

Duncan was badly battered. There wasn't an inch of him that wasn't bruised or bleeding. When he flicked his tongue out gingerly along his lower lip, it tasted metallic. Every breath was an agony. His eyelids were so swollen, he could barely see Clave coming toward him with the dagger. God save him—he was in no condition for what he was about to do. And yet he knew he must.

The instant Clave severed the cord at Duncan's wrist, Duncan whipped his hand out of its prison, catching the reiver by the arm. With a violent wrench that took every ounce of his strength, he twisted the blade until it pointed at the Spaniard's belly.

The man's jaw fell open in frozen disbelief. Before he could scream, Duncan plunged the dagger to its hilt beneath Clave's ribs. The reiver let out one final rattling breath as a trickle of blood dripped from his still gaping mouth.

"Clave!" the other reiver bellowed.

Duncan flinched in pain as he wrested the steel from the dead man's falling body. Half on faith, half on instinct, he flipped the dagger around and sent it racing through the air. Luck was with him. With a hard thunk, the blade pierced deeply the remaining foe's black heart. Duncan slumped back on the bed even before the Spaniard's lifeless body hit the floor.

After that, he drifted off. It seemed an eternity passed in that limbo of unconsciousness, though it couldn't have been long. It was still dark when he revived, and the silence of death hung like a cloud over the room. His eyelids were gummed shut, and his lip stung where it was cut. The linen had fallen from his mouth, but his tongue was as thick and stifling as the cloth had been. He poked it around experimentally. Thankfully, there were no loose teeth. The smell of blood permeated his nose, but it wasn't broken. His ribs ached, and his stomach felt as if a cart had rolled over him. God—he was as helpless as a kitten.

He had to get away before more of them came. He couldn't endanger his host by remaining here. First, however, he had to free himself.

Every muscle in his torso complained as he rolled over to tug at the leather cord around his left wrist. He lifted his heavy head and tried to discern the secret of the convoluted knot. After a moment, he let his head fall back. If only the wool merchant could see what she'd wrought, he thought bitterly.

When the dizziness abated, Duncan inched himself across the pallet until he could reach the cord with his teeth. With frustrating awkwardness, he gnawed at the leather until it was bitten through.

He rested again. It seemed as if the sky outside were lightening, at least the narrow patch of it he could glimpse through the arrow loop. He'd have to hurry.

Fortunately, Tomas had fallen toward the bed. When Duncan pushed himself up on his elbows, he saw he might be able to retrieve the dagger from the dead man's chest. His bones screaming in protest, he stretched out backwards across the bed, dangling over the edge so he could reach the blade. All the blood rushed to his head, the pressure causing an enormous throbbing behind his eyes. Finally, flailing at the dagger, he closed his hand on the haft and drew it sharply from the victim. Blood oozed like honey from the wound.

Leaning forward, he cut his ankles loose and cautiously swung his legs over the side of the bed. They seemed to be unbroken. He located his undergarments and performed the slow, painful task of dressing.

Kneeling by the Spaniards' bodies, he searched for anything he could scavenge. Pocketing a few coins and an extra dagger and buckling on a sword, he glanced one final time at the disheveled pallet. There were dark spots on the bed linens—blood. It wasn't all his own. Some of it was Linet's—maiden blood she'd surrendered in the heat of passion. Their blood would mingle eternally on the white linen. As their lives should have. He tensed his jaw. He couldn't bear to think about it.

As silently as a shadow, he stole into the dying night to find Linet. Whether he would kiss her or kill her, he was uncertain. But he had to find her before El Gallo did.

The great hall of de Montfort castle was extravagantly furnished, almost to the point of gaudiness. Richly detailed Arras tapestries hung from the walls, and the wainscotting that ran the full length of the room was painted with intertwined vines and blossoms in shades of green, rose, lavender, and yellow. A row of ornate, carved mahogany screens blocked the entrance of the buttery, where servants scurried back and forth making preparations for supper. Wall sconces with lit beeswax candles were located between each of the tall, shuttered windows. The beamed ceiling had been plastered and painted with biblical scenes. Glancing at her surroundings, Linet developed a new appreciation for all her father had sacrificed.

"The medallion?" she inquired politely. The man before her, her uncle, Lord Guillaume de Montfort, so resembled her father that it took her breath away. And the hope in his eyes when he beckoned her to join him in the great hall had been raw and anxious. She wished she could give him any other answer but the one she must.

The blood rose to her cheek, but she smiled graciously and tried to swallow her keen embarrassment. "I . . . it has been lost, my lord."

"Lost?" The word sounded hollow in the huge room. He doubted her. She saw it in the subtle flattening of his eyelids. He was disappointed.

The trial of her long journey—the chill of the forest, the sleeplessness, her futile attempts to make herself presentable after a night of trudging along the road to de Montfort—reared its head to torment her. She longed to throw herself upon her uncle's mercy, to tell him everything, to bury great wrenching sobs against the shoulder that seemed so like Lord Aucassin's. But that was fatigue motivating her—fatigue and frustration and heartache—not common sense. And it wasn't befitting a lady.

Instead, she took a shaky breath and fingered the fine, soft, forest green velvet of her new surcoat, the one she'd purchased from a local seamstress at the soul-wrenching price of the gypsy's ring. "I know I must seem a stranger to you. And I know my father was . . . exiled from . . ."

"No!" Lord Guillaume cried. Then he turned his face aside. "Not exiled from me. He was my brother . . . God rest his soul." He pressed a finger to his forehead, reliving some past agony. "Our father was too stubborn to beg Aucassin's forgiveness, and I watched him suffer for it. I watched our mother grow old for want of a son's love. But he was always my brother, by blood and in my heart. When he wrote that he was dying . . ." He choked back a sob.

Linet felt her own throat constrict. Her nose stung with unshed tears.

Lord Guillaume steeled himself, clearing his throat. "Aucassin wrote that he had a child of his . . . marriage—a daughter. He said that if aught should happen to her, if ever she needed the help of de Montfort, she would be known by the medallion about her neck."

Linet's vision grew watery.

Lord Guillaume studied her. "Your eyes are so like his," he whispered. Then he sighed. "But without the medallion . . ."

Linet sniffed. She understood. Without the medallion, she was no better than a peasant masquerading as a lady. She'd been a fool to hope she'd find salvation here. She executed a quick curtsey, then wheeled away to flee before her exhausted emotions could turn her into a blubbering bowl of custard.

"Wait!" he called.

She stopped, but could not find the courage to face him.

"There is enough doubt in my mind and enough shame

staining my soul to extend you common courtesy at least." He
sounded very tired. "Until I discover otherwise, you are welcome as a member of this household." He clapped his hands
twice, beckoning a servant from behind the buttery screens.
"Marguerite, see that Lady Linet is made comfortable in the
Rose Chamber."

Linet, her throat thick with emotion, turned and gave him a
deep, grateful nod. Then she followed the maid across the hall
and up the stairs to her new quarters.

The chamber was exquisite. Rose-colored velvet hung from
the canopy of an immense bed, caught at the posts with yards
of thick silver cord. The walls, freshly plastered, were painted
with roses in every shade of pink imaginable—salmon, cerise,
coral, mauve. Candles were copiously arrayed atop every
piece of delicately carved furniture—table, chest, and desk all
bearing the design of entwined roses. A pair of thick tapestries
depicting lords and ladies a-maying framed the tall window,
into which was set a panel of stained glass in the design of a
rose. Even the freshly laid rushes were sprinkled liberally
with rose petals, scenting the chamber like a garden.

She'd seen wealth before, but never had she seen a room so
luxurious. The maid drew open the shutters, and the sunlight
streaming in illuminated the chamber until it almost hurt
Linet's eyes to look at the bright walls. Surely, she thought,
heaven could not be so wondrous.

Once the maid vacated the room, Linet fell headlong onto
the thick furs upon the bed. The pallet enveloped her in its
feathery embrace. And despite her resolve to lay aside her
new garments with meticulous care, despite her intention to
explore every opulent corner of the room, to pick up and examine every ivory comb and silver candlestick, it was the
matter of but an instant before she drifted into a deep slumber.

A cloud slipped in front of the moon, shrouding Duncan's
face in complete shadow within the cowl he pulled over his
head. From the trees, he could see the sentries atop the wall
walk as they strolled back and forth, guarding de Montfort
castle.

Then the pale moon emerged again, and anyone able to see

Duncan's bruised and battered countenance would have
thought him a monster.

His guise, one of the reivers' cassocks, helped to conceal
his injuries. It would also gain him entrance, if no one noticed
the three feet of Spanish steel hidden beneath his holy robes.

He let his gaze travel up the two tall corner towers of the
castle and wondered if Linet was somewhere within. Did she
rest peacefully, he wondered, irony twisting his lips, or was
her sleep troubled by dreams of betrayal and vengeance? He
grimaced at the bitter taste in his mouth and spat on the
ground once before he emerged from the forest to beg entry to
the castle.

Linet awoke with a start, gasping at what seemed sudden im-
mersion in a sea of darkness. At first, she couldn't remember
where she was. The objects in the moonlit room shimmered in
ghostly blue, unrecognizable shapes. She raised up on her elbows and stared at the thin panel of light slashed upon the
wall through the open shutters. Suddenly, it all came back to
her—the gypsy, her betrayal, this new home she didn't deserve. With a guilty heart, she pushed the hair back from her
eyes, wondering what hour it was. She came to her feet,
smoothing the crumpled fabric of her ill-gotten surcoat as best
she could.

The vertical beam of light crossed her face as she padded
over to the window to peek out. A queer tingle of anticipation
crept up her back as she drew close to where a chill draft
slipped through the space between the shutters. She could see
the barbican of the castle from her chamber. Two guards were
standing watch over the cold, clear night.

There was a visitor speaking with them, a late-arriving
monk from the looks of him, probably seeking shelter. Something in the carriage of his body, his size and shape, disturbed
her. But the vague sensation vanished almost as soon as it appeared. They let the man in, and she watched the shrouded
figure until it disappeared from view.

A low growling from her belly intruded upon the quiet. She
hadn't realized how hungry she was. No one had disturbed her
nap for supper, and she hadn't eaten since dinner of the night

before. Perhaps she could find her way to the kitchen and turn up some scrap of meat or crust of bread.

She plucked the stub of a beeswax candle from the holder beside the bed and tiptoed into the hallway, lighting it on a wall sconce. Shadows jumped out eerily, heightening the unfamiliarity of the steps as she descended.

A hundred people or so lay strewn in the great hall in various postures of repose amidst the rushes. Their presence was some comfort to her in the vast room. Some snored loudly, others slept the sleep of death. Every now and again, one of the hounds would chuff briefly, aware of her, but apparently unconcerned. In the midst of it all, the fire blazed healthily, tended by a single little girl who poked at it with a stick as tall as she was. Linet smiled. Here was someone who could help her.

Duncan huddled against the wall, his head hung wearily between his knees. He still shivered with cold from his long trek. But it was as nothing compared to the chill of his heart, the chill that bore the name Linet de Montfort. He peered up beneath his heavy brows toward the fire crackling with false cheer. Then, almost as if he'd summoned her with his thoughts, Linet herself appeared, eclipsing his view, her silhouette stark against the orange glow. He sat breathless, watching her every move like a hawk.

Her new status suited her well, he thought bitterly as his gaze coursed down her body over the costly velvet surcoat belted with silver. But someone should have told the naughty girl that one didn't sleep in such garments. It was horribly rumpled. Evidently, he sneered, Lady Linet wanted her hard-won trappings of nobility surrounding her at all times, even in slumber.

Still, as bedraggled as she was and as harshly as he felt her betrayal, he couldn't deny that Linet was breathtaking. The fire cast a coppery glow upon her unbound hair. The deep shadows beyond her made her skin nearly translucent in contrast. The dark surcoat molded to her body as perfectly as his hands. Sweet Christ, he thought, how could such an angel have dealt such treachery?

Somehow, some way, he'd find out. And he'd repay her for her heart's treason, if it was the last thing he did.

Linet couldn't shake the queer feeling that someone was watching her. Even as she bent to speak with the little girl, she cast uneasy glances about the hall. Did reivers lurk in the black corners? Was she truly safe in this fortress? She doubted that she'd ever feel secure while El Gallo lived, not without . . . someone . . . to protect her.

Shaking off painful memories and swallowing her trepidation, she followed the little girl into the kitchen for cold meat and ruayn cheese. She never noticed how her skirts nearly brushed the feet of the monk reclined against the wall, the monk peering out at her with vengeance in his eyes.

15

FOR SEVERAL DAYS, LORD GUILLAUME AND HIS KIN AP-
proached Linet with tenuous respect. She understood.
They didn't want to invest too much faith in her claim, a claim
that would only bring disappointment later if it proved to be
false. Still, she was astounded by the regal treatment she received from the household. Maidservants fussed over her as if
she were a spun sugar subtlety. She was bathed and adorned
and perfumed until she was sure she'd be attacked by bees if
she went out of doors. Complex, colorful dishes the like she'd
never tasted before were offered her at the high table. The
lord's three daughters, pitying her lack of belongings, even
slipped her a few of their older surcoats to wear.

She should have been elated. Everything her father had
worked for had been achieved at last. She'd been returned to
the bosom of nobility. His indiscretion had been healed.
Though the de Montforts' acceptance was tentative, already
the family had begun to show a fondness for her. It was only
a matter of time before they accepted her completely.

And yet it was difficult for her to fit into this new garment
of nobility. She'd left too many loose ends in her life—her
mesnage, the Guild, Harold . . . the gypsy—and like a length
of poor cloth, the fabric kept threatening to unravel.

Everywhere she looked, *he* haunted her. She would peruse
a box of jewels and be drawn immediately to the pair of sapphires, so like his eyes. The palfrey Lord Guillaume let her
borrow was the same ebony shade as the gypsy's hair. The

jongleurs' songs could never compare to his, and their wit was never as sharp.

She tried to forget the gypsy, tried to immerse herself in the opulence around her. But no matter how many nobles offered her friendship and kindness, a pervading melancholy surrounded her like a thick, gray fog. She wondered if it would ever lift.

High now upon the wall walk, in a rare moment of solitude, Linet gazed off across the darkening countryside toward the place where she'd last seen . . . him. She wondered where he was. He'd be free by now. She doubted he'd come looking for her. She'd wounded him. Only a fool would seek out the thistle that had pricked him so sorely.

Besides, she reasoned, swallowing the thought like an acrid draught, she had probably been but another conquest for him in a long line of dalliances. Peasants engaged in many such affairs. Women no doubt swooned over the likes of him, lapped up his sugared flattery like a kitten would cream. The gypsy surely would not want long for company.

As for her . . .

An unwelcome lump swelled her throat. She stared up at the first star of evening winking in the mauve sky until it grew blurry from the sudden welling of tears in her eyes. Damn, she cursed wretchedly, she mustn't think of him, mustn't remember the wine-sweet taste of his lips, the clear crystal of his eyes, the reassuring strength of his arms around her. She'd not dwell on the memory of his ebony hair curling about her neck, the powerful play of muscles along his arms, the large, callused hands that stroked her body as skillfully as they did a harp.

Dear God—she sobbed wretchedly as the truth hit her with numbing force. She'd betrayed him. She'd betrayed a man she was trying desperately to make into a scoundrel—faithless and cruel and uncaring. But it wasn't true. He'd been more than kind. He'd been patient, gentle, understanding. He'd protected her with savage swordsmanship and made love to her with savage grace. He'd shown her nobility—this peasant—and honor and strength. Possessing no title, he'd shown her dignity. Possessing no wealth, he'd shown her generosity. She closed her eyes as the terrible, wonderful truth poured into her soul.

She loved him. God help her, she *loved* him.

He was gallant and clever and intelligent and brave, all the things she'd ever imagined a nobleman to be. He could enflame her desires with a glance and stop her breath with a word. For as long as she lived, no voice would ever sound as pure as his. No arms would feel as secure. No smile would light up her heart the way his could. She'd fallen wholly, desperately in love with the gypsy.

For one sweet moment, she rejoiced in the confession, tears of relief streaming down her cheeks. Never would she deny him again, she promised, clutching her hands to her breast as if to enclose him within her heart. Never. Yet, even as her tears dried, she realized it was too late for absolution. There was naught to be done. She'd made her choice. She'd chosen her father's dictates over her own heart. She'd denied true love in the name of honor. Now she'd have to live with that legacy.

She raised her trembling chin and gazed solemnly at the early rising moon. She was a lady now. There would be no more trafficking with peasants. Hers was a world of refined airs, civilized manners, tamed passions. She must forget what had passed in that bittersweet entanglement as thoroughly as if it had never been. And let her heart be damned.

Perched high atop the wall walk, her figure a graceful silhouette against the low-slung moon, Linet appeared an archangel haloed by the orb of golden light. But Duncan knew better. He spit the bitter dregs of his ale onto the straw of the stables. Linet de Montfort was no angel.

She'd readily discarded her past life, he thought bitterly. And she'd dismissed him with nary a backward glance. It didn't matter that for days now she'd wandered the castle like a lost soul, her face drawn by some wistful yearning. It didn't matter that the smiles she offered her newfound kin never quite reached her eyes or that her step seemed heavy upon the wide stone steps of the keep. Whatever misery she suffered, he told himself, she deserved no less. If she believed that untold riches would ease her suffering conscience, she was mistaken. And if she was lonely . . .

She turned on the parapet and seemed to float down the steps on a wave of green velvet, moving with a natural grace found among those highborn. Her hair was arrayed in a fantastic tangle of braids and ribbons that tumbled artistically over her bare shoulders. She was the very picture of nobility, her skin paled with powder, her lips stained a dark shade of crimson, the rich verdant fabric of her gown making her skin an even more delicate shade of cream.

But he could see by her shadowed eyes that she'd been crying. Pity welled in him like leavening in bread, and he cursed his own weak will. Never had he been able to endure a woman's tears.

Surely she'd bewitched him. For days now he'd been able to think of little else. He remembered too well the silkiness of her skin and the weight of her in his arms. His lips hungered for the soft flesh of her neck. His eyes craved the sight of her pale bosom, her narrow waist, the gentle flare of her hips. When she chanced to pass near, the clean, sweet scent of her intoxicated him like no wine could.

But it went far deeper than that. He felt incomplete, as if a part of him had been severed. His heart thumped hollowly in his breast. For days, he'd found pleasure in nothing, but only flailed along like a falcon with a bent wing, anchored miserably to the earth for want of her.

It was madness. And he was a fool to torment himself by remaining here. Tonight, he decided, clenching his fists within the concealing sleeves of his cassock, he would finish it. Tonight he'd confront her with her crime and break her hold over him. Tonight he'd end his suffering.

Linet lifted her heavy silver chalice and sipped at the spiced wine, peering over its lip. The tables groaned with their succulent burden—steaks of venison, galentyne sauce, cold shrimp in vinegar, pandemayne bread so light that it melted in the mouth, a colorful salad of parsley and fennel, watercress and mint, tossed with petals of primrose and violet, and dried and sugared figs.

She lost what little appetite she had, however, when she looked beyond the high table. There the smoky candles guttered, and the stench of unwashed bodies competed with the aromas of peppered meat and thick ale. The peasants supped on the meager leavings of the nobility—the stale, stew-soggy trenchers, the tough ends of the meat, the coarse ale, the food to which *he* was accustomed. She lowered her dagger. She couldn't eat.

She only toyed with the sumptuous fare all through supper. Even her appetite for entertainment was curtailed when Lord Guillaume presented a long list of diversions to catch her fancy. It seemed nothing would lift her melancholy.

A consort of viols played, then a harpist, and a lutist. Finally a quartet of dancers demonstrated the latest steps from Italy. She feigned interest, nodding at her uncle's remark that the circling and twining of the dance seemed akin to the intricacies of weaving cloth. She politely applauded the completion of a particularly complex dance pattern and repressed a sigh as the musicians played a seemingly endless roundelay.

Linet glanced at her silver chalice. A servant had filled it yet again with wine. She pushed it away. If she drank any more on her empty stomach, she'd never be able to keep her eyes open for the remainder of the entertainment.

A shrouded monk hobbled up to the dais, a harp clutched to his breast. The hall quieted. Linet stifled a yawn. He struck a single soft chord. Then his fingers caressed the strings one by one. There were murmurs of awe about the hall as he played with sweet delicacy at first, then embraced the music with the fervency of an impassioned lover.

Linet studied him intently. His playing *was* beautiful, but there was something . . .

A prickling began at the back of her neck, as if she'd backed into a spider's web. Those hands, those broad shoulders, that music . . . it couldn't be.

When the monk raised his voice at last in song, Linet's heart leaped unbidden in her breast, and she sucked in a quick breath of recognition. Lord Guillaume looked sharply over at her, and she forced a reassuring smile to her lips. It took all her resolve to keep from throwing herself at the gypsy's feet and begging his forgiveness.

The song was a melancholy ballad, his voice ragged and compelling. But as the words of love and treachery spun outward, the relief Linet had felt upon seeing him slowly curdled into fear. She knew for whom he sang.

The blood drained from her face. The gypsy had come after her, but it was to be no sweet reunion. Nay, he had come for vengeance. Sorely wounded by her betrayal, he'd come to ruin her, to expose her. The song was a message for her ears alone, but soon, he'd tell the tale of how this de Montfort *lady* had lifted her skirts for a peasant. Her father's dream would be shattered, and she would relive a nightmare.

Everyone stood and cheered for the shrouded monk with the heavenly voice as the song came to a close. Linet groped for her chalice, accidentally sloshing its contents over the rim onto her precious surcoat, where it spread into a nasty stain. She gulped down what was left of the wine, half-choking, then used her cloth napkin to dab at her clammy forehead. By the time she looked up again, he was gone.

She had to flee. That was all she could think about. She must excuse herself, go to her chamber, and bolt the door. She didn't even want a servant with her tonight. She must be alone to think, to plan. Dear God—she couldn't let him corner her here. He could destroy her with one well-placed word whispered in the wrong ear.

She shuddered. She mumbled to Lord Guillaume that her head ached, that she wished to retire. Alone. He shrugged a concerned consent and bid her good night.

Once out of sight, she dashed up the steps with her skirts in her fists, running as if she were pursued by ghosts. She pushed open the heavy door of her chamber and slammed it behind her. Her heart pounded painfully in her breast. Only when she shoved the bolt home did she dare to turn and lean back against the door in relief.

Too late, she saw him.

He was only a black silhouette against the fire on the hearth, standing motionless, but she recognized him at once. With a panicked gasp, she swiveled and began scrabbling at the bolt with suddenly clumsy fingers. In a moment he was behind her, his breath hot upon the back of her neck.

She took a gulp of air to scream. But before she could even turn to face her attacker, he clapped a hand over her mouth and shoved her against the door. For an endless time he held her there, immobile, letting her panicked breath moisten his palm. When he finally spoke, it was in a harsh whisper.

"Why?"

Her eyes darted about nervously, cataloguing the whorls of

woodgrain on the door. His scalding breath at the back of her neck sent shivers down her spine. What did he want from her?

Duncan wanted just one thing from the woman quivering like a trapped bird.

"Why?" he repeated. He slowly removed his hand from her mouth, still pressing her against the door.

"What do you want?" she asked breathlessly. "I'll give you whatever you want. Just please don't tell them . . ."

"Don't tell them what?" he rasped. "That I trusted you and you betrayed me?"

"Nay, I . . ."

"How long did you plan it all?" he snarled, bitterness rising in him like a boil. "From the very first? Keep me as long as you have to, let me risk my worthless neck, use me as a plaything, then desert me when my services are no longer required?"

Linet's gasp tore at his heart. But now was not the time to weaken. "And now your greatest fear is that I might humiliate you by telling your precious newfound loved ones about us. Am I right?" Her lack of a reply was answer enough. "I trusted you," he growled. "Damn you, I *trusted* you!" There was a long silence as he battled the hurt that threatened to unman him.

"I meant you no harm," she murmured feebly.

His chuckle came out hard and bitter. It would be a wintry day in hell before he'd believe that. He was no fool. Despite the innocence in those wide emerald eyes, he wasn't going to leave himself vulnerable this time. As bad as the beating had been, it was nothing compared to the anguish she had dealt him. "No harm?"

The fire popped on the hearth. Linet flinched.

His voice turned deathly quiet. "You left me naked and unarmed, bound to the bed. Do you know what happened to me after you left?"

He wheeled her around to face him. It was time she saw what she'd wrought. He slammed her back against the door and flung off his hood.

"Jesu!" Linet covered her mouth, stricken with horror. She staggered. Her eyes darted wildly as she surveyed his injuries—swollen eyes, purpled jaw, split lip, a long gash healing on one cheek, a lump rising from his forehead. His beautiful face had been . . . destroyed. She braced herself against the door for balance, hardly able to speak. "How . . . who did this?"

"El Gallo's reivers," he said flatly. "They followed us. They found it great sport to have their victim trussed up for their pleasure."

"Oh, God," she breathed. She felt sick to her stomach. "They did this to you?" She shook her head. "You must believe me," she said weakly. "I had no idea. I would not do this . . . to my worst enemy." She reached out a hand to brush a bruise on his collarbone. He recoiled, but she sensed it was not so much from pain as it was from her touch. "Your wounds need tending," she murmured. "Please allow me to make amends."

"You cannot make amends for the damage you've done."

Linet's chin quivered. She forced it to still. As much as his attack hurt, she deserved it. She'd injured him profoundly, more profoundly than just his superficial cuts and bruises evidenced. His eyes were bleak with a deeper pain, like once lustrous gems clouded by neglect.

Driving the lightheadedness from her brain by sheer will, Linet met his gaze. Somehow, she vowed, she would set things aright. Somehow, she would heal him. Even if it broke her heart in twain, she'd render him whole again.

"I cannot give you excuse for what I did," she said, "but I tell you this." Her voice quavered. She had to look away. "Never have I . . . and never shall I . . . love another as I have you."

Duncan's heart leaped into his throat. For a long moment, he didn't breathe. Surely he had heard amiss. She had wronged him, logic argued. She had turned her back on him, abandoned him, left him as reivers' carrion. "Nay!" The word was wrenched from his throat.

"Aye," she whispered. And it was there, within the anguished depths of her eyes—she spoke the truth.

The memories of their sweet coupling—how he had felt beside her, inside her, possessing her—came rushing over him like the quenching sea over parched sand. And yet he knew he had to stem that tide for the sake of his sanity. "You think your words absolve you?" he asked quietly.

"Nay," she hollowly admitted. "I will never be absolved, neither by you nor by my father. But I owe you the reason, at least." He remained silent as she drew a deep, shuddering breath and tried to explain. "On his deathbed, my father made me swear him an oath. I didn't question him. He was dying, and I . . . I thought the vow an easy one to keep. I was wrong." She swallowed hard. "I promised my father I would never . . . never fall in love with a peasant."

She hazarded a glance at him, but his expression was unreadable. "Had I known how impossible that vow would prove . . ." she murmured, her eyes blurry with moisture. "Ah God, I cannot imagine what hell it will be to live without you, knowing the heaven I have found in your arms."

Duncan squeezed his eyes shut, battling control of his senses. Part of him wanted to soar at her words. Part of him wanted to weep. "I offered you that heaven, for all eternity. You cast it aside."

"Because I had to. Because I must," she sobbed. "Because of my promise."

Duncan swore and seized her by the shoulders. "What kind of promise makes you cast aside the greatest love you'll ever know? Or makes you betray the man who has thrown his heart at your feet? What kind of promise makes you sentence yourself to a life without this?"

He dragged her to him, arching her backwards over one arm and burying the other hand deep in her tresses, loosing half the pins. He pressed his mouth to hers, savagely, as if to brand her his own. Her lips were as warm as flame, and she tasted of honey mead. He crushed her to him, oblivious to the pain, kissing her with the desperation of a condemned man.

Linet's fingers closed like talons in the fabric at the front of his cassock, drawing him nearer. She returned his kiss, so fiercely she bruised his swollen lip. She drew breath in long, shaking gasps against his cheek and moaned deep in her throat. Duncan's control evaporated.

"The devil curse me for a fool," he muttered hoarsely against her hair. "I want you, Linet."

"Then the devil curse us both," she breathed.

Linet felt as if she were diving into a raging ocean of sensation. Every nerve in her body drew taut. Everywhere his flesh brushed hers, she burned with desire. Her lips were swollen, her breasts ached with wanting, and though he pressed hard against her, still she needed to be closer. Every inch of her longed to join with him.

Once more, she thought, just once more. Before she had to meet her destiny—the bleak, barren destiny that seemed to stretch into eternity before her—she wanted to glimpse heaven one final time. Then she would accept the consequences. Then she would go willingly to that existence to which she'd been condemned by the cruel trick of fate. But she had to feel his love just once more.

"Please," she begged, clawing at his cassock.

The gypsy needed no second plea. Wincing only once when she slammed into his ribs, he swept her off her feet and carried her to the pallet, laying her out atop the rose-scented coverlet.

She wanted him now, quickly, before she could think about it. As his unbelted cassock fell open, freeing the potent evidence of his passion, she bunched her velvet surcoat and linen undergarments up to her waist.

With a groan, the gypsy swooped down upon her, his cassock covering them both like a feeding falcon's wings. He buried his face against her neck, his breath almost a sob on her skin. She whimpered impatiently as the warm flesh of his loins brushed hers, seeking, finding. Penetrating.

The burning never came this time. A breathtaking fullness almost paralyzed her as her body closed welcomingly around his. She squeezed her eyes tightly in ecstasy as he simply held her. Then she wrapped her arms about his neck and lay her head against his shoulder. He belonged here, she thought, savoring the pressure of his loins against her.

For a long moment he lay motionless, letting waves of arousal wash within her in their own sweet cadence. Then, slowly, he began to move. Each inward thrust was like the perfect crossing of yarn across a loom, steady and smooth. Linet, like a novice woolmaker, moved beneath him impatiently. But though he trembled with the effort, the gypsy was the master weaver, forcing her to the slower, surer pace. Surrendering to his lead, she reveled in the rhythm of their lovemaking.

Together they wove the fabric of their need, kissing and stroking and drawing each other toward a shared destiny. For now, no life existed beyond the clasp of their souls—no reivers, no title, no promise. Nothing could separate or distract them from that perfect merging. The fire crackled in response to their ragged pleas and throaty whispers, bathing them in warm golden light.

Quickly, Linet learned the tempo of pleasure and sought to prolong the sweet agony, retreating slowly and drawing out the sensations. But the gypsy would not long endure such play. With a low growl, he pushed into her with his full weight, and his bones ground against hers in a primitive pulse. She wrapped her thighs around his waist, squeezing the tender ribs they had both forgotten.

His movements grew more and more deliberate. Soon she matched his every thrust, burying her head against his strong neck and clinging to him like to a runaway steed.

She could have ridden that way forever, but her body began to build to a fever pitch of sensitivity. She felt some inner core expand into a glowing ball of light, rising slowly toward the heavens until it reached a zenith. Her back arched impossibly, and she cleaved fiercely to the gypsy for an endless, breathless moment of absolute still.

Then she was shaken by the tremors of a million shards of crystal exploding into the sky, showering upward and outward and finally, finally falling softly back to earth.

While her body was still racked with uncontrollable shudders, the gypsy made his own powerful ascent. Seized by the throes of passion, oblivious to the torture of his bruised muscles, he surged forward with the force of a wild beast and spilled his bounty deep into her womb.

For a long while, the only sounds in the room were the snapping fire and their own labored breathing.

Duncan gazed solemnly down at the woman he'd just bedded against all his better judgment. She'd left him as weak as a new foal. He shivered with the force of his release, and his nostrils quivered with each breath. On the morrow, every muscle and bone in his body would be complaining about the abuse it had endured for his pleasure. But it would be worth it. No one compared to Linet. She was everything—passionate, strong, and yielding. She demanded and she surrendered, gave and received with equal ardor.

He'd meant to punish her for betraying him, but now that seemed like a distant and foolish obsession. Later, they would sort out their misunderstandings. She would apologize. He would forgive her. Eventually he would wean her from her snobbery. But for now, he only wanted to hold her.

"I may live to regret these words, Linet, but still I must say them." He ran his thumb across the curve of her chin. "I love you."

Linet dissolved instantly into tears. She didn't mean to. She intended to bask in the afterglow of their lovemaking, to bid the gypsy a fond, if bittersweet, farewell, and to gracefully resign herself to whatever the dismal future held for her. But she didn't expect their union to be so soul-wrenching. And she didn't expect the thought of leaving him to hurt so much. Sweet Jesu—how was she ever going to live without his love?

"Did I hurt you?" he whispered, his forehead wrinkling.

"Nay," she sobbed. And yet she ached with an anguish far beyond physical pain.

"Shh," he soothed, smoothing the hair back from her brow. "There's no need for tears, my love."

Her weeping worsened. She didn't want him to call her that. She didn't want to hear that he loved her. Their coupling, however sweet, did nothing to change the fact that he was a peasant and she, a noblewoman. It did nothing to alter the vow made to her father. Before the tears dried on her cheek, he would be gone from her life . . . forever. And she'd have nothing of him save memories and his . . .

A sob caught in her throat. Sweet Christ, she realized, she didn't even know . . .

She wiped her nose on her sleeve. "Will you give me one thing . . . before you go?"

He screwed up his forehead. "Before I go?"

"Tell me your name, your *real* name?"

He was silent a long while. Then a smile seemed to tug at the corners of his mouth. "You don't know my . . ."

He got no further. The door to the chamber opened with a whoosh of air that made the fire dance crazily, then banged back against the wall.

Linet's heart stopped.

"It sounded like she was in trouble," Linet's maidservant was chattering as she swept into the room.

"What the devil!" In strode Lord Guillaume, his chin still greasy from supper, his face fast purpling with rage.

Linet felt the air crystallize inside her like the first chill breath of winter. She was paralyzed.

The gypsy moved away from her with quick dignity, pulling her surcoat down over her numb legs before he wrapped the cassock around himself. He stood tall and solemn, with the confidence of a highborn knight able to defend his honor and that of his lady love.

"What is the meaning of this?" Lord Guillaume demanded.

Linet trembled, certain her guilt was branded onto her forehead.

"Guards!" the lord shouted.

"I can explain," the gypsy assured him.

"Does this man mean anything to you?" Lord Guillaume asked pointedly, ignoring the gypsy.

Linet was too stunned to speak.

"Show him the ring I gave you, Linet," the gypsy murmured. "It will explain . . ."

"Silence!"

Linet clutched her finger where the ring used to be. She glanced guiltily at the gypsy. A muscle in his jaw tensed.

"Guards!" Lord Guillaume shouted again.

"Tell him who I am," the gypsy insisted.

Linet's mind was a blur of confusion. Her uncle must not find out. After all her father had endured to earn his title back—all the years of hard labor, all the sacrifices—it wasn't in her to shatter his dreams like cheap glass. Her uncle must not discover she'd fallen into the same gutter wherein she was spawned.

Duncan tried to remain calm. He didn't flinch a muscle when two burly guards appeared at the doorway. He knew, despite the missing ring, Linet would somehow explain his presence.

"Linet?" Lord Guillaume prodded.

Her voice was numb, wooden, quiet. "I don't know his name, my lord."

Duncan's heart turned to stone. He stared at her in disbelief. She wouldn't meet his eyes.

And then he felt nothing, even when the guards grabbed his

arms and shoved him roughly through the door. He remembered nothing of the trek to the cold, dank cell below the castle. And when they clapped the iron rings around his wrists, he thought only that they were no colder nor harder than Linet's heart—her black, lying heart.

16

LINET COULD RECALL ONLY VAGUELY WHAT HAPPENED THE
rest of the night, and that only in fragments. A numbness
descended upon her, enveloping her like a bubble, shielding
her from the buffeting of the outside world. A flurry rose up
around her. A pair of whispering maidservants stripped the
linens from the bed and replaced them. A woman made her
drink a huge cup of opium wine. Lord Guillaume paced the
length of the chamber in agitation, repeating over and over
that no word was to leave this room. And someone kept on
sobbing and sobbing like to wake the dead. But within her
sphere of protection, she seemed to float freely above it all.

If an occasional shaft of pain lanced suddenly through her
all the way to her heart, it was soothed soon enough by the
wine's balm of oblivion. And by the assurance that she could
count on Lord Guillaume to take care of everything.

She hadn't counted on a kinsman's wrath.

Deep in the bowels of de Montfort castle, Duncan sat on a
filthy mound of hay crawling with lice. Moisture oozed from
the dank, mossy stone walls, and the stench of rotting rushes
and rat excrement was nauseating. Not a sliver of light could
find its way into the cell. Duncan could only imagine what
creatures scratched and skittered in the corners of the cramped
hole he'd been thrown in.

He slumped forward, not bothering to pull the edges of the
cassock together, in spite of the fact he was shivering violently, his lips blue with cold. He was too devastated to care.

He refused to think about Linet. He knew that if he let himself dwell on her betrayal, he would be torn apart with rage. Instead, he thought about his family—his gracious mother, his good-hearted father. He thought about his brothers—Holden, so brave, and Garth, so brilliant—and the dozens of black-haired, blue-eyed children who huddled around him after supper every night to hear their favorite stories.

Who would tell them what had befallen their father? Who would know? Not even the wool merchant could say who he truly was. Without his crest ring, he was utterly anonymous. He blew out a slow, icy breath.

He was going to die. He knew that. No nobleman would settle for less than a tortuous end for a peasant who had dared to defile his kinswoman. It was only a matter of when and how. She wouldn't be there, of course, when they executed him. She couldn't abide the sight of blood. It was just as well. He never wanted to see her deceiving face again. He only prayed that when the time came to die, he'd do so bravely, like the de Ware that he was.

With a prayer for courage on his lips, he curled into a ball on the damp stones and fell mercifully asleep.

The sun rose, and a stillness hung in the air with the promise of stifling heat by mid-morning. A hawk made lazy circles across the pinkening sky, hunting for its breakfast. Within the gray castle walls, most of the inhabitants were already well into the day's activities.

But Linet still slept. Only a young maidservant, bustling about the room, at last woke her from her drugged stupor. The girl was jabbering away all at once about a scullery lad burned in a kitchen accident, some public flogging, and her latest love. Linet sat up dizzily, annoyed that she had overslept, mostly ignoring the servant's babble.

She shook the cobwebs from her brain. The sleeping draught had left her dazed. As she perched on the edge of the bed, some ugly memory kept trying to bob up to the surface of her thoughts, but always it was pulled under again before she could grasp it. She rubbed her throbbing temples. Never again, she swore, would she drink opium wine.

Finally, she stumbled from the bed and began digging

through her wooden chests, searching blindly for something to wear. The servant giggled and shook her head, gesturing to the garments already laid out for her.

Linet yawned, rubbing the crust from her eyes with the back of her hand. As shaky as a newborn colt, she wobbled to her feet, leaning upon the servant's arm.

Then, from outside the window, she heard a hollow thumping. It was the sound of a distant, solemn tambour.

"What could that be?" she remarked, mostly to herself.

"Why, that's the prisoner I told you about, my lady," the servant told her. "No doubt they're taking him up now."

Linet frowned. She supposed she should have paid more attention to the maid's prattle. "Prisoner?"

"Aye, my lady," the servant said, holding up a linen shift for Linet, "the one they're to flog." She clucked her tongue. "A pity we won't get to watch. But Lord Guillaume bade me keep you here until it's finished."

Linet made a grimace of disgust as the maid slipped the shift over her head. She would just as soon stay in her chamber. She had always detested public humiliations and punishments. They were just an unwelcome reminder that in some ways, no matter what her father held, nobles were not so far removed from savages.

"'Tis scandalous, really," the servant confided, crossing herself. "They say he is a monk."

Linet's heart stumbled. "What?" She could scarcely draw breath. "What did you say?"

"The man's a monk. They won't say what he did, but Lord Guillaume . . ."

Linet ceased listening. Memory jolted her like a clap of thunder. In the distance, the tambour echoed hauntingly.

It could not be. It could not be, she reasoned, she hoped. But somehow she knew for whom the tambour sounded.

"A monk?" she whispered.

"Aye," the young maid replied, wary of the look in her mistress's eye.

The cadence of the tambour's dirge seemed her own death knell as Linet walked to the window. Her nerves vibrated with tension. A thin stream of air swept spiritlike through the arrow loop. She squinted her eyes against the harsh light of the sun.

What she saw made her knees turn soft as custard. She clutched the stone sill for support.

A somber procession made its way out of the barbican gate. A dozen nobles rode on horseback, Lord Guillaume at their fore. Throngs of peasants crowded about—curious children, gawking old women, scowling crofters. She could hear the hungry jeers of rabid spectators, barking insults and slurs. In the midst of the procession, a blackened cart rolled with reluctant sloth along the road toward Gallow's Hill. Its passenger was half-naked, his soiled brown robe hanging from his hips by its rope tie. His legs were braced apart so he wouldn't fall from the swaggering cart. His chest and arms bulged against the heavy chains wrapped round his body. Though his head hung limply upon his breast, the cords of his neck strained in obvious discomfort. His face was concealed, but there was no mistaking that muscular form, those sable curls.

Linet's throat constricted with dread as her gaze was drawn inexorably toward the man in the cart. She longed to look elsewhere, to forget what she had glimpsed, but some compelling force pulled at her, willing her to watch. Only when the retinue passed beneath an obscuring canopy of trees did she finally tear her eyes away, staggering back from the window, her face bloodless.

"Oh, my lady!" the servant gasped, rushing forward, misunderstanding. "Do not distress yourself! Your own uncle has seen to that devil's punishment. They say the man was already beaten half to death. The flogging will assuredly finish him. There is naught to worry about."

Finish him? Linet's brain screamed. Dear God—Lord Guillaume couldn't mean to kill the gypsy, could he? Panic shortened her breath. This couldn't be happening. She couldn't let it happen, not when she . . .

She loved the gypsy. Sweet Mary, she understood that now. She loved him. Beyond reason. Beyond hope. Beyond any vow she'd given her father.

And by God, if it cost her everything, she had to save his life. It was in her hands, she realized. It was up to her to cease this travesty. Biting her lip, she seized a gray cloak from a hook on the wall and swung it over her shoulders atop the shift.

"My lady!" the servant shrieked. "What are you doing?

Where are you going? Lord Guillaume gave me strict orders . . ."

Linet pinned the cloak closed and raked her fingers through
her hair.

"My . . . my lady! You're not even properly dressed!
You've no kirtle, no slippers. I haven't even run a comb
through . . ."

"There is no time . . . I must go now," Linet chanted breathlessly. "I must go now."

A specter couldn't have flown more swiftly from the room.
Still, by the time she rushed down the cold stone steps, raced
across the deserted courtyard, and bolted through the barbican
gate, drawing the curious stares of the guards above, the procession was already cresting Gallow's Hill.

With a whimper of despair, she picked up her skirts and ran
up the long, twisting road. Sharp rocks and wayward thistles
cut the soles of her feet. Once, she tripped on the hem of her
cloak, wrenching her ankle, and fell heavily to the ground,
tearing the frail fabric of her shift and bloodying her knees.
She staggered to her feet and cast off the culprit cloak, but still
she ran, favoring the injured leg, closing the distance between
her and Gallow's Hill.

Limping forward, she caught up at last with the stragglers in
the crowd. Ahead, the ominous finger of the gallows pointed
accusingly at the heavens. Suddenly she was chilled by the dis-
abling thought of the souls that had departed here unshriven,
souls like her gypsy. She quickly crossed herself and continued.

Duncan let his face betray no fear when the cart ceased its
jostling and rolled to a stop. He wasn't afraid to die. As a
knight, he faced death every day. Nay—all he felt was bitter
wrath. The shame of this slaughter, the real torture of it, was
that he, Duncan de Ware—expert swordsman, heir to one of
the wealthiest estates in the land, loyal vassal answering to
King Edward himself, hero of the common man—was about
to die nameless, the death of a pauper, unable to defend himself against a crime he didn't commit. The futility of his life
crushed him like an unconquerable wrestler against whom he
nonetheless intended to struggle with his last breath.

A burly man, his face covered by an ominous black hood,

wrenched the chain loose from the cart and shoved him forward. Duncan stumbled and fell against the side of the cart, bruising his tender ribs, unable to catch himself with his bound hands. Brutally, the executioner pushed him from the cart and up the incline toward a whipping post. Peasant boys threw sticks and pebbles. Their fathers spat obscenities.

Linet cursed softly. Already they dragged the gypsy forward. God help him, he was going bravely. She cried out for them to halt, but her hoarse, breathless voice was lost in the taunting of the mob.

His gait, though awkward, never faltered. When he faced the crowd from the stained wooden block that served as a floor before the post, fierce pride burned in his cold sapphire eyes. Even when Lord Guillaume stepped before him, the venom of the nobleman's gaze couldn't cow him.

Linet pushed and prodded her way forward through the stubborn wall of spectators, shrieking at them to cease, but it was too late. The blood was already hot in their veins.

Duncan could feel the bloodlust surround him like a wash of molten lead.

"Have you any last words to say?" Lord Guillaume hissed.

Duncan fixed him with a steady, icy stare. "I am a de Ware. Tell Linet de Montfort that she may wear the trappings," he rasped out in a low voice, just loud enough for the lord to hear, "but she does not know the first thing about being a lady."

Lord Guillaume sputtered in outrage and nodded to the executioner. The great hooded beast raised a fist and smote Duncan heavily across the face.

Linet gasped, along with half of the ladies in the crowd, as the gypsy's head drooped.

"Prisoner!" Lord Guillaume shouted.

Slowly, the gypsy lifted his head. Linet sobbed when she saw the darkening bruise under his eye and the trickle of blood so like a tear wandering down his cheek.

"Prepare to receive the lash for your crime," the lord advised, signaling the whipsman.

The hooded man wheeled the gypsy around and wrenched his arms up to attach the shackles to the whipping post. Then he backed away and unfurled his whip so it writhed on the ground like a languorous snake ready to bite.

Time seemed to slow as Linet reached forward, running with dreamlike sluggishness toward the man bound to the whipping post. The eager cries about her grew muffled, and with sudden acute vision, she perceived the subtle clenching of the gypsy's fingers, the tensing of his body as he anticipated the pain of the lash.

Suddenly, she heard a scream, as if from a distance, some tortured soul crying "Nay!" to the marking of this flesh. All eyes turned to her. At last she broke free of the mob and surged forward to the platform, her hair streaming wildly out behind her. She dropped on her knees to the wood block, ignoring the sharp pain, adding her own blood to the stains there, and spread her arms wide, placing herself between the gypsy and the whip.

The whipsman stood with his lash poised to strike. For one terrible moment, Linet felt icy fear tease her spine as the man paused uncertainly.

The hooded giant then flung the whip forward. Linet cringed but held her ground. It was already slicing menacingly through the air when Lord Guillaume cried out, "Linet! No!"

As soon as Duncan heard her name, he whipped his head over his shoulder and sought her out.

The whipsman snapped the lash back in mid-flight. It fell short of the block, whistling its complaint and slithering harmlessly on the ground. Lord Guillaume clapped a hand to his chest.

Rage filled Duncan's breast. What was Linet doing here? Was it not enough that she'd caused his ignoble end? Did she have to witness it also?

"Begone, woman," he growled at her.

"Linet! Niece!" Lord Guillaume cried, clearly distraught. "You were not to be present for this!"

"Please," Linet begged her uncle in a voice raw with emotion, "please do not flog this man."

Duncan scowled. Surely he'd heard wrong. He glared at her, on her knees in supplication, her hair loose and uncombed, her feet bare. Sweet Jesu—she wasn't even dressed. The fine white linen of her shift was so insubstantial that it was nigh transparent. He clamped his jaw shut, confused by mixed feelings of anger and pity, and tore his eyes away.

Her words had an entirely different effect on the man studying the scene from the midst of the crowd. His black glove
tightened on the pale, feminine fingers draped over his arm,
and the corners of his mouth twisted downward.

Up to now, Sombra had found the whole spectacle highly
amusing. It seemed that rogue gypsy from the *Corona Negra*
had managed to procure his own execution. Without Sombra's
intervention. But that cursed wool merchant had just stepped
in the way, literally. And worse, if the pained look on Lord
Guillaume's face was any indication, she'd already earned her
uncle's trust.

There was no time to waste. He'd have to make his move
now or lose his chance. Schooling his features into an expression of great offense, he raised his voice. "Niece! Niece?
What outrage is this?"

Lord Guillaume almost looked thankful for the distraction.
"Who speaks?"

Sombra stepped forward with the wench. "I am Don Ferdinand Alfonso de Compostela, and I am appalled by the travesty I see before me!" The wool merchant blanched at his
words. The gypsy wrenched futilely against his bonds. But
Sombra ignored them. They were as harmless as pups now.
"How dare you call this . . . this half-naked strumpet your kin
when I bring your true niece to you myself?"

With a flourish, he presented his imposter. She sank into an
elegant curtsey with no prodding from him. Sombra smiled
appreciatively. He'd certainly chosen the right wench for the
task. She was taller than the real Linet de Montfort. Her hair
was blonde, though not as fair nor as long, and her eyes were
a somewhat murkier green. Though her looks hardly compared to the blushing beauty of the real woman, she wasn't
uncomely. But, working as a whore to the nobility for so long,
she'd picked up some of the graces of that class. With the
medallion about her neck and her cultured manner, she'd easily fool the lord.

Linet felt for an instant as if she were looking into a mirror,
a mirror that subtly distorted the features of her face. Though
she could see the de Montfort medallion swinging forward in
the sunlight as the strange woman curtseyed, Linet reached up
reflexively between her own breasts in disbelief, as if it might

somehow still lie there. But Sombra had indeed stolen it, cleanly and easily. And with it, he had stolen her birthright.

Her shoulders slumped in defeat. She'd come to that point at last—the point where a warp too tightly wound and a weft of faulty dye and a skipped thread all converged to create an irreconcilable flaw in the fabric. She'd made too many mistakes. She'd trusted the wrong people. She'd betrayed the wrong people. And now she was paying dearly for it—with her title, with her trade, with her servant, who was surely dead, with her heart, and possibly with her soul.

Linet gazed at Lord Guillaume through a watery veil of tears. He pursed his lips thoughtfully, rocking slowly back and forth on the balls of his feet. How like her father he was— outwardly strict and demanding, all bellow, but inside, blunted claws. Even now he looked as if, despite all the evidence to the contrary, he wanted to believe her.

She could convince him. There were things she knew about Lord Aucassin that no imposter could possibly duplicate. There were her looks—Linet had her father's eyes. There was her impeccable knowledge of the family line. And she had the word of the Guild. In sooth, it might take time to unravel the wayward threads of her ordeal, but it could be done.

And yet, what would it gain her? She could prove she was indeed Linet de Montfort. But how would it preserve her father's pride and her promise unless she also owned that the gypsy had ravished her without her consent? And if she claimed that his peasant hands had soiled her noble person against her will, was she not condemning him to death?

She clamped her eyes shut. There was no easy answer. She had to choose. Would she cling to her nobility, or would she confess her soul's longing? It was not a dilemma solved as one solved trade matters, by scrawling calculations on parchment. Nay, she had to listen to her heart. Fate had left the decision in her hands. It burned there like a cinder in her fingers.

The whipsman impatiently tapped the butt of the lash against his palm. Lord Guillaume knitted his brows and rocked back on his heels. The crowd whispered, waiting.

And at last her heart spoke to her.

She lifted her chin. "I beseech you, my lord, to spare this

man from the lash, for . . . for he is not guilty of the crime for which you punish him." Her voice quavered. "I am."

The mob of peasants gasped collectively at this new development. Linet awaited her uncle's word like a prisoner awaiting sentencing. Lord Guillaume only blinked at her in confusion.

"What are you saying?" he asked quietly at long last.

"Oh, my lord, forgive me," she said, her voice breaking. "I cannot let him bear the blame for what has passed. It is all my fault."

"So you are not Linet de . . ."

"He is my lover," she blurted.

"Nay!" the gypsy snarled.

The crowd hushed. Lord Guillaume stared at her a long time, his face painted in lines of bewilderment. "There is no need for you to protect him, Linet," he said sternly. "I assure you, he knew full well his crime when he committed it. If you are upset by the bloodlust here, perhaps you had best return to the keep."

"Nay!" she shouted. "I'll not leave him!" She murmured, "I'll not leave him again. I . . ." She gazed at the gypsy, *her* gypsy, bound to the whipping post. "I love him."

Whispers of amazement echoed through the crowd like wind through a wheat field.

"So you deny . . . that you are Lady Linet de Montfort?" Lord Guillaume growled. "You claim instead that you are this . . . this monk's mistress?"

Words wouldn't pass her lips when she saw the bleak resignation in Lord Guillaume's face. Instead, she nodded her assent.

Lord Guillaume waved to the executioner with obvious reluctance, releasing the gypsy from the whipping post. Then he closed the key to the prisoner's shackles within Linet's hand. "He is yours then," he whispered, clasping her hand tightly. He dug in his pouch and pulled forth a piece of silver. "My servants will escort you to the harbor at Calais, to a ship bound for England. The coin is for your passage . . . home." His eyes were bleary and red, and his chin quivered as he made the next pronouncement. "Henceforth, you are duly exiled from this holding and all lands belonging to de Montfort."

The weight of what she'd done sank upon her like a smothering cloak. Silent tears streamed unchecked down her face as her uncle turned his back on her and prepared to take the imposter to his bosom.

She couldn't watch. Around her, the crowd of spectators dispersed, muttering in disappointment at the bloodless outcome, and the procession filed back toward the castle. Soon no one was left on Gallow's Hill but her, the shackled gypsy, and a half dozen crows that hopped about, baffled by the absence of spoils. Her tears waned until they finally ceased and she was plagued only by an occasional hiccough. She wiped her bleary eyes, clutching the key in her fist. Slowly she rose on shaky legs, plucking the sticky linen from her bloody knees, and turned to face the man for whom she had sacrificed everything.

The gratitude, the relief, the adoration she expected from him were nowhere to be found. He looked down his nose at her with eyes as flat and gray as a sea squall and a sneer of disdain so intense that she almost recoiled from him. Her heart felt as if it would break.

Duncan forced himself to look over her head. He ignored the blood stains on the front of her shift and the womanly curves beneath it. He made himself think only of her deceit, her betrayal, not of the price she had paid.

He was no fool. She had likely only saved his life because she feared the damnation of her soul if he should die. The woman was heartless. He'd been burned twice by her tempting fire. He'd not be burned again. He closed his eyes to her, hardened his heart against her soft entreaty, and told himself he cared not what happened to her.

Linet felt as if she skated on the thin ice of her emotions. "Give me your shackles," she bid him in a faltering voice. "I shall free you."

With a sullen glare, he walked away, speaking over his shoulder. "I would rather live in chains the rest of my life than be beholden to you for my freedom."

"Please . . ." she whispered. "Forgive me, I pray you."

"You will have to look to God for absolution. After what you've done, I'd be a fool to offer you forgiveness."

"Please, don't go!" she cried.

He stopped in his tracks, but he refused to turn around or even acknowledge her. She stared helplessly at the muscular back she'd caressed only last night, the thick black curls she'd run her hands through, and swallowed the bitter despair that threatened to choke her. Dear God—she had lost him, too. Despondent, she circled until she stood directly before him. How she yearned to rest her head upon that wide chest, to feel his arms secure around her. But she knew she'd find no comfort there today. Fresh tears filled her eyes. She took one of his unresponsive hands in hers and pressed the shackle key into it.

Then, with a soft cry, she rushed blindly off—homeless, nameless, loveless.

El Gallo crumpled the neatly scrawled parchment in his fist and threw it to the deck. He'd have done the same with the messenger, that wool merchant's quaking old servant, had they not been in port, under the watchful eye of the Flemish magistrate. Fury rose in him like a boil, and he could feel the veins of his forehead bulging with ire.

"So," he bit out, flecks of spittle popping from his mouth as he spoke, "Sombra thinks to prick me with his great accomplishment."

He twisted the hairs of his beard. This whole de Montfort ordeal had been a curse to him at every turn. First he'd been humiliated and robbed in England. Then his attempts to seek retribution at the spring fair had been foiled. There was one glorious moment when he'd held the wool merchant captive on his ship. But even that had been short-lived. He'd lost two of his best men somewhere in Flanders. God alone knew if they yet breathed.

But this! This was the crowning glory of his shame. According to the missive, Sombra had somehow managed to not only find the de Montfort wench, but also to tweak fate to his benefit. The wily Spaniard had endeared himself to the de Montfort family with an imposter. Sombra was returning to Spain a rich man.

The envy was bitter on El Gallo's tongue. But he was not one to accept defeat, even when he could taste it. The battle was not over.

"And yet," he thought aloud, combing his fingers through the strands of his beard, "perhaps Sombra has not been so clever, eh? He let the real de Montfort wench go. It is only a matter of time before she sails for England, for her home. There is certain to be proof of her birthright there—her father's possessions, a legal document, some heirloom trinket perhaps, an illuminated family Bible—items that will prove beyond doubt that she is the real heiress." The corner of his mouth quirked up. "And of course, it would be remiss of me to not offer my ship and my escort for her safe passage back to Flanders to reclaim her title—her title and my reward for restoring the true heiress to de Montfort." He barked out a laugh. "To think, I for once will be doing the noble thing." The thought tickled him immensely. "Perhaps my countrymen will return my holdings in Spain to me for my good deed, eh, Harold? What do you think?"

The servant cowered, ready to bolt. But El Gallo wrapped a companionable arm around the skinny man, nearly crushing him in his embrace. "No, no, my friend. You will stay with me now. Together we will right this terrible wrong!"

His hearty belch and guffaw ruined the effect of nobility he was striving to achieve, but it was of no consequence. There were preparations to make—crewmen to round up from the brothels, a week's provisions to procure, the unfortunate death of Sombra to plan. It was nearly sunset now. He wanted the *Corona Negra* ready to sail at midnight.

The waves lapped gently against the planking of the barnacled English vessel. The canvas of its sails snapped in the crisp breeze. That sound would have stirred adventure in Duncan's spirit but for the fact that this morning, each smack of cloth sounded and seemed like a slap across the face. His head throbbed with dull pain, and he groaned, keeping his breakfast down by sheer dint of will. He didn't want to think about what would happen when they rounded the arm of the inlet and headed for the open sea. He was probably a sorry sight, green with nausea and purple with bruises, leaning upon the ship's railing. Never again, he swore, would he drown his woes in drink.

Yesterday, he'd gone straight from Gallow's Hill to the nearest alehouse in Calais. Slumping into the smoky plaster corner of the Cheval Blanc, he'd spent most of the reivers' remaining coins, staring into cup after foamy cup of ale, believing his answer lay at the bottom of the next one. Until he'd reached the point of conversing with himself.

"I should leave her for the reivers."

"Nay," he'd argued. "Nay. You swore to protect her."

"She betrayed me! I owe her nothing."

"An oath is an oath. No matter how much you detest that angel witch, you made a vow. After all, one doesn't have to bear affection for the King to swear fealty to him."

Finally, he'd sunk his head onto his hands in surrender. The ale had pared his troubles down to the bone: Linet de Montfort was sailing back to England on the morrow. He'd be aboard that ship. He had to be. Someone had to keep her out of trouble.

That had been his brilliant decision last night, made upon the counsel of malted grain. Today, it seemed less than brilliant.

He glanced sideways and saw her again by the far railing. Damn, the ship was too small. He kept having to look at Linet's bleak, guileless face as she gazed off across the empty sea ahead like an angel bound for purgatory.

A knot of foolish guilt began to form in his chest. He tried to squelch it. Why should he feel remorse? It was *she* who had caused this, all of it. It was *she* who had been the betrayer. He would tell her so, damn her. It was about time he set her straight. He clenched his fists. He'd march over and confront her now. Right after this bout of nausea passed.

At the aft end of the ship, Linet picked morosely at the peeling paint of the railing. For one bright moment, spying the gypsy at the Calais dock among the passengers bound for England, she'd imagined he'd forgiven her. She was wrong. The rancor in his eyes had been clear. And now, a few hours into the voyage home, she was weary, wearier than she'd ever been in her life. All night, lying awake in the room her uncle's coin had paid for, she'd languished over her losses, cursing, weeping, praying. Fortune could not have cast her into a deeper pit, she was certain. She'd lost . . . everything.

And yet, she considered, letting reason steer her course where emotion had failed, nothing had changed. She was still a de Montfort in her soul, whether anyone believed it or not.

She was still a successful wool merchant, even if her profits might suffer this year. As for love . . .

She took a deep breath to drain the dregs of her melancholy. She'd made mistakes. And like a poor business decision, naught could be gained by dwelling on them. She had laid in her course, and whether for good or bad, she would sail onward. It was the noble thing to do. She'd just have to salvage what she could.

No sooner had she begun to imagine dealing with the sobering life ahead of her—a life of reduced pride, reduced respect, perhaps even reduced livelihood—when the bottom fell out of even her most bleak aspirations. Dear God, she thought with a jolt, what if she carried the gypsy's child?

She gripped the railing to steady herself. Why hadn't she thought of that before? They were two hale adults. They had committed the required act. The more she thought about it, the more she became convinced that it was likely she *had* conceived. And that would be devastating.

She couldn't subject a child to the humiliation and ridicule that came with bastardy. She knew how cruel people could be. No matter what she'd done to lose her own dignity, she couldn't sully that of an innocent child. She swallowed the lump in her throat. There was only one solution to her dilemma. She would have to marry. And it would have to be soon. She might not be able to afford the luxury of a long courtship if she was with child. It was the only way, she thought. She had to wed for the child's sake, to salvage its honor.

But even as she resigned herself to the decision, she steeled her jaw against the sudden, inexplicable urge to weep. What was wrong with her? she wondered. She was aware of her duty, her responsibilities. Hers would not be the first marriage made for practical reasons. Surely, with her merchant's skills and her not uncomely appearance, some eligible man would overlook her less than pristine condition in the marriage bed.

But the thought made her throat close. She couldn't envision anyone in her marriage bed except that wild-haired, fiery-eyed gypsy. She couldn't conceive of letting someone else touch her in that intimate way, couldn't imagine losing her soul to another man.

Sweet God—she wanted only him. Honor be damned, pride be damned, she wanted the gypsy.

And he despised her. She chewed at her lip. Or did he?

A stray gust of wind blew the hood of her cloak back, lifting her hair away from her face. And suddenly the answer was clear. Aye, she'd seen hatred in the gypsy's eyes when he glared at her from the whipping post—icy, raw hatred. His words had dripped with acid scorn. Still, there had been something more, something beneath the rage. And it hadn't been loathing. There had been . . . pain in his eyes, terrible hurt and longing, she realized.

Why hadn't she noticed it before? He was like a wounded wolf, snarling and hiding his injuries so he could be hurt no more. Linet's heart lifted, and a glimmer of possibility was born in her breast. Once, he had confessed his love. And while that love might lie buried deep beneath a mound of betrayal and mistrust and pain, perhaps it wasn't dead. Perhaps she could earn it again.

Closing her eyes, she murmured a prayer for fortitude. She had a strong will when it came to business. She never backed down from a fight. This battle might prove difficult, but she vowed she'd do whatever it took to regain the gypsy's affections.

The sudden hand gripping her shoulder startled the resolve right out of her. She whipped around to look into the gypsy's scowling face, her newfound hope completely deserting her.

"Do exactly as I say," he commanded under his breath.

She frowned. His tone did not bode well.

"Come!" he barked.

"I am not some . . ."

"For the love of God, woman," he quietly snarled, "do not defy me. Not now."

He nodded toward the north, around the last narrow point of land. A ship was rapidly approaching, a ship bearing the unmistakable colors of El Gallo.

17

"NAY," LINET WHISPERED, CLUTCHING HIS SLEEVE, HER VOICE as insubstantial as air.

"I'd wager my blade our Spanish friend is searching every vessel that crosses from Flanders to England," Duncan muttered. "He must want you very badly." Instantly, he regretted his words. Linet looked as if she might faint. "I won't let him have you," he promised. As much hell as the wench had put him through, he didn't have the heart to frighten her.

At best, it was a tenuous vow. There was nowhere to run. And no time. In another moment, the vessels would be close enough to pick out individuals by sight.

He cast about for a suitable place to cache a small wench. His eyes alit on a wooden trunk beside the mainmast. He was upon it in two strides, had broken the rusty lock in another moment. Ignoring the captain's indignant protests and the passengers' remarks of outrage, he upended the chest, emptying its stash of raw wool across the deck.

"Stay calm, all of you. Captain Campbell," he told the frowning Scotsman, "we are about to be boarded by sea reivers." The captain's scowl deepened. "They are looking for me. If need be, I will go with them . . ."

"Nay," Linet argued.

". . . so there will be no trouble for the rest of you. Simply do as they say."

"Nay!" Linet repeated more vehemently. " 'Tis not you they seek . . ."

Duncan had no time for her protest. El Gallo was coming.

He swept her off her feet, dropped her into the chest, tucked a layer of wool over her ere she could draw breath to complain, and slammed the lid shut, anchoring it closed with his raised boot.

There was, thankfully, a loud commotion on board as the two ships came abreast of one another and El Gallo's grappling hooks clawed the merchant ship closer. Otherwise, Linet's muffled cries of outrage might've alerted the Spaniards to her presence.

Linet spat the foulest word she knew. To no avail. Damn that scheming gypsy! It was as black as midnight inside the chest. She pulled a tuft of cloying oily wool from her mouth and pressed up hard against the box's lid. It wouldn't budge. She tried not to think about how like a coffin the chest was, dark and stifling and sealed by whatever part of the gypsy's anatomy he'd chosen to apply to the lid. Already the air felt thick and stale, and wool adhered to her sticky brow.

Something sharp poked her in the back. She patted her hand over the object. Of course, she thought with gallows irony, a pair of wool shears. She was going to be buried alive with the tools of her trade.

She could tell by the tortured creaking of the deck planks that El Gallo himself had come aboard. She stilled her movements and strained to hear the conversation.

Duncan felt the reiver captain's gaze scrape down him like a crofter's rake.

"Ah, my *friend*, what a surprise!" El Gallo sneered. "I had not thought to encounter *you* again in this world. But see how impetuous fate has brought you to me." He paced in a half-circle before Duncan. "Ah, I must say you look a bit more . . . weathered than before."

Duncan set his elbow on his knee and cupped his chin in his hand as casually as he could, given the circumstances. "Indeed, captain," he replied with a grim smile, "though not as weathered as the ones who visited this upon me . . . God rest their souls."

El Gallo's face remained as passive as a clump of dough. "Where is she?"

"She?" Duncan feigned puzzlement. "Ah, the wench," he chuckled. He planned to tell El Gallo that he had long since

tired of Linet de Montfort. He planned to tell him that she was
dead. But then he spotted Harold, Linet's servant, cowering in
chains to one side of the reiver captain. He swore silently. He
couldn't let Harold believe that his mistress was dead. It
would devastate the poor man. After a brief pause, he shook
his head in self-mockery. "Alas, the vixen escaped her tether
some days past."

El Gallo stared at him with cold pig eyes for a long while.
Then he snapped his fingers once, and two crewmen brought
Harold forward. The man trembled like an autumn leaf.

"You do not know where the girl is?" El Gallo repeated,
strutting like a smug rooster between Duncan and Harold.
"Pity, I had some rather good news for her."

Duncan shrugged, feigning disinterest.

The reiver captain smiled humorlessly and perused Duncan
again from head to toe. "What colorful bruises you have
earned, my friend," he crooned. "Perhaps my men shall give
your companion here some of the same . . . decorations?"

"Companion?" Duncan tossed off with a lightness he didn't
feel. "I am not acquainted with this man." Hopefully, his lie
would keep the servant from harm.

"Really? You do not know old Harold here?" El Gallo said,
flexing his fingers. "Then you do not object if I . . ."

Before Duncan could stop him, he hauled back one meaty
fist and plunged it into Harold's face. There was a sickening
crunch. The passengers gasped. Harold staggered back with a
moan, clutching his injured nose with shackled hands. Already, blood dripped through his fingers.

Duncan clenched his jaw. He fought the compulsion to fly
at El Gallo, wrap his hands around that fat neck and squeeze
the life out of him.

"You devil's spawn! What have you done to him? I pray
you rot in hell!"

The words didn't come from Duncan's lips, though his
thoughts were running along the same course. Nay, the audacious protest had come from within the wool chest.

"Harold!" Linet cried. "Harold!"

Damn! Duncan thought. She couldn't have picked a more
inopportune time to break her silence.

El Gallo smirked slowly, crossed his arms over his thick

chest and eyed the wooden box. He motioned to his men. "Remove him," he ordered.

To Duncan's credit, it took four of them. But the reivers ultimately wrestled him away from the chest, securing him at swordpoint.

With the pressure of his foot removed, Linet sprang up out of the chest like a coney from its burrow. Tufts of wool fell from her, and her hair hung in disarray. But there was fire in her emerald eyes as she faced the Spanish reiver captain, dangerous fire.

"You leave my servant alone!" she commanded.

El Gallo was highly amused. "Leave him alone?" He pretended to ponder the idea. "Leave him alone. Perhaps you are right. I know of no place more alone than here, in the middle of the sea. Oso!" he called. "Leave the man alone."

"Nay!" Linet shrieked. She flew at El Gallo like a kitten against a hound, batting ineffectually at his great stomach and clawing him with her nails.

The captain subdued her within seconds, squashing her against his side. But the distraction of her struggle had been enough to allow Duncan to duck his captors and confiscate one of their swords. In the blink of an eye, he swung the point of the blade to El Gallo's throat.

Even with the reiver captain's ruddy flesh quivering beneath his blade, Duncan knew his leverage was shaky at best. El Gallo's crew far outnumbered the men of fighting ability aboard the English vessel. Somehow Duncan had to offer the sea reivers something sweeter than their captain's revenge.

"Listen and listen well, El Gallo," he said in a low voice. "You and I know that reivers are about as loyal as rats on a sinking ship. This crew of yours might just as soon see their captain perish as live, if it means gain for them. So I suggest you weigh your options carefully." Then he announced, "Release these two now, and I will come with you in their place. They're useless to you anyway. The old man is but a poor servant, and the wench is an imposter to the title of de Montfort."

Linet squirmed in protest.

"You have a far more valuable hostage in me," he added. "Have your men contact the de Ware holdings in England to demand my ransom. I am Sir Duncan de Ware, my father's oldest son, heir to the castle."

He heard Linet moan almost inaudibly. Of course, she wouldn't believe a word of it. But he'd garnered the interest of the Spanish crew.

"My family, de Ware, is wealthy," he said in Spanish, eyeing the reivers individually. "They will pay well for my safe return, enough to make each of you captain of your own ship."

There was impressed muttering amid the crew.

"De Ware?" one man repeated.

"I've heard that name before," another said.

"Of course you have, imbecile," El Gallo said, his eyes shifting dubiously. "The brothers are said to be matchless with a sword."

Duncan pressed his weapon's point against the flesh of El Gallo's neck. "Would you care to find out?"

El Gallo's placating smile and the lack of a reply couldn't mask the fury in his eyes.

"Why should we believe you?" one of the Spaniards challenged.

"You deceived us before," a second added.

"If you choose to disbelieve, so be it," Duncan said. "A moment after I have slain your captain, I shall turn the blade on myself. Not only will you lose your hostage, you will have all of de Ware hunting you down for murder." He let the message sink in. "On the other hand, if you choose to believe me, you could all live quite well the rest of your days on the ransom. It's a risk you'll have to take."

Duncan had no intention of giving the Spaniards one coin from his father's coffers—he would die first—but he knew he'd used the right bait. Avarice lit up the crewmen's faces as they considered the idea.

"Let these two go," Duncan pressed El Gallo, "and I'll come willingly with you."

"Nay." Linet breathed the word.

"Very well," El Gallo hastily agreed before his men could conspire against him. "It is a risk worth taking." He waved anxiously at the steel against his neck. "Put up your sword."

Linet could only stare in disbelief as the gypsy tossed the

weapon to the deck and bravely raised his head. El Gallo nodded for Harold's release and called for the shackles to be placed on the new prisoner. She could scarcely breathe, so tightly was El Gallo squeezing her against his ribs. He lugged her across the deck, and then, with no more ceremony than one would give laundry, hefted her up and dropped her back into the wooden chest. Too stunned to move, she watched as the gypsy held his wrists out for the shackles.

It was a stupid thing for him to do, she thought as her chin began to quiver. The gypsy owed her nothing. Now that she had no reward to offer him, there was no good reason for him to continue protecting her. El Gallo would assuredly kill him when he found out he'd been deceived yet again, and it would be an ugly death. The damned fool was risking his life for a servant he'd met once and a wench who had cruelly betrayed him. It was an utterly stupid thing to do.

She wiped at her wet cheek.

It was the kind of stupid thing a nobleman would do.

She raised her eyes to the gypsy. He looked indeed the very picture of nobility, standing there courageously before the notorious reiver captain. Bruised and beaten, he was willingly offering himself up for yet more. To protect them. To protect *her*. As the irons were locked about his wrists, he flinched not at all, but only gazed stoically off across the sea toward the shore he might not live to see again.

Linet bit her lip. She'd been wrong. Her father had been wrong. Nobility was not a matter of birth. It had nothing to do with manner or dress or speech. It was a matter of principles, of priorities and sacrifice. A fresh pool of tears gathered in her eyes. This man—this gypsy—was right. He had more nobility in his little finger than most nobles she'd met could boast of their entire lineage. He was good. He was honorable. And he was . . . about to be stabbed!

Linet saw the damning wink of steel in El Gallo's fist. Time stretched as the reiver captain slowly pulled the dagger from his belt.

The gypsy turned his head toward her as if in a dream, oblivious to the danger, looking his last at the woman he'd once claimed to love.

The blade came free of its sheath. Linet opened her mouth

to scream. This couldn't be happening, she thought. But El Gallo drew the knife slowly back.

Her voice came out in a long shriek. "Nay!"

She reached beneath her to push herself up out of the chest, and her hand closed around something cold and hard.

El Gallo's dagger paused at its zenith, then reversed direction, drifting forward toward the gypsy's chest.

Linet leaped at what felt like a snail's pace out of the box and lumbered toward El Gallo. Her heart thundered once, twice, as she closed the distance, then thrust her hand forward with all her might.

The blades of the shears sunk deep into the soft flesh of the sea reiver's belly. He twisted upon the steel, his enormous weight plunging them deeper. His dagger fell from nerveless fingers and clattered harmlessly at his feet. His mouth opened and closed like a fish's. He staggered backwards. His disbelieving eyes grew wide, then vacant, then glazed. He fell to his knees, swayed, and crashed to the deck in a widening pool of blood.

Linet shook. Blood was everywhere. It oozed from El Gallo's horrid wound. It spattered the wood planks of the ship. It soaked the green wool of her surcoat. Her hands glistened with the bright red fluid, and she smelled its coppery, faintly garlic scent on her fingers.

But she didn't faint.

She'd done it, she thought, staring down at her grisly handiwork. She had slain the bastard. And she'd saved the gypsy. She'd done it.

Duncan was too astonished to speak, let alone move.

Harold was the first to recover. His nose still trickling blood, he snatched the sword from a gaping reiver and managed to send the stunned man to oblivion with a lucky punch.

After that, all hell broke loose. Two reivers came at Captain Campbell. He tossed a heavy coil of rope at one of them, knocking him to the deck, and turned to battle the other. Harold called out feeble challenges to any comers. A young boy began vigorously kicking the shins of whatever reiver he could find, and squeamish maids recoiled even as they hurled tankards and weighty purses at the heads of the enemy.

Duncan had to help them. He rattled the chain of his shackles.

On board the *Corona Negra*, several of El Gallo's crew began to grow suspect of the chaos on the merchant ship.

"The grappling hooks!" Duncan called out to the captain.

"Right!" Campbell ordered his mates to the task.

"Harold!" Duncan called, lifting the shackles.

Harold battled his way toward Duncan. Then he raised his plundered sword to break the shackle chain asunder, nicking the blade in the process.

"You owe me a new weapon, my lord," Harold complained in jest, his old eyes twinkling, when Duncan was free.

"I owe you a new nose." Duncan clapped him on the shoulder. "Now promise me, old man, out of loyalty to your mistress, that you'll stay out of the way. Trust me. I can handle this alone." He heaved a quick sigh. He hoped he was right.

Without an instant to spare, he pushed Harold out of the path of an oncoming dagger and into the belly of a reiver armed with two swords. As the two disentangled, Duncan filched the swords and braced himself for battle.

The grappling hooks were disengaged now. The two ships drifted apart. Only a few foolhardy Spaniards were willing to brave the widening chasm to leap onto the merchant ship.

Linet couldn't move. She couldn't feel anything. She sank down upon a giant coil of rope. Her hands had frozen to the ship's rail, but she was content to leave them there as the battle raged around her.

The gypsy planted himself in the middle of the deck, drawing the reivers' attention. Two of the Spaniards charged at once. He easily met them, one with each of the two swords he wielded. A third reiver tried to strike while he was engaged, but the gypsy spun, slashing to clear a full circle around himself. El Gallo's men split up then to attack him from all sides like a pack of wolves.

She clasped a shaking hand to her breast. The English captain and his crew were occupied securing the ship's escape from the *Corona Negra*. Two passengers lay wounded on the deck. Aside from them, there were little else but a handful of young lads and a bevy of maids left to battle the armed ruffians. The gypsy was surely a dead man now, unless old Harold could hold the Spaniards at bay. Desperately, she sought out her servant.

To her chagrin, her man was leaning against the ship's railing, his hands idle upon the pommel of his stolen sword, watching the progress of the battle with something akin to amusement.

Linet was utterly appalled. How could Harold allow a man so obviously outnumbered to be slaughtered? She watched the fight with growing concern as sparks flew from the colliding blades.

The gypsy fought the reivers in a circle at first, lunging with his right arm at one, then slashing unexpectedly with his left at another. He goaded them with words and jabs until they struck out at him with ill-controlled fury.

Only when he began to taunt them with the swords did Linet realize this was child's play to the gypsy. He tossed a sword into the air, and while one reiver was distracted, came up with the other blade to sever a tie from the first's jerkin. He spun the swords in a blinding acrobatic display, their steel snicking like the gnashing of dragon's teeth over the Spaniards' heads, then slashing horizontally to ventilate their shirts.

Linet frowned. The fool was enjoying himself.

Finally, he seemed to tire of the entertainment. Using sheer power, he struck the sword away from one of the reivers, and it sailed end over end into the sea. Then he kicked the churl in the seat of his braes, sending him over to Harold, who calmly grabbed him by the jerkin and levered him over the railing, as if by design.

The gypsy surprised the second reiver. He ducked and rolled at the man's feet, bowling him over. The reiver fell on elbows, knees and chin, his sword skirring across the deck. Harold offered to help the dazed victim up, then assisted him in climbing overboard.

Finally the gypsy faced the last Spaniard, a sword in each hand and ferocity in his eyes. The reiver reconsidered the odds and his limited alternatives. He wisely dropped his sword and sidled over to the edge, voluntarily diving into the water below to swim for the *Corona Negra*.

Duncan wiped his brow with the back of one sweaty hand.

A cheer arose, and the passengers waved the tools of their victory—satchels, cloak pins, pots—threateningly toward the departing mob of the *Corona Negra*. With Captain Campbell's help, Duncan heaved the last of the reiver crew overboard. But he only shook his head at the huge bulk that was El Gallo. Disposing of that body would require several strong men.

Campbell clapped Duncan on the back in his excitement, then, remembering himself, grinned sheepishly, removed his coif, and made a proper bow. Duncan smiled faintly in acknowledgment. But something else was on his mind. He had some choice words for the fool wench who so recklessly put herself at risk.

When he spotted her, sitting primly on a coil of rope, covered with blood, looking small and bewildered, all his self-righteousness vanished. His heart softened at once. He shook his head. He could never resist a hapless waif. And Linet de Montfort was the sorriest soul he'd seen in a long while. He slowly walked to where she sat. Crouching beside her, he took her shaking, bloody hands in his and looked up into her face. She was in shock.

"Are you all right?" he whispered.

Her voice faltered as she murmured, "I thought he would s-slay you."

Duncan tried to grin and failed. "He nearly did."

Linet looked down at her quivering hands, wincing at the scarlet stains. "So much b-blood," she stuttered. "But I d-didn't swoon, did I?"

"Nay," he said with a faint smile. "Nay, you didn't swoon."

"Good," she said, satisfied. Then her eyes rolled back in her head, and she collapsed against him in a dead faint.

18

"ARE YOU CERTAIN HE'S STILL ALIVE?"

Garth's question was innocent enough, but it drove Holden instantly to the brink of violence. "Of course he's still alive!" he insisted, pounding a fist on the locked garden gate and narrowing angry eyes at his brother. "How dare you even suggest . . ."

"Holden!" Robert shouted. Then he lowered his voice, looking to make sure no gossip-mongering servants dawdled in the moonlit corners of the walled garden. "If you can't be civil . . ."

Holden rolled his eyes and began plucking the luminescent blossoms from the jasmine bush beside him.

Robert spoke consolingly to Garth. "Duncan has to be alive. I'm sure of it. But your father . . ."

"He's beginning to ask questions, Robert," Holden said through his teeth, loosing a snowfall of crushed blossoms from his fist. "You've sailed to Spain and back, and you've nothing to show for your efforts." He spat on the ground. "Nothing but a Spanish harlot to warm your bed . . ."

Robert's blood seethed. "You . . . miserable . . ." He roared in outrage and lunged at Holden, knocking him hard against the garden wall. "Do not speak thus of my betrothed again, you slutching . . ."

"Your betrothed!" Holden yelled, poking him in the chest. "Is that so? And while my brother languishes . . ."

Robert drew back his fist with a snarl.

"Cease!" Garth cried, prying the two men apart. "Your petty insults do naught to help Duncan!"

Holden cursed and threw Garth off him. Then he kicked guiltily at the sod.

Robert lowered his eyes and shook his head. He didn't know what had come over him. When he'd calmed, he murmured, "I was so sure Duncan would be here when we returned."

"Well, now the fuel's been added to the fire," Holden said, idly snapping a twig off the peach tree. "The King's asked me to join him in Scotland on campaign."

"Scotland!" Robert exclaimed, his anger forgotten in his excitement. "That's wonderful! It's what you've dreamed of, Holden!"

Holden's smile was grim. "And now I cannot go."

"What do you mean?"

"I'm . . . the next in line, Robert." He ploughed a weary hand through his hair. "With Duncan gone, God knows where, chasing after his latest mistress . . ."

"She's not his latest mistress." Garth's eyes shone silver in the pale moonlight. "I think he plans to wed her."

"What?" Holden asked.

"Linet de Montfort. I could see it in his eyes . . . before he left. I wouldn't be surprised if they married."

"What!" Holden exploded. "That's absurd! He cannot marry! Not without the King's permission!" His laugh was a bark. "And I doubt Edward will look favorably upon one of his finest knights wedding a wool merchant!"

Robert stroked his chin. "She *is* a de Montfort. It *is* possible."

Holden threw his arms up toward the sky. "You cannot even find my brother, and already you are marrying him off! Meanwhile, I must invent some excuse to decline the King's offer—one that won't leave me swinging from the gallows as a traitor!"

While the men continued to bicker, Lady Alyce, who'd been quietly planting mint and borage nearby since twilight, heaved a weary sigh and emerged from the deep shade. She'd heard enough. It was time to intervene.

"No son of mine will swing from the gallows as a traitor. And put that sword away, Holden."

Holden sheepishly slid the blade he'd drawn in alarm back into its sheath.

Lady Alyce shook her head and stuck her planting stick in the ground. Never, she thought, had three grown men looked so culpable. Holden shifted anxiously back and forth on his feet. Garth hung his head like a penitent priest. And if the sun had shone overhead rather than the moon, she was sure Robert's face would've matched the color of her roses.

She dusted off her mud-smudged hands. "Is there something you wish to tell me, gentlemen? Something besides the news you've been shouting to the entire household?" She wasn't sure she wanted to hear the rest of it. What she'd heard already was enough to make her heart thump as unsteadily as a three-wheeled cart. But it was obvious the men weren't going to come up with a solution on their own.

The three of them looked back and forth between themselves. Finally, Garth stepped forward.

"We took a vow of silence on the matter, Lady Mother," he recited gravely, looking for all the world like Galahad speaking of the Holy Grail.

"A vow of silence?" She tried not to laugh. The three of them had been yelling fit to wake the dead. But she schooled her features to sternness. "If a son of mine is in danger . . ."

Robert glanced at Garth. "We've reason to believe he may be."

"All right," she replied, carefully controlling the quaver in her voice. "All right." She forced her heart to calm. "You said he was lost. Where was he bound?"

Robert cleared his throat. Holden clamped his lips firmly together. Garth closed his eyes. Dear Lord, how she despised the guessing games the de Ware men's insufferable chivalry forced upon her.

She drummed her fingers on her chin. "At least answer my questions then. Did he go to the wool merchant's village, as you led me to believe?"

"Nay," Garth replied guiltily.

"Did he go to the forest?"

"Nay," Garth replied.

"Is he . . . on your father's land at all?"

"Nay."

"Is he . . ."

"On a ship," Robert blurted, earning a glare and an elbow jab from Garth.

"On a ship?" she gasped.

Garth was still glaring at Robert.

"For God's sake, Garth," Robert muttered, "he's your father's heir."

Garth frowned. For him a vow was a vow.

"And this ship is bound . . ." she began, one hand settling nervously on her bosom.

"We know not," Holden answered, raising himself to his proud height.

Robert frowned. "We have a fairly good idea."

The brothers scowled at Robert.

"The merchant girl, Linet de Montfort," Robert said, "she was abducted."

"And naturally Duncan could not stand idly by," she supplied, nodding. Duncan's inherent heroics, she'd discovered long ago, were a matter completely out of his hands. "Who was the abductor?"

"El Gallo." Garth had mumbled the words so low that she almost missed them.

"El Gallo!" She crossed herself. This was more urgent than she'd expected. "Duncan has stowed himself on a sea reiver's vessel?" She unpinned her filthy apron, thinking aloud. "El Gallo. It's about those letters of marque, I'll wager." She wadded the apron into a ball with the muddy side in. "We'll have to notify her family. Perhaps they can help."

"Family?" Holden said. "Whose family?"

"Linet de Montfort's. She has kin in Flanders, powerful nobles."

"Flanders?" Holden asked.

"'Tis where she's from. All the best wool merchants are. And she's somehow related to the de Montforts there."

"But how . . ."

"Did I know?" she said, plucking up her planting stick. "A bit of gossip. A good deal of inquiry. A woman carrying royal letters of marque does not happen by every day, and I've been poking about. Her story is quite interesting." She tapped the stick to her temple. "Besides, 'tis a wise woman who learns the history of the merchants she employs and keeps an ear to the doors of her demesne. Aye, de Montfort may be able to help us."

Holden fidgeted with his swordbelt. "Then we'll go to Flanders. Robert, ready a crew . . ."

"Wait!" she protested, laying her palm on Holden's formidable chest. "Do you not have a king to serve?"

Holden scowled. His face became a study of torment. He had an obligation to his brother, both moral and emotional. But the King was handing him an opportunity most men would kill for—a chance for a second son to earn wealth and holdings.

"I cannot abandon Duncan," he murmured at last.

The turmoil in his eyes pained her. "Do not worry. Duncan is safe . . . for the moment. You know there is naught a reiver likes more than silver. El Gallo only cuts his own purse if he lays a hand on Duncan de Ware."

The reassuring smile she gave him was less than heartfelt, but she couldn't bear to see Holden suffer. She reached up loving fingers to tuck one of his stray curls into place.

How glad she was of her three sons, even the two not of her womb. Holden and Duncan were like portraits of their father, but painted in two different seasons. Duncan had hair of coal black, where Holden's looked like mahogany kissed by the sun. Duncan's eyes shone steadfast and blue, Holden's a mutable green. But both of them had a sense of honor and loyalty to make any mother proud. And afraid.

Holden was always off fighting some battle or another. But if anyone was able to pull trouble out of thin air, it was Duncan.

She plucked an unexpected tear from her eye before it could ripen. The thought of losing one of her sons was unbearable. If Duncan were returned to her, sound of mind and body—if he would but promise to stay out of harm's way in the future—she vowed she'd give him anything he desired. A dozen new destriers. A great hall of his own for all the strays he brought home. A bride of his heart . . .

Her mind perked up at once, as alert and scheming as when she played chess. That overbold son of hers had gotten himself into this scrape over Linet de Montfort. He'd followed her onto a sea reiver's ship, risked life and limb for her. It was as plain as a nun's habit that Duncan was in love with the lass. Perhaps Garth was right.

Linet de Montfort had much to recommend her. She was striking, intelligent, and spirited, just the perfect foil for Duncan's wit and kindheartedness.

Lady Alyce felt a smile tug at her lip. When Guillaume de Montfort ransomed the girl from El Gallo, as he no doubt would—the family was notoriously wealthy—Lady Alyce would petition for a wedding between Duncan and Linet. De Montfort would certainly give his assent. An alliance with de Ware would gain him much political favor.

As for El Gallo, what her husband would do with him— whether he strung the reiver up by his ballocks or let him sail merrily back to Spain—was of no concern to her. She just wanted Duncan home and happy, with a wife to look after and to keep him out of trouble.

It was the perfect solution.

Only one thing stood in the way of securing the banns for them at once—the King. And Holden could do something about that.

"You have our blessing to go to your King, Holden. Tell Edward he may have you." She pursed her lips. "But he will have to recompense us in kind. I have a favor to ask of him, a betrothal I want arranged immediately."

"Mine?" Holden nearly gagged on the word.

"Nay, nay—Duncan's."

She hadn't seen relief so blatant on Holden's face in a long while as she brushed past the men to unlock the garden gate. But she had no time to tarry. She had a bath to order, one with an extra sprinkling of dried violets. She'd don the red silk, the sheer garment James had brought back from Turkey. And she'd see if Cook had any of those cherry coffyns left. A challenge awaited her—convincing her husband that a union between de Montfort and de Ware would be profitable and wise—and she looked forward to every delicious moment of it.

Sombra gazed down at his handiwork, but he felt nothing. No satisfaction. No justice. Only emptiness and the cold wind that slid up the wall of the cliff, ruffling the girl's blonde hair.

Her eyes were glassy and wide. Her skin was as pale as alabaster. The blood had quit pumping from the thin slit he'd carved in her throat. There was only a feeble trickle now, soaked up by her cheap woolen undershirt like broth by bread. Even the abandoned sprawl of her limbs across the rocky ground, the way her skirts bunched high above her quivering knees in her final portrait of death, did nothing to inspire him.

He needed more, more than just the whore's death to console him for all he'd lost. It hadn't been her fault anyway. To be truthful, despite his possession of the medallion, despite the dramatic scene divesting the real Linet de Montfort of any hope of claim to the title, Lord Guillaume de Montfort had never really seemed to place complete faith in Sombra's story. Melancholy had persisted in the man's eyes from the moment he'd reluctantly taken the imposter's hand in his and placed a kiss upon it. And the daughters had been just as hesitant, in spite of Sombra's most charming efforts.

Fate decided to play a cruel trick on him then. It let him believe for a day that he had everything in his grasp. Coin beyond counting was pressed into his palm. He was showered with gifts of inestimable value—cloth and spices and jewels—gifts of gratitude for the safe conveyance of the heiress of de Montfort to her rightful home. For one day he basked in the warmth of victory. For one day he dreamed of his manor in Spain and of the toothsome revenge he would take upon those who'd stolen it from him.

And then all of it was snatched away. Some lowly seamstress from the neighboring village, hearing the gossip and hoping to incur a healthy reward for her trouble, came crawling to the lord with a heavy silver ring she'd obtained from the woman claiming to be Linet de Montfort. And this Linet de Montfort was quite different from the one who now assumed the title. This lady, she said, had surrendered the ring tearfully and then proved so particular and knowledgeable about the quality of the garment she desired that the seamstress had nearly turned her shop upside down trying to please her.

The story was little proof of anything in and of itself. The ring, bearing a wolf's head, could have been stolen. But de Montfort recognized the crest and made the connection between the ring and the monk's claim of de Ware heritage. De Ware was an old family, a powerful family. One didn't offend such families. If there was any chance that the monk truly was kin to de Ware . . .

Sombra didn't want to think about the humiliation that had followed—the seizing of his rewards from him, the stripping off of his precious garments, the shackles rattling about his wrists as he and his harlot imposter were led down the dank, stinking steps to the dungeon.

He escaped within the hour. Gaolers were notorious half-wits, and castles were busy places. The wench and he fled through the wood, stealing food, filching clothes, never resting until they made their way to the sea. Of course, he couldn't let the girl go. She'd turn him in to the authorities for the reward. And so he'd killed her.

He kicked gently at her with the toe of his boot to be sure. There was no response. Wary of staining his garments, he nudged her body with his foot until she rolled over the cliff and broke upon the white-spattered rocks below.

The sun was on its last legs when he arrived at the docks of Calais, faint with fatigue. He raked his lank hair back with his fingers and straightened the brown woolen surcoat, silently cursing. It had been the best garment he'd been able to snatch in this backward country. But soon, he told himself, he'd don black velvet again—black velvet and cloth of gold and silk from the Orient.

As soon as he met up with El Gallo.

Luck was with him. At the furthest end of the Flanders dock, fluttering from the tallest mast in the harbor, hung El Gallo's pennon—the scarlet cock strutting proudly against the ground of gold. Grateful tears sprang to Sombra's weary eyes. He swiped at the undignified evidence of his desperation and started forward.

For the last several miles, he'd practiced the speech that would have El Gallo feeding from his fingers again. Providing his strength held out, he'd deliver it with the proper amount of remorse, cunning, and promise to garner the captain's attention. El Gallo could never resist an opportunity for coin. If Sombra could pique his interest in something new and profitable—whether it ultimately bore fruit or not—he could have his life again. He could have his cabin on the *Corona Negra* back. And he'd work in the shadow of the great sea reiver once more.

He stumbled eagerly forward through the crowd, his eyes bleary with emotion. Just ahead, coming down the gangplank, he could make out the crew of the *Corona Negra*: Diego, soaked to the skin, his head wrapped in bloody linen; Roberto, limping, half-dragged by a deathly pallid Diaz; an unconscious Felipe carried between two others. Something was very wrong.

Sombra pushed his way through the throng, taking long strides toward the ship. His heart beat against his ribs like a moth caught in a child's fist. At the foot of the gangplank, he seized Diego's arm.

"What is it?" he demanded. "What has happened?"

"Sombra!" Diego wheezed. "It's the captain. El Gallo is dead."

Sombra stumbled backward. "No," he whispered. "No." He crumpled to his knees before the *Corona Negra*. "No!" he cried hoarsely. He buried his face in his hands upon the splintered wood of the dock, unmindful of the muttering strangers passing by. All his hopes, all his schemes—crushed in a single, final blow. There was no doubt in his mind now. He was fortune's foe.

By afternoon, the Dorwich harbor teemed with merchants and travelers and young boys itching to clamber onto the sailing vessels anchored at the dock. After two days of breathing the wretched stink of her grisly cargo, the ship's passengers from Flanders disembarked enthusiastically, eager to tell the tale of the defeat of El Gallo, some of them exaggerating their own part in it. A few brazen souls even climbed aboard the ship for a peek at the rotting corpse of the infamous reiver.

Linet still looked dazed, despite the fact Duncan had done his best to comfort her. And now he didn't want her to have to answer a lot of questions. She could hardly be found guilty of murder under the circumstances. El Gallo was a notorious criminal, and there were plenty of witnesses to the incident to exonerate her. But unless and until a trial became necessary, there was no sense in adding to Linet's distress by exposing her to gawking bystanders.

"I need to wash my hands," she said.

Duncan looked down sadly at her fingers, rubbed raw with washing the blood from them. But in sooth, he was more concerned with the huge stain on her surcoat.

He obliged her wishes before she could attract too much attention, guiding her below deck and into the captain's cabin. He poured water from a pewter aquamanile into the wash basin beside the captain's pallet. "Give me your hands," he bade her. Then he gently laved away the evidence only she could see.

The ritual seemed to calm her. As he handed her a linen towel, she murmured low, "Can you ever forgive me?"

"Forgive you?" What did she mean? She'd saved his life. If she hadn't acted swiftly and, he was reluctant to add, with characteristic de Montfort brashness, it might have been *his* blood soaking the ship's planking.

"I was . . . wrong," she said. "I was wrong to judge you, wrong to . . . betray you."

He rubbed his thumb nervously along the back of her hand. She was softening his resolve. That was the last thing he wanted. Aye, he'd listen to her. She deserved that much. But though he had no qualms about offering her protection, he wasn't about to let her commandeer his heart again.

She let out a shuddering breath and picked at a nub in the wool of her skirt. "My father taught me never to trust a peasant," she said quietly. "You see . . ." Her eyes took on a far-away cast. "My mother was a peasant. And my father was so in love with her that he forsook all that was de Montfort to wed her. He gave up . . . everything—his title, his wealth, his land, his family." She frowned. "After she found that he no longer had those things to offer her, she ran off, making him a gift of their newborn child." She smiled faintly. "Father said I was still wet from the birthing when he heard me squalling at his door."

Duncan swallowed. He'd found such a child once in a heap of refuse. The little girl lived at de Ware Castle now.

Linet closed her eyes. "My father taught me that peasants

are ignoble, unworthy. He said I must never put faith in them. You must understand . . ."

"I understand," he said brusquely.

"But you," she began, the frustration of the paradox wrinkling her forehead, "you are an exception. You've been kind and brave and . . . and . . . nobler than any gentleman I've ever known."

Duncan's hands grew very still. He didn't want to hear this. He wasn't ready to forgive her. But when Linet looked at him with those wide, angelic eyes, he could feel his control slipping.

"If you'll still have me," she murmured, "I will consent to be your wife."

Duncan ceased breathing. Suddenly it felt as if his heart was being held between Linet's palms over a deep chasm. A hundred emotions swirled through his head.

She had saved his life. He owed her much for that. Yet once she'd left him like carrion for his enemies. She was the loveliest, most clever and engaging woman he'd ever met. Yet she'd callously stolen his crest ring. She had made love to him with a passion and unbridled zeal he'd never before experienced. Yet she'd betrayed him while his seed was still warm inside her.

He had offered her marriage once. She had refused him most dramatically. He wasn't inclined to repeat his mistakes. Still, there she was, looking up at him with a rapt breathlessness that was rapidly turning to embarrassment as he delayed answering.

"Why?" he asked bluntly.

"Be-because I see you are not the man I thought you were," she stumbled. "You are honorable and . . . and worthy . . ."

"Worthy?"

She blinked in confusion.

"I see now," he said bitterly. "You are no better than your mother. Now you know I am Duncan de Ware. *Now* I am worthy of you—me with my wealth and position."

"Duncan de Ware?" she exclaimed. "Don't be absurd! You may have fooled El Gallo and his crew, but I am not so gullible."

He shook his head, incredulous. "You don't believe me?"

"That you are Sir Duncan de Ware? Of course not."

"Then why do you want to be my wife?" he demanded.

"I told you . . ."

"I've *always* been honorable and worthy," he said dismissively. "Why now? Why not before?"

She squirmed under his regard. "Because . . ."

"Because?" he prodded, boring into her soul. Then his eyes suddenly flattened, and his gaze slipped pointedly toward her belly. His voice was like ice. "You fear you might be with child," he guessed, "and you don't wish to bear a bastard."

"Nay!" she cried, but her blush revealed how close he'd come to the truth. Aye, two days ago marriage had seemed a reasonable solution, but she'd been to hell and back since then. She'd had two days to reflect on everything they'd been through, on the gypsy's decency, on her betrayal, on what truly had meaning. She was a changed woman.

"You needn't fear, lady," he bit out, his eyes like splinters. "I always provide for my offspring."

"You don't understand. I . . ." Linet stared at him, incredulous. "How many do you have?"

"Nineteen." A thoughtful frown flitted across his brow. "Or twenty."

At first, she thought he was jesting. But there was no mistaking the severity of his expression. All the air went out of her. He was serious.

"And when I marry," he told her, teeth clenched, "it will be for far more substantial reasons than to give my name to a child I've sired."

Linet eked out a desperate protest. "Please, don't give answer yet." Dear God—she wished she'd never asked. She couldn't yet face the possibility that there was no hope for their love. "Think about it for a time."

His mouth worked in indecision before he finally replied. "I will . . . think about it."

He slipped a cloak from the peg on the cabin wall and draped it around her to hide her bloodstained kirtle. Then he ushered her briskly away from the ship and the inquisitive crowd, pausing only to send a young lad on to the castle with news of their safe return.

The rickety wagon and its sorry nag made slow progress along the northern road the next day. Usually, Linet made the journey in a few hours. At this speed, it had taken most of the afternoon. Still, she thought, thank God Captain Campbell had seen fit to provide them coin for transport, else they'd have gone afoot, for the three travelers—Harold, the gypsy, and she—hadn't a farthing between them.

She didn't know how they'd managed to afford shelter at the inn last night. In sooth, she remembered little of what transpired after she disembarked. But she awoke refreshed upon a comfortable straw pallet after a blissfully dreamless night, and someone had left her an underdress and a clean kirtle to wear.

When the gypsy showed up with horse and cart, insisting upon accompanying her to Avedon, she almost wept with relief. She was going home at last.

And now the journey was almost over. The amber sun dipped behind the mountains as they crested the top of the rolling hill below which nestled Avedon.

Linet's spine straightened with pride. The beautiful, thick-grassed glen was dotted with sheep and ribboned through by a silvery stream that meandered about the walls of the little town. In the distance lay fields of young wheat and barley, oats and rye, spread like a patched cloak over the fertile ground. From atop the hill, the thatched buildings of the village huddled together like gossiping neighbors.

As they passed through the city gate and along the cobbled streets, Linet breathed in the familiar smells of home—fresh cut fodder, mellowing ale, the acrid stench of the dye house, evening pottages warmed over a hundred different home fires. Most of the merchants had closed up shop and gone inside their dwellings. Twilight would soon wink its watchful eye over the land, and the city gate would close for the night.

A mistiness touched Linet's eyes as she thought how much her life had changed since she was last here.

Duncan watched with narrowed eyes as they rolled past cottage after cottage. He sought, out of habit, the penniless waifs tucked into the crevices between the buildings, and he wished he had his purse of silver coin.

At long last, they neared a sizeable walled mesnage, and Harold gestured proudly toward it, letting him know they'd arrived at the de Montfort home.

A wisp of smoke curled up from the roof of the tall thatched cottage, though little light shone through its shuttered windows. The yard was well-kept, and the flagstone forecourt was clean. But no servants bustled out to greet their mistress. Duncan felt uneasy.

Linet, throwing caution to the wind in her eagerness to be home, hopped down and ran forward to the wooden gate, preparing to shove it aside so the cart could enter the forecourt. No sooner had her hands touched wood than Duncan grabbed her forcibly by the shoulders, setting her aside.

"Let me go first," he murmured. He peered into the forecourt, back to the outbuildings, and saw nothing immediately suspect. "Wait here. I'm going inside."

"But you'll . . ." Harold protested.

"Wait here. I don't want you walking into a trap."

"I don't think you'd better . . ." Linet began.

He slipped off before she could finish. Drawing his dagger, he approached the door of the mesnage with the stealth he used to stalk deer. Slowly he pushed the door open.

The inside of the cottage was lit only by the fire burning on the hearth. The shadows cast by the room's furnishings did a macabre dance upon the plaster walls. He strained to make out the faint details of the room. He took a tentative step forward.

The quick, slight breeze should have warned him, but it had been too brief for him to move away in time. Stars burst suddenly upon the darkness as he was bowled over by a tremendous bang against his forehead.

19

DUNCAN REELED LIKE A DRUNKEN MAN FROM THE BRUISING blow, shaking his head to clear his double vision. Somewhere, echoing in his addled skull, he heard the incongruous cackling of an old woman. Was it his disoriented brain, or was some ancient wench actually egging him on?

From outside, Linet smothered a gasp at the loud clang.

"I'll see to the horse and cart, my lady," Harold muttered.

Linet picked up her skirts and hurried toward the cottage. She'd tried to warn the gypsy. Now she could hear the old woman threatening him with more violence.

"Margaret!" she shouted. "Margaret, it's me, Linet."

"Ah, my Linet, you're home early! Don't you worry, lass!" the old lady beamed. "I've got the rascal! He won't be seein' straight for a few days, that's for certain."

"Margaret!" Linet scolded, squinting into the dim room. "What have you done? Where is he?"

Before Margaret could answer, Linet stumbled against the gypsy's weaving body. He clutched at her shoulders for support, nearly knocking her to the ground.

"Didn't get past me, he didn't," Margaret rattled on. "I was ready for him, the slippery rascal."

"Margaret," Linet said, trying to remain calm. "Put down whatever weapon you've got and light a candle. I fear you've attacked a . . . a friend."

"A friend?" Margaret shrieked. "He's not a thief?"

"Nay, Margaret, and why you must toddle about in the dark when we have plenty of candles . . ."

"Candles won't help these old eyes of mine," Margaret complained. "And if he's not a thief, then why was he sneakin' about like that?"

There was a painful ringing in Duncan's head that wouldn't go away. Only when a candle was finally lit did he discover the origin of that pain.

He almost wished he hadn't. To his chagrin, a tiny woman at least seventy winters old clung tenaciously to a huge iron cooking pan, wielding it like a cudgel. Despite Linet's reassurances that he was not the enemy, suspicion yet lurked in the woman's bright, beady eyes, particularly when she perused his already battered countenance.

"You'd best sit down," Linet said in concern as he cradled his forehead. She pressed him carefully into a chair. "Margaret, I hope you're satisfied. You've addled his brains."

To Duncan's horror, Margaret did look rather pleased with herself.

She sniffed. "Looks like I'm not the first to take a whack at his head. If he's not a thief, then who is he?"

"He's . . . ah . . ."

"Sir Duncan de Ware," he supplied, ignoring Linet's surreptitious kick at his shin.

Margaret's eyebrows rose at the mention of his title. "Sir . . . Duncan de Ware?"

"Nay!" Linet blurted.

"Aye," he countered, pressing a palm to his throbbing forehead.

Margaret lifted a suddenly fluttery hand to her cheek. "Well then," she said, nervously clearing her throat, "I must fetch the servants and fix up a proper meal." Aside to Linet, she whispered loudly, "Why didn't you tell me, my lady, that you were comin' home early and bringin' a guest? A proper knight. *Sir* Duncan de Ware. Imagine. And me near brainin' the poor lad." She turned and marched to the pantry, the iron pan thumping against her thigh.

Linet stood with her mouth agape. He'd told Margaret he was a knight. And worse, the old woman believed him.

"Why did you tell her that?" she hissed.

"Tell her what?"

"That you were Sir Duncan de Ware?"

"What would you have me tell her?"

Linet ran frustrated fingers through her mussed hair. She didn't know. It had been her idea to shield the servants from the truth. After all, she couldn't very well dance in with a stranger on her arm, proclaiming him a gypsy and the possible father of her child. But she feared the pool of deception was going to grow deep around her ankles if she didn't curb it now.

Three pairs of curious eyes peered around the corner of the pantry screens. Margaret had obviously just broken the news to the servants—supper was going to be graced with the presence of a knight.

Linet glared at the whispering girls. They ducked their heads back into the pantry.

"Perhaps you shouldn't have come here so soon," Linet muttered. "After a few days, after things have settled . . ."

"Linet," he whispered, taking her hands in his, "you have just slain one of the most devious Spaniards to roam the seas. He has accomplices everywhere. I cannot leave you alone here, defenseless."

"I can . . ."

"Defend yourself? I think not." He quirked a brow upward, then rubbed at his forehead. "Although the old woman might do some damage with her pan."

The "old woman" made her entrance then from behind the pantry screens, maids in tow. She sang out, "I hope you like mutton, sir knight."

Did she have to call him that? Linet wondered peevishly.

"Mutton? It's one of my favorites," he assured Margaret.

The girls fairly beamed.

The brash gypsy picked up the candle Margaret had brought in and began lighting all the others about the room, like King Midas turning every object he touched to gold. They were nearly as *costly* as gold, Linet thought, irritated at the way he lit so many of them.

She wondered how long he intended to maintain his pretense at nobility. Already the maidservants cooed over his bruises and flitted flirtatiously about him, taking his cloak, questioning after his every whim. Damn him—right before her eyes and in her own household, he was usurping the authority from her.

Harold came in through the back door.

"Wipe your feet!" Margaret yelled from the pantry.

"And a good evening to you," Harold muttered back. He apologized to the gypsy. "She's a good-for-naught old woman, my lord. I hope she's made you welcome?"

The gypsy massaged his temple. "Aye, Harold, that she has. Already offered me the hospitality of the kitchen."

"So I heard. Is there anything I can do for you, my lord?"

Before Linet could make a bid for Harold's attention, the gypsy began making demands of his own.

"Aye, Harold. Perhaps you could prepare a pallet for me somewhere? And I'd like to meet the servants, so I can learn their faces, know them by name. Will you invite them all to table for supper?"

"Aye, my lord." Harold's eyes gleamed at the unexpected invitation.

Linet drummed her fingers on the back of a chair while Harold went about his work. "If I might remind you, gypsy," she said under her breath, "*I* manage this household."

"Would not your servants think it strange if Sir Duncan de Ware did not exercise the authority he was born to?" His sly smile was enraging.

If Linet had been a cat, Duncan thought, the fur on the back of her neck would have stood straight up. She would've raked him with furious claws. But he wasn't worried. With so many witnesses bustling in and out of the room, she could do little more than hiss at him.

He turned his back to her and took a moment to survey his surroundings. Even by *his* standards, the cottage was impressive. The main chamber was large. The floor was made of neatly fitted flagstones, and the walls were of light plaster, but for the areas around the fireplace and the wall sconces that had turned a smoky gray. The screens dividing the hall from the pantry were painted with vines and flowers of red and gold. In one corner of the room rose the staircase leading to the upper story, where the sleeping quarters were.

A half dozen chairs were placed about the room, as well as a large carved chest with matching cabinet, a desk furnished with parchment, a quill, and some sort of ledger, a stack of finished wool beside a loom, and a trestle table that could be set up for meals. The copious candles about the room lent a cheery glow to the cottage.

He opened a single pair of shutters and peered through the unglazed windows. The night was quiet, and the first stars of evening were just winking on their points of light.

When Harold returned, the two of them assembled the trestle table. Margaret and the serving girls brought in great platters heaped with food and a bottle of expensive French wine. Duncan could see by the tense curve of Linet's mouth that she didn't approve of the maid's generosity.

"I'm going to check on the outbuildings," she said tightly.

"Don't trouble yourself, my lady," he said magnanimously. "'Tis grown dark. *I'll* check on the outbuildings."

Margaret hummed as she fetched pewter goblets from the cupboard, and Linet hissed at Duncan out of her hearing. "This is *my* house! You may not order me about!"

Duncan bent to pile kindling on the cold hearth and smiled grimly. "Nonsense, my lady, don't worry about me," he said, loudly enough for Margaret to hear, "although it is good of you to express your concern."

Linet muttered an oath.

He lit the kindling with the candle flame, blew gently till it caught, then rose commandingly above her. "Do watch your language," he whispered, nodding toward the servants fetching napkins from the cabinet. "There are ladies present."

With that, he swept past her, past the screens, out the back door, and into the night to the outbuildings.

How Linet suffered through supper she never knew. The impudent gypsy, obviously relishing the authority he'd appropriated, played the role of de Ware to the hilt, inviting even the filthy stable boy to the table and impressing everyone with colorful tales of his own fictional past.

"My father was furious, of course, when I came home empty-handed," he told them as he picked at the mutton in his trencher. "You see, I'd given my first kill to a hungry peasant I met on the ride home."

The stable lad's eyes grew round in admiration. The serving girls giggled adoringly. Linet frowned. The way the gypsy told them, *she* could almost believe his stories.

Then it struck her. She knew how the gypsy made his living. She should have realized it long ago, with his penchant for disguise, his ability with the sword, his quick wit.

He was a player. He had to be. And a player's very profession was deception. It was no wonder he could convince Margaret he was a gentleman, Sombra he was a reiver, El Gallo he was the cousin of King Philip. He'd spent his life perfecting those skills. She sat back, smug in her newfound knowledge.

"Pray tell us more, Sir Duncan," Margaret bubbled, refilling his cup.

"Oh, nay!" Duncan wiped his mouth with his napkin and looked pointedly at Linet. "I fear I begin to bore my audience."

"Nay!" the servants cried.

"Your stories are marvelous," Margaret gushed. "Are they not, my lady?"

"Oh, they're quite imaginative," she dryly agreed. "But Gwen's head has nodded thrice now, and Elise's eyes will scarce stay open. We have some rather large orders to fill in the weeks ahead. I want you all at your looms at dawn with your heads clear and your eyes sharp."

Margaret clapped her hands. "Lady Linet is right, girls. Maeve and Kate, you may remain to help clean up. The rest of you, off you go!"

The girls protested softly, but rose to obey.

"Harold," Duncan said, "see them to their quarters." Then he added under his breath, "And tonight, keep a dagger close at hand."

"Aye, my lord. And where shall you bed down?"

Linet stiffened. She wondered just how presumptuous the gypsy would be. Would he dare to demand her father's chamber? The chamber that lay but a thin plaster wall from her own?

"I shall sleep here by the fire if you've an extra pallet," he decided.

She should have been relieved. He obviously didn't intend

to compromise her under her own roof. But for some curious reason, she felt a twinge of disappointment.

"Very well, my lord," Harold replied. "Truth to tell, Sir Duncan, I would rather your sword arm be close to the front door anyway."

Duncan winked at him.

Maeve and Kate began clearing the remnants of supper from the table while Margaret fussed over a cauldron hung over the fire.

"I believe the water for your bath should be hot now, my lord," she announced with relish.

Horror blossomed in Linet's eyes. Duncan's smile broadened. It was considered, of course, an irrefutable honor for the lady of the household to bathe visiting nobility.

Lady Alyce tapped the rolled parchment upon the solar table with a great deal of satisfaction, making the candle flame dance merrily upon its perch. This afternoon a boy from the village had brought home welcome news of Duncan's return and El Gallo's demise. Less than an hour after his arrival, the parchment came, still damp with the sweat of the diligent King's messenger who'd rushed it there.

King Edward approved the match. Linet de Montfort was a suitable bride for Duncan. Whether it was Lady Alyce's arguments or her surrender of Holden to Edward's cause that convinced the King, she didn't know and didn't care. The two lovers—and if she knew Duncan, they were lovers by now— could be wed with the blessing of the King.

Her eyes gleamed as she imagined what a handsome couple they'd make, and what beautiful children, *her* grandchildren, children dressed, she thought wryly, in the most fashionable and fine woolens. Ah, yes, it would be especially delightful having a wool merchant in the family.

She slid a fresh piece of parchment across the table, dipped her quill in the bottle of ink, and began writing up the banquet order for a lavish wedding feast.

Margaret dipped a wrinkled finger into the cauldron of steaming water hung over the fire. "Do tell us, my lord, how the two of you came to meet at the fair."

Linet stiffened as the gypsy stretched his arm out possessively across the back of the bench he shared with Linet.

"Ah," he said, "I'm certain I blush to tell it, but I admit it was a matter of love at first sight."

Maeve and Kate sighed. Linet glared at them.

"Yes," he continued, toying with the end of Linet's waist-length braid, "Linet de Montfort took one look at me and informed me she'd trust me with her life."

Linet couldn't believe what she was hearing. She snatched up her goblet of wine and took a big gulp to stifle her scream of outrage.

The gypsy shrugged. "What else could I do but comply with her wishes?"

She choked on the wine.

"Are you all right, my love?" Duncan asked, clapping her on the back a few times.

She felt ready to kill him.

Margaret clapped her hands together suddenly. "Sir Duncan de Ware! Why, you must be related to Lord James de Ware himself!"

"Aye," he replied without embellishing the fact. "Are you certain you're well, Linet?"

"I'm fine," she managed to choke out.

"Well, then," Margaret said, actually giving the gypsy a little wink, "I'll have this ready in a moment, and then you may have the honor of bathin' Sir Duncan."

"I'm sure Sir Duncan can . . ."

"Haul in the rinse water and the heavy tub, of course," he finished smoothly, laying his napkin down upon the table.

Margaret screwed up her wizened face. "Did you say, sir, how you are related to Lord James?"

Linet held her breath.

"Nay, I did not," he smiled, downing the last of his drink and handing the cup to Kate. "This wine is excellent, Margaret. I commend you on your choice. My own steward could not have selected better."

Margaret blushed with pride, effectively distracted.

"Let me do that," he offered as Kate and Maeve began to dismantle the trestle table. "You two get some sleep. Young hearts need time to dream."

The girls sighed dreamily and scurried off.

Linet sat stunned. Curse his arrogant hide! It was enough that she'd accepted him as a peasant, that she'd sworn her love for him despite his lack of lineage. But for him to put on the airs of a blue-blooded noble . . . He'd certainly outdone himself with this guise. And now he had an accomplice in her servants. It irritated her beyond words that everyone was so gullible to his charms. No doubt Duncan was enjoying himself immensely with women fawning all over him.

Dear Lord—now *she* was calling him Duncan.

"I'll go prepare your room for you, my lady," Margaret said with a curtsey.

When Margaret was gone, Linet finally found her voice. She rose and wheeled on the gypsy. "You may bathe yourself!" she whispered.

"I thought you'd say that."

"Duncan de Ware indeed! I know what you are now." She poked him in the chest. "You're a player, aren't you?"

He grinned that disarming, lopsided grin of his, but Linet held firm.

"Don't try to deny it. I've discovered your secret now."

He leaned back against the cupboard and crossed his arms, apparently eager to hear her conclusions.

"You had me puzzled for a while, I admit, with your lack of skills and your abundance of coin," she told him frankly, "but I've not survived in the wool merchant's trade without a nose for this sort of thing."

He sighed dramatically. "Alas, so you have found me out. Where did I go astray?"

Linet smiled smugly. "It was in your choice of roles, *my lord*. If you were going to pretend to the nobility, you should have chosen a fictional title, not one known in these parts."

"Margaret believed me. Harold believed me." He blinked. "Gwen and Elise and Maeve and Kate . . ."

"Pah! They'd not know a king from a kitchen boy. They are . . ."

"Mere servants?"

Linet pursed her lips.

"Ah, inferior intellect," he said.

She frowned. It sounded so harsh when he put it like that. "They do not understand these things. But *I* . . ."

"You can tell," the gypsy nodded, digesting this information.

"Of course."

"Ah, well then, I hope I can rely on your guidance concerning my performance. You will tell me if you spot any grave blunders?"

"You can rest assured," Linet threatened with a triumphant smile. "And now I'm off to bed."

Duncan watched her as she ascended the stairs, her hips swinging victoriously. "Margaret won't approve, you know," he called after her.

"Approve of what?"

"Your declining the privilege of bathing me."

Linet cursed him with her eyes. "The devil take Margaret."

Duncan chuckled and shook his head as Linet disappeared behind her chamber door. Then he went outside to search for whatever buckets he could find. There were several beside the well in back of the house. He set to work filling them. He worked quietly, alert always for stray sounds that might indicate an intruder. Then he hauled the buckets into the cottage.

The tub, cached in a corner of the buttery, was large and well-padded with linen. As he lugged the heavy wooden thing across the flagstones, he could hear the dissonance of feminine argument coming from above. He poured the cauldron of simmering water into the tub, tempering it with a bucket of the cold, and still the conflict continued.

The angry voices were muffled by Linet's door, but he heard the word "bath" mentioned a half dozen times. After several minutes of serious battle, the victor emerged. Margaret, stern-faced and smug, came strutting out of the chamber. She brought down a stoppered bottle, a ball of soap, a stack of linen towels, and a deep blue velvet robe, which she pressed into his hands.

"There you go, my lord," she said sweetly. "The lady of the house will be down shortly to do her duty."

Duncan stifled a grin. "Thank you, Margaret."

"Well then, if you'll not be needin' me, I'll go to my bed now, clean things up in the mornin'."

"Fine."

"You're certain you won't be needin' anythin' else? I won't
be peepin' my head out again," she said with a meaningful
wink. "And, well, I wouldn't wake up to the Crack of Doom."

Nonplussed by the wily old maid's frankness, he watched
her bustle upstairs and into Linet's chamber. Shortly afterward, Linet boiled out of the room, looking as if she'd like to
poison someone. Duncan wondered what vile threat Margaret
had made to ensure her mistress's cooperation.

Linet ground her teeth and swore for the hundredth time
that she'd turn Margaret out of the house—no matter that the
old woman had been in her father's employ for over twenty
years. She stomped down the stairs in her velvet slippers and
the linen underdress, tossing her unbound hair over her shoulder. She'd already half undressed for bed by the time Margaret won the battle. She saw no reason to ruin a perfectly
good surcoat with the splashes of a careless bather. So she
hadn't bothered to dress again.

It was an outrage, this bathing of strangers, she thought as
she stormed down the steps—an archaic, stupid practice that
her father had never once required of her. And now she was
going to be performing the dubious *honor* for a peasant.

She hit the bottom step and froze. The tub was already
brimming with steamy water. A large linen towel was slung
over the gypsy's shoulder, and he was whistling. While she
watched, he unstoppered the bottle of sweet woodruff, sniffed
at it, then dumped its entire contents into the tub.

She gasped. Woodruff petals weren't cheap. She rushed forward and grabbed the bottle from him. Dear God, she thought,
this wasn't going to work. She still loved him, aye, and still
desired to be his wife, but this deception in her own household was proving too much of a strain for her.

"On the morrow," she told him in a harried voice, "I'm
afraid we must find you other lodging."

"Must we?" He seemed amused.

"You deceived my servants. When they discover you are
not Sir Duncan de Ware . . ."

"And how will they discover that?"

The simplicity of the man was uncanny. She pressed her

fingers to her throbbing temples. "You cannot go on pretending to be a nobleman when . . ."

He frowned in concern. "My performance is flawed?"

She groaned. "Your performance is . . . is . . ."

"Not up to the standard of nobility?" he asked bleakly.

"Nay," she replied, confused. "I mean, aye, but . . ."

"But your servants may suspect," he ventured.

"Nay, it is not that at all," she answered, scowling. "They are convinced. They are *thoroughly* convinced."

"Ah. I think I see. You fear you may give away my guise, because *you* are not convincing. You're not properly trained in bathing nobles, are you?" he guessed brightly. "That's it, isn't it? You didn't wish to expose your ignorance."

Linet looked at him as if he'd fallen from the moon. How could anyone so misunderstand her?

"This will be educational, then," he declared enthusiastically. "I've seen dozens of baths given to nobles. I shall be happy to instruct you."

Linet couldn't for the life of her figure out how the gypsy goaded her into it, but not a quarter of an hour later, his clothing was draped over the screen, and she was wringing out a linen cloth, sponging his back for him as if he were the King himself.

After she ran out of curses to whisper under her breath, she ladled water up over his shoulders at his behest, gritting her teeth and forcing herself to ignore both his lordly air and what lay beneath the surface of the water.

As he leaned forward so she could wash his back, it was difficult not to notice the muscled contours of his body. When his arms flexed, they seemed as thick and strong as oak limbs. She remembered how those arms felt in her grasp, how her hand couldn't even reach halfway round the bulging muscle there.

Suddenly her knees felt weak, and her heart began to thump erratically. She took a deep breath to clear her mind and lathered the soap into Duncan's thick hair. She scrubbed vigorously, hoping to dispel her desirous musings, muttering all the while about what a spoiled child he was.

The gypsy sighed elegantly. "Ah, perhaps I shall have to

consider more seriously your suggestion of marriage, Linet. I think I should like having a bath such as this every night."

Whether it was his cocky reminder that she'd proposed a lifetime together or the way her body was playing traitor to her, Linet didn't know. But she'd had enough. Her fists clenched. Before she could even think about what she was doing, she reached with a soapy hand for one of the buckets of cold water and poured it without warning over Duncan's lathered head.

His intake of breath was sharp. Linet dropped the bucket with a loud crash, backing away from her handiwork. The gypsy shivered once and shook his head like a wolf coming from the stream. Then he turned and fixed her with eyes that took on a lupine gleam.

"Margaret," Linet mouthed silently, then prepared to scream the word.

His gaze was unwavering. "Do you really want Margaret to know what you just did to Sir Duncan de Ware?"

"Perhaps it was . . . an accident."

He smirked slowly at her effort. "Aye, well, one never knows what accidents may occur in the bath, does one?"

With that, he rose up out of the tub in all his naked glory, and for one moment, the only sound in the room was the ominous dripping of water as it rolled slowly off his body and back into the bath.

20

THE GYPSY TOOK ONE STEP FROM THE TUB. LINET COWERED back, bumping the screen. He towered over her, his body strong and dark and blatantly male. He took a second step just in time to grab her upper arm, preventing her from toppling the screen completely over.

She squirmed in his grasp, unable to do much more than spit quiet curses at him and pry at his fingers with her other hand. His head lowered to hers, and she leaned away from the wicked glint in his eyes. With his free hand, he scooped up the linen rag from the tub, dipped it into a cold bucket, and brought it near. Her eyes widened as she saw what he meant to do.

He let it drip in a tiny, icy stream down the neckline of her kirtle. She squealed. Then he squeezed his fist, and water gushed onto her bosom, spilling down over her breasts. She jolted with the shock of both the chill and what he'd dared.

He clucked his tongue. "Another accident," he murmured, laying the rag across a chair and lowering his gaze languorously to the front of her gown.

She fought to breathe. Her kirtle was soaked now. The damp linen clung to her breasts like a second skin. She could feel their peaks stiffening in protest of the cold water. The cad released her arm then, stepping back as if to admire the view.

Linet wasn't about to surrender the battle. She snatched another bucket from the floor, and before the gypsy had time to duck, she flung its contents directly into his smug face. The smirk vanished.

"You little vixen," he sputtered.

The bucket hit the floor with a loud thunk, and Linet clapped her hands over her mouth, certain Margaret would come bustling down any minute. He quickly caught one of her wrists in a viselike grip and tossed his dripping hair back from his face, spattering her in the process.

"So it's to be war, is it?" he growled.

For reply, she snatched up the wet rag from the chair and smacked it across his chest, where it stuck for a moment, then plopped to the floor. His grip on her wrist let up, and she easily wormed away from him, scuttling around to the opposite side of the tub.

Duncan hadn't had so much fun since he and Holden had loosed frogs in Lady Alyce's solar as boys. He was thoroughly enjoying himself. In wet linen, Linet looked like some bare-breasted Siren emerged from the water with naught but mischief on her mind. Her green eyes sparkled dangerously.

He advanced with cool stealth. She made a slight retreat, but her narrowed eyes told him she was confident with the tub between them that he couldn't reach her. He stared at her a long while. Then he curved his lips into a secret smile.

God—he adored her. This was the woman he wanted for wife. The thought warmed him to the core. He watched the excited rise and fall of her chest as she breathed, the quick pulse beating in a vein at her neck. And there was no doubt in his mind. This was the woman he wanted by his side for the rest of his days—the woman who dared fling insults in a sea reiver's face, the woman who could be taught to milk a cow, the woman who conformed to his body like chain mail, who challenged him over a bathtub like it was a battlefield.

She watched him warily now, like a cornered rabbit, ready to spring should he dart around one end of the tub or the other. He did neither. With a sly grin, he bent forward, dipped his hands into the water, and bombarded her with great splashes of water until she shrieked at him to cease.

Surely she'd surrender now, he thought. She was drenched from head to toe. Her kirtle and hair were studded with flowers from the bath. She looked as helpless as a drowning cat. But the clever vixen used his false assumption to her advantage. Grabbing up whatever rags she could find, she began dipping them in the bath and firing them at him with both alacrity and skill.

Laughing, he ducked out of the way a few times, blocked one rag with his arm, then received one full in the face. Growling like a wolf pup, he rounded the corner of the tub and almost laid hands on his attacker. But the flagstones were slippery with spilled water. His feet went out from under him. With a dull thud, he landed hard on his hindquarters.

Linet gave a great whoop of victory as she watched her foe fall, dodging out of his way. Unfortunately, that triumph was short-lived. The stones were just as wet where she was, and her drenched slippers betrayed her. One hand caught at the screen as she slid and slammed painfully onto her backside. The sections of the screen listed dangerously for an interminable moment, then crashed to the stones with a powerful bang in a cloud of plaster dust and ashes. Rubbing her bruised bottom, Linet coughed in the settling dust.

"Now look what you've done!" she whispered in panic, surveying the damage. She glanced nervously at her chamber door. Surely Margaret would come stomping out any moment. The old woman slept so lightly, she swore Margaret could hear a spider spinning a web in the next room.

He grinned. "What *I've* done?" He winced as he lifted his hips from the flagstone floor. "I seem to recall that it was *you* who struck the first blow."

"Well, if you hadn't been so cursedly condescending in the first place, ordering me about and . . ."

He laughed. "Condescending, is it?" He came to his feet and wrapped a large wet linen square around his waist. "Well, isn't that what one expects from a nobleman? I thought I played my part rather well."

"Rather too well," she bit out, struggling to her feet. "Don't imagine you can enjoy the privileges of nobility simply because you've slipped the bloodlines on like some costume."

"Why not?" he challenged her. "Why should I not enjoy the same comforts as my fellow men?"

"Because you're . . . you're not . . ."

"Worthy?"

Linet bit her lip and searched the wet flagstones.

"Then why do you want to marry me?" he whispered.

"I told you."

He shook his head. "You could find another man, a noble-man, one who would overlook your past sins."

Linet pursed her lips. "Perhaps I shall."

"Nay, you'll not," he told her in a voice as smooth as hon-eyed wine.

"Why not?"

"Because there is a bond between us."

Linet froze. Those were her very thoughts, as much as she wanted to shut them out. But she could hardly admit it to her-self, let alone the gypsy. How could she possibly explain that no matter what his birthright, no matter how little coin or hope of coin he had, no matter how coarse his manners were, in her heart she knew he was as good a man as her father had ever been? How could she reconcile the fact that she'd fallen in love with a commoner? Yet how could she even imagine sharing the sacrament of lovemaking with anyone else?

Duncan could feel the current between them even now as she stood shivering before him—beautiful, vulnerable, an-gelic. She reminded him of a lost, wretched orphan he'd once brought in from the rain. The little girl, he had set by the fire in the great hall so she could warm her feet. He had other ideas about warming Linet.

The pale linen of her kirtle left nothing to his imagination, from the rosy hue of her nipples to the narrow column of her waist. The wet fabric clung and caught between her legs, and his heart quickened as he remembered the softness there.

Linet felt his eyes upon her as if they touched her. The damp cloth covering him couldn't hide the evidence of his budding desire. Suddenly she felt unguarded. She wrapped one arm protectively about her waist and trained her eyes on the tub. The water there still sloshed back and forth in a lulling, sensual motion.

"You want me," he murmured. "We both know that."

She blushed at his frankness and mumbled, "Those are not the words of a nobleman."

His eyes raked worshipfully down her body. She nervously licked her lower lip.

"And," she said haltingly, "and a nobleman wouldn't look at a woman . . . the way you do."

One side of his mouth curved up. "How would a nobleman look at a woman?"

She swallowed. "With respect. With honor."

"But, my lady, I do respect you," he assured her, humbly bowing his head, "and I plan to honor . . . your wishes."

That was what she was afraid of. Lord—he looked so dangerously compelling, his wet hair slicked back off his forehead, his mesmerizing blue eyes trained on her like a wolf's on its prey.

He came closer. She fought off the insane urge to flee. What was wrong with her? She acted as if she were about to be devoured. She was in her own home, damn it, she who had bullied dyemakers and battled reivers.

"What words would a noble use?" he asked quietly. "Would he tell you your lips are as ripe and sweet and inviting as cherries?"

Linet felt the blood rise in her cheeks.

"Would a gentleman tell you," he murmured, "that your skin looks as delicious as warm cream? That your breasts . . ."

"Nay!" Linet cried out to stop him. "A noble wouldn't speak of . . . of those, and well you know it."

He gave her an amused frown. "You've never been to Court, have you, my lady?"

She straightened defensively. "Not yet."

"I have," he told her, moving ever so slowly closer to her, "and do you know, the noblemen are just as bawdy as the peasants?"

Linet felt the warmth of his aura press in on her, even though he was still a good yard away. "You have never been to Court," she accused hoarsely.

"Don't players often perform for royalty?" was his evasive reply.

He was so close now that she could sense the dampness of his body.

"The men at Court, the nobles," he told her, "are just as driven by their baser instincts as the men aboard the *Corona Negra*. They are just as lusty, just as raw, just as savage."

He was close enough for her to see the azure and indigo flecks in his eyes.

"The women at Court," he breathed, "are every bit as desirous as the women in the marketplace. Once they've shed their gowns, their flesh is much the same, willing and soft, their legs long, their breasts sweet . . ."

"Stop!" Linet hissed. Lord—her body responded to his words as if they were caresses. She really should slap him for such speech.

"Sheathe your claws, kitten," he whispered, reading her thoughts. " 'Tis not me you fear, but yourself."

Linet stared at the hollow of his throat, unable to meet his eyes. It wasn't the first time he'd told her that. Slowly she unclenched her fists. Was it true? Was she only afraid of the way her body responded to him, of the way her control abandoned her when he was near?

He brushed her cheek with the back of his knuckles. She closed her eyes languidly. He traced her lips with a finger. She parted them, her breath quick and shallow. He circled the shell of her ear with his thumb, stroking the sensitive place beneath it.

"You want me now, don't you?" he murmured. "Whether I'm a noble or a peasant."

It was useless to argue with him. Not while his breath was warm upon her face. She moaned softly.

"Tell me," he said. "Tell me it makes no difference who I am." There was strain in his eyes, as if everything depended on her answer to his question.

She swallowed hard and finally saw him as he was. A man. A man with dreams like any other man. A man with a heart that could swell with love or break in despair. A man with eyes the color of a summer sky, eyes full of wisdom and delight and all the devotion a woman could ever desire in a lifetime. A man with a soul assigned neither by king nor country, but by God alone, who measured souls by their goodness and not their birthright. Who was she, then, to judge him?

Breathless with discovery, she gazed at him forthrightly, past his tormented eyes and into the heart of his being, and spoke the words he longed to hear. "I care not who you are," she said. "I love you." Then she astonished them both by flinging her arms about his neck and kissing him for all she was worth.

A wave of desire caught Duncan unawares and nearly collapsed him in its wake. Joy bloomed in his chest at her confession, and rational thought deserted him. Her lips were like fire branding him, and the way she clung to him, her body molding erotically to his, sucked the breath from his lungs.

Gone were his restrained intentions. Gone was his iron control. All he wanted was her. Now.

She cleaved to him like a wild, desperate animal. She tangled her fingers in his wet hair, devouring him with her lips and teeth and tongue. Her hands roved across the muscles of his shoulders and chest, and she pressed wantonly against him with her hips.

Sweet Lord—he didn't even know what he was doing with his hands. They'd wrapped around her back, holding on for dear life. He'd have laughed at his own sudden ineptitude if it weren't for the fact that Linet's hand had dropped to his waist and was scrabbling at the linen towel.

He let out a great, growling breath and yanked the towel off himself, then picked her up bodily and looked for a place to set her down. He eyed the staircase. He'd never make it up the steps. The trestle table? It had been packed away. And if Margaret or one of the maidservants walked in . . .

Linet whimpered at the delay, clawing at his shoulders. His eyes glazed over with need.

"Sweet Christ," he sighed.

Carefully he laid her out upon the flagstones. In a heartbeat, he tossed up the hem of her dress and plunged into her, the perfection of their mating as inevitable as the roll of thunder after lightning. He thrust into her again and again, his arms trembling as he rose above her. She lifted her knees and brushed her calves against the sides of his hips, clutched at the curls at the back of his neck.

He shifted his weight subtly, rubbing erotically against her, and she cried out in wonder. To his amazement, she suddenly wrapped one arm and leg over him and rolled, coaxing him onto his back. Stunned, he pulled her down on top of him. She was the aggressor now, holding him down against the stones, riding him with ruthless abandon.

Duncan writhed in ecstasy, oblivious to the hardness of the rock beneath him. God—she was so tight about him, he thought he might burst. Her thighs were like velvet against his belly, and the scoring of her fingernails across his chest sent shivers through his body.

Sooner than either wanted, their passion began to build until the air around them was charged with it. The heat of their bodies sealed them together, flesh and mind and spirit, like the welding of iron to steel on a forge. They moved together toward the white-hot culmination of desire. And the instant they reached it—gasping, clawing, screaming—they became forever fused.

Coming home was a long journey. But gradually, Duncan felt the roughness of the flagstones beneath him. He shifted his hips over the sharp crack in the floor. But still he surrounded Linet with his arms, enveloping her with a deeper love than he'd ever extended. He wanted her—not just now, but for all time—her passion, her depth, her willfulness, all of her.

Linet knew she should be ashamed. Her body had acted of its own free will, driving her to do things surely only a strumpet would dare. And yet, lying here, her head upon the gypsy's breast, listening to the strong beat of his heart, she'd never been so content. When he began to stroke the back of her head with long, gentle, soothing motions, she closed her eyes against his chest.

Duncan smiled in contentment. When his breathing slowed to its normal pace, he lifted his head up to look at Linet. The poor exhausted wench was asleep atop him, her body limp with trust, her mouth parted in repose. He chuckled lightly and cradled her in his arms as he sat up, stirring her from her nap.

"Margaret may have given her oath to keep the door closed tonight," he whispered, "but I warrant she'll be up before the sun tomorrow. Let's get you into bed. I'll clean up the mess."

He pulled the wet gown from her and wrapped her in the blue velvet robe Margaret had left for him, then, squeezing into his wet braes, carried her up the steps and quietly swung open the leather-hinged door of her chamber. Margaret was snoring loudly on the low pallet beside her mistress's bed.

The luxury of the room was astonishing. Fresh, sweet rushes covered the floor, and the lamps Margaret had lit earlier were redolent of spiced oil. Linet's bed dominated the chamber, covered in green silk and draped at the corners in swags of burgundy velvet. A huge carved chest stood at the foot of the bed, and a table pushed against one wall was littered with quills, parchment, a comb and mirror, a ewer and basin for washing, and folded linen rags. It was obvious

Linet's father had tried to recreate, in Linet's world at least, the life of a noble.

He whistled low. "I think I could easily grow accustomed to such accommodations," he murmured, tiptoeing around Margaret's pallet. Pulling back the silk coverlet, he lay her out on her bed. "Sweet dreams." He kissed her tenderly on the forehead, then made a hushed exit.

Linet snuggled down into the bed, but she wasn't yet ready to sleep. Glancing about the chamber at her familiar possessions—the creaky loom in the corner, the worn, velvet-cushioned chair beside the hearth, the rich tapestry of the unicorn chase her father bought her when she was twelve autumns old—she felt a sudden foolish yearning for the innocence of her youth.

One way or another, when she finally made her confession to the Guild, she'd bid a final farewell to it all. She closed her eyes tightly and prayed that, unlike her mother, the gypsy peasant would not desert her when she'd lost everything, that the bond he spoke of was more than just pretty words exchanged in the heat of passion.

A wisp of a cloud like the tangled web of a spider drifted across the face of the full moon, dimming for an instant the sleeping town of Avedon. The hour was late—even the village's midnight revelers had gone home to sleep off their customary overindulgence in ale.

Lurking in the eery shadows outside the de Montfort mesnage, Sombra knew nothing of what had transpired earlier within and cared little. He knew only that Linet de Montfort was inside. He had but one thing on his mind—to destroy the bitch who had slain El Gallo and ruined his life.

He choked back a curse and stroked the haft of the sword that had been El Gallo's. With the captain gone, Sombra felt like a changed man, a shadow with no substance. His cheap clothes, torn to shreds in a rage of grief, were stained with wine and sweat. His hair was unkempt, his beard bedraggled. Lack of sleep had bleared his eyes and left him prone to strange hallucinations. But the dream of vengeance, so close now, sharpened his wits and his vision to almost unnatural clarity.

In sooth, he hardly needed the small flickering lantern as he slunk along the stone wall of the cottage toward the outbuild-ings. Not for light anyway.

He'd start with the warehouse, he decided. He wanted her to feel the pain of watching her livelihood vanish before her eyes. Just like he had.

The warehouse was unlocked. Sombra smiled thinly. Fate owed him as much. Lifting the lantern, he slowly pushed the door open and peered into the room. A dozen looms stood in neat rows, some laden with half-woven cloth, others empty. Bolt after bolt of fabric lined the walls of the warehouse, and the straw-covered floor was littered with scraps of wool and bits of fleece.

The old man's wheezing breath, coming from behind the door, gave him away. Sombra instantly punched hard toward the source of the sound and was rewarded with a groan and a thud as the body slumped to the floor. He raised the lantern. It was Harold. With a dagger.

Sombra kicked his miserable carcass. After all he'd done for Harold—saving him from El Gallo, releasing him from captivity—the old man had tried to kill him. He wouldn't live to see another day. Sombra would make sure of it. It was the work of a moment to secure the old man to a chair in the mid-dle of the warehouse with the copious wool yarn lying about the room. Nature would take care of the rest.

The fire was easy to start. The lantern lapped up the rushes on the floor like a hungry hound. Flames bounded across the straw to dance upon the looms. Sombra stared, mesmerized with mad delight.

It was beginning. First he'd destroy her wealth. Next would come her home, her servants, her lover. Then he'd kill her slowly, inch by inch, torture her in the name of El Gallo until she begged for death.

Grinning in ecstasy, he retreated from the warehouse and into the shadows of the night to wait. It wouldn't be long now.

Linet tossed in her sleep, uneasy. Her eyes flew wide, blind in the dim room, but she knew instantly that something was amiss. Raising herself up on one elbow, she peered groggily toward the starry night.

She wrinkled her nose. A faint thread of some familiar scent insinuated itself through the crack of the shutters. Tugging the coverlet back, she hastily went to the window and eased one shutter open.

The gray shadow of some devilish cloud roiled across the moonlit lawn. Then Linet recognized the intensifying acrid stench.

"My wool!" she cried, startling Margaret awake. "My wool!" Without bothering to don her slippers, Linet rushed from the window and flung the chamber door open, intent on racing below.

Linet's outcry roused Duncan with such alarm that he neglected to bring his sword in his haste to come to her. He caught her in the doorway. She struggled in his grasp, her eyes rolling in panic like a wild colt's.

"Fire!" she shrieked. "The warehouse!"

"I'll go!" he shouted. "You stay here."

He knew he had about as much chance of preventing her from following him as he had of stopping the sun from rising, but he could at least make his way downstairs before she did. He elbowed past her, ignoring her protests, and hurtled down the steps.

Linet followed at his heels, her gown brushing the steps like a whisper urging her to hurry. The gypsy was halfway out the back door when she reached the bottom. Through the open doorway, beyond his silhouette, she could see an orange glow coming from the warehouse. Thick grayish smoke billowed out from the building, and she heard the sound of coughing from inside.

"Stay back!" the gypsy yelled.

"Harold!" Linet screeched, stumbling forward.

She never saw the grim determination on the gypsy's face as he turned to rush onward—the unquestionable knowledge that he must try to save the man caught in the fire. All she saw was a lone, half-naked, unarmed man taking on the fires of hell in a hopeless battle. Before she could draw breath to scream, he ran headlong into the bowels of the fiery beast.

Duncan didn't stop to think. A man was trapped. He had to rescue him. It was as simple as that. He didn't even feel the flame as it singed the hair on his arms.

He burst into the hellish conflagration. The room looked

like the devil's workshop, with looms weaving fire into some infernal tapestry of destruction. Through the wisps of foul smoke, Duncan could make out Harold, bound to an upset chair by a spider's web of wool yarn. The old man's face was red, and he coughed hideously, cringing from tongues of flame that licked at his legs. But he was, miraculously, alive.

Drawing on all his strength and speed, Duncan reached the servant in two strides, hefted him up, chair and all, and carried him out through the demonic blaze.

For Linet, it seemed forever that the gypsy remained in the dragon's fiery belly, an eternity before he emerged from the devil's jaws. In sooth, her relief as the gypsy finally appeared, Harold safe in his arms, was so great that she forgot for a moment the blade that had just moments before come to rest against her throat.

The gypsy would be disappointed in her, she knew. She should have listened to him, stayed in the cottage. Now she had literally run into the hands of the enemy again. Sombra's spindly arm gripped her about the waist so tightly she could scarcely breathe. This time, she feared, she wouldn't survive.

Duncan scanned the perimeter of the demesne. His smoke-filled eyes watered, and the night seemed as black as pitch after the bright glare of the fire. But he knew the danger was far from over. Somewhere within these walls lurked a foe so diabolical he'd torture a helpless old man by burning him to death.

He knew Linet had followed him out of the cottage. It was only a matter of time before the enemy laid hands on her. He prayed she was still alive. He wished to God he had his sword.

He had to think quickly. He spilled Harold out onto the soft earth of the garden. Then, doubling over, he made a show of repeated coughing while he peripherally surveyed the mesnage. Linet's servants were emerging now from one of the other outbuildings, stumbling on the wet grass and screaming in terror. It was difficult to make out anything in the chaos.

Then he saw a black shape amid the shadows at the back door, a blackness broken only by a glistening fall of hair and the glint of steel. He had her. Sweet Christ—someone had Linet.

Without looking up again, Duncan staggered to the small

cookhouse and pushed his way inside. He had to arm himself. He glanced about in the darkness and let his hands move over oaken casks, a cheese press, iron cauldrons. At last, squinting in the shadows, he detected the dull shine of silver utensils hanging on one wall. With unerring acumen, he selected the two longest carving knives.

Linet gasped as Sombra's bony hand clamped about her waist and he exhaled his rank breath against her ear. He was angry. He'd apparently wanted the gypsy to see them. And he hadn't.

The servants dashed about like ants now. Soon neighbors would arrive to extinguish the fire. But already smoke obscured the yard, wreaking confusion.

All at once, the cookhouse door exploded open. The gypsy careened around the corner of the building, falling headlong to the sod. Sombra's fist tightened reflexively, and he nicked her with the knife.

Linet let out a little cry. Dear God—was the gypsy dead? For a full moment, she watched the still body on the ground, the only sounds the shrieking of servants and the rumbling and crackling of the fierce fire beyond as it digested its timbered meal. Finally, Sombra pushed her forward. The ground was damp and chill beneath her bare feet, but her heart felt much colder as she gazed at the gypsy with dread.

Two yards away from the gypsy, Sombra drew his sword and reached out tentatively to poke at the lifeless form. He snickered at his own misplaced fears as the body failed to respond to his prodding.

Duncan winced as the sword jabbed at his back again. But he forced his body to lie absolutely still. Then he counted to ten. With a burst of strength, he rolled and pitched forward, then shot up to face his doomed foe with the two carving knives.

He should have guessed. "Sombra," he croaked, his voice hoarse with smoke.

Sombra's surprise was short-lived. And he still had the advantage. He held Linet's life beneath his blade. "I had wished to kill you first before her eyes," the Spaniard sneered, "but it is enough now that she knows I will kill you next."

Duncan's fists tightened on the knives. A tiny drop of Linet's blood dripped down Sombra's dagger. The bastard would do it, he thought. He'd kill her in cold blood. With a calm he didn't feel, Duncan chuckled. "You are spineless then, Sombra. It is no wonder you were always merely the shadow of the great El Gallo."

"You are a fool to provoke me," Sombra warned him.

"And you are a coward, hiding behind a piece of woman-flesh." He could almost see steam curling out of Sombra's ears. "If you are a man, then meet me like one."

The Spaniard's nostrils flared in anger.

"You are afraid to fight me?" Duncan scoffed. "I am armed with kitchen knives."

Sombra made the fatal mistake of daring to hope he could win in a battle against a de Ware. His hold on Linet loosened marginally.

"Be quick about it, unless you want witnesses," Duncan hissed. "The neighbors in these villages watch out for their own."

Sombra's eyes darted about. It was true. Shouts filled the air, and shutters banged open from beyond the mesnage wall. He roughly cast Linet aside.

Linet bit back a cry as she tumbled painfully onto the cob-blestones.

"My lady!" Margaret shrieked, rushing from the cottage to see what all the fuss was about.

As Linet watched with mounting horror, Sombra drew his sword and squared off against the gypsy, his arms wide.

Margaret gasped. "I'll get my pan!" she decided, wheeling about.

"Nay!" Linet shouted. "Go to my father's room and bring Sir Duncan a proper sword!"

A shower of sparks shot upward from the warehouse as the two enemies faced one another. Sombra swung first, his sword whistling through empty air as the gypsy dodged the blow. His dagger followed, glanced aside by the gypsy's kitchen knife. Again, Sombra's blade came round, and the gypsy caught its edge with the second knife.

Sombra advanced, grinning, emboldened by the advantage of his longer blade, and the gypsy danced out of its path. But in the midst of retreat, the gypsy's bare foot set down upon a slick patch of moss, and he slipped backward. Sombra's sword flashed in an arc before him, shallowly slashing the gypsy's bare chest.

Linet sucked in her breath. The gypsy scrambled backward till he could regain his feet, but Linet could see a thin ribbon of red had begun to drip down his stomach. Sombra flapped his arms in savage glee, like a bat excited by the sight of blood. He stabbed forward with both weapons, and the gypsy blocked them, crossing his own blades.

Behind them, the warehouse creaked and rumbled ominously, and men began to call for water to douse the flames. Clouds of smoke climbed into the night sky, eclipsing the stars with their ghastly ascent. Children clambered up on the walls of the mesnage to watch their fathers battle the dragon that threatened to claim their own homes. The men were too busy fetching water and sand, shouting orders to spouses and servants, to notice the duel that transpired by the light of the holocaust.

Linet was afraid to interfere with the battle. She'd learned her lesson. She longed to drive a dagger into Sombra's heart herself, but she feared she might distract the gypsy or wind up a hostage again. Instead, she crawled across the damp earth to where Harold lay captive and began to loosen his bonds.

Duncan flexed his fingers on the weapons. They tingled from gripping the unleathered hafts of knives not meant for warfare. The steel of Sombra's blades was far superior to these carving knives, and Duncan feared they'd not last long.

No sooner had doubt crossed his mind than one of the kitchen knives snapped in twain under a hard chop of the Spaniard's sword. Cursing, Duncan cast it aside and held his remaining weapon before him in both hands.

Sombra cackled and came at him, slashing and thrusting. Duncan could do little more than sidestep out of the way. Once, when the Spaniard swung a little too broadly, Duncan was able to rush in and knock the dagger from his grasp, but there was no time to pick it up for his own.

With a terrible clang, Sombra's sword crashed down upon the weakened steel of Duncan's second knife, breaking it off blunt halfway down the blade.

Sombra's eyes gleamed in triumph. "El Gallo is avenged," he said. Then he lifted his sword high to split Duncan's head.

21

LINET'S THIN SCREAM PIERCED THE NIGHT, BUT THE RAGE IN Duncan's blood left no room for fear. Angered by Sombra's cruelty, appalled by the fire's destruction, furious with sinister plots that would dare deny him the woman he loved, Duncan drew strength from his wrath.

"Nay!" he roared.

Heedless of the menacing sword, he charged. He collided hard with Sombra and held him close, almost as if wishing a fond farewell to a dear friend.

"I will finish what my brother did not," he hissed.

Sombra's eyes widened in terrified recognition.

Then, drawing back the blunted knife, Duncan shoved it forward with all his might. The dull remains of the blade drove in between Sombra's ribs.

The Spaniard stood dazed for a moment. He swayed with Duncan in a grisly embrace. His black glove crept up Duncan's chest like a spider, as if he'd claw what life remained from Duncan with his bare hand if need be. But then his eyes went glassy. His hand curled shut. His sword dangled from strengthless fingers, then fell futilely to the cobblestones. And Sombra's last breath rattled out.

Duncan eased the body to the ground, shaking with the violence of what he'd done. Gradually, he grew aware of the activity around him. Women laden with heavy buckets struggled past, and men poked at the burning warehouse with long poles, trying to control its demise. Ashes floated like drab snow over everything.

In the midst of the maelstrom, in the soot-frosted grass, knelt Linet. She stared at him, almost reverently. He swore under his breath and wiped his bloody hands on his braes. He felt awkward before her, oddly unworthy of her awe, ashamed of the grotesque act he'd committed before her.

But then she came to him, her robe billowing out in the warm draft, her figure a stark silhouette against the orange inferno. And all Duncan's guilt vanished.

Linet gazed at her gypsy in wonder. Her knight—and she now believed that no man more richly deserved that title— had risked his life for her sake. Jesu—he had even risked his life for the sake of her servant.

He had vanquished the enemy. He had ended the nightmare.

She flung herself into the gypsy's arms with abandon. Never had she felt so safe, so warm, so welcome. Here was her hero. Here was her noble knight. Here was her destiny.

Nestled against his chest, she wondered how she could have ever doubted it. She took a deep breath, inhaling the smoky, sweaty, masculine scent of the man in whose arms she so certainly belonged. Her eyes filled with happy tears as he held her close.

She was still clinging to him when Margaret came tearing out of the cottage, Lord Aucassin's sword in hand. The maid stopped cold when she saw them. Linet cleared her throat and pushed the gypsy gently from her. It was time, she decided, to set matters straight once and for all.

"Margaret," she began.

"Are you puttin' out a fire or startin' one?" Margaret asked.

Linet took one of the gypsy's large hands in her own two and clasped it defensively. "You'll keep your nose out of it, Margaret. This is the man I love," she declared as the fire snapped behind her. "He is noble and good and brave and . . ." She raised her chin. "And he is a peasant. But I don't care. It doesn't matter what my father believed. I intend to marry him . . . if he'll have me," she added hastily.

Margaret looked back and forth between the two. She blinked. "Peasant . . ."

"That's right. He's a peasant," Linet confirmed with a stubborn set of her chin. "But he is worthy, Margaret, the most worthy man I've ever met. He saved Harold from the fire, and he slew that Spaniard, the one who abducted me. He followed me on the ship to Flanders and kept me safe from the reivers and . . . well, he threw me into the sea, but it was all for the best, and . . ." Linet felt herself chattering on like a nervous squirrel, and she could tell by the puzzled frown on Margaret's face that she was making little sense. "Say what you will, Margaret. Curse me for my father's fool, but I will follow my heart in this. I love him." She looked up into her beloved's sapphire eyes. "I *love* him."

Margaret still scowled.

Linet sighed. "I shall discuss the changes in the household later, Margaret. At the moment, we have a fire to quell. But I warn you, no matter how you argue, I'll not change my mind."

She pressed a quick kiss to the gypsy's cheek.

Before Duncan could frame a reply, Linet was off in a flash of linen, whirling away to help organize the battle against the fire.

"Hmph," Margaret snorted as her mistress departed. "Well, I suppose you won't be needin' this, then?"

She held out the sword. He took it from her. It was heavy but well-balanced, a nobleman's weapon.

"You know, I was upstairs," Margaret said, "tryin' to get to sleep with the racket you two were makin', when it came to me all at once." She tapped her temple. "Duncan de Ware. You're one of Lord James's brood, his oldest son, I'm thinkin'."

"Aye."

"I thought so." She wrinkled her nose affectionately at him. "We'd best be lendin' a hand with the fire, don't you think?"

Duncan nodded and reached for an overturned bucket near his feet.

"Of course, her father wouldn't have approved," Margaret said.

"Nay?"

"He'd always wanted to present her at Court." Margaret picked up another bucket and hobbled to the well. "Let her choose a husband from among the nobles there, settle into a nice, old, established family."

"My family *is* . . ."

"I knew Linet was headstrong," Margaret said with an indignant sniff, "but I never thought she'd pick a husband without my blessing."

"In sooth, *I* was the one . . ." Duncan began, hefting his bucket atop the well's stone wall.

"You *will* marry her, of course." There was no doubt in the old woman's voice as she tied the rope to her bucket and lowered it into the well.

Duncan raised a brow.

Margaret continued. "She's a proper lady, no matter what the rest of her family says, and I assure you the de Montfort lineage goes back at least as far as that of de Ware."

"Margaret."

"She has a fine talent and a keen mind. She'll keep your household in good order."

"Margaret."

Margaret shook her head. "I should have known she could no more govern her heart than her father could. Well, at least she's had the wisdom to choose well. As far as the dowry . . ."

"Margaret."

"What is it?" Her round eyes narrowed in suspicion. "You are not promised to another?"

"Nay, Margaret. I love Linet, and I fully intend to wed her."

Margaret grunted in satisfaction. "Now then, what's this nonsense about . . . a peasant?"

Duncan was spared having to answer that question. The warehouse suddenly collapsed with a great whoosh of flame. Every man available was needed to douse the burning tinder.

The midnight sky was already paling by the time the fiery beast was at last brought to its knees. Blackened timbers lay about the yard like the smoking bones of a dragon, their heat only an impotent reminder now of the savage animal that had reared its destructive head.

Duncan leaned against the wall of the well. Linet trudged toward him, rubbing an arm across her forehead, smearing soot over her face. She looked exhausted. Her hair hung in clumps about her shoulders, her clothing and skin reeked of smoke, and there were black streaks at the bottom of the overlong velvet robe where she'd waded through the charred remains of the warehouse. But Duncan had never seen a more beautiful sight.

The way she'd organized the extinguishing of the fire to save her neighbors' homes—putting idle children to work to watch for live cinders that might rekindle, pushing up her sleeves and climbing into the wreckage herself—she would do the de Ware household proud.

"Will you marry me, Lady Linet de Montfort?" he called.

Linet smiled weakly at her gypsy. She knew she looked like hell. Her eyes felt scraped raw. Her father's blue velvet robe was streaked with oily black. God only knew what color her hair was. It was just like him to ask her that now.

And yet, nothing could be more appropriate. His face, too, was grimy with soot. Blood from his gash had dried on his chest, and his hair was dull with ashes. But his was the face she wanted to dream about each night and wake up to each morning.

"Absolutely," she murmured. She collapsed against him, happier than she'd ever been in her life.

"You're near dead on your feet, my lady," Margaret interrupted, dusting the ashes off her hands as she came up. "Will you see her to bed, then, my lord? I'm afraid I've got my hands full with Harold. That moon-eyed alewife down the lane put so much drink in the dodderin' fool—to cut the pain, she says—I doubt he'll be able to find his own feet."

"Please put Harold in my chamber," Linet said. "His burns could use the soft pallet." She looped her arm around her intended's waist. "As for me, I'll curl up before the fire. From now on I'll sleep in no better quarters than he who is to be my husband."

Margaret harumphed. "Oh no, you won't. I'll not have you and 'he who is to be your husband' dallyin' on the floor of the hall again and disturbin' everyone in the house. Harold will be fine downstairs. You'll both go to your chamber . . . and secure the door."

Linet's jaw was still hanging open when her gypsy swept her off her feet and carried her up to her bedchamber. A hundred questions rattled at her brain, but she was too exhausted to seek answers. By the time he'd lain her gently on the feather pallet, all emotions save longing had deserted her.

"You need to rest, Linet."

"Aye." Rest was the furthest thing from her mind.

"We've had a long day."

"Aye."

He loomed over her like a guardian angel, his black hair hanging in dirty clumps, his forehead streaked with soot, his eyes red-rimmed. God—he was handsome.

"We'll have to assess the damages tomorrow," he said.

"Mm-hmm."

"I'm afraid you lost . . . everything," he said softly.

She gave him a sultry gaze. "Not everything."

Duncan took a deep breath. His breast swelled with quiet joy. Linet looked beautiful, lying there on the silk coverlet, even with strings of her hair sprawling across the pillow, her eyes smoke-ringed, her cheek smudged with ashes. And if she only knew what that look of hers did to him. Lord—he longed to kiss those sweet lips. "It's late," he said hoarsely. His eyes locked with hers.

"We should get some sleep." She stared back.

He cleared his throat. "You need your rest," he said, more to himself than her.

"Aye," she lied.

And then he bent toward her, drawn by the clear message in her eyes as irresistibly as a spiraling eddy in a stream. Jesu—he'd starve if he didn't taste those lips soon. He lowered his head until Linet's trembling breath mingled with his. His mouth tentatively closed over hers, his tongue flicking out once to sample the yielding petals of her lips before he finished the kiss.

Now he'd withdraw, he thought, tell her good night, let her rest. Foolish man. Linet melted into his embrace as smoothly as a hand into a well-worn glove. Her tongue gave answer of its own, licking delicately along his bottom lip. Before he could stop himself, he was deepening that kiss and beginning another. His arms curved to surround her more fully, and he tucked her securely against his chest. Her matted hair seemed silky in his fingers, her grimy skin like velvet to his touch. No woman had affected him so profoundly.

It was the moan that pushed him over the edge, the little mewling sound she made against his lips. What little control he'd mastered was gone in an instant. He covered Linet's eager face with kisses. He slipped the velvet robe from her shoulders with practiced ease, fairly devouring the exposed flesh. His hands explored further, tracing the contours of her throat and bosom, seeking the ripe fruit still hidden from his view.

She gasped as his fingers closed around one vulnerable nipple, hardening it to a stiff peak. He groaned as she pressed impatient hips against his thigh.

He tugged her stained garment down past her waist. She wriggled out of it the rest of the way. The breath caught in his throat. His own dark, massive hand looked almost brutal against the pale flesh of her stomach.

Her fingers scrabbled impatiently, ineffectually, at Duncan's braes, and she frowned as if she could will them away. Duncan half-chuckled deep in his throat. The poor lass obviously had little experience undressing men. But her determination was encouragement indeed. He had his braes off in a matter of a heartbeat.

Their embrace stole the breath from both of them. Everywhere they touched was fire, purer and more powerful than the flames they'd battled earlier. Flesh burned against flesh. His coarse, muscular textures rasped across her soft, sensitive places. Lips sought to quench their thirst on silken nape and rough-stubbled cheek. Hands caressed and teased and persuaded until rapture took them both up into its arms.

With a soft roar that was like a claiming, he pressed into her, and she received him with a sweet wantonness that brought tears to her eyes. Their consummation was gentle, languid, loving. He moved against her willing body with care and tenderness. She answered him with exquisite leisure. They savored each glance, each kiss, each moment. Only in the final throes of desire were they forced to abandon their measured grace. Then they strove against each other with the devotion of novice nuns and the recklessness of new-trained knights.

Linet sobbed in ecstasy as her patience was at last rewarded. It felt as if a halo of fire surrounded her and burst into a thousand flames, each brighter than the sun.

Duncan's seed pulsed out like an endless fount of honey,

and he shuddered with the force of his release. He kissed her on the mouth, a firm, grateful kiss, then for once at a loss for words, had to settle for merely sighing her name.

She hugged him to her with what strength she had left. Then she drifted off even as the sun began to lighten the sky, dreaming of their long and happy future together.

It seemed to Duncan just minutes ago that he'd fallen blissfully asleep in Linet's arms. But the sun streaking in through the eastern windows and penetrating Duncan's slumber was already high enough in the sky to light up the straw-covered floor of the chamber. His eyes were gritty, and his throat burned. He gave a great stretch of his arms, groaning at the ache, the result of several hours of hoisting heavy buckets of water.

Someone was scratching on the chamber door. "My lady." It was Margaret. Beside him, Linet stirred. "My lady, you must come down."

"It cannot be morning yet," Linet rasped, her voice smoke-roughened. She sat up and groggily peered out the window, as he had, to gauge the time. She shook her head to clear the fog of sleep. Suddenly her red-rimmed eyes grew round. "God's wounds!"

"What?" he shot back, startled, fearing another fire had begun.

"What day is it?" she demanded.

He only stared stupidly at her as she flung herself from the bed. She began hurtling aimlessly about the room, wringing her hands. The fact that she was completely nude helped to wake him.

"We must . . . first . . . nay! Margaret. Margaret!" she shrieked, trying to run her fingers through the hopeless tangle of her hair. "Hurry!" she yelled at him. "There is no time!"

Duncan ran a filthy hand across his unshaven chin, still baffled by her panic.

"I promised Lady Alyce her cloth today," Linet explained as she struggled into a kirtle, "and the day is half gone. She'll think I've cheated her."

Duncan smiled. So it was her reputation she worried about. Her concern was unwarranted. Cloth was probably the last thing on his mother's mind. It was the last thing on his mind as well when Linet drew her hands up the graceful length of her thigh.

"Oh," she wailed in misery as she found a huge rip in the kirtle, "this will never do. I stink of smoke, my clothing is a shambles, and I have no goods to deliver! Just look at me! Margaret!"

Duncan just looked at her indeed. He couldn't help but grin at the spectacle of his future wife dashing about the room, deliciously half-naked. She snatched up a robe from her clothing chest and threw it on just as a knock sounded at the chamber door.

"My lady?"

"Margaret! Come in, come in! Fill a basin with water as quickly as possible. We will need food and the horse and cart . . ."

"But, my lady, the villagers wait . . ."

"And make sure the nag is fed well. The way we'll have to drive her, this may be her last journey!"

"Journey? But, my lady, what shall I tell the ones who wait below?"

"The ones who . . ." Linet stopped her pacing. "Who waits below? Is it the Guild?"

"Nay, my lady. 'Tis the villagers."

"The villagers?" Linet frowned.

"Tell them she'll be down as soon as she's dressed," Duncan said.

Margaret went swiftly to do as she was bid.

When the basin arrived, both of them scrubbed ruthlessly at their blackened skin and sooty hair until the water resembled a murky moat. Linet wriggled into her best surcoat of deep green wool. Duncan didn't have the heart to tell her that her wet hair was already staining the material.

He had no change of clothing. He pulled on the filthy braes and the tunic he'd worn yesterday. The tunic was still fairly clean, but someone had lain atop it all night, so it was creased in several places. He smoothed his tangled hair as best he could with Linet's silver comb.

"My lady," Margaret crooned from behind the door.

Linet's nerves were stretched to the limit. "What is it!" she snapped. Then she sighed. She didn't mean to be rude to the old woman, but her reputation as a wool merchant rested upon how she handled the awkward situation today. Every moment was critical.

"My lady, you must come below." Margaret seemed unaffected by Linet's tone. In sooth, she sounded absolutely delighted. "They're waitin'."

"The villagers?" Linet asked. "What do they want?"

"Please hurry, my lady."

Linet looked askance at the gypsy, who only shrugged. Then she tossed her wet locks over her shoulder and opened the chamber door. When she saw what awaited her in the great hall, she came within a hair's breadth of retreating and closing her chamber door on the impossible sight.

All the peasants of the village must have come to camp at the de Montfort mesnage. The hall was packed with their milling, unwashed bodies and the various meager possessions they carried. A leather-skinned crofter grinned toothlessly up at her, lifting a basket of leeks in salute. A grimy-faced old woman clutched a bundle of rags to her sagging bosom. A pair of dirty young lads drove a small pig forward with sticks. A buxom lass cradled a clucking hen in her bare brown arms. And more still pushed their way through the front door.

For a brief moment, Linet feared they were taking over the household. The thought dizzied her. She faltered back. The gypsy caught her.

"What do they want?" she whispered, trembling.

"Why don't you find out?" he said. He sounded so confident, so unconcerned.

It took all her courage to descend the steps. Halfway down, the offers began. A gangly youth hoisted up a brace of slaughtered hares. "I caught 'em myself yesterday." He slung the carcasses across the trestle table.

"My wife won't be needin' these, God rest her soul," an old man mumbled, elbowing his way forward and dropping a pair of thick leather shoes onto the table.

A pair of giggling maids bounced out of the crowd, their arms draped with crudely embroidered linens, which they deposited beside the shoes.

"It's got a limp!" a barrel-chested, black-bearded man bellowed, pushing a rusty wheelbarrow toward her. "But it'll serve ye well enough!"

One by one, the villagers came forward, yelling out the virtues of what they'd brought, leaving their humble offerings in a growing pile in the midst of the great hall. There were livestock and linens, flour for the pantry and seedlings for the garden, some things she needed desperately and some for which she had absolutely no use.

But they were for her. These peasants with scarcely two coins to rub together had managed to scrape up enough to help a neighbor who'd lost her warehouse and outbuildings to fire. They had brought her gifts of their hearts.

Tears brimmed in Linet's eyes, and she couldn't stop her lips from quivering as the villagers eagerly dropped their parcels on the table.

"This isn't right," she whispered to the gypsy on a sob. "I can't take these things."

His voice was warm and kind against her ear. "You have to take them. You will offend them if you don't."

Linet sniffed. The last thing she wanted to do was to offend them. In all the years she'd lived in Avedon, she'd scarcely breathed a word to any of them. Yet here they were, offering her comfort and sustenance they could ill afford. It touched her deeply.

She'd accept the gifts. It was what they wanted. But somehow she'd repay their generosity. She dashed the tears from her face with the back of her hand and raised her chin.

"Good people," she called out clearly, "I cannot thank you enough for your kindness." She swallowed hard, praying God would somehow grant her the wherewithal to keep her next promise. "I vow to you . . . all of you . . . that when my warehouse is restored, when the looms of de Montfort are operating again . . ." She looked at all the faces, faces that had before always seemed a blur, and found in them decency and affection and encouragement. She smiled proudly through a new welling of tears. "I shall weave for each of your families a length of fine worsted such as the nobles wear, enough to make you Sunday garments."

The villagers remarked in wonder among themselves, smiling their gratitude, until someone started a great cheer. In a moment, the hall of de Montfort was ringing with her praises.

How she'd restore her warehouse she didn't know. The Guild would probably oust her for marrying a commoner, preventing her from selling her wares at market and hiring apprentices. Even if she could somehow raise the coin to purchase a loom or two for her home, it would take her years to fulfill her promise, weaving alone.

But somehow she'd do it. Somehow she'd struggle to her feet and repay these people for all the years she'd scorned them. Somehow she would redeem herself.

She descended the rest of the steps cautiously, like a swimmer approaching a cold pond. A snaggle-toothed man shot forward and snatched her hand between his two dirty paws, pumping it roughly. She gasped at first, afraid he meant her harm. But his eyes twinkled with affection. She smiled, then withdrew her hand, placing it atop a shy little girl's head. A wizened old woman hobbled up, embracing Linet suddenly in a grateful squeeze. A tiny boy sucking his thumb tugged at her skirts.

It wasn't as disconcerting as she'd expected. She moved forward through the crowd as through water, touching a shoulder here, receiving an embrace there, wading deeper and deeper into the midst of the humanity. And yet she felt neither fear nor repulsion. They were only people, even with their dirt-stained aprons and their sticky fingers, their stringy hair and their bare, lanky limbs. They were *her* people.

She was still floating on a current of good will when she climbed aboard the cart to make the journey to de Ware Castle. The gypsy had to drive the nag at a breakneck pace through the countryside to get them there by nightfall. Fortunately the weather had been kind—no rain had fallen to turn the road into a mucky mire.

Maple, oak, and birch passed in a blur as they sped along. Even the merrily twittering sparrows couldn't catch them. The odor of damp earth and the faint scent of apple blossoms wafted by like fleeting memories. The few clouds above seemed like faraway nomads drifting across the sky, sky that was almost the exact color . . .

Linet sobbed suddenly. The gypsy reined the horse to a halt, turning to her in concern.

"What is it?" he asked.

How could she explain? It seemed so trivial. "My blue worsted . . ." she wailed. Suddenly the weight of all she'd lost in the last year came crashing down on her shoulders—her father, her title, her warehouse, her looms . . . But at this particular moment, nothing seemed so devastating to her as the loss of her precious blue worsted, the worsted dyed with rare Italian pigment, the worsted that matched the color of his eyes. It was silly, she knew, insignificant in the face of her greater losses. But it moved her to tears.

"It's gone," she blubbered, burying her face in her hands. "My blue worsted is gone."

Duncan didn't hesitate to comfort her. He reached across the seat and gathered her into his arms. He'd soothed enough weeping women to know that their words often had naught to do with their tears. It was no matter that she'd narrowly escaped death at the hands of sea reivers, that she'd been hunted halfway across Flanders, that she'd singlehandedly slain a Spanish criminal, that she'd lost the source of her livelihood to fire. That damned blue cloth was her biggest concern now. And he couldn't get it back.

"Everything will be all right," he said, combing her hair with his fingers. "I promise you."

Duncan smiled to himself as the cart wobbled through the gates of de Ware. If Sir Duncan de Ware had ridden up to the castle astride Freya, his adoring vassals might have recognized him. But atop this merchant's cart at twilight, in the shadow of a beautiful angel with curls of gleaming gold, he passed through the throng at the gates without notice.

Linet seemed oblivious to most of the stares. She had been uncharacteristically quiet for the past hour. It was probably nervousness. They circled the courtyard, and Duncan dropped her off before the door of the great hall so he could stable the horse.

"Fear not," he said, squeezing her hand in reassurance. "I'm sure Lady Alyce will understand."

Linet scarcely heard him. She was occupied with choosing

words of diplomacy for the confrontation ahead. How she'd explain it all she didn't know. She had no cloth for the lady, nor did she have the advance payment she'd received from her. Worse, she had neither warehouse nor wool even to complete the order. But she had her honor. She hoped it would serve her now.

She stared at the imposing front doors of the great hall until the gypsy was gone. Then, taking a shaky breath, she broached the entrance.

The cavernous hall was empty except for a few servants and a man-at-arms, to whom she gave her request for an audience with Lady Alyce. She attempted to still her trembling heart and hands. Lady Alyce was a kind woman, she reasoned. Surely she could rely upon her patience and understanding.

She waited for what seemed an eternity, counting her steps along the length of the vast room, tapping her fingers against her thigh, watching the servants travel back and forth from the buttery to the pantry.

This hall was much more inviting than her uncle's castle, she decided. It was warmer, brighter somehow, the tapestries cheerier, the rushes fresh and fragrant. It seemed like a place of harmony, where wealth wasn't displayed for wealth's sake.

She fidgeted with her skirt. Damnation! The hem was muddy. She hoped Lady Alyce wouldn't notice. The gypsy, at least, seemed confident that everything would work out. Where *was* he? He'd had enough time to stable the nag by now. She'd feel much more sure of herself with him at her side.

The gypsy, she mused. He still hadn't told her his real name. Everyone in her household seemed content to call him Duncan. She supposed he'd tell her in his own time.

Her thoughts scattered as a small commotion ensued at the far archway of the hall. A tall, gray-bearded nobleman entered, his surcoat a luxurious sweep of black velvet. Instinctively, she curtseyed.

At first, Lord James thought the diminutive girl in the middle of the hall was wearing a coif of spun gold. Then he realized he was seeing her hair. She lifted her head again. Her face was as beautiful as her hair—her cheeks rosy, her eyes brilliant. Alyce had been right. Duncan's betrothed looked like an angel.

But suddenly the girl's face contorted with horror. He wondered uneasily for a moment if he'd forgotten to don his braes.

"Are you mad?" she hissed across the empty hall.

22

LORD JAMES GLANCED ABOUT HIM. PERHAPS THE DAMSEL WAS addressing someone else. But there were just the two of them. He regarded her curiously.

"Aye, I'm speaking to you," she said, continuing to gape at him. "Lady Alyce will be here at any moment! What do you think you're doing?"

"I?" he asked indignantly.

"Are you looking for a flogging?"

He raised himself up to his full height. How dared the girl speak to her future father-in-law in this way?

"Please go," she begged. "You'll only make matters worse, Duncan."

Ah, here was the coil, Lord James thought. The damsel wasn't the first to remark on the resemblance his son bore to him. And with Duncan's penchant for disguises . . .

"I am not Duncan," he announced, hoping this would set things aright.

"Of course you are not," she whispered sarcastically. "You are not Venganza or Gaston de Valois either."

"My name is . . ."

"Nay, I don't want to know now. I want you to leave immediately, get out of that ridiculous costume, and wait for me outside."

Lord James smiled. No doubt Duncan had been up to his well-known pranks with her in the recent past—ridiculous costume indeed. He stroked his beard and looked hard at her. She didn't budge. This was obviously one spirited woman, just the sort of partner his eldest son needed, one who wouldn't be overawed by Duncan's wealth and position, but would speak her mind freely. Damn, but Alyce had chosen well.

"I shall send my wife out presently," he told her.

"Your wife? Really!" she fumed, her hands on her hips. "Where in heaven did you procure those garments, by the way?"

Lord James glanced down at his clothing. "You mean my . . . ridiculous costume? My wife ordered it."

"Stop staying that, Duncan. You know . . ."

"I am not Duncan."

"I'll not put up with this nonsense when we are wed."

"Ah," Lord James replied, quite satisfied with her decree. Aye, he decided, this woman would suit his son very well. He saluted her. "Until we meet again then."

Lady Alyce stifled a smile.

Duncan stood before her, challenging her with a gaze of un-yielding iron. Already he'd made the mistake of coming to the solar, *her* domain, to confront her. Apparently he was compensating for that tactical error by puffing out his chest and staring at her with a grim expression that said he'd brook no argument from her.

How out of place he looked here, she thought. His size and that fierce, dark countenance of his were at odds with the blithe tapestries, soft furnishings, and warm candlelight flooding the room. And he was obviously uncomfortable. He wouldn't know what to do with his arms if he unfolded them from across his chest. He'd likely stand for hours before attempting to sit on one of the delicate cushioned benches he was certain would break beneath his weight. It was all too amusing.

Before he misunderstood the smile that threatened to crinkle her eyes, she turned her back to him and gazed out the window.

"I know you're upset," he warned, "but . . ."

"I am *extremely* upset," she told him, but somehow she couldn't make her voice reflect that.

"Be that as it may, I will not change my . . ."

"Do you smell smoke?" she asked suddenly, turning to him and sniffing.

"I helped to put out a fire last night. Linet's warehouse burned to the ground," he mumbled, obviously eager to get back to the other topic. "I want you to know it was entirely my idea."

"The fire?" she asked, eyes wide.

"The marriage."

"Ah," she sighed, pressing a hand to her breast in relief.

"Linet is blameless," he insisted.

"Well," she laughed shortly, "that much is a comfort. I'm glad to know the *girl* at least has more sense than to try to marry without the King's permission."

How like his father he was, she thought, this firstborn son she'd raised as her own, stubborn and principled and utterly charming. He never doubted for a moment that he'd get his way. Most of the time, he was right.

"However," she continued, crossing her arms and turning her back on him again, "that is not why I am upset."

His sigh was loud.

"Linet de Montfort is lovely," she said, "brilliant, hard-working, courteous. I couldn't ask for a more suitable daughter-in-law. In fact, I told the King so when I sent for his approval. All it needs now is your father's final blessing. He should be with her now."

There was an instant of delay while he digested this information. "What?" he finally exploded.

"I told you I think she is lovely."

"How did . . ." Duncan stumbled.

"I purchased quite a bit of cloth from her, you know—superior quality stuff."

"Mother," he threatened, sounding very like his father now, "what have you done?" He stepped behind her and turned her around by the shoulders.

"Only assisted fate, my dear," she said with a shrug.

Duncan was at his wit's end. He ran a hand through his hair. He wondered how his father had endured this woman's capricious logic. "Mother, how could you possibly know what fate has in store for me?"

"Duncan, Duncan," she chided, patting him lightly on the cheek. "I *always* know."

He shook his head. It was no use trying to interpret her reasoning. His ire should have been pricked by the fact that his stepmother had made his wedding arrangements with the King without consulting him. But in truth, he couldn't help but be content with the outcome. Looking down at her radiant expression, he knew he couldn't stay angry with her for long.

"If you had my future planned all along," he said, arching a brow, "then why are you upset with me?"

"I am upset, you big lout, because I know you've bedded her, and that means we must make haste in case she is with child. There is scarcely time to prepare for the kind of ceremony your father will insist upon for his firstborn."

He grinned, and she pushed him aside to pace.

"We must have a hunt," she decided. "We'll need quail and heronshewes, at least, and a dressed swan as the processional centerpiece at the wedding feast. We have pickled salmon from Scotland, and river eels will be simple enough to come by, but . . . oh, how I do wish we'd gotten more figs and dates from that Turkish merchant after Lent . . ."

Duncan heard little else Lady Alyce chattered about. He bussed her soundly on the mouth, startling her from her discourse, then gladly fled the room that seemed to mock his masculinity.

Linet made a deep curtsey when Lady Alyce at last swept into the great hall with two of her maids-in-waiting.

"There you are, my dear," the lady beamed, gliding closer. "Why, what lovely hair you have. It's as golden as the sun."

Linet touched her curls self-consciously, keenly aware of the fact she'd forgotten to wear a proper coif and veil. "My lady . . ." she began nervously.

"And your gown—what a beautiful shade of green," the lady continued, circling her with her maids until Linet felt like an object of art. "Did your dyers do it?"

"Aye, my lady, thank you."

One of the maids began sniffing suspiciously. Linet would have sworn Lady Alyce kicked surreptitiously at the girl, though she remained smiling all the while.

"I smell smoke," the other maid declared.

Linet colored.

Lady Alyce took Linet's arm and walked with her to the

dais at the end of the hall. "Do go and prepare a bath, ladies," she called over her shoulder. "One of you smells of smoke."

Linet bit her lip. "I fear 'tis me," she whispered.

"Now," Lady Alyce said, ignoring the comment, "I wish to have new attire for a special ceremony. How long would it take you, from the raw wool to the dyeing and the weaving, to complete enough cloth for garments for my immediate family—that is, my husband and myself, two of my sons, and . . . let me see, the men will wear their own colors . . . five of my ladies?"

Linet was overwhelmed by Lady Alyce's babbling. How could she tell her that the raw wool was gone and all her looms destroyed?

God must have been smiling on her.

"I have a store of raw wool," Lady Alyce said, "quite fine I am told, though I'd like your judgment on that, and I would prefer the work to be done on my looms here, except for the dyeing, of course. 'Tis a smelly business, is it not, best left to the furthest end of the village?"

As Linet nodded her agreement, a flicker of hope began in her breast. "Have you a quill, my lady?" she asked. "I must tally it all."

"Come," Lady Alyce beckoned.

She ushered Linet upstairs to a vacant chamber. Linet liked the room immediately. It seemed warm despite the rich, dark colors, and the furnishings looked well-used and cared for. The chamber was comfortably cluttered with coins tossed across a table, a velvet robe hanging over a chair, wax drippings on a half-finished parchment on the desk.

"My son's," Lady Alyce disclosed. She pushed the inked parchment aside and gave Linet a fresh one, along with a quill.

Linet perched upon the large leather-seated chair and scrawled out figures, asking the lady to refresh her memory about the number of garments. Then she rose from the desk. "The cloth can be ready in a week's time, two at the most, depending on how many weavers we employ," Linet told her. "Of course, after that, the garments must be cut and sewn."

"Of course," the lady agreed. "Very well. That timing should suffice."

"You would like to know the cost?" Linet ventured.

Lady Alyce fluttered her hands. "It's immaterial."

Then the woman chattered on for nearly half an hour while Linet took notes concerning the colors and textures she desired. Lady Alyce certainly had impeccable taste, Linet decided. It was a fortunate thing the cost was of no import.

When their negotiations were finished, Linet stood humbly before Lady Alyce and bit her bottom lip. She had to tell the woman about the rest of her order.

"My lady, first let me say that, I assure you, upon the . . ." She meant to say, the name of de Montfort, but somehow that seemed inappropriate now. "Upon my honor as a wool merchant of the Guild, I will not fail you in this. There is another matter, however, of most dire consequence, which I must confess."

"The fire?"

Linet looked aghast. "Can you smell it on me?"

She could have cut out her tongue for blurting out the words, but Lady Alyce only smiled gently.

"I believe, my dear, your bath should be ready by now."

"You see," Linet tried to explain, "there was a fire. All my cloth, all *your* cloth . . . my bath?"

"Aye." Lady Alyce said warmly. "I know all about the fire. Don't fret over it."

"You know?"

"Aye. Duncan told me all about it."

"Duncan?"

"Mm," Lady Alyce nodded. "Come now, let's find that tub."

Linet followed her in wonder. When had Duncan spoken to Lady Alyce? Whatever the truth, the gypsy had told her everything would be all right, and it looked like it would. She was going to have a nice hot bath. There was the promise of much coin in her pocket. And in two weeks' time, she would journey with her new husband back to the village and her warm, comfortable, cozy home.

Linet's hair was only half dry from the bath, blessedly clean and scented with jasmine, when she decided she'd better seek out her betrothed. She hadn't had time to explain to Lady Alyce the loss of her title. Thus, the lady had invited her to sup with them at the high table. While that idea pleased Linet, she wished to seek Duncan's permission first. The last thing she wanted was to embarrass him by enjoying the rights of her now empty title while he sat alone at the lower tables.

Slipping into the blue brocade surcoat Lady Alyce so generously provided, Linet crept down the stairs into the great hall. Servants rushed about setting up trestle tables for supper, but there was no sign of her gypsy.

She ventured up to the chapel next, afraid to intrude upon other floors which might house private chambers. She hoped to God *he* hadn't done so. But he wasn't in the chapel.

On the way downstairs, she crossed paths with one of the guards who had come to her rescue in Lady Alyce's solar. That seemed like a lifetime ago.

"You," she said, stopping him on the stair.

"My lady?" He bowed. "All is well, I trust?"

"I am looking for Dun . . . the man who accosted me in Lady Alyce's solar. You remember me? The wool merchant?"

"Duncan?"

Lord—did everyone know him? "Aye."

"The last I saw of him, he was below stairs in the armory. You might look there."

She thanked him, wondering at the amused expression on his face.

Duncan was not in the armory, although a half dozen other men were, in various stages of armament and wearing diverse expressions of pleasure or hostility at finding a woman in their midst. She made a hasty retreat.

Where could he be? she wondered, sauntering down the corridor. A series of steps off one end of the hall led down a dark passage. That could be the way to the dungeon, she surmised. And then a horrible thought occurred to her. Perhaps Duncan had gotten himself into trouble already. Perhaps he'd been thrown in the dungeon! She supposed she should take a peek, since it was so near.

Slowly, tremulously, picking her skirts up from the slimy looking steps, she inched down into the cold world below the castle. There was no sound from below, only the smell of damp earth.

Oh God, she thought suddenly, what if there was another prisoner down there, or the remains of one? She shuddered, and her eyes dilated as she slowed her descent into the cavernous black ahead. She felt for the edges of the steps with her slippered toes and placed one hand upon the wall for balance, but she recoiled quickly from the eery, slick moss growing in the joints of the stones.

Finally, becoming claustrophobic in the lightless, thick air, she stopped, leaning forward into the darkness to whisper.

"Duncan?"

"He is not here." The gentle voice immediately behind her startled Linet so badly that she almost took a tumble down the steps. Fortunately, whoever it was caught her in time. She clung to his tunic until he picked her up by the waist and set her above him on the stair.

"You frightened me!" she gasped at the unseen man.

"I saw you wander down here. I imagined you were lost," he explained in a soothing voice. "Did you know this was the dungeon?"

"What? Oh, aye, I thought it probably was."

"And you thought Duncan was down here?"

Linet didn't know how to answer him. "You know, I think I'm feeling a bit faint from the close air. Might we go above?"

"Certainly." He grasped her firmly by the elbow, and together they climbed back into the light.

"You," she said to him when she saw his handsome face, his misty gray-green eyes, "you were the other guard in Lady Alyce's solar. I remember you."

He inclined his head slightly in a nod.

"I am Lady . . . I am Linet de Montfort, the wool merchant," she told him.

"I know. I am pleased to make your reacquaintance, my lady. I am Sir Garth de Ware."

Linet looked at him for signs that he was teasing her, but he continued to stare, unwavering. She dropped into a hasty curtsey. "My lord, I had no idea. Please forgive my trouble here. I am looking for . . ."

"Duncan."

"Aye."

"He wouldn't be in the dungeon."

What an odd conversation they were having. The young man seemed to possess no sense of humor.

"He wouldn't?" She chuckled sheepishly. "Of course he wouldn't."

"Unless he were having it cleaned."

Having it cleaned? Cleaning a dungeon? One of them had obviously lost their mind.

"I see," she replied, not seeing at all.

"He doesn't like to see anyone suffer, not even the prisoners," Sir Garth explained.

That sounded like Duncan.

"The dungeon goes empty most of the time anyway," he told her.

"Ah." She smiled. "Well, should you see Duncan, will you tell him I am looking for him, my lord?"

"Of course," he said with a nod. "He'll be at supper, naturally."

"Naturally," she agreed.

"I shall see you then, my lady," he murmured.

He left her to her search then. It turned out to be fruitless.

Supper was an entertainment in itself for Linet, marred only by the fact that Duncan was nowhere to be found. The fire in the midst of the room blazed brightly, and the great chamber was filled with the sounds of laughter and shouting, jesting and scolding, so different from the dignified halls of her Flemish uncle. Candles burned on all the tables, and there were linen napkins at each place. Children scurried to find their spots on the benches, and the hounds in the corner of the hall yipped for morsels of food.

Linet sat at the high table in a place of honor beside Lady Alyce, a placement she didn't fully understand, but she wasn't about to argue about it. The place next to her was empty, and beyond that were Sir Garth de Ware, a lady-in-waiting, and the guardsman she remembered from before, who clung to a raven-haired woman beside him like moss to a stone.

She wondered which two men were the other de Ware sons. She had just leaned over to ask Lady Alyce about it when she noticed the woman's husband seated on the other side of her.

Her eyes grew round.

Then she chanced to look up behind Lord James, and her heart nearly stopped beating.

It was Duncan, a Duncan she'd never seen. This one was freshly shaven, scrupulously clean, his hair combed and shining. He was dressed in a rich tunic of gray wool overlaid by a tabard of deep blue velvet, a color that echoed the blue of his eyes, eyes that were identical to . . . his father's, she realized.

Duncan bent to kiss his mother's cheek, then sidled by her to take his place beside Linet. He grinned. "You look lovely," he murmured.

Linet's hand trembled as she reached for her goblet of wine and took an awkward sip. Frantically, she tried to remember everything stupid she'd said to Lord James, Duncan's father. She gulped down a swallow of wine. Hadn't she referred to his clothing as ridiculous?

What had she said to his mother? His brother? Suddenly, the room seemed to sway out of kilter, and she longed desperately to leave the table.

Duncan clasped her hand and turned to her in concern. "What is it?"

"You are Sir Duncan de Ware," she whispered in accusation.

"So I have said," he answered, raising his brows, "numerous times."

"You are not a player," she said under her breath. "You are not even a peasant."

"I never said I was."

In spite of the delectable scents of roasting meat, mustard, and freshly baked bread, Linet felt sick to her stomach. She pressed her napkin to her bloodless lips and tried to breathe steadily. But it was no use. This revelation was the final log placed on the cart, the one that brought the entire precarious load of wood tumbling to the ground.

Her eyes brimmed with tears of humiliation. Without a word, she staggered to her feet. Then she fled the hall. Thankfully, the chaos of supper let her escape without too much undue attention. But she could feel the eyes of the family at the high table following her all the way.

Duncan pursued her, out the door of the great hall, up the steps, into the chapel. She pushed the door closed between them, but he forced it open again, invading her place of asylum.

"Leave me," she cried, backing down the aisle of the chapel, "leave me alone!"

Duncan frowned. What was wrong with her? She should be deliriously happy. In all the star-crossed lover legends he'd ever heard, the heroine was delighted to discover that her hapless hero was in truth a prince.

Gently, he pressed the door shut behind him. A dozen candles flickered against the whitewashed walls, illuminating Linet as she retreated to the center of the chapel, trying to catch her breath.

"I thought you'd be pleased," he breathed, coming toward her.

"Pleased? To be made a fool of?"

"I never intended to . . ."

"Never intended?" she shrieked. Her chin quivered. "For weeks you've had the opportunity to let me know! When did you *intend* to tell me?"

"I *did* tell you, but you wouldn't believe me, would you?"

She had no answer for that.

He came close and set his hands atop her shoulders, but she ducked away from his touch.

"Was I just some conquest for you?" she sobbed. "Were you bored with the ladies of the Court? You noblemen think you can snap up any woman you like, just because you are who you are! Well, you may not have *me*, sir . . ."

"What?" Duncan exploded, incredulous. This was too much for him. She was like a hotheaded knight fighting against the quintain. The harder it hit her in the back of the head, the more she swung at it. "Don't you see?" he demanded. "That is *exactly* why I did what I did!"

"You conniving, blackhearted son of a . . . !"

"Do not swear at me, not in the chapel!"

"I'll do what I like!"

Duncan ran both hands through his hair in exasperation. He was getting nowhere. "You agreed to marry me, did you not?"

She only glared at him.

"You agreed to wed me, in spite of the fact you believed me to be a peasant."

She lowered her eyes.

"Admit it. You wanted to marry me. Why?"

She was chewing on her bottom lip. That was a good sign. At least he was forcing her to think.

"Was it because you knew I was the heir to the de Ware title, the eldest son of the lord?" The chapel was still, but for the dust motes that filtered down in the candlelight. "Was it because you knew I was wealthy, and you couldn't wait to get your hands on all that coin?"

"You know it wasn't," she muttered.

Duncan sighed and rubbed his chest. "It used to be that when a woman professed to love me, I never knew if it was for my title or my wealth, or both. Until now. At last, a woman has agreed to marry me without knowing what title or wealth I possess." He cupped her chin, forcing her to look up at him. "Can you understand what that means to me?"

Linet's jaw clenched stubbornly. For a moment she seemed prepared to deny everything. But then her eyes softened, and her shoulders dropped in surrender.

"Tell me why, Linet."

"It's because . . . damn it all . . . I love you."

He grinned and ran his thumb across her pouting bottom lip. The candlelight made a golden halo around her hair. Never had she looked more holy. "And I love you, my angel."

The affection blossoming in Linet's eyes was so warm, one would've thought he'd given her the universe.

In a way, to Linet, gazing lovingly up at her peasant lord, he had.

There was an abrupt rattle at the door. They drew apart self-consciously.

"Come," Duncan called out.

Lord James himself entered and swung the door shut, closing off the stares of the handful of others behind him. He cleared his throat. A strange combination of embarrassment and pride played over his features. Duncan knew instantly that Lady Alyce had sent him in.

"My lady." Lord James nodded stiffly. "Please accept my sincere apologies for . . . for neglecting to properly introduce myself when we first met . . . due to the fact I scarcely had time to get a word in edgewise." The last words came out in a rush, and Lord James's chin lifted haughtily, daring Linet to challenge him.

Duncan quirked a brow. What kind of an apology was that?

Before anyone could comment, the door swung open again, and in crept Lady Alyce. As she pressed the door closed, she squinted suspiciously at her husband. "Did you apologize, my lord husband, or did you try to excuse your behavior?"

Lord James turned on her fiercely, his fists balled, but she didn't even flinch. She was well accustomed to this show of temper from him. Lady Alyce then approached Linet, taking her hands in her own. "These men," she confided, clucking. "They think they can only win a woman's heart with elaborate scheming."

"Scheming?" Lord James thundered. "Was it not you, my lady wife, who contrived to secure the King's approval for this match by bargaining with our other son's commission?"

The ladies gasped in unison. Lady Alyce paled, pulling away from Linet.

"How did you find out?" she sputtered, shamefaced.

"Garth," Duncan and his father said simultaneously.

As if on cue, Garth made his way into the chapel. He nearly made a hasty exit as well when he saw the accusation in his parents' faces.

"Robert and I . . ." he began. He looked behind him for his companion, but Robert had made a timely disappearance. "I," he amended, "wish to express my sincere apologies . . ."

He was nearly knocked off his feet as a familiar little old woman came barreling into the chapel.

"Margaret!" Linet exclaimed.

"I had your household follow us here," Duncan explained.

"Don't you worry none," the maidservant soothed, pride blazing in her eyes as she turned to Lord James. "I know what you think. You think my Linet is not noble enough for your son!"

"God's blood!" Lord James boomed.

Lady Alyce cuffed him. "We're in the chapel!"

Margaret continued, "I will have you know she has been endowed with all the right and privileges . . ."

"I care not if she is the Queen of Faeries!" Lord James countered.

"Faeries?" Garth mouthed, completely baffled.

"She is a de Montfort!" Margaret proclaimed. "Her family . . ."

"Goes back hundreds of years," Lady Alyce recited. "We know."

"Perhaps your son is not noble enough for my Linet," Margaret told her haughtily.

"Old woman, are you suggesting . . . ?" Lord James demanded.

"God's wounds!" Lady Alyce cried, throwing up her hands.

"Not in the chapel," Lord James and Garth chided in unison.

"I see no reason Lady Linet should continue with this farce of a . . ."

"You mean to say my son brought her from Flanders for . . ."

"The King himself has sanctioned the match. Will you counter . . ."

The remainder of their argument was lost on Duncan. Suddenly, the rest of the world didn't matter. He only had eyes for the angel before him—his bright, beautiful, intriguing angel who had been willing to sacrifice everything for him.

Linet thought, as he bent to fit his lips to hers, that at least she'd never grow bored of this man. Sometimes he kissed her like a gypsy bent on breaking hearts. Sometimes he kissed her like a pilgrim pressing reverent lips to a sacred relic. Sometimes he kissed her like a sea reiver claiming his riches. But always, he kissed her like a man desperately, passionately, hopelessly in love.

All around them the battle raged, but they took no notice. They were embroiled in a battle of their own, dueling to see who would tire of kissing first.

epilogue

"Who shall it be tonight? The minstrel? The gypsy? The sea reiver?" Duncan murmured.

"Hmm . . ." Linet replied, twining her fingers through one of his sable curls. "I think perhaps the old crone Robert said you do so well."

"She *is* the lascivious sort."

The fire flickered on the hearth as the weak December wind wheezed through the room. But Linet had no desire to leave the comfortable haven of the bed to close the shutters. Beyond the open window, snowflakes floated down from the close black sky like angels falling to earth. Linet shivered and snuggled further down into the soft wool coverlet of Italian blue, tucking her cold nose against her husband's shoulder.

"Cold?" he asked her, pulling her into the circle of his arms.

"Mmm," she purred.

"I know how to warm you." His voice was rough and seductive. Its promise sent tingles along her spine. She sighed luxuriously, relaxing back against his warm body.

Suddenly the hand upon her shoulder seemed to wither into a claw, and he cackled in her ear. "Yes, dearie, I have just the sort of caudle to warm yer bones. Let me see. Was it two wings of a bat and one eye of a beetle, or . . ."

She beat at him, giggling all the while, until he caught her arms and pulled her roughly against him. Flesh to flesh, there was no mistaking his desire for her, and her laughter subsided when he trapped her in those gypsy eyes of his. Then, step by delicious step, he showed her his best method for chasing away the cold.

Afterward, as she lay entwined with him like ivy clinging to a stone wall, she sighed and gave him a pout. "I suppose I won't be seeing much of you next week," she complained.

"Why?" He closed his eyes contentedly.

"I shall be busy supervising the weavers I've sent for."

He opened one eye. "Weavers?"

"Aye." She traced a circle on his chest with her fingertip.

"Whatever for?"

"Someone has to operate all the looms."

"The looms?"

"The looms I asked Uncle Guillaume for as my dowry. I'll have to weave cloth for the villagers of Avedon first, of course. But after that . . . have you seen the rags our waifs are running about in? Really, Duncan," she scolded, "I'm surprised at the neglect."

Duncan wondered if she knew how much her words pleased him. She'd said "*our* waifs." He caught her wrist, stopping her ticklish design on his chest. "Thank you," he murmured, then added in his thoughts, *for your understanding, for your generosity, for your faith.* "You're an angel." He kissed the top of her head.

The candlelight glanced off the heavy wolf's head ring he wore, catching his eye, and he recalled the moment during their wedding that he had slipped its twin on Linet's finger. He'd had the matching rings made for them from the melted metals of his expensive silver de Ware crest ring and her cheap bronze de Montfort medallion, returned to his possession by Lord Guillaume. The combined alloy suited them, they had decided, noble champions of the common man that they were.

Linet smiled faintly as she studied her wedding ring. It seemed ages ago that she'd stood before the chapel, enveloped by a thronging mass of nobles and peasants alike, reciting the vows that would bind her to her husband. Never would she forget the lump in her throat at his whispered words to her as they stood upon the steps that morning, nor how true they rang as she studied the hundreds of faces surrounding her.

"This division of men into noble or peasant overlooks the common bonds between them," he'd said, clutching her hand. "All men want sons. All women crave affection. All people search for some sliver of immortality. You and I can forge those bonds, if you will only stand beside me in this."

From that moment forth, she'd vowed in her heart to do just that, to support him faithfully in the many battles to come.

She was part of the de Ware family now, she reflected as she watched the snowy drifts collect at the edges of the narrow window.

And she was safe. Robert's new bride had assured that. Anabella was with child, and her father, a prominent Spanish gentleman, was so relieved to have his daughter wed well and quickly to an English noble that he'd personally guaranteed the de Ware family full protection against any recourse for El Gallo's death.

Linet sighed contentedly. Tomorrow was Christmas Day, replete with feasting and entertainments and the exchanging of gifts. She couldn't wait to give Duncan his present. She had made a beautiful green wool coverlet with the black de Ware crest on the magnificent loom that had been his wedding gift to her.

Her only regret was that one of Duncan's brothers wouldn't be home for the festivities. She'd never met Holden, but he was so beloved by the family that she felt as though she knew him. She also felt she owed him a debt. After all, it had been Holden's commission that bought King Edward's approval of their match. According to Duncan, his brother was off winning Scotland for the King even now.

"I wonder if it's miserably cold at the border," she murmured.

"Worried about that fool brother of mine?"

She nodded.

"You've never even met him."

"He's a de Ware," she said, as if that explained everything.

"Oh, he's a de Ware all right. If he gets too cold, he'll find himself something to warm his bed. Like I did."

Linet tickled his ribs for that remark. "You," she announced, climbing atop him and planting a kiss on the end of his nose, "are pitiless." She kissed his forehead. "And vain."

She licked his earlobe. "And naughty." She bit his neck. "And overbearing."

Duncan lost track of his virtues as she ticked them off one by one, and it was only when she rocked smugly back astride him, her toasty bottom nestled against his stomach, that he realized she had tied his wrists to the bedposts with the cord from the bed curtains.

His eyes grew smoky. "Those wouldn't be weaver's knots?"

Linet grinned at him like a wolf at dinner. Duncan shivered in anticipation.

Turn the page for a preview of . . .

MY WARRIOR

the exciting new novel by Glynnis Campbell
coming soon from Jove Books!

*

CAMBRIA SAW HER FATHER IN THE DREAM, WALKING TOWARD her with his arms outstretched. She smiled as he crossed the sunny meadow toward her. But suddenly a great gray wolf appeared between them, its paws massive, its eyes penetrating. The beast opened its jaws in a mournful howl, and a great black shadow fell across the Laird.

She woke with a scream stuck in her throat. Her heart raced like a sparrow's as she tried to break the threads of the nightmare. She rested her damp head in trembling hands. They came more frequently now, the prophetic dreams that haunted her sleep, forcing her to glimpse the future. This one was a warning, she was certain. The wolf boded ill for her father.

Shaken, she rose on wobbly legs, dragging the fur coverlet with her, and peered out the window. Damnation! The sun was in the sky already. Katie had let her oversleep, probably out of kindness—Cambria had been up past midnight polishing armor—but she couldn't afford to be late, not today. She let out a string of curses and tossed the fur back onto the pallet.

A loud crash echoed through the stone corridors and shook the oak floor, bringing her instantly alert.

The shouting of unfamiliar voices rumbled up from

below the stairs, and then she heard the frenzied barking of
the hounds. Her heart began to pound in her chest like an
armorer's mallet. She scrambled over the bed, snatching
her broadsword from the wall. With frantic haste, she
struggled into a simple gown, cursing as her tangled hair
caught in the sleeve. The crash of hurled crockery and
women's terrified shrieks pierced the air as Cambria finally pulled open her chamber door and rushed out.

She was fairly flying down the long hallway when she
heard the unmistakable clang of blades colliding. She hurtled forward, descending the spiraling steps that opened
onto the gallery above the great hall.

At the top of the landing, she froze.

The scene before her took shape as a series of grue-
some paintings, none of which she could connect to make
any sense: brightly colored tabards flecked with gore;
servants huddled in the corners, sobbing and holding
each other in terror; hounds yapping and scrambling on
the rush-covered stone floor; lifeless, twisted bodies of
Gavin knights sprawled in puddles of their own blood;
Malcolm and the rest of the men chained together like animals. For a moment, a numbing cold seemed to enclose
her heart like a great helm warding off the attack of a
blade.

But as her eyes moved from the overturned trestle tables
to the slaughtered knights and cowering servants, trying to
make reason out of the confusion before her, that armor
shattered into a million fragments.

The Laird. Where was the Laird?

Panic began to clutch at her with desperate claws. She
shifted her death grip on the pommel of her sword, her
eyes frantically seeking out her father. If she could only
find him, she thought, everything would be all right. The
Laird would explain everything. He always took care of
the clan.

She ran trembling fingers over her lips. Dear God, where
was the Laird?

As if she'd willed it, two lads came forth from the side

chamber, struggling with the weight of the grisly burden they carried between them.

Dear God, no! Cambria silently screamed as she recognized the tabard of her father. Not the Laird!

Even as her heart clenched in her breast, she dared to hope he yet lived. But his body was limp, drenched with blood, far too much blood, and when his head flopped back, the glazed eyes stared sightlessly toward the heavens, where, 'twas clear, his spirit already resided.

The shrill keening initiated in her soul pierced through her heart and escaped her lips. "Nay!" she screamed, hurtling down the steps, her gown floating behind her like a wraith. "Nay!"

Cambria dropped her sword and shook the pale body, unwilling to accept the Laird's impossible stillness. He had to wake up. The clan needed him.

She stroked his forehead, but there was no response. She took his big hand in hers, but 'twas as heavy and slack as a slain rabbit. Blood soaked her linen gown, smearing across her breast as she embraced his silent form.

"Nay," she whispered, "nay."

He couldn't be dead. He couldn't. He wouldn't have left her alone. She'd already lost her mother. He wouldn't have made her endure that pain again.

And yet there he lay, as silent as stone.

A wretched sob tore from her throat, choking her. Dagger-sharp pain lanced through the empty place in her chest.

The Laird was lost to her forever.

Hot tears spilled down her cheeks onto her father, mingling with the blood of the Gavin who was no more. She wept as all around her the nameless invaders murmured on, calmly wiping the blood from their blades, blood of the brave Gavin men who'd not live to fight again. She peered at them through the wild strands of her hair, the obscene enemy who had massacred her people.

Who were they? Who were these bastards who had in one bloody moment destroyed the Gavins?

The pain in her heart twisted into a bitter knot of hatred.

Nay. She refused to believe it. These strangers hadn't destroyed the Gavins. No one could destroy the Gavins. Gavins had lived for hundreds of years. They would never die. They lived in her. She was the life's blood of the clan now.

Wiping the tears from her face with the back of one hand, she reached down to clasp the pommel of her fallen sword with the other. She kicked her gown out of her ankles' way and tossed her hair over her shoulder. Whirling, she came up with the blade and faced her foe. Several of the servants crossed themselves as she turned toward the knights with all the fury of a madwoman.

"You bastards!" she shouted. "You have slain my father!"

The knights scattered, dodging her slashing broadsword, and her steel flashed wildly as Cambria attempted to take on the entire company. She slashed forward and back, using both hands on the pommel to strengthen her blows. Two men who underestimated her sincerity received serious wounds.

But the element of surprise couldn't remain long on her side. Though Cambria kept them at bay briefly, the enemy far outnumbered her. Two of the knights finally caught her from behind, squeezing her wrists till she dropped the sword, which clattered heavily to the floor.

One of the knights yanked her head back by the hair. She bared her teeth, and her eyes narrowed like a cornered animal's.

Suddenly the unguarded doors of the great hall burst open. An enormous black destrier galloped like thunder across the hard floor, bearing a helmed knight. He was flanked by several other riders who hauled their horses to a skidding stop on the stones. Rushes scattered everywhere, and the knights fought to control their mounts in the close quarters.

Cambria was forced to her knees by the hulking dark captor beside her, and she squinted against the rising dust.

"My l-lord," the golden knight stammered in surprise, inclining his head toward the newcomer.

Tension hung in the air as he awaited a reply, but the silence was only broached by the snorting of the horses, the squeak of leather tack, and the sniffling of maid-servants.

Cambria sucked in great gulps of air through her open mouth and tried to center her mind. She could feel her body drifting toward unconsciousness, toward the place where nothing could harm her, but she resisted its lure, clinging desperately to reality by reminding herself over and over that she was the Gavin. She clenched her nails into the palms of her hands to keep from fainting and focused intently on the rider at the fore, who was nudging his mount closer.

The knight set his huge destrier into motion, Cambria noted, using only the slightest pressure of one of his armor-plated knees. The steed tossed its head proudly and ambled forward. Man and beast no doubt made a formidable foe in battle, their carriage that of champions.

With bullying arrogance, the rider let the steed come to within a foot of the golden knight till it huffed its breath into the man's eyes.

Cambria scowled up at the helmed rider. This had to be the monster responsible for the Laird's murder. She swayed momentarily with nausea, recalling too clearly her father's bloody surcoat and his dead, glassy eyes. She swallowed to control her rising gorge. She prayed God would give her the strength to hold out until help came, until de Ware's knights arrived. The English lord was bound by his word, after all, to protect Blackhaugh from enemies such as these. He'd be obliged to capture and punish these murderers. She hoped The Wolf would tear them limb from limb.

She watched, unable to move, unable to speak, as the knight before her removed his helm, eased the mail coif from his head and ran a hand through his dark curls.

Then her heart stilled as well.

A heavy weight seemed to press on her chest, making it nigh impossible to breathe as she looked upon his face.

He wasn't at all the villain she'd expected. In fact, he was the most striking man she'd ever beheld. His face was evenly chiseled, so perfect it might have been pretty were it not for his furrowed brow and the scars that told of many seasons of battle. His hair, damp with sweat, reminded her of the rich shade of roasted walnuts, and it fell recklessly about his corded neck. His jaw was firm, resolute, but something about the generous curve of his lips marked him as far from heartless.

Most startling, however, were his eyes. They were the color of the pines in a Highland forest, deep and almost sad, eyes that had seen violence and suffering, and had endured. Those eyes caused her heart to beat unsteadily, and she wasn't entirely certain 'twas from fear.

He angled his mount with another nudge of his knee and cocked a brow at the golden knight. "Have you finished here, Roger?" His voice was low, powerful, and laced with irony.

The golden knight regarded him with ill-concealed hostility. "Aye, my lord. They resisted, as you see, but . . ." He shrugged.

The lord shifted in his saddle, tossed his helm to his squire, and blew out a long breath.

The carnage before him was inexcusable. As he'd suspected when he set out this morning to intercept Roger's advance, something here was amiss. He should never have trusted Roger Fitzroi. The man obviously didn't understand the proper use of violence. Judging by the age of the shields of the conquered lining the great hall and the frayed edges of the Gavin knights' garments, this poor clan could have hardly posed a threat. Good Lord, there weren't even that many of them, he thought as he let his gaze roam over the broken bodies.

And then he saw her, kneeling at his knights' feet, in the

midst of all the slaughter. The breath caught in his throat. For a moment he forgot where he was.

It was an angel. Nay, he corrected as he continued to stare at the eyes that were too fierce, the jaw too square, the hair too dark. Not an angel. Something more fey—a sprite. Accustomed to the fleshy, languorous women at Court, this lass's exotic looks were as refreshing as the dip he'd had yesterday in the cool loch.

He couldn't take his eyes from her. She looked the way he'd made women look many a time in his bed—hair spilled carelessly, lips a-quiver, cheeks flushed—and all at once, he wished to caress that fine-boned cheek, run his fingers through those too dark, tangled tresses, kiss that spot on her neck where her pulse visibly raced.

The wench was glaring at him with those cut crystal eyes, and he was amazed to see her defiance falter only infinitesimally beneath his regard, a thorough scrutiny that usually made his foes tremble.

She reminded him of a wildcat he'd seen once on his travels through the moors, one caught in an abandoned snare. Before he'd cut the animal free, it had looked at him just this way—frightened, hateful, suspicious. He suddenly had an absurd longing to remove the pain from the liquid pools of her eyes as he'd done for the wildcat.

Ariel nickered softly beneath him and stamped an impatient hoof, jarring him back to reality. Damn, he thought, shaking off his insipid dreaming with a toss of his head. This new life of lordly leisure was making him soft.

He frowned into the girl's face. Then his gaze dropped lower. Her body strained against the thin linen of her gown, and he could clearly see a perverse crimson streak across her fair breast.

Desire fled. He grew instantly livid. "Have we taken to wounding innocents?" he demanded.

Roger answered belligerently. " 'Tis not her blood, my lord. 'Tis that of her traitor father, Laird Gavin. Though this *innocent* wounded two of my men!"

He snorted in disbelief. A wee Borders lass was hardly

capable of fighting off the formidable de Ware knights. He looked dubiously down at her again to see if he'd over-looked something. He was sorry it was the sprite's father who had died, but if the Laird was indeed a traitor, it would only have been a matter of time before he was executed for his treachery. Perhaps it was better he'd died nobly, with a sword in his hand.

"Who is your father's successor, lass?" he asked her quietly.

The girl lifted her chin bravely and replied, "I am."

He should have guessed. "And your husband?"

"I have no husband."

"Your betrothed?"

"I have no betrothed. I am . . . the Gavin." Her voice broke as she said it. He could see she was fighting back tears.

Several of his countrymen smirked at the idea of a young woman claiming a castle, but he knew there was nothing odd about it for the Scots. He stared at the girl with a mixture of pity and disgust at the Laird's foolish-ness in leaving his daughter unmarried and, therefore, un-protected. He swore he'd never understand the Scots' ways.

"I'll spare your life if you swear fealty to me."

To his amazement, the girl fixed him with a jewel-hard stare and shook her head firmly once. "Even now the cas-tle is being surrounded by an army of the King," she pro-claimed. "You'll not escape alive."

"Lass . . ." a burly old Gavin man called from the corner, but his captor jerked his chain, ordering him to silence.

He scowled down at the girl and held up a hand to quiet his men's snickering. "The King . . . Edward's army?"

"Aye!" she hissed, her eyes sparking like sapphires. "Lord Holden de Ware will slay you for the murder you've committed! He is a powerful warrior, known to all as The Wolf for his savagery, and he has sworn to protect this keep!"

He stared at her, stunned. Her eyes gleamed with victory,

and the thrust of her chin was confident and proud. He almost hated to dash her hopes.

But he had to.

He held her gaze with his own and explained softly, "I am The Wolf. I am Lord Holden de Ware."